PRAISE FOR THE HELL DIVERS SERIES

DISCARD

"Relentless action and danger in a gritty postapocalyptic world where survival depends on a few brave men and women. *Hell Divers* is one hell of a page-turner!"
—BOB MAYER, *NEW YORK TIMES* BESTSELLING AUTHOR

"An action-packed page-turner...You won't be able to put this book down until the last searing page."
—MIKE SHEPHERD, *NEW YORK TIMES* BESTSELLING AUTHOR, ON *HELL DIVERS*

"*Hell Divers* is action-packed, gritty, and wholly original. A rare combination of a high premise, solid storytelling, and heart."
—DANIEL ARENSON, *USA TODAY* BESTSELLING AUTHOR

"A well-told, action-packed tale...This story has something for even those who don't favor military science fiction and Mr. Smith is to be applauded."
—*SFREVU* ON *HELL DIVERS II: GHOSTS*

"Literally skydiving into the apocalypse, *Hell Divers* delivers more of Smith's trademark breakneck action and suspense. Amazing settings, great characters, the end of the world shouldn't be this much fun!"
—MATTHEW MATHER, BESTSELLING AUTHOR OF *CYBERSTORM*

"A terrific blend of high-concept and wild action... A must for fans of smart postapocalyptic storytelling."
—SAM SISAVATH, BESTSELLING AUTHOR OF THE PURGE OF BABYLON SERIES

"An exciting new take on the end of the world and a thrilling race to survive...Sure to delight fans of survival and postapocalyptic thrillers."
—A. G. RIDDLE, BESTSELLING AUTHOR OF *THE ATLANTIS GENE*, ON *HELL DIVERS*

"I love it! The whole book was awesome... It was creative and intense and there was never a dull moment... You should definitely give this one a try!"
—*HOOKED ON BOOKS* ON *HELL DIVERS*

HELL DIVERS IV
WOLVES

Books by Nicholas Sansbury Smith

The Hell Divers Series (Blackstone Publishing)
Hell Divers
Hell Divers II: Ghosts
Hell Divers III: Deliverance
Hell Divers IV: Wolves
Hell Divers V: Captives (coming 2019)

The Extinction Cycle Series (Orbit)
Extinction Horizon
Extinction Edge
Extinction Age
Extinction Evolution
Extinction End
Extinction Aftermath
Extinction Lost (A Team Ghost short story)
Extinction War

The Trackers Series
Trackers
Trackers 2: The Hunted
Trackers 3: The Storm
Trackers 4: The Damned

The Orbs Series
Solar Storms (An Orbs Prequel)
White Sands (An Orbs Prequel)
Red Sands (An Orbs Prequel)
Orbs
Orbs II: Stranded
Orbs III: Redemption
Orbs IV: Exodus

HELL DIVERS IV

WOLVES

NICHOLAS SANSBURY SMITH

BLACK STONE

PUBLISHING

Copyright © 2018 by Nicholas Sansbury Smith
Published in 2018 by Blackstone Publishing
Cover design by Kurt Jones
Series design by Kathryn Galloway English

Printed in the United States of America
Originally published in hardcover by Blackstone Publishing in 2018

First paperback edition: 2018
ISBN 978-1-5385-8948-9
Fiction / Science Fiction / Apocalyptic & Post-Apocalyptic

1 3 5 7 9 10 8 6 4 2

CIP data for this book is available
from the Library of Congress

Blackstone Publishing
31 Mistletoe Rd.
Ashland, OR 97520

www.BlackstonePublishing.com

For those that battle the darkness,
may you see the light ...
never stop fighting.

"Luck is a very thin wire between survival
and disaster, and not many people
can keep their balance on it."
—Hunter S. Thompson

ONE

The third day of the sky pelting rain was when Xavier Rodriguez felt the first tingle of annoyance. Over the years, he had become a very patient man. Trekking across the radioactive wastes for the better part of a decade allowed him to claim patience as a virtue. But by the fifth and sixth day of rain, his patience was nearing its end.

He hated being cooped up in a boat, and the new storm brewing overhead wasn't helping his mood any. Sitting around gave him plenty of time to think. There were still moments of deep anger and resentment when he reflected on those ten long and perilous years on the surface. For hours at a time on the journey, he found himself either lost in his thoughts or jerking away from the nightmare images.

Lightning webbed across the horizon—a welcome distraction from the memories. Each rumble of thunder shook the *Sea Wolf* with a gentle vibration.

X sat in the control room, eyeing his enameled mug on the dashboard. The precious contents sloshed inside, blending the tea spiked with good old shine from the *Hive*. Miles, his trusty Siberian husky hybrid, sat on the floor, muzzle on his paws, crystal-blue eyes glancing up every few minutes.

The twin hulls flanking the command center groaned as the two turbo engines pushed the craft through the heaving seas that slapped the port side. X flipped a switch on the dashboard, and the high beams lanced through the inky darkness, illuminating waves like snowcapped mountains as far as he could see.

The reinforced fiberglass-and-metal frame suddenly didn't seem all that sturdy. He considered taking the boat off autopilot but didn't want to risk veering off course. So he tried to relax in his leather seat and put his trust in Timothy Pepper, the AI program guiding the *Sea Wolf*.

A glance at the on-screen map showed they were still sailing east of an island once known as Cuba. They had already passed through the dark Bahamas, with no sign of the Metal Islands or the Cazador ships.

He checked the circular navigation monitor on the control panel to look for landmasses, other vessels, or mutant creatures that he assumed lived in the cold, dark waters.

A green light blinked, revealing no contacts. The view through the windshield revealed nothing but open water as far as he could see.

While he wasn't at all opposed to having an uneventful first leg of their maiden voyage, he was starting to get bored. He twisted in his chair at the screech of the hatch opening. Magnolia Katib stood in the entryway, a hand on her pale forehead.

"How you feelin', kid?" X asked.

"How's it look?"

She lurched over to the other chair. Slumping against the cushioned leather, she let out a groan. "I think I prefer diving to sailing."

To conserve energy, X flipped the lights off on the dashboard. The dark waves stretched into dark infinity, making it difficult to see where the ocean ended and the sky began. If not for the sporadic flashes of lightning, it would have felt as if they were sailing through the void of space.

"I always wanted to see the ocean," Magnolia said, "but this really sucks. I've puked four times this morning."

X gave her a quick glance. Her short-cropped hair, dyed blue, hung over her sapphire-blue eyes. It used to give X the creeps, but he had warmed to her style.

"Better drink some water to stay hydrated," he said. They had a good supply of water and a recycler unit to help it last, but at this rate, she would need more than her daily ration.

"Yeah, yeah." She turned her attention back to the dashboard, tapping the fuel-gauge monitor with a purple fingernail. "Is this right?"

"What?" X leaned over to double-check.

"Looks like battery two is losing power," she said. "Why didn't Timothy warn us?"

"Pepper?" X said. "He was annoying me, so I shut him off."

Frowning, Magnolia swiveled her seat to another section of the control panel and hit a button.

The AI's voice broke over the speakers.

"Good afternoon, Miss Katib and Mr. Xavier."

"'X.' I told you to call me 'X.'"

"My apologies, sir."

"Just '*X*'!" he said in a voice just shy of a shout.

Magnolia smirked, giving X a cockeyed glance. "He's really getting on your nerves, isn't he?"

"I'm not used to robots."

"Timothy, what's the deal with the battery power?" Magnolia asked, returning her attention to the monitor.

"The boat, as you may know, is equipped with two batteries that charge the twin turbo engines," Timothy said.

X groaned. "Cut to the chase, pal."

After a pause, Timothy continued. "Battery two has malfunctioned, although I'm not certain of the cause. It may require a manual assessment, as it could be something as simple as a faulty sensor."

X checked the gauge for battery two. Sure enough, Mags and the AI were right: it was down to 25 percent. But how the hell could that happen, and how had he missed it? Both batteries were lithium-ion, and Chief Engineer Samson had said they were two of the best ever recovered from the surface.

"*Shit*," X said. His tone drew the attention of Miles, who glanced up from his paws and then went back to sleep after letting out an exasperated sigh. X could empathize. Despite having spent most of the journey in this chair or his bunk, he was exhausted.

Boredom had a way of creating fatigue, leading to mistakes, and even in these churning seas, X was bored as hell. He wasn't used to being cooped up in a small vessel, and part of him missed the freedom of roaming the wastes—although he didn't miss the *Hive* one bit.

"I'm going topside," he said, unbuckling his harness.

Magnolia's eyebrow went up. "You serious?" Her eyes flitted back to the windshield. "In this downpour? Can't this wait?"

"No," he said firmly. Truth be told, X wasn't overly worried about the lithium-ion batteries—he just needed some space and air. He was used to being on his own, and as much as he appreciated Magnolia wanting to join him on this adventure, he missed his solitude, and the AI was getting under his skin.

X moved over to check the readout on the main monitor, looking closely for radiation and any trace of mercury in the rain. Both were in the yellow zone, and he decided he would suit up on the second deck above them.

"Stay here, boy," he said to Miles.

The dog let out a whine and sat on his hind legs, watching as X prepared to leave the room.

"Be careful," Magnolia said, wrapping a strand of blue hair behind her ear.

"Shall I assist you, X?" Timothy asked.

"Nope. You just keep us from capsizing, okay, mate?"

Timothy's hologram flickered and then smiled. "'Mate'—that's a new term to me, and I'm pleased to find in my database that it means 'friend.'"

X shook his head as he stepped out into the narrow hallway belowdecks. He didn't trust the AI—or any other robot with a conscience. If Katrina hadn't insisted, he would never have allowed the program on board. But he couldn't deny that Pepper was useful, especially when it came to guiding the *Sea Wolf* through rough weather.

The hatch clicked shut behind X, and he made his way past his quarters on the left. Magnolia had taken the quarters on the right. The third room included a shared eating space with a stove, small kitchenette, and oval table where they ate most of their meals.

The next two rooms were bathrooms, and aft of these, a maintenance room and storage closet, where they stockpiled their extra rations and medical supplies.

He climbed the ladder to the second cabin, which they had transformed into a staging area for future missions. Racks of weapons were bolted to the bulkhead on his right. Brand-new submachine guns, a speargun, and even fishing rods were stocked and secured throughout the room. Crates bolted to the deck contained scuba gear, life jackets, and buoys.

X made his way over to the crate containing his

suit, armor, and helmet. The metal gleamed in the overhead light, but the polishing did little to obscure the scratches, dents, and other abuse inflicted during his decade on the surface.

After throwing on his new suit, he donned the trusty old armor. Back on the *Hive*, when Michael Everhart had asked him whether he wanted new gear, X had declined. Why give up something that had saved your life countless times? The gear was old, sure, but he had made modifications to his helmet and battery unit that made it more useful than ever before.

He secured the helmet, clicking it into place, and made his way to the rack of weapons, opting for an automatic rifle with a grenade launcher attachment. He left the bandolier of grenades on the rack, slung the gun over his shoulder, and spun the wheel handle to open the hatch to the weather deck.

Gusting wind peppered his suit with rain. He fought his way out onto the seventy-foot-long deck using the glow from lightning flashes. A fork speared through the sky and into a wave. The glow lit up the stern. X examined his handiwork. Two strands of razor wire were looped around the rails to dissuade any mutant beasts lurking in the seas from coming aboard.

Three spearguns were mounted on the deck, in slots retrofitted from fishing-pole mounts. X had welded them on himself, taking a lesson from the Cazadores, who had mounted such weapons on their ships.

In the center of the deck stood a twenty-foot mast with a crow's nest at the top. There was a second mast in the stern, but neither had sails up right now, and they weren't extended to full length, to present less of a target for lightning.

Chinning his comm pad, he opened the channel to the command center.

"Mags, you copy?"

"Copy that."

"I'm on deck and heading to the engine compartment."

"Please try to keep water out of the compartment, mate," Timothy said.

X chuckled in spite of himself. "Let's lay off the 'mate,' okay?"

"Okay … X."

"Please be careful, X," Magnolia added. There was trepidation in her voice. Not that he blamed her for being nervous at this point—she was sick as a dog, and he was starting to think she regretted coming along.

X uncoiled a rope from the bulkhead outside the hatch and looped it through two carabiners. He tested the hitch before setting out across the slick deck, keeping his eye on the silhouette of a Siberian husky painted on the deck not far from the mast. The name *Sea Wolf* was painted on the rectangular hatch that opened into the guts of the boat.

That was his objective. The sails were stored inside the compartment, close to the engine and battery units. The only access was from the hatch he was walking toward.

Battling the fierce winds, he slowly made his way forward. Beneath his boots, the entire boat rattled from the booming thunder. A wave slammed into the starboard side, sending a cascade of water over his armor. The shower didn't bother him, but he did fear taking a bath in the ocean.

He made cautious progress, pulling on the rope for slack on his way to the hatch. Bending down, he grabbed the handle and prepared to open it when the vessel crested a wave. X braced for impact.

The boat continued rising, then crashed back down with enough force to knock X off his feet. Water came over the side, hitting him with the force of a hurtling Siren. He scrambled back to the hatch and wiped his visor with a gloved hand.

"Be advised, I'm picking up a heavy electrical disturbance about two knots southwest," Timothy said.

"You picked a crappy time to go topside," Magnolia stuttered over the comm channel.

"Just keep us steady, Pepper," X said. He reached out for something to hold on to, but the only other thing to grab was the mast, which wouldn't do him any good. Clinging to the hatch, he prepared for the next wave.

He couldn't see over the cabin forming the bow of the boat and had no idea when it would hit. The vessel climbed again, engines purring beneath the deck, straining against the rough water.

"X, I highly recommend you come back inside before—"

X cut Timothy off. "And I'd highly advise you not give me orders, Pepper."

The boat rose onto a wave, and X gripped the handle tighter, gritted his teeth, and waited. This time, the bow slapped back down so hard, water broke over the top of the cabin. He looked up through the spray as lightning slashed the sky, illuminating a wall of waves in front of them.

"Magnolia, take over for Timothy," he ordered.

"But …"

"Do it, Mags. I trust you over him. No offense, Pepper."

"None taken, sir," Timothy replied.

Still clinging to the handle, X looked over his shoulder at the hatch leading back into the boat. It wasn't even twenty feet away, but he couldn't risk getting flung over the side, not even with the rope hitched to his armor.

"X, you should follow Timothy's suggestion and get back inside," Magnolia said.

"That's a negative, Mags. I'm going inside the battery room."

Static crackled over the channel with her reply. "Okay, but do it soon."

X prepared to open the hatch and climb inside. He couldn't risk flooding the compartment. While he waited for the right moment, his eyes darted to the razor wire on the rails. He had looped the wire there to protect them from sea creatures, but if he should get caught in it …

The boat rose up on a wave again, lifting X to a fleeting view of the ocean in all directions. Miles of dark, churning water surrounded the tiny boat. In the wake of a lightning flash, he thought he saw something moving in the murk.

Slapping back down, the vessel creaked from the impact. Although he had braced himself, the force still rattled his bones.

He shook off the shock.

Magnolia continued bringing the boat about, but the damage was already done. A sensor beeped over the comm system, and X didn't need to hear her frantic report to know the *Sea Wolf* had taken damage.

"We've got a crack in the right hull," she said. "Sealing it off."

A clanking sounded, and he looked up as the sail mast began to extend, the three-piece pole rising toward the storm clouds.

"What the hell is happening!" X shouted. "The mast is raising!"

"Must have malfunctioned," Magnolia quickly replied. "I can't stop it."

X looked back down at the hatch. He had to get inside before the mast took a lightning bolt and fried him where he stood. He spent the next few seconds timing the waves and waiting for his opportunity to climb inside.

"X, I'm picking something up on ..."

The rest of her transmission cut off. He clicked the handle left and pulled the hatch open. With seconds to spare, he unclipped his tether and turned to climb inside, when his peripheral vision caught a darting movement over the port gunwale.

In the split second it took his mind to process what he was seeing, a thick sucker-covered arm the size of a tree trunk slapped the deck and quickly slithered back over the railing, taking a coil of razor wire with it.

"What in the hell ...?" he mumbled. His pounding heart skipped as three more arms curled out of the water and rose above the railings. These weren't the snakelike creatures from the swamps. These were all arms of the same beast.

"X, something's attached to the boat!" Magnolia shouted. "Something—"

"Big? Yeah, I see it!"

X finally ducked into the hatch and had started to close it when one of the arms grabbed the handle, forcing it open. A third arm curled around the mast, twisting and curling its way to the top, where it bent the pole just below the crow's nest.

Using all his strength, X tried to force the hatch shut. But the *Sea Wolf* crested another wave and came slamming back down, dislodging X from the hatch and lofting him into the air.

He flailed for something to hold on to. With the rope gone, he had nothing to hold him steady. He crashed onto the deck, sliding as soon as he hit. The port rail stopped him with the clunk of his rifle on metal. The impact knocked the air from his lungs, and red encroached on the edges of his vision. When it cleared, he had no more than an eyeblink to avoid another arm darting over the deck.

Kicking it away, he pushed himself up and fought his way back to the hatch leading inside the boat. Lurching past one of the spearguns, he grabbed it, his boot sliding on the slick deck. He swiveled the weapon toward the nearest arm and harpooned the meaty flesh.

A howl rose above the cacophony of the storm— the voice of a monster. The dark, dead seas weren't so dead after all. It was why he had brought such weapons with him.

He grabbed the hatch to the cabin, opened it, and slammed it shut. An arm crashed into the metal a moment later. Backing away, X unslung his rifle, and flinched as an arm hit the hatch again.

"X, get down here!" Magnolia shouted from the command room.

Keeping the barrel aimed at the hatch, he back-pedaled over to the ladder. Then he climbed down to the lower deck and bolted for the command center. A wave smacked the starboard hull, and he thumped into a bulkhead. Stars broke before his vision, but he kept going to the next hatch.

Inside the control room, Magnolia gripped the wheel and stared at the glass. She had flipped the beams back on, and the bright glow captured the side view of a meaty orange body covered in flaps and bumps.

"X …" she stammered, "what the hell is that?"

Miles was up and growling at the glass.

Part of the sea creature had surfaced, giving them a view of glistening flesh crisscrossed in deep scars. Longitudinal wrinkles and flaps covered its mantle and narrower head.

"Pepper can probably answer better than I," X said.

"I believe it's an Enteroctopus, or a giant octopus," the AI replied.

The massive cephalopod tightened its grip around the *Sea Wolf*'s twin hulls. It reminded him of another monster—not as big and with fewer arms, but a monster all the same. El Pulpo, king of the Cazadores.

Something in his gut told him they were getting closer to the Metal Islands.

"This creature does not register in my database," Timothy replied after a few seconds' pause.

Thick arms covered in scars pulled the boat closer to a gaping hooked beak. The monstrous beast brought a tire-size eyeball to the windshield. Magnolia turned the wheel to the right, but the rudders didn't respond. The engines whined.

"Stop," X said, holding out a hand. "You're going to burn them out."

"I'm detecting a problem with engine two," Timothy said. "I recommend shutting it off."

Magnolia looked over to X.

"Do it and get back," he said.

Ever so slowly, Magnolia unbuckled her harness. The enormous eye with the strange elongated pupil followed her actions, and before she or X could react, an arm slapped against the windshield. Spiderwebs spread across the reinforced glass, which cracked audibly from the impact.

Magnolia moved out of the seat, and X shouldered his rifle, training the muzzle on the bulbous lump-covered head of the giant octopus.

"Take Miles into your quarters," X said. "Timothy, you take control of the boat as soon as I get done with this fucker."

"What do you mean, when you 'get done with it'?" Magnolia asked, not moving.

"Sir, I don't think your weapons will have much …" Timothy started to say.

Water trickled through the cracked glass as a long arm smacked the window again. This time, its suction cups pulled away a triangular chunk of glass, letting in the howling wind and salt spray.

"Go, Mags!" X shouted.

He moved his finger to the trigger, held in his breath, and fired at the huge elliptical eye.

* * * * *

Michael Everhart stabbed the rotted melon with his garden fork and blinked away the sweat in his eyes.

The diseased fruit splattered the dirt with green and red mush.

A bright glow from the ceiling-mounted grow lights captured the depressing scene. Other workers were carting off their first crop. The hybrid seeds had resulted in large melons, but a disease had putrefied the fruit.

"What the hell happened?" asked Cole Mintel.

The burly middle-aged man had joined the new team of farmers on *Deliverance* to help get the produce growing. He rolled up his sleeves, exposing strong forearms shaped by a lifetime working with wood.

Michael shook his head as he examined the three rows of melons. "Some sort of blight, I guess."

Cole looked over the open space at the other crops. Twelve rows of corn were already maturing, and plump, healthy red tomatoes hung from dark-green vines. A large patch of potatoes had already begun to break through the rust-hued dirt.

"We'll be fine," Michael said. "We'll try the melons again, or maybe we'll try something else."

He scooped the mess into a bag and handed it to Cole, who was collecting the ruined fruit. The older man hadn't said much since losing his son two months ago, and Michael could tell he had lost his passion for woodworking. Lately, he spent more time at the farm than in his shop.

"How's your wife?" Michael asked.

"She … we miss Rodger."

"I miss him, too. He was like an older brother to me." Michael put a hand on Cole's shoulder. He seemed to sulk under the touch.

"His sacrifice saved a lot of lives," Michael said.

Cole nodded again. "I better get these to the composters."

"Right." Michael watched the man leave and let out a sigh. They had lost too many friends over the past few months. Commander Rick Weaver, Andrew Bolden, Rodger Mintel, Ty Parker—the list went on and on.

But a ghost from the past had returned. As if in partial compensation for all the heartbreak and sacrifices, Xavier Rodriguez had come back from the dead. Humanity now had a future—an uncertain one, to be sure, but there was hope.

The most dangerous of emotions. Michael pulled the shirt from around his waist and used the bunched material to wipe the sweat from his forehead.

"Commander Everhart."

He followed the voice to the clean-room entrance, where Lieutenant Les Mitchells had ducked under the flap. "Sir, you're needed on the bridge."

"I'll be there in an hour," Michael replied.

Les remained where he was, and even at this distance, Michael could see the worry in his eyes.

"Give me a few minutes," Michael said.

That seemed to satisfy Les, who slipped back into the clean room.

Throwing on his shirt, Michael picked his way

through the rows of crops, careful not to step on a stem or tendril. He felt eyes following him across the dirt.

Most of the crew didn't understand why he spent his time off from diving and engineering to work in this place. But for Michael, farming had become therapeutic. Every tomato he held in his hand, every stem of potatoes he pulled from the ground, and every apple he plucked from their tree was a tangible success—something you could smell and taste. Something that sustained the human race.

Layla joined him here from time to time, but she didn't love it the way he did. She preferred to be in the new library aboard *Deliverance*, combing the archives and learning about the history of a destroyed world.

Michael got out of his work clothes, cleaned off, and then threw on his red coveralls. Walking through the corridors, he drew looks from nearly everyone he passed. There weren't many Hell Divers left, and even though Michael was helping in the effort to recruit new ones, the divers would never reach the numbers they had during his father's tenure under X.

The real legends were almost all dead now.

Two workers painting a bulkhead outside the farm stopped to salute Michael. He simply nodded and continued on his way. After Captain Jordan's death, both ships had returned to the roots of the *Hive*. The artwork was being restored, and destroyed and deleted archives were slowly being recovered, but there was still much work to be done.

Michael turned down a passage still being retrofitted into new quarters. More workers in yellow uniforms were carrying equipment into the small rooms, preparing them for their new tenants.

A third of the *Hive*'s population had already moved into quarters on *Deliverance*. There were still issues to deal with, primarily involving lower-deckers who felt that they got the short end of the stick in reassignment. But the committee formed to deal with such issues was working every day to make sure food, medical care, and shelter were being distributed equitably.

For the first time in recent memory, the passengers of the two airships were experiencing something that approached an egalitarian society.

Now that they had a second ship, there were more jobs. More jobs meant more food. More food meant a healthier population. A healthier population meant that Michael had a stronger pool of possible recruits for the next Hell Divers team.

Some days, he was really starting to feel that there was still hope for the human race, especially now that X and Magnolia were on the surface, looking for a permanent home.

He pulled his long hair back into a ponytail before approaching the hatch to the bridge. Only one militia soldier stood guard—another sign of change. With Jordan's henchmen either in the brig or dead on the surface in Florida, there was no reason to have a bulky security force. The executive team had reassigned most of the militia to other jobs, such as farming.

The hatch opened, and Michael walked out onto the clean bridge, blinking in the dim light.

Layla stood at the helm beside their new captain, Katrina.

"Commander Everhart on deck," said one of the officers.

Katrina and Layla both turned to face him, and both smiled, though the smiles seemed fraught, almost forced. In an instant, the optimism he had felt rising inside him drained away.

"Captain," Michael said.

"Follow me, Commander," Katrina said.

Layla remained at the command center while Michael followed the captain into the small conference room off the bridge, not bothering to ask why she wanted to meet with him personally. It could be any of a hundred things, since the ships were always one step away from disaster. But this time, it wasn't an engineering problem, or a new strain of flu afflicting the passengers, or a lower-decker resentful about reassignment.

"We just received a distress signal from the *Sea Wolf*," Katrina said. "Something happened to them, Michael."

His heart sank at the news. Everything had been going so well. But Michael had learned long ago that life was seldom fair.

"We tried to hail them," Katrina said, "but their radio is either damaged or offline. Right now, we have no way of knowing what happened."

She put a hand on his shoulder. "I wanted you to know. I loved X once, too." Her eyes flitted to the deck. "A part of me will always love him."

Michael blinked back a tear. He stiffened, trying his best to stay strong, because that was exactly what X would want him to do.

"Try not to worry," Katrina said. "If anyone can survive out there, it's Commander Rodriguez."

TWO

A violent shaking startled Magnolia awake. She coughed up a mouthful of salt water, gagged, coughed again. A curtain of short-cropped blue hair hung over her face, blocking her view. She pulled it back and looked up at the blinking emergency light spreading its pulsing red glow over the room.

Between blinks, she spotted the wet, furry heap that was Miles. The dog lay a few feet away, curled up, unmoving.

"Miles," she whispered. Reaching out, she nudged him, and he let out a whimper and moved a leg.

That was good. At least, he was still alive and could move.

But where was X?

Magnolia touched the goose egg on the back of her head and winced. She pulled away fingers slick with blood. She had taken a beating and had no idea how long she was out.

"Timothy, do you copy?" Magnolia said.

There was no answer but the creaking of bulkheads.

At first, she couldn't remember why she was inside her quarters with Miles, but an otherworldly call reminded her.

The screeches of the giant octopus carried through the small vessel. But something about this melancholy sound was different from the one she had heard in the command center.

The scent of smoke drifted belowdecks. That got her attention.

She pushed herself up in the puddle of cold water, cursing a blue streak that would have made X proud.

X … Where the hell are you?

Miles tried to get up, too, but slipped and fell in the water, splashing it over Magnolia's black fatigues. She helped him up onto a bunk and told him to stay put.

Then she fumbled her way over to the hatch and opened it to a passageway that was ankle-deep in seawater. Another emergency light winked outside the command center.

The hatch was ajar, providing a view inside the room. The red swirl from the light fell over standing water and a shattered windshield. A failsafe mechanism had activated, covering the broken glass with a metal hatch to keep the water out and at the same time blocking her view of the dark sea.

"Timothy?" she said.

The AI did not respond.

She closed the hatch and sealed it to keep the rest of the boat from flooding, then began her search for X.

The ladder to the upper deck was slick, and a quick glance revealed that it wasn't just water.

Blood coated the rungs.

She climbed to the staging area and stepped cautiously into the dark space. There were no emergency lights up here, and all the porthole windows were sealed off with metal hatches.

"X," she said quietly but firmly.

There was no response.

She reached into her cargo pocket and pulled out a small flashlight, which she pointed at the floor. A trail of blood led to the hatch.

"X, you son of a …"

She hurried over to a gun rack, freed her carbine, and slapped a full magazine into it. The gun felt good in her hands, but she wasn't sure the rounds were going to do much against such a massive beast.

The hatch opened to darkness and a spray of cold water that hit her face. Howling wind greeted her as she stepped onto the deck with her rifle shouldered and the flashlight clamped against the stock.

The trail of blood ended on the deck, where the ocean water had washed away any further evidence. She played the beam back and forth, but X was nowhere to be seen.

"X!" she shouted, but her voice was lost in the howling wind.

The *Sea Wolf* swayed as she took her first step out. The engines continued to propel the craft through the mountainous waves that crashed and rose, over and over.

"X!" she yelled again.

Her light fell on a limp arm lined with suction cups, nailed by a spear to the rail.

Another sucker-covered arm hung off the cabin behind her, severed and dripping red off the second deck.

Her flashlight moved to the gore spattered behind the mainmast. Smoke rose away from a charred spot and a gaping rent in the deck.

"Oh, shit," she whispered. The damage was, without a doubt, the result of a grenade. The blast had blown off two more of the creature's arms, and a hunk of meat that she didn't recognize.

"X, where are you!" she yelled, frantic now.

A reply came over the wind.

"Mags!"

The voice was faint but recognizable.

She hurried over to the side of the boat, cautious not to slide into the razor wire. Lowering her rifle, she used her flashlight to scan the ocean.

"Mags!" X yelled again.

But this wasn't coming from over the side.

She looked up at the top of the bent mast and spotted X, hanging on to the crow's nest. Another torn snaky arm was wrapped around the metal lookout, part of it coiled around his leg.

"You crazy bastard," Magnolia whispered.

She stared for a second but quickly moved away from the side of the boat. Judging by the spatter around her, the beast was dead, but if she had learned one thing over her years of diving and fighting, it was never to turn her back on a monster.

With the rifle up and trained on the starboard rail, she backpedaled to the mizzenmast, boots slapping in the constant wash. "That thing still out there?" she called up.

"Nope, nothing but fish bait now!" he shouted.

She stopped when she got to the mast.

"You need me to come get you, or you coming down from there?"

X swung his legs over the side of the crow's nest and kicked the hanging arm, but the suction cups had him and wouldn't let go, even in death.

She kept an eye on the rails on both sides of the *Sea Wolf* as X made his way down the bent mainmast. One of the engines was still running, but if they continued losing power they would be forced to use the sails, which was going to be difficult with the mainmast so severely compromised. The mizzenmast looked fine, but if they lost the engines, they would need both sails.

A beeping came from her wrist monitor, and she held up the cracked screen to see the radar come online. The small computer was synced with the boat, and she had manually created a program to go off if the radar picked up anything.

Her heart leaped at the small green bleeps east of their position.

"X, uh, we got a problem," she said.

"Yeah, I accidentally blew a small hole in the boat,

I know, but I had no choice ... and the mast is bent."

He jumped to the deck and, pulling a machete from the sheath on his back, cut away the yard of octopus arm still clinging to his leg.

"No, we got other problems."

"I know this already, Mags!"

Magnolia held her monitor in his face.

"Ah, damn!" he shouted.

"Either that thing was just a baby or it brought a lot of friends," she said.

"I'm going to need more grenades."

The boat swayed from side to side as they rushed back across the deck to the staging area and armory. Magnolia followed him down the ladder and into the passageway.

"Where's Miles?" X shouted.

"In my bunk."

Magnolia opened the hatch.

"You okay, boy?" X said, bending down by his dog. Tail whipping, Miles confirmed that he was just fine.

X led them back to the command center and took a seat in front of a console dripping with water. The metal hatch now covered the cracked and shattered windshield.

"Timothy must be offline," she said.

"Shit, just when we need him." X punched at the screen to reboot the system while Magnolia checked the navigation screen and the contacts to the east.

Timothy's voice suddenly cracked from the console. "Sir, I am unable to retract the mainmast."

"That's because it's bent," X said. He looked over to Magnolia. "Those contacts seem funny to you?"

"What do you mean?" Mags asked.

"They aren't moving toward us … We're moving toward them." X reached forward and flipped the metal hatch off the windshield. Another flip of a switch activated the searchlight beams. They penetrated deep into the darkness, capturing mountains above the waves on the horizon. These mountains weren't more waves or giant sea creatures, or anything else that moved.

"Dry land," Timothy said. "We've found another island chain."

Magnolia studied the jagged silhouettes.

"You think this is the Metal Islands?" she asked.

X shook his head. "I don't see the sun, and it's only five o'clock."

Magnolia picked up the radio handset. "I'll inform the captain." She pushed the button several times, but it wouldn't come on.

"The radio has been damaged," Timothy said. "I've activated the distress beacon, but we have no way of contacting the airships."

"Why the hell did you do that?" X said. "Now they're going to worry about us and possibly even send help—help that we don't need."

Magnolia didn't reply right away, but she couldn't hold back her thoughts. "X, I hate to break it to you, but we *do* need help. The boat has some serious damage."

"I do *not* want them sending anyone. It was my decision to come out here, and you made your choice, too, Mags."

She put down the radio handset, realization setting in. "You don't want Michael to come after you, do you?"

"You just figured this out?"

"So what if we find the Metal Islands? Then what?"

X didn't reply. He grumbled to himself under his breath. Magnolia was used to that; X still acted crazy from time to time. She had been fine with his rants and his conversations with himself, even when he screamed at night, but it was happening more often, and he was really starting to scare her.

She looked back at the islands. She wasn't sure what was out there, but whatever it was, they would have to face it on their own.

Captain DaVita wouldn't be coming to help them, nor would Tin and Layla. The storms in this area made a rescue mission impossible, and diving through the clouds was a death sentence.

"Pepper, shut that distress signal off," X ordered.

"Sir, if we do that, they won't be able to track us."

"That's the point," X replied. "We can fix the boat on our own. Now, do it, or I'm shutting you off for good."

Magnolia saw the anger in X's face, and for the first time on the journey, she felt the tendrils of despair creeping in. What had started off as a new adventure to locate a place for humanity to call home—and a chance to avenge Rodger—was turning into a nightmare. She just hoped she could trust X to do the right thing if they found the Metal Islands.

* * * * *

Les Mitchells pulled on the cuffs of his white uniform as he approached the brig with his wife, Katherine, and seven-year-old daughter, Phyl. Both of them had recovered from their cough weeks ago and were slowly regaining their strength. But they both had a long way to go, especially Phyl, who had lost almost ten pounds and looked like a stick. Katherine brushed back a strand of dirty-blond hair and heaved a sigh as they stopped outside the brig.

Today was a big day for the Mitchells family, for today they were to be reunited with Trey, who had spent nearly a year in the brig for stealing from the trading post. Captain DaVita had greatly reduced his sentence after Trey's vital help in overthrowing Captain Jordan, but they couldn't just let him out, even with his father now serving as executive officer on *Deliverance.*

To keep the system working as it was designed to work, the rule of law had to be respected.

Les rapped the hatch with his fist, and Lauren Sloan, the recently promoted sergeant of the militia, opened it, her lazy eye moving from Les to Katherine to Phyl.

"Wait out here," she grumbled, clearly unimpressed with Les' new rank as lieutenant of *Deliverance*.

Les smiled at his wife and bent down slightly to wrap his tall daughter in a hug.

"Is Trey really coming home with us?" Phyl asked, looking up with her hazel eyes.

"He sure is."

Katherine returned the smile with one of her contagious grins and put her arms around Les and Phyl. They were still huddled together when Trey finally emerged. Two months shy of his eighteenth birthday, and the boy was the thinnest Les had ever seen him—even thinner than Phyl.

"Hi," Trey said, his voice timid.

"My baby," Katherine said, pulling away from Les to hug her son.

"Trey, you look really—" Phyl said, but Sloan interrupted her.

"Sign here, and you can be on your way, kid," she said, handing Trey a clipboard. He let go of his mother long enough to sign his name to the page.

And just like that, Trey Mitchells was a free …

Man. Your boy is a man, Les thought. He exchanged a nod with Sloan. He respected her for helping them take down Captain Jordan, and she had treated Trey with dignity. It wasn't her fault the rations for prisoners were barely enough to survive on.

"Congratulations again on your promotion," he said.

She shrugged. "Just means more work for me." She gave a mirthless grin. "Congratulations on your promotion as well, LT."

"Thanks," Les replied.

Her lazy eye stopped on Trey. "Stay out of trouble, kid," she said.

"I plan to, Sergeant."

Les put his hand on his son's back and herded his family away from the brig on the *Hive*, anxious to get them all together around the small table in their quarters.

Although he worked on *Deliverance* now, he, like many of the other Hell Divers and officers, had opted to remain living on the *Hive*. Something about deserting the airship had felt wrong, and when given the opportunity for a new cabin on *Deliverance*, he had politely declined.

A smile broke across his face at the sight of fresh paint on the bulkheads. Trey grinned, too, seeing the fresh artwork covering the metal with images of the Old World: fluffy clouds, exotic animals, and cities.

"How are you feeling?" Katherine asked Trey.

His smile broadened. "I'm just glad to be out of that hellhole and back with my family."

They arrived at their home a few minutes later, where a meal of guinea pig stew, fresh bread, and warm potatoes waited. They even had a healthy spread of butter.

Les hadn't eaten butter for as long as he could remember.

"I bet you're hungry," Phyl said. "You look like a beanpole."

"Takes one to know one," Trey replied. He brushed his long hair out of his face and pulled out the familiar creaky wooden chair he had always sat on for meals.

"We need to get you a haircut and a bath," Katherine said.

"I'll eat, bathe, and then I'm off. I want to see Commander Everhart," Trey said.

Les took a seat at the head of the table, studying his son in the glow of the single bulb dangling from the overhead. The friendship between the two young men went way back but Les found it odd his son would want to see Michael right after leaving the brig, unless …

"For what?" Les asked.

"I've had a lot of time to think about what I'm going to do with my life," Trey said. He looked over at his mother, who had stopped scooping stew into bowls.

She looked just as nervous as Les felt about whatever this was that Trey had decided behind bars. He was hoping his son would reapply to engineering school or come to work on the bridge with him, but his gut told him Trey wasn't interested in either of those opportunities.

"I'll tell you after we eat," Trey said, licking his lips. "I'm starving."

Katherine finished pouring the stew and distributed the bowls one by one. They bowed their heads together and held hands just as humans had done centuries earlier.

"I'm thankful today to have my son Trey back home, and our entire family together once again," Les said. "Today, I pray to whatever God might be out there, to keep the *Hive* and *Deliverance* in the sky long enough for Xavier and Magnolia to find us a new home."

He let go of Trey's and Phyl's hands and waited for Trey to tell them of his decision, but the boy was busy shoveling food into his mouth.

"Mom," he said with his mouth full of stew, "this is so-o-o-o-o good."

"We were lucky to get a guinea pig. First time we've had meat in months."

Phyl took a bite of bread, but she still hadn't touched her stew.

"What's wrong, sweetheart?" Katherine asked.

"I don't feel so good." Phyl looked up at her brother.

"Your stomach feels sick?" Les asked.

Phyl shook her head and put her hand on her chest. "It's my heart. It hurts. I missed Trey really bad, and now I'm worried he's going to leave us again."

Trey laid his hand on Phyl's. "I'm not going to leave you guys again. I promise."

"But you told me you want to be a Hell Diver," Phyl said. "And Hell Divers die."

Les suddenly felt his own heart grow heavy. "Is this true, son?"

"Yes." Trey laid his fork, with a skewered new potato, down on the table. "I've decided it's the best way to give back to the ship and my family. We'll get more rations, and—"

"I'm the XO now, Trey," Les said, cutting him off. "You don't have to risk your life."

Trey's lip quivered. "We can't afford to lose you, Dad. And I know for a fact you'll keep diving despite your new title. I heard Sloan talking about it."

Les couldn't dispute that. He had agreed to remain a Hell Diver when he accepted the position of XO.

"It's time for me to be a man," Trey said. "It's time for me to take your place as a Hell Diver."

Katherine looked across the table at Les, her eyes pleading with him to talk some sense into the boy.

But his son was no longer a child. He had helped overthrow Jordan, had served his time in the brig, and was now free to do what he wanted.

Les wiped the corner of his mouth and put his handkerchief on the table. Today was supposed to be a joyful reunion and a wonderful meal with his family, but he had lost his appetite. After finally getting his son back, the thought of him diving into the apocalypse made him feel sick.

* * * * *

Katrina DaVita was starting to feel at home on the bridge of *Deliverance*. All around her, officers worked at their stations in the circular space, monitoring the skies for storms, watching the life-support systems on the ship, and communicating with the crew of the *Hive*.

Technically, she was the captain of both ships, but she had chosen to lead from this control room. For the first few weeks, she had tried to work on the clean white bridge of the *Hive*. It was larger and comfortably familiar, but that familiarity was the problem.

Memories of her former lover, Captain Leon Jordan, made working there too painful. If she was going to focus on saving the human race and leaving a positive legacy as captain, she needed to do it aboard *Deliverance*. The *Hive* would always be her home, but she needed a fresh start.

She had considered adding a new captain to the *Hive* but had no one she could entrust with the job quite yet. Former Lieutenant Hunt and Ensign Ryan were serving time in the brig for conspiracy convictions, and everyone else was too green.

Humans continued to let her down. That was why she had transferred the AI Timothy Pepper from the Hilltop Bastion to the other airship, to serve as her cocaptain.

She knew that the ship was in good hands with the AI, and being able to trust Timothy allowed her to concentrate on the most important part of her job: keeping the two airships in the air.

Today, she had a few things on her plate. Shortly, she would check the finished renovations of forty new living quarters on the ship. When finished, they would house over a hundred people from the *Hive*, bringing the total occupancy on *Deliverance* to just shy of two hundred. The other 273 passengers would remain on the *Hive*.

But now she had a bigger problem on her hand than just angry civilians chafing under what they saw as unequal treatment.

Katrina made her way over to the comms stations, where Ada Winslow, a twenty-year-old engineering student turned communications officer, sat in a chair facing the radio equipment.

After losing the experience of Ensign Ryan and Lieutenant Hunt, Katrina had been forced to pull several new staff members straight from the school. Ada was at the top of her class, and though she hadn't majored in communications, she learned quickly.

"Ensign Winslow, have we heard anything from Commander Rodriguez or Miss Katib?"

Ada twisted, her brown eyes eager to help. "Negative, Captain. I've been combing the channels all evening just in case they are trying to broadcast on a different frequency, but nothing so far."

"Keep trying." Katrina gave her a reassuring nod. She made her way down the line of new crew members. Ensign Dave Connor, a forty-year-old engineer who had lost his leg in an accident involving one of the *Hive*'s turbofans, manned the navigation system, tapping his prosthetic leg on the deck. He also doubled as a weatherman and was an expert at reading the storms, which made him invaluable to her.

"How are the skies looking?" she asked.

"Ma'am," Dave said, exposing a mostly full set of yellowed teeth, "winds out of the south at eight knots. Barometer has dropped slightly. I'm detecting an electrical storm that appears to be along a fifty-mile front. We're keeping our distance, but if we get any closer, we're in for a rocky ride."

"Keep an eye on that storm and let me know if anything changes."

"Will do, ma'am."

Katrina continued to the next officer, Ensign Bronson White. By far the oldest man on the ship, he seemed to be named for the color of his thick hair and beard. Thick spectacles magnified his pale blue eyes. He was the former chief engineer of the ship, replaced by Samson upon his retirement ten years ago.

"Ensign," Katrina said.

Bronson nodded politely. "How are you this evening, Captain?"

"I'm well. How are our ships?"

He shifted his glasses down his nose to look at the display. "Gas bladders on the *Hive* are all functioning properly, and the engines on *Deliverance* are fully operational. We haven't had to use a turbofan on the *Hive* for several days."

"And the supports are holding firmly?" she asked, referring to the aluminum struts that Engineering had used to tie the two ships together.

"Yes, Captain."

Katrina patted White's shoulder before walking away.

Layla Brower was the other crew member working the night shift, and by her slouched posture and tired eyes, it was obvious she missed Michael.

But Katrina needed Layla on deck tonight. Her job was an important one: using the new archives from *Deliverance* to restore the archives that Jordan had destroyed. Tonight, she was also working with Sergeant Sloan of the militia to keep the peace on the airship.

"How's it going?" Katrina asked.

Layla shook her head. "It's been quiet so far, but the night is still young. We have four soldiers on patrol throughout *Deliverance*, and another ten on the *Hive*."

Not a lot of boots, but to Katrina's thinking, the fewer the better—especially since the militia had willingly carried out Captain Jordan's orders to kill Janga, Ty Parker, and many others.

The passengers didn't trust the militia, and that made Katrina's job as captain difficult. Very difficult. It did help that she had been the one to kill Jordan, but even this had not gained her the trust of everyone—especially former lower-deckers.

Missing from the bridge was Lieutenant Les Mitchells, who was with his family, celebrating his son's release from the brig. It was a happy day for the Mitchellses, and one that Katrina was glad to finally see. Ordering Trey back to his cell after he had helped overthrow Jordan was difficult, but she had to be fair. Shortening his sentence by a year was the best she could do without upsetting other passengers who had family members serving time.

Katrina went back to the captain's chair and sat. Her crew was new, with both young and old officers, but they were *her* team, and she was proud to have them working with her.

They had been granted a new beginning with *Deliverance.* But no matter how well things were going in the sky, their future really depended on what was happening on the surface. If X and Magnolia were dead, then the one shot at finding the Metal Islands was over before it really began.

"Ensign Connor, bring up our current location on-screen," she ordered.

The wall-mounted monitor in front of her chair flashed to life, showing an old-world map. The airships were still flying about fifty miles off the coast of Florida. A curved red line showed the location of the *Sea Wolf* ever since *Deliverance* dropped the vessel into the water.

X had sailed southeast from Florida, between Cuba and the Bahamas. They were just west of the Turks and Caicos Islands when the distress signal activated, but it had shut off not long after being turned on.

She wasn't sure precisely where they were now, but it had to be close to those islands. Pushing another button on her monitor, she pulled up the weather overlay map.

A red cloud swallowed most of the screen, intensifying over Cuba and the Bahamas.

X had seen this map. He knew what he was getting himself into, and that was why he had opted for the route between the islands. Another dense fog of red covered most of Jamaica, Hispaniola, and Puerto Rico. Only a small chain called the Virgin Islands was visible in the blur.

In her mind's eye, Katrina pictured the nuclear-tipped missiles striking each of the larger islands two and a half centuries ago, incinerating millions of people and destroying in minutes what had taken humanity an eon to create. But maybe the smaller groups like the one on the map hadn't been touched. Maybe it was some sort of Goldilocks zone that had been deemed not worth destroying. And maybe the radiation and electrical storms never reached this place.

Or maybe it was just another mutated wasteland.

The sound of the hatches opening pulled her away from her reflections. Les ducked under the bulkhead and walked onto the bridge, his normally pale cheeks red. Katrina knew right away something was wrong.

She rose from her chair.

"Captain," he said.

"That was a quick dinner," she replied. "How's Trey?"

Les sighed at his boots. "He wants to be a Hell Diver."

Katrina stroked her jaw. She remembered the look on her father's face when she had told him the same thing. He wasn't happy about it, but he hadn't lived long after she decided to join the ranks of the divers.

"Trey is a man now and has to make his own way," she replied.

Les swallowed, his prominent Adam's apple bobbing, and rubbed his tuft of red hair. "I know."

"Try not to worry, Lieutenant. The next time we dive, it will be into a green zone, and even if Trey does decide to go through with this, it will be months before he dives. Besides, we have bigger problems right now." She motioned for Les to follow her over to the central table.

"Listen up, everyone," she said.

Layla, Dave, Ada, and Bronson all stood to attention at their stations. Even the older ensign, who had a natural slouch, stood ramrod straight.

"As a few of you already know, we have received a distress beacon from Commander Rodriguez and Miss Katib. The last ping we got from their distress beacon was just west of the Turks and Caicos Islands before it went offline. For now, only a few of us, including Commander Everhart, are privy to this information, and for now I want to keep it that way."

"Should we change course, Captain?" Layla asked.

"No, we hold steady where we are. The electrical storms in this area are too dangerous to try mounting a rescue op. X and Magnolia are on their own for now."

"The *Sea Wolf* is our best hope of finding a new home for humanity," Layla said.

Katrina sighed. "I know this, but X and Magnolia

can take care of themselves. Right now we need to focus on keeping our ships in the sky ..."

Her words trailed off as realization set in. Her predecessor had often used that same line. The thought chilled her.

So this was how it felt to lead the final bastion of civilization. The burden of having so many lives in her hands wasn't even the worst part of leading—it was the secrets she had uncovered on *Deliverance* that she still hadn't told to anyone.

THREE

The island sure didn't look like a potential home for the human race. X stood in the off-kilter crow's nest twenty feet above the *Sea Wolf*, roving his rifle scope across the shoreline and looking for any sign of the Cazadores or Sirens.

The same bleak scene from back on the mainland filled the scope. A cold, dead world the color of rust waited on the other side of a wide bay. Along the base of a mountain, the ruins of a city stood at the far edge of a gray beach. The crumbling structures weren't blackened from the nuclear fires, but the years had not been kind to them.

It was a place of broken windows, sinking foundations, rotted wood, and cracked roadways, just like every city he had ever seen. The jungle had crept into the heart of the town, covering most of the structures in vines and red foliage.

No, there weren't any Cazadores here. This wasn't the Metal Islands that el Pulpo had spoken of back in

Florida. This was just another radioactive old-world city, cursed to die in the darkness.

And once again X had no choice but to scavenge the wastes while nursing an injury. Blood crusted around his arm where a suction cup had held him tight enough to draw blood through his skin. And his flesh wasn't the only part of him injured.

Smoke fingered away from the stern of the *Sea Wolf*, swirling into the storm clouds above. The vessel had taken severe damage in the storm and the attack. He had blown a three-by-three-foot hole on the port side with the grenade that killed the giant octopus, flaying open the metal deck and splattering the rail with hunks of gore stuck in the barbed wire. Even worse, engine two was destroyed, and battery two was at zero percent charge.

"Pepper, how long will battery one last us?" X asked over the open channel.

"Battery one is currently showing an eighty percent charge, which should last roughly two more weeks before requiring a recharge."

X twisted for a better view of the deck, examining the damage from above. The beast had done a number on the twin hull, leaving deep rents in the stern and starboard rails. The command center had a broken windshield and a damaged radio.

"Michael better not come for us," X muttered to himself.

"Come again?" Magnolia said.

"Nothin'."

X hadn't meant for her or Timothy to hear his thoughts about Katrina or Michael coming after him out here. He was terrified that the distress beacon Timothy had activated would provoke the captain into sending them help.

I can do this on my own, with Miles' help and maybe Mags' if she gets smart about shit.

Grabbing the metal rail, X went back to scanning the island. A few clicks to his wrist monitor brought up a map of their current location. They were in the West Indies, dead north of Hispaniola, which meant he was looking at a part of the Turks and Caicos Island chain.

"Take us in, Mags," X said over the comm link.

"You sure about that?"

He grumbled. "You need to start trusting me, kid."

"And you need to stop calling me 'kid'—although I won't hold my breath for that day."

The single working engine purred beneath the deck, and the rudders turned slightly. He felt a little guilty about having yelled at her in the command center, but she had to understand, he didn't want *Deliverance* risking their hides for him. This was his decision, his mission.

He wanted el Pulpo's head on a pike, and he wasn't going to stop until he found the bastard—and, with any luck, discovered humankind's future home in the process.

He wedged his boot between the metal ribs of the crow's nest and trained his rifle scope on the shore as the *Sea Wolf* began cutting through the shallows.

Lightning forked over the mountains, spreading a blue glow across the jagged cliffs and the mutated jungles surviving in near darkness.

This was the third island they had come across in the past few hours, but the first showing any sign of civilization.

X was hoping to find the tools to help repair their radio and fix the *Sea Wolf*. His vantage point gave him a panoramic view of their surroundings, and he continued to scan the ocean, beach, and city beyond for contacts.

He didn't need to activate his night-vision goggles to see the island in detail. The sky retained a blue tint from the constant flashes across the mountain chain, casting an eerie glow on the terrain and the surf.

Several large vessels stood aground on the shallow bottom, the waves beating their rusted hulls. On shore, a dozen shipping containers sat in the sand. X recognized the language marking the side.

It was all in Spanish—the language of the Cazadores.

Shadows flickered beneath the clouds. He zoomed in with his scope on what looked like missiles firing from the sky toward the jungles.

At first, he passed them off as some trick of the light. But then he realized, this was no optical illusion.

His heart skipped at the realization—they had to be Sirens.

But when he zoomed in further and followed one of them in his sights, he saw these weren't the genetically modified humans at all. These were massive birds.

"I got potential hostiles," X said.

"I see 'em. Do you want me to change course?"

X watched the beasts for several seconds. There were a dozen of them, and several were headed out to sea. From this distance, he wasn't sure just how large they were, but they were big.

They weren't just big—they were monsters.

An ethereal wail made him flinch. He ducked down just as one of the creatures swooped overhead from behind, giving him a close-up glimpse.

This one had a bald head the color of blood, and a wingspan longer than two men. The yellow beak was big enough to swallow a child. It flapped black wings, heading toward the shoreline with an eyeless fish clutched in its talons. A flashing antenna hung from the skull of the fish, blinking and giving the bird's underside a purple glow as it flew back to its nest on the island.

These weren't just birds. They were monstrous vultures.

X checked his six for more of the flying beasts, but the sky was clear in that direction. He ignored the water until he saw something cresting the waves back in the bay. A spiky dorsal fin broke through the water, cutting the waves.

The birds weren't the only hunters prowling these waters.

"Great," he muttered, flipping his NVGs on. In the green hue, he saw the silhouette of a shark half the boat's length, just below the surface. The predators had survived nearly half a billion years on Earth; it should have been no surprise that they made it through the apocalypse.

"Mags, better pick up speed," X said into the comm.

"It's pretty shallow in here. I have to—"

The crunch of the hull hitting something massive nearly sent X tumbling out of the crow's nest. He looked over the side of the cage at more silhouettes beneath the surface. But these weren't giant sharks or cephalopods.

A graveyard of boats lay in the shallows, their carcasses strewn over the bottom, where they had sunk at their moorings hundreds of years ago. They no doubt made perfect homes for all sorts of monsters.

"Hurry it up, Mags!" he shouted.

The *Sea Wolf* clipped the stern of an ancient vessel just below the water, shaking X inside his aerial cage. He watched in horror as they plowed toward the minefield of sunken wrecks.

"I can't see," Magnolia shouted over the channel.

Miles barked in the background. The poor dog wasn't used to the confines of a boat any more than X was. He was meant to be free, to be able to run on the surface, but like humans, Miles had been dealt a cruel hand.

The anger flowed through X as he tried to form a plan to get them out of this mess. There was always a way out—always an option.

"I'll be your eyes, Mags, just calm down," X said. "Now turn a hair to the right … now!"

The boat veered around a barnacle-encrusted wreck. Beyond it, several more derelict hulls broke the surface. Radio towers protruded from them like twisted rebar. The sight gave him an idea, but he tabled it for now and checked the status of the shark.

Still trailing them, the sea monster lazily whipped its tail back and forth, moving through the water with ease—the perfect predator. X aimed his rifle and prepared to fire, then decided that the noise might attract more hungry things.

The creature swerved away, sinking beneath the waves and vanishing into the boneyard of ships.

X slowly lowered his rifle.

It would be back.

The *Sea Wolf* moved into the center of the bay at a good clip. At the helm, Magnolia steered around the clearly visible obstructions, and X continued to warn her of those buried beneath the dark surface.

Piercing chirps from the birds hunting over the land filled the night. At least, X thought it was night—it was hard to tell in perpetual darkness. Day or night, his biological clock and his growling stomach told him it was time for supper.

He fought both the pain radiating up his arm and the grip of exhaustion.

"Screw off," X muttered, raising his weapon and firing at a bird that swooped toward the boat. The rounds lanced through its red-plumed wings, sending the creature arcing down toward the bay.

Magnolia steered to port, avoiding the broken hull of a fishing vessel that had split in half on a submerged rock.

Hearing a splash off the starboard side, X turned to see the bird he had shot, flailing in the water. In a blink, the shark hunting in the shallows emerged, opened a mouth rimmed with two rows of teeth, and swallowed the struggling bird in a single bite. The sea beast vanished beneath the waves.

"Almost there, Mags," X said, trying to focus on the beach.

Their vessel squeezed through a gap between two ships aground in the tide. X got a view of their decks, still laden with shipping containers marked in the Cazadores' language.

This wasn't the Metal Islands, but they had to be getting close.

The starboard hull of the *Sea Wolf* screeched against the hull of the ship on the right. X kept his rifle up, roving for contacts on the decks to either side.

A moment later, and they were free and sailing right for the shore.

"Beach us," X ordered.

Timothy, who had been silent until now, spoke up. "Sir, I would highly recommend avoiding contact with solid land. The impact could dam—"

"Mags, shut our AI friend off, please," X said.

"Sorry, Timothy," Magnolia said. "Nothing personal."

The shark's dorsal fin surfaced again, and X wasted no time lining up the crosshairs on the head and pulling the trigger. The rounds punched into the dark skin around the open mouth, which yawned open to reveal feathers still stuck in the double rows of teeth.

Blood trickled out of the bullet wounds, and the beast veered away, its tail slapping the starboard hull before it swam off into the bay.

The impact knocked the *Sea Wolf* to the side, so that the port hull caught the next swell of surf. Escapes like this were never based on pure logic, and sometimes, with just seconds to make a decision, a good option didn't present itself.

This time, the only option was to hang on for his life.

He clung to the cage as Magnolia tried to get the bow pointed ashore, but the surf was too strong. The waves slammed them broadside onto the beach, where they skidded until they fetched up against a rock.

X slid out of the crow's nest, losing his rifle in the process. His left boot caught on the rail, leaving him hanging upside down twenty-odd feet above the sand.

Dangling there, he would be easy pickings for one of the oversized vultures. And dropping to the sand would leave him with broken legs, or worse.

"X!" Magnolia shouted.

She emerged on the deck below with Miles, who barked up at him.

It took only a second to see that the dog was actually barking at three birds swooping in from the sky.

X suddenly got a crazy idea. He swung his body until his boot dislodged, and using the momentum, he reached for the rungs. He fell several feet before finally catching one.

Somehow, the force did not dislocate his shoulder, though pain lanced up his shoulder and neck. Wasting no time, he put his boots against the mast, clear of the rungs, and slid down until he could safely swing off onto the sand.

Magnolia, with a rifle in each hand, and Miles were waiting for him there. She tossed X the rifle he had dropped, and they stood together, back to back, firing on the swooping birds.

They emptied their magazines, plucking a dozen from the sky with calculated shots to conserve precious ammo. The meaty bodies whapped into the sand a hundred feet away, twitching and squawking as they died.

X looked back over his shoulder to see whether the shark was still hunting in the surf. The *Sea Wolf* had pushed up a berm of sand on the port side, and smoke continued to drift from the deck.

"You still don't think we need any help?" Magnolia asked while changing magazines.

The potshot got under X's skin, and he couldn't hold back his words.

"Remember the Hell Diver motto?"

"Uh … 'We dive so humanity survives.'"

X dipped his helmet and gestured for Miles to join him. "This mission isn't about destroying humanity;

it's about saving it. We dived for humanity; now we're sailing for humanity. And I'm not going to risk *Deliverance* or the *Hive* just to save our sorry asses. We're on our own out here, and the sooner you start accepting that, the safer humanity is going to be."

* * * * *

The men and women inside the launch bay of the *Hive* were a diverse group. Les could see many shades of skin standing in front of the tubes that, for centuries, had launched Hell Divers onto the postapocalyptic world.

But there was one thing these people all had in common: youth.

Les hated seeing so many young volunteers standing in a room that most people stepped into only a handful of times. Seeing his son among them was especially painful.

Trey will have to make his own way. Captain DaVita's words repeated over and over in his mind as he looked over his son and the other volunteers.

Trey stood between Sandy Bloomberg, the daughter of the head farmer on the *Hive*, and Jed Snow, an orphan that had lost his dad to diving and his mom to cancer. They were just months shy of their eighteenth birthdays, and it showed.

Jed sported a thin beard that didn't quite cover all of his pimples, and had his long dark hair slicked back. Sandy tried to make herself look older by liberally applying homemade makeup, but it only served to emphasize her lack of experience with the stuff. She directed light blue eyes at Les and smiled, two crooked front teeth showing.

The veterans, Commander Michael Everhart and Layla Brower, weren't much older than Jed, Sandy, and Trey. Only Erin Jenkins was in her midtwenties.

Vish Abhaya and his twin brother, Jaideep, were also young, only nineteen years old. They were both handsome: tall and dark-skinned, but they had spent the past few years in and out of trouble. They came from a Buddhist family that still practiced traditions of the Old World. But the boys didn't shave their heads, wear robes, or meditate multiple times a day—or at all.

Ordinary brown jumpsuits draped their skinny frames, and gold hoops hung from their ears. Like many youths, the boys had rebelled, not because they were evil at heart, but because they were bored.

Hell Diving seemed to attract kids like this until they realized what it really entailed or until they died, whichever came first. Les had seen it plenty of times before, and he wasn't sure how to feel about their presence. Both Abhaya twins were failed students and had spent most of their teenage years working odd jobs or in maintenance. Their last name meant *fearless*, but he wasn't sure they were cut out for the world of diving into the apocalypse.

"You sure about this?" Vish whispered to his brother.

Jaideep punched him on the arm. "I told you to keep your trap shut."

"Jeez, man." Vish gave his brother a cockeyed look and rubbed his shoulder.

"What you lookin' at, old man?" Jaideep asked Les.

Vish laughed. "You sure you're not too old to dive?"

"And too tall?" Jaideep added with a chuckle.

"That's *Lieutenant Mitchells* to you," Trey said. He took a step toward the twins, but Les shook his head. The last thing he wanted to deal with right now was a fight that could end in Trey heading back to the brig.

"Yeah, I'm tall, and I'm old enough to be your father, but if you're serious about diving, you both better get serious, because diving isn't a joke," Les said.

Jaideep smirked, but Vish nodded, apparently getting the message.

The twins weren't the only potentially problematic divers.

Erin Jenkins had a chip on her shoulder. Her Mohawk glistened with paste under the overhead lights. She wore a sleeveless shirt that showed off her ropy, defined arm muscles. Michael and Layla were discussing something with her in private.

"We have no choice," Michael said loud enough for everyone to hear.

Layla put a hand on his arm—a subtle gesture to calm the commander down. Les had seen her do it a hundred times, but this time it didn't seem to have any effect.

Michael stalked over to the porthole windows to look out at the swirling storm clouds. For the past two months, both he and Erin had developed anger problems. Erin's was related to losing her dad, but Les wasn't sure where Michael's was coming from, unless it had something to do with X.

Layla walked over to join Michael, and Les moved closer to Erin.

"Everything okay?" he asked.

Erin shrugged a shoulder.

Les liked the young woman, but he wasn't sure he liked the idea of diving with her again until she got her emotions in hand. A prickly attitude could lead to poor decision making, and a single poor decision could kill someone.

For Les, with Trey standing just a few feet away, more was at stake now than ever before. Les had to protect his son at all costs, but he wasn't sure there would be a way to prevent Trey from diving with Erin in the coming months.

The problem was simple math. They didn't have a very big pool of people to recruit from. The passengers were getting stronger, thanks to an increase in food production, but the only volunteers so far were those now standing inside the launch bay.

Katrina had privately communicated orders to Les, Michael, and Layla. She didn't want any of them diving unless absolutely necessary. Their focus was to be on the airships, not the surface. X and Mags were in charge of the ground, for now.

The metal doors screeched open, and everyone came to attention as Katrina finally walked into the room. She wore her braided hair over her shoulders, and her crisp white uniform pulled up over her forearms to proudly show off the Raptor and Angel tattoos.

"Good evening, Captain," Les said.

"Evening, Lieutenant." Katrina stopped in front of the group, who gathered in a loose rank before her. She spent a moment taking them in, and Les did the same.

Jed, Trey, and Sandy stood stiffly and respectfully, eyes forward like soldiers. Jaideep and Vish were more relaxed, and Jaideep seemed to be whistling a tune under his breath. Les realized if you added up all their ages it still wouldn't equal the amount of dives Xavier Rodriguez had completed over the years.

"Welcome, and thank you, all of you, for volunteering," Katrina said. "I started diving when I was about your age."

Moving down the line, she looked at each of them in turn, stopping to give Jaideep and Vish another once-over. Then she moved on to Trey and Sandy. Finally, she walked past Erin, Layla, Michael, and Jed.

"Jed, I'm happy to see you here. Your dad would be extremely proud, and your mom would be, too," Katrina said.

"I'm proud to be here," Jed said. "If it weren't for some health problems, I would have been here when I turned sixteen."

Katrina forced a smile, and then looked at Les.

"Lieutenant, may I have a word?" She gestured toward Michael and Layla. "You, too, Commander Everhart, and diver Brower."

The three followed the captain over to the conference room, where hundreds of Hell Divers had received briefings over the years. Les saw Sandy's curious gaze follow them across the room before Katrina closed the door behind them.

"This is not enough," she said.

Michael and Les exchanged a glance.

"These are the only volunteers," Les said.

"We will need more."

Michael stepped forward, his back stiff. "I thought we didn't have any upcoming missions."

Les was equally baffled. Did she have something planned that he didn't know about? Just last night, she had told him there wouldn't be any dives for months.

He wanted to ask what had changed in the past twenty-four hours, but his job as her right-hand man wasn't to question her in front of others. He would do that in private—unless she told them first.

Katrina took a seat in her chair and put her hands on her head.

"Ma'am," Layla said, walking over to pat Katrina's back in a sign of support.

Les didn't know what to do. He hadn't seen Katrina like this since she first took the helm. But the trauma of losing her child, killing her former lover, and seeing X leave—again—and the burdens of being captain had likely stacked up.

She was a strong woman, but in the end, she was only human.

Katrina pulled her hands away from her flushed cheeks and stood again.

"Sorry. I'm fine. There's just a lot on my mind, and I'm worried about our friends on the *Sea Wolf*."

"X is still out there," Michael said. "I can feel it in my bones."

"He's definitely a hard man to kill, but he isn't immortal." Katrina sighed. "I should never have sent him out there alone with Magnolia. We should have sent more boats. More …"

After a pause, she looked to Les. "Lieutenant, I want you to meet with Sergeant Sloan as soon as possible. Tell her I need the best militia soldiers she can spare."

Michael raised a hand. "Captain, I thought I was in charge of finding new divers."

"Things just changed, Commander," Katrina replied, still looking at Les. "I need you for something else."

He had finally figured out what had her so bothered. She wasn't looking just for people who could dive—she wanted people who could fight.

FOUR

"I feel like I haven't spent any real time with you in weeks, Tin," Layla said as they walked down the passageway connecting the *Hive* to *Deliverance*.

News of the *Sea Wolf* had rattled him, but he couldn't do anything about it right now.

They need you here, X had told him before leaving. *If something happens, don't come after me.* Maybe so, but Michael was having a hard time sitting idly by while X, Mags, and Miles were potentially in trouble. To do nothing felt like abandoning them.

He knew that Layla was upset, too, though she wasn't showing it.

"Have you missed me?" she asked.

He squeezed her hand. "Of course. I always miss you."

"Great answer." Her smile still had the same effect on him as when they were kids. The cute dimple and gleaming white teeth still sent a little shiver through him.

"I don't know what to do about X and Magnolia," he said.

Her grin vanished, and her hand went slack.

"Don't do that," Michael said, taking her hand again. "I know you're upset, too, and I think we should talk about this."

"Why talk about something we can't control? We can't go searching for them in those storms. You know that."

"Yeah, but …"

"You can't beat yourself up over this. Magnolia and X made their choice when they set off for the Metal Islands. They knew the risks, and besides, you said it best back in the launch bay: X might be in trouble, but he isn't dead."

Michael looked at the Team Raptor patch sewn over his chest. Inside his vest pocket were the words he had given X over a decade ago.

Accept your past without regrets. Handle your present with confidence. Face your future without fear.

He carried the quote with him even though he had it memorized. He had lived his life by the motto, and handing the quote to people was his way of giving back. Each time he gave it to someone, he wrote it down again for the next person.

"Everything's going to be okay, Tin," Layla said.

Michael kissed her softly on the cheek. "I know. Come on, I have a surprise for you."

Her smile returned, and she followed him down the empty passage.

Around the next corner, two technicians were installing a monitor inside the relocated engineering school. Places like this gave him hope. This was where they would train the next generation of engineers—the men and women who would help keep both ships in the sky. Many of them would also become Hell Divers.

The cog continued to turn, spitting out the innocent youth aboard the airship.

Young men and women like Jed Snow and Sandy Bloomberg, who were still just kids in Michael's eyes. He could still remember Jed and his mom in the trading post that day Layla and Michael had given him a fortune cookie.

He memorized it a long time ago.

Accept your past without regrets. Handle your present with confidence. Face your future without fear.

Michael and Layla walked past several kids drawing on the bulkhead, and he wondered if they too would end up in the cog someday.

Fresh paint glistened in the light. There were four kids, all about eight to ten years old. One of them was Phyl, Les Mitchells' daughter. She reminded Michael of Layla at that age: innocent, fun, aggressive.

"That drawing stinks, midget," Paul said to his friend Jimmy Moffitt. "You should just give up already."

Michael shook his head. "Hey, there—"

But Layla beat him to the punch. "Paul, you apologize right now. I happen to think Jimmy's drawing is really good."

The short boy turned away from the bulkhead, where he had painted a stick figure of some sort of animal.

"Oh, yeah? What is it, then?" Paul asked.

Layla stuttered. "It's art; that's what matters. And name-calling is just going to get you into trouble."

Paul lowered his paintbrush, looked at Jimmy, and said, "Sorry. Your drawing doesn't suck."

"And …?" Layla said, hands on her hips.

"You're not a midget."

"There, that's better," she replied. "Now, have fun, and don't get that paint all over the place."

She left Michael standing there with the kids. He cracked a half grin at Jimmy and then hurried to catch up with Layla.

"That totally reminded me of something from when we were kids," he said. "Remember the time we were standing outside the school, and Pipe was teasing me about my tin hat?"

"That happened a lot."

"I'm talking about the time you did something about it."

Layla blushed. "Oh, *yeah*, I kicked him in the balls."

"I believe you called them 'marbles.'"

They both laughed as they walked on through the ship.

"Pipe was a good man," Layla said. "A bit of a dick when he was younger, but I miss his jokes."

"Me, too. And Rodger, and Ty, and Weaver, and …" Michael let the words trail off. "But enough about the past. Let's focus on the present and how lucky we are."

"Deal." She gave him a sly grin. "So where are you taking me?"

"I told you, it's a surprise."

They passed several technicians and engineers in yellow coveralls, readying quarters for more lower-deckers from the *Hive*.

Michael and Layla had kept their quarters there. *Deliverance* had saved their lives, but the *Hive* would always be his home.

Until they found a place on the surface.

The thought reminded him yet again of X, Magnolia, and Miles. They were down there somewhere, in danger while he took his girlfriend on a date.

As if sensing his thoughts, Layla took his hand again. "Just you and me right now, remember?" she said.

"Right."

Leaving the construction site behind, they turned into a passage already occupied by new passengers. Several hatches were propped open, providing glimpses into the lives of people who had lived below-decks on the *Hive* for most of their lives.

Chloe and Daniel sat on a bunk in the room to his left. Both kids wore fresh bandages on their hands and over their heads.

"I'll be right back," Michael said.

Layla waited for him as he knocked on the hatch.

"Where are your parents?" he asked the kids.

They both gave him a nervous look.

"It's okay, I'm not going to get us in trouble or anything," Michael said. He pulled two pieces of candy from his vest pocket.

"Here you go."

"You're a Hell Diver, aren't you?" Daniel asked.

"I am."

"What happened to that old guy?"

"Old guy?"

"Rick," Chloe said. "That's what Janga called him. He gave us candy jam."

Michael felt Layla's presence behind him.

"He's gone," Layla replied. "He died so we could have this new home."

Chloe looked at the ground and then overhead, chomping nosily on the hard candy. She and David were just two of the many kids who had deformities from the radiation poisoning.

"Will you come back sometime?" Chloe asked.

Michael smiled. "You betcha."

He waved, and they continued down the next passage. Neither spoke at first. They had grown up privileged—the child of a Hell Diver or of parents who worked in the brig. Seeing how these kids lived made his heart hurt. But at least, they had a future now, for the first time in their lives.

"Here we are." Michael stopped outside the armory, where two militia guards stood sentry.

"Commander Everhart," said O'Toole, a fit-looking man with a crossbow cradled across his chest armor.

"We weren't expecting visitors," said Monk, the other sentry.

"That makes three of us," Layla replied, looking at Michael.

"We're just checking something out," Michael said.

O'Toole punched an access code, and the double doors unlatched. He nodded at Monk, who stepped back.

It still felt odd to Michael that men twice his age held him in such high regard, especially after thinking him a traitor just two months ago. But after capturing *Deliverance* and helping overthrow Captain Jordan, he was now one of the most respected men on the ship, second only to X, who was legend.

Empty darkness greeted Michael and Layla as they stepped inside.

"Lights," Michael said. The voice-activated overheads clicked on, spreading a cool blue glow over metal bulkheads that flickered like water.

"You brought me on a date to the *armory*? How romantic!" Layla quipped. "You really know how to get a girl out of her jumpsuit."

"We're not here to look at weapons of mass destruction. This way."

They walked past six glass-covered bomb tubes. This was the equivalent of the launch bay on the *Hive*, but with nuclear bombs—loaded, primed, and ready to drop.

"Katrina should just dump this arsenal in the ocean," Layla said. "Bury it in the dark, cold depths."

"I couldn't agree more."

Layla followed Michael to the pair of sealed hatches across the room. He pulled a key card out of his vest as they approached.

A warning sign with the symbol for explosives hung from the bulkhead to the right. Layla halted outside the hatch. On the other side were assault rifles, missile launchers, grenades, and just about every other type of weapon humans had used to kill each other in the past.

"This is decidedly *not* romantic," she huffed.

Michael grinned. "You don't trust me enough." Using his key card, he swiped the button for the hatch on the left. It opened onto a staircase that spiraled down into the guts of the airship.

Layla stepped to the side for a better look, then frowned. "You are full of surprises, Tin."

He laughed and led the way down to a command room just big enough for two leather chairs and a console mounted with various instruments and screens.

"What is this place?" she asked.

"Combat direction center, or CDC, also called the launch operations center."

"Excuse me?" Layla said, folding her arms across her chest.

"Relax. We're not launching any missiles or dropping any bombs."

Michael sat in front of the controls and flipped on the central main monitor. He used his key card to access the mainframe, then pushed a button to open a metal hatch covering a rectangular glass screen that looked like a mirror. In the reflection, Layla remained standing behind him with arms crossed, looking at once stern and a little confused.

The hatch opened to darkness. In the bowl of swirling black, a flash of lightning looked like branching blood vessels. The light faded away, leaving them with only the weak lighting from the main screen.

Michael typed at a keyboard, entering his credentials a second time.

A robotic voice came over the speakers. "System online."

Layla put a hand on Michael's back. "Okay, you're starting to freak me out a little. What are we doing here?"

"You're about to find out." He tapped the keyboard, scrolling through historical records. Twisting around in his seat, he said, "Timothy found an old-world video in the archives and thought you might be interested."

"We're here to watch a video of the past?" she asked. "I thought we were focusing on the present."

Michael sighed. "I know I said that, but you've been spending a lot of time at the library, working to restore the archives, and I think you might find something here."

Layla finally sat beside him, intrigued and annoyed, judging by her body language. "You think there might be something new here? Something that isn't in the archives upstairs?"

"Timothy sure seems to think so," Michael said. "He asked me what you're looking for, and I said oh, nothing much—just the history of the world and humanity. So he told me to come down here. He said we'd find information we had never seen in the archives, and it would help restore the history we lost."

Layla's hands squeezed his shoulders. "So have you watched it yet?"

"Nope, wanted to wait for you." Michael started to hit PLAY, but Layla touched his arm.

"That's really sweet, but don't you think we should tell Katrina, or maybe Les?"

"Why?"

"If this information is new, then maybe Katrina should see it first."

Michael pulled his hand back from the monitor. "Far as I know, this is just a history video, like those we watched back in school. But if there's information on a hidden paradise that humans colonized, I'm happy to share it right away."

"Okay, deal." Layla looked at the screen. "Let's get to it, then."

Michael grinned and hit the play button. The screen jittered, and the video started in an old-world metropolis. The streets between scrapers were packed with thousands of people. The sun, high in the sky, spread warm gold over cheering crowds—hands in the air, whistles blowing, confetti raining from buildings.

A deep baritone voice spoke.

"In the year two thousand thirty-five, people took to the streets in every major city across the world, rejoicing in an agreement that brought all governments and all races closer together with a single currency and a shared economy. Business worldwide was booming with the creation of artificial intelligence and the solution to problems that had plagued humankind for centuries. A shared commitment between governments tackled the one thing that threatened peace: the energy crisis."

The video zoomed in on people from all countries and walks of life—every ethnicity, religion, and nationality. This was humanity. This was how the world once looked.

But there was something he didn't recognize among these people. Machines strode around with their human handlers. Some were humanoid in appearance, but others were contraptions like the robot vacuum he had taken apart as a kid, in the days following his father's death, when X was looking after him.

"Are those what I think they are?" Layla whispered.

"AIs—like Timothy, only machines instead of a hologram."

The video feed moved from city to city, all of them showing robots and humans in the streets, joined in celebration.

"Industrial Tech Corporation, the most powerful company in the world, led the charge to combat the energy crisis and rising temperatures across the globe," said the narrator.

An image tagged "Chicago, Illinois," came on-screen, featuring the ITC symbol and headquarters building.

"Hades," Michael said. He would never forget the place that claimed the lives of everyone on the *Hive*'s sister airship, *Ares*. But the city looked far different from the wasteland X and the other divers had seen ten years ago.

"ITC had built facilities in hundreds of locations all across the world," the narrator continued. Images flashed of headquarters in Dubai, Shanghai, Sydney, Mexico City. "Food production was more efficient than ever, and hunger, even in developing countries, had been all but eradicated."

Next came the images of robots driving massive machines, harvesting vast tracts of cropland that stretched to the horizon.

Images of a laboratory came on-screen. Men and women wearing white suits with helmets and breathing apparatuses worked in sterile environments.

"Medical advances continued throughout the world, including cures for cancer and rare genetic diseases. The average life expectancy jumped to one hundred and five. Thanks primarily to the work of ITC scientists, tissues, limbs, and organs—even brains—were now being grown inside labs."

The video went inside a hospital room, where a baby born without limbs cried on a table. The parents stood by with tear-streaked faces. Next came an image of the same parents, smiling over a bed where their child happily flailed its perfect little arms and legs.

"Amazing," Michael said, thinking of Chloe and Daniel.

"Some of this stuff I've seen before, but not like this," Layla said. "I didn't realize science had advanced so far before the world ended, or that ITC was behind so much of it."

"Doesn't surprise me," Michael said. "What we still don't know is what ended it all."

Lightning flashed outside, and he pushed the button to seal the hatch and block out the distracting sporadic light.

"Despite medical and scientific breakthroughs," the narrator continued, "the energy crisis threatened to reverse the advances in food production. Overpopulation, pollution, and depletion of fossil fuels led to the threat of war."

The video showed an aerial view of a desert, but as the camera zoomed in, Michael saw that it was really a farm field, its crops shriveled and the dirt cracked. Dry gullies ran through the terrain, and barns were packed with ranks of idle robots.

"Rising temperatures and drought quickly destroyed the achievements that scientists had made in the past decade. In the year two thousand forty-one, humanity was once again spiraling toward war over dwindling resources."

This time, the video came from inside the Senate Chamber in the United States. Michael recognized the seal and the podium from his history classes.

"Today, both parties have come together to tackle the issues of climate change and the drought afflicting the southern states," said a florid-faced senator with a flag pin on his lapel. The audience stood, clapping.

The narrator continued in the background. "Once again, governments and scientists around the world banded together, led by ITC. Within two years, they found an economical way to harvest water from the ocean by desalination."

The video returned to the cracked fields, and in a fast-moving time lapse, the feed showed the checkered acres transforming into lush green Edens, with robot farmers harvesting bountiful crops.

"In two thousand forty-three, humanity was closer than ever before to solving all the problems that had led to war over the millennia. There was no need to fight over resources or territories. For the first time in a thousand years, peace reigned in the Middle East."

"Sometimes, I don't believe this world was ever real," Layla said.

"What doesn't seem real is that humans could have destroyed such a paradise."

Layla brought her knees up to her chest and watched as the video continued. But Michael's eyes left the screen and turned to his lifelong best friend. He moved over to her side, kissing her cheek, then her neck. Layla giggled and smiled the smile he had fallen for so many years ago.

Their lips connected, and a moment later they were pulling each other's clothes off. His shirt caught around his head, and when he finally freed it, she was standing before him, naked. She pushed him back into the chair.

And for the next half hour, they ignored the video and made love in the cramped command center, their bodies sliding against each other, mouths pressed together in an act that would continue until the last humans perished.

And for that brief ecstatic interlude, Michael forgot everything that was wrong with life in the sky and the horrors on the surface.

* * * * *

Nature had reclaimed the derelict city. Vines stretched across the sagging, broken streets and consumed the structures. Most of the buildings were debris piles, having collapsed long ago under the sheer weight of the vegetation.

On a rocky bluff east of the city stood a single building, its ten stories still firmly supported by sturdy concrete pillars. Tenants had once lounged on its balconies, drinking cocktails and watching the surf lap against the beach.

Lonely toppled statues of mermaids and satyrs littered the courtyards around swimming pools, their hands and panpipes pointing at the dark, putrescent water.

Magnolia pulled one of two double-edged sickle blades sheathed on her lower back and sliced through a red plant growing on her path. Goo sluiced out onto the dirt.

"Careful with those," X said. He was just ahead, with Miles behind him, sniffing the air.

She wasn't sure what X had planned, but she wasn't about to ask him now. He was already peeved at her. His words on the beach repeated in her mind.

I'm not going to risk Deliverance *or the* Hive *just to save our sorry asses. We're on our own out here, and the sooner you start accepting that, the safer humanity is going to be.*

The otherworldly calls of the birds X had called "vultures" brought her back to reality. She decided to embrace their solo adventure and give X the benefit of the doubt.

"I really think we should keep an open channel to Timothy," she said as they walked.

"So he can annoy us? I don't think so."

"But he's just trying to help."

He stopped and walked back toward her. "I don't trust robots, okay?"

Thunder boomed over the mountain, and Magnolia glimpsed several vultures flying out of the jungle canopy. Most of them had vanished sometime during the night, when she was sheltered in the boat with X.

Apparently not that concerned about the giant birds, he jumped over the twisted guardrail along the road. He helped Miles over and moved to the edge of a jungle. A bandolier of grenades hung across his chest armor and over his back, and extra magazines were stuffed into his duty belt and the cargo pockets of his suit.

He looked like a man going to war, which didn't ease Magnolia's mind. She sheathed the blade and unslung her rifle as she trotted to catch up.

"We'll have to cut through the jungle to get to that building," he said, pointing at the hotel in the distance.

"You sure that's a good idea?" She instantly regretted the words.

"You want to lead?" he asked. "Maybe you and Pepper know where we can find parts to the radio— or, better yet, a new boat."

"Pretty sure we're not going to find a new boat up here," she whispered.

X continued into the jungle. At the base of the mountain, gangly trees with thick green bark formed a fence along the shore, like soldiers standing guard. It wasn't so much the spike-covered branches or the hourglass trunks that bothered her. These weren't the flesh-eating trees she had fought in Florida.

This bark didn't glow, and the vines didn't try to swallow them whole. This was just an old-fashioned jungle. What bothered her was knowing how much Rodger would have enjoyed seeing this place. She could picture him stumbling down the path, gaping in awe at trees that somehow adapted to an environment without sunlight.

She set off after X. Beetles the size of her boots scuttled across the path, and two-headed lizards perched on rocks along the path. A mammal that looked like an oversize rat crunched through the undergrowth, blinking its saucer eyes at Magnolia before disappearing back into the jungle.

Everything on this island had adapted, either to see in the darkness or to get by with no vision at all. Radiation levels here were mild, but that didn't mean they had always been. Each creature had evolved to survive here.

Even the fish and birds seemed to have undergone transformations. Some hadn't changed much, but the changes always made them better predators. The shark and the octopus had grown to gigantic proportions, as had the monstrous vultures.

As they moved along the trail toward the eastern edge of the city, several structures rose over the dark canopy. Houses built onto the bluffs had their foundations and rooftops largely intact. She tried to picture a time when people had lived in places such as this—places once called "paradise." But try as she might, she couldn't imagine what the Old World was really like before the nuclear fires and the monsters.

"You okay back there, Mags?" X whispered over the comm channel.

"Yeah. How's the arm?"

"Just another scratch."

He ducked a low branch, and Miles turned to her as if to say, *hurry up*. Even the dog seemed impatient with her today.

A clicking sound on the trail made Magnolia whirl. The source was a purple beetle on the center of the path. It opened mandibles, exposing a row of teeth that looked sharper than necessary for a beetle, clicked again, and then scuttled away into foliage.

Raindrops pattered on the canopy above. The sound was calming, and even the sporadic thunder and lightning had a soothing effect. Still, the dangers of this mutant paradise weighed heavily on her. The journey to the Metal Islands hadn't exactly started off well, and being stranded on unknown shores didn't help.

On a section of trail unprotected by the tropical canopy, the dirt had turned to mud. She followed the tracks of X's big boots.

The trail rose to a bluff, giving her another view of the ocean. X had stopped at the top, crouched low with Miles by his side.

Magnolia took a sip of water from the straw in her helmet and looked out over the dark ocean. To the west, where the *Sea Wolf* lay beached, the tide was starting to recede.

"Come on," X said, waving her onward. Miles followed without complaint, but Magnolia finally raised her hand.

"Hold on," she said. "I don't like the idea of going farther without a plan."

X halted and, instead of replying, angled his rifle toward the mountains, at a slope covered with thick undergrowth.

At first, she thought he was pointing at the vultures flying above the canopy. She ducked when she saw them, but X remained standing. Miles, too, stayed on his feet. Only then did she realize that he wasn't pointing at the birds at all.

Sheathing her sickle, she raised her carbine, zooming the scope in on a mushroom-shaped structure in the middle of the vast jungle.

"What in the …?"

"Satellite dish," X said. "I saw it on the way in. That's where we're headed."

Magnolia lowered her rifle. "I thought we were headed to the hotel. Why didn't you tell me this?"

"Because I figured you'd complain when you saw vultures up there. But I didn't want to just leave you at the boat, either."

"Listen, X," she said, frustration rising in her voice. "I know you may have a hard time believing it, but I've grown a lot since Hades. I'm not a little girl anymore." "You never were a little girl."

Magnolia tilted her head, waiting for the rest.

"I've always known you had it in you to be a good Hell Diver. You're a damn fine one, but you need to trust me and stopping rushing to do everything. That's always been your problem." He paused. "Your attitude doesn't help, either."

So I'm the one with an attitude?

"Yeah, I know what you're thinking," X said. "But save it for later and keep moving. We've got a long hike ahead."

He turned and continued up the trail, rifle cradled across his chest.

A vulture wailed in the distance. This time,

Magnolia didn't lag behind. She hurried to catch up with X, keeping quiet and trying to trust that he wasn't leading them into a nest of monsters.

FIVE

X stood like a statue in the darkness, searching the belt of jungle in the green hue of his night vision. A camouflaged lizard perched on a rock ahead. He saw it only when it blinked reptilian eyes that apparently could see him just fine in the dark. All three of them were tracking a bug.

A long tongue flicked out, and the lizard's face split down the middle, like a cracked egg, to swallow the insect. The head sealed shut, and the lizard skittered away.

X continued looking for the real hostiles he was worried about—the vultures. Though he didn't hear them, he knew they were out there.

Patience first, he reminded himself. *Always patience first.*

Years of trekking across the ruined wasteland had taught him that. There was a reason people back on the airships had called him "the Immortal," and it wasn't because he had some magical immunity to death. He had survived through patience and strength and, more than once, pure blind luck.

X didn't know how Magnolia, on the other hand, was still alive. She was always rushing missions. Speed and agility were useful, but they weren't everything—especially when the monsters were faster. It seemed she survived on blind luck all the time.

She tapped her foot as he continued to scan and listen to the jungle. Before the journey he had updated the microphones built into his helmet. Now he could pick up specific sounds in noisy places, such as this place.

He filtered through the racket of bugs, thunder, and rain—and even Magnolia's tapping foot—to pick up sounds of movement from the ground and sky: a faint rustle in the undergrowth, the soft whoosh of wings above.

The microphones didn't make his hearing as acute as Miles', but X certainly had an advantage that he never had back in the cold wastes—although he was having second thoughts about the enhanced audio now, given how much Pepper and Magnolia talked. At least he didn't have to deal with the AI right now.

Looking up, he checked to see whether any of the vultures had left their nests. He had to take a step back for a view through the canopy. His boots sank into the mud. Arching limbs reached far into the sky. If he could only climb them, he would have a great view of the area, but the sharp thorns on the bark made climbing nearly impossible.

And did he really want to risk falling?

"Want me to scope things out?" Magnolia whispered over the comm channel.

"No. Stay put."

After another few minutes of waiting and hearing nothing, he decided to move. He flipped off the safety on his rifle. He had a fresh magazine loaded, and a grenade in the launch chamber. Using a hand signal, he motioned for Magnolia and Miles to follow him deeper into the jungle.

Red mushrooms with a purple glow lined the path. The largest suddenly pulsed like a heart and sprayed green fluid into the air—a defense mechanism, he supposed, and probably poisonous. Reaching up to make sure his helmet was secure, he maneuvered around the mushrooms and pointed them out to Magnolia and Miles before moving ahead.

A snake as long as his leg slithered across the dirt. X halted when he saw that the creature had two heads: one where it was supposed to be, and the other where the tail should be.

"Gross," Magnolia whispered, jumping back. Miles let out a low growl, and X held up a hand to silence him.

The farther they trekked, the more X wondered what else was hiding in this deformed jungle. He kept pushing on, alert but undeterred by external threats. He could deal with whatever lurked out here.

The trail curved up a hill, giving him a look at the mountain above. Storm clouds drifted over the jagged peaks, dumping more rain on the island. The temperature dropped as they climbed higher.

The cold rain hit the canopy, and a stream carved its way down the muddy trail. Slinging his rifle, he grabbed the tree to his right, then planted his boots, found purchase, and climbed around the slick spot.

He turned to help Magnolia, but Miles moved with ease, bounding up the hill to stand beside him. The three continued toward the summit, where the jungle thinned, and the first sign of civilization gradually emerged.

It was hard to see the building at first. Thick undergrowth surrounded the concrete rubble of the structure, and vines clung to the foundation. Half the building had collapsed over the centuries, but the roof over the standing section was still intact. To the right, tucked between two trees, was the satellite dish X had seen from the beach.

The metal dish, angled southward, was draped with vines.

Magnolia took up position beside him, and Miles sat on his haunches, looking, listening, smelling. Behind the dish and building, X spotted movement. Magnolia saw it, too, and pointed at the birds perched on the branches.

They counted thirty of the flying monsters.

High on the branches, under an awning of pale banana leaves, there were twisted vines and thin branches which formed the bowl of what looked like a nest.

"Babies," Magnolia said.

X zoomed in on the vulture nestlings. Even those were the size of a human child. Bald red skulls bobbed up in the nests, their yellow beaks clanking with hunger. As he watched, a full-grown vulture descended on the nest, something large and squirming gripped in its talons.

These vultures were both hunters and scavengers. Another change brought on by mutations and, perhaps, evolution.

He considered using his grenade launcher to blow the little demons out of the nest, but really didn't like the idea of going head-to-head with one. Nor did he like the idea of starting a fight that could draw more monsters to their position.

No, the best way to get into the compound was to sneak in and not make any noise. He pulled back the charging handle of his rifle to chamber a round, then tilted his helmet toward the building.

Magnolia shook her head.

"Let me take point, X," she whispered over the comms. "I'm faster than you, especially right now."

He checked the birds again to make sure they couldn't hear the hushed conversation. But the perched creatures remained quiet, the only movement a fist-size blob of white shit that splattered on the ground.

"Remember that time in Hades when you didn't trust me, and—"

X cut Magnolia off. "And you almost died? Yeah, I remember it perfectly. I don't want a repeat of that near disaster."

He really didn't want Magnolia pouting or complaining. A deep breath helped him dial back the frustration. "Patience first. Always patience first."

"I know. So does that mean I can check this building out, or not?"

X thought on it another moment, checked the vultures again, and nodded. Magnolia moved out of the tree line, where the rain beat down on her. She sprinted in a low hunch across the field.

Miles took her place, and X put a hand on him to calm him. X wasn't the only one slowing with age. Miles was ten now, and even with his genetic modifications, he didn't move the way he used to.

X raised his rifle at the trees, keeping the birds in his sights. Their long beaks were down against their feathery chests, their eyes closed.

The nearly constant flash of lightning overhead was messing with his night vision, and he switched it off with a bump to his chin pad. The entire sky was illuminated by the storm, spreading weak blue light over the terrain.

He checked the baby vultures with his scope, confirmed that they hadn't seen Magnolia, and then moved his scope back to her.

She was almost across the field. Hopping over a patch of red mushrooms, she made a run for the building. When she reached the foundation, she hugged the wall and crept toward the door.

As X watched, the noise-reducing microphones picked up a mushing sound. Miles must have heard or sensed something, too. He suddenly stood up, back ridged.

X moved his scope back to the trees, scanning the branches for movement. But the vultures were still sleeping, and their babies weren't moving.

The mushing sound came again, like boots hitting mud.

"What do you see, Miles?" X whispered.

The dog was looking toward Magnolia and growling softly. She grabbed the handle of the closed metal door, then hesitated, turning to her right. As she reached for the curved blade at her back, something slammed into her, knocking her to the ground in front of the building.

X stood, holding in a shout. He trained his rifle on the area where something had tossed Magnolia across the dirt like a rag doll.

"Mags!" he yelled.

The birds in the trees burst into flight, their great wings kicking up a draft fierce enough to rustle the leaves on branches far below them. They screeched in alarm as they crossed the skyline.

But it wasn't X's shout that set them off.

The grunt of the thing that had Magnolia pinned to the ground came over the speakers in his helmet, and he flipped on his night-vision goggles to finally see the abomination.

The lizard that could split its head in two wasn't the only camouflaged creature out here. But this was no lizard—it was a hoglike beast covered in thick brown fur the color of the terrain.

Miles growled at the mutant, apocalyptic version of the pigs on the *Hive*. Covered in thick fur with a spiky mane, it was four times Miles' size, and it had Magnolia pinned to the ground. Tusks, upper and lower, protruded from a long jaw, dripping saliva onto her visor.

"X!" she shouted, flailing, writhing to get free.

Hold on, kid …

He was still trying to get a shot, but she was in the way, and the thought of hitting her made him hesitate. He flipped the selector switch to semiautomatic, and a second later, the beast's jaw moved into view. He squeezed off a shot that shattered an upper tusk. He pulled the trigger again, and an eyeball exploded.

The beast leaped off, squealing in agony, and looked at X with its remaining eye. He kept the creature in his sights, just in case it decided to make a run for him, but instead it turned and bounded into the foliage. The birds screeched overhead, circling and watching from a safe distance.

By the time the beast vanished into the jungle, X was running. Miles chased him through the thick weeds and around the patches of mushrooms.

Magnolia lay in the dirt about twenty feet from the building. She reached up for her helmet, and X grabbed her by the arm and helped her to her feet.

"Can you run?" he asked.

A distant snort came in reply. Then three more, from different locations.

This beast had friends.

"Move!" X shouted.

He pulled one of Magnolia's arms over his shoulder and moved with her toward the building.

X raised his rifle with his free hand. They slipped and fell in the mud, landing snared together. The first thing he did was grab his rifle, plucking it from the muck. Then he grabbed Magnolia and pulled her to her feet.

"Work with me here, kid," he grumbled.

"My head. I …"

X hadn't noticed the crack in her helmet until now. The beast had definitely done some damage. The tusks had scarred the metal, and a puncture wound dripped blood over the Team Raptor symbol.

"Hold on," X said. "We're almost to the door."

Miles barked behind them, but X kept his gaze on the building. When they finally got to the door, he propped Magnolia up against the foundation and rattled the handle. It was locked.

Using his muddy boot, he kicked it once, then twice, breaking it off the hinges. The metal door banged open into a dusty room.

He helped Magnolia inside, then motioned for Miles to follow. But when he looked for the dog, all he saw was the muddy field and knee-high weeds.

A bark sounded from the sky, and his eyes darted toward the storm clouds, where a vulture was flapping away with Miles in its talons.

"*No-o-o-o-o!*" X shouted at the top of his lungs.

* * * * *

Katrina was already nearing the halfway point of her cardio workout. She finished lap fifty around the launch bay of the *Hive*. Some routines she wanted to keep, despite the painful memories on the ship. Her workouts were one of them. She had trained here as a Hell Diver for most of her adult life.

Sweat coursed down her skin, and her muscles burned. By the fifty-first lap mark, she was starting to fight to keep the pace.

But not just her body was struggling. Her mind and heart were fighting the battle of regret, and the poison was starting to infiltrate her soul. Everything that had happened over the past few months came rushing over her during her run.

Normally, exercise helped reduce stress and let her concentrate on what mattered. Not this evening. She couldn't stop thinking about the child she lost to malnutrition. The thoughts prompted a rush of energy that pushed her harder through lap fifty-five. She ran the fifty-six at a record pace, the pain in her muscles yielding to the flood of warmth pumping through her veins.

She tried to block the images of her child from her mind, but no amount of mental discipline could repair her heart. The anguish was torture, but she deserved every bit of it.

The porthole windows flashed by, and the launch tubes blurred as sweat dripped into her eyes. She tried to tell herself she didn't want to lose her baby—but the truth was, she had decided she couldn't live in a world where Leon Jordan was in control. The man had been mad, trying to kill her friends and executing anyone who threatened him.

She had wanted to die herself, but instead, she lost her child. And she was still alive.

It wasn't right. Part of her wished she had died, but she still had a duty to humanity.

Grunting, Katrina ran even harder, her muscles pushed to the edge, her endurance stretching to its limits. Her lungs took in the oxygen greedily, but no matter how much air she sucked in, she couldn't get enough.

Stars broke across her vision.

Sweat trickled down her pale skin.

At lap seventy, she squinted into the dimly lit space, trying to focus on the banners hanging from the bulkheads above the lockers. The symbols of the Hell Divers were displayed proudly there: Team Raptor, Team Angel, Team Phoenix, Team Wolf.

The banners were a useful distraction from the pain of her other thoughts. For a moment, she felt as though she could keep going.

Just ten more laps, she told herself. *Only ten more and you've hit ten miles.* As she ran, she continued to look at the banners, picturing the ghosts of Hell Divers throughout the room.

In her mind's eye, she saw Rick Weaver sitting at a card table, looking over his hand with a sly grin. Aaron Everhart closed a locker and held up a hand at her as she passed. X was there, too, winking at her the way he had all those years ago, when a spark of love had united the two of them. Ty Parker, the technician who had once manned the launch tubes, was polishing one of the lids, chomping on an herb stick.

The images were all just figments of her imagination, but seeing the launch tubes reminded her again how many people had died over the years. It wasn't just the ghosts of the men and women who had perished diving that made her heart pound; it was also what these tubes had been used for long before the Hell Divers ever came into this world.

The ghost of Captain Maria Ash, hair all but gone from the radiation treatment, stood in the center of the launch bay with her hands cupped behind her back, stoical and strong despite the cancer eating her throat.

She looked at Katrina and said, "The future of these airships is in your hands now. You must not concentrate on the past if you are to lead humanity to a new home in the future."

Ash disappeared, replaced by her successor. That Jordan was on his knees the moment before she had killed him helped ease some of that pain.

Killing him was one thing she didn't remotely regret.

Adrenaline rushed through her veins, and Katrina ran her fastest lap yet, her shoes slapping the metal hard and echoing through the vaulted room.

On the seventy-ninth lap, she stumbled, tripped, and crashed to the floor with such force, she flipped onto her side and landed on her back. The ghosts were gone now, and she was alone.

Katrina remained there several minutes, taking in deep breaths, her body tingling, legs finally relaxing.

Tears welled in her eyes, and one streaked down her face. She clamped her eyelids shut, trying to block the mental torture as the poison of regret sank deeper into her pounding heart.

"Captain, are you okay?" said a deep voice across the room.

"Yes, one moment," Katrina replied. She quickly pushed herself up and got to her feet to face a figure across the room. He was standing in the entrance to the launch bay, but the light was too dim to make out his features.

She pulled down on the bottom of her tank top and turned to wipe the last tears from her eyes. Then she turned back to the figure who still hadn't identified himself, and saw the shadow of what looked like a sword.

Her heart froze, a terrifying image surfacing in her mind. For a fleeting moment, it was as if Jordan had come back from the dead to get his revenge. "Captain," the person entreated. He walked into the light, and she saw Lieutenant Lester Mitchells, his red hair ruffled as usual. "I'm sorry to bother you, ma'am …" He paused and tilted his head slightly. "Are you okay?"

She nodded, sucked in a breath, and started across the room. "I'm fine—just thought I saw a ghost, is all."

SIX

Magnolia slapped the floor with her palm in frustration, tears steaming down her face. Outlandish wails rose into a cacophony outside—a mixture of howling beasts and screeching birds. The macabre music assaulted her ears as the minutes passed by. She strained to hear anything that would tell her X was still alive. Gunfire, a bark from Miles, a message over the comms—anything to let her know he was still alive.

She had blown it. Bad.

Had she paid more attention while crossing the field, maybe she would have seen the beast sneaking up on her. Maybe she could have brought her rifle up in time to shoot it between the eyes. Or she might have stabbed it with her blade. Instead, she had rushed across the clearing as fast as she could to get to the compound.

X was right. God *damn* it, he was always right—which, of course, was why he had survived so long in this dangerous world, and why she had a hole in her helmet.

She reached up to check the damage. The tusk had punctured the crest but not her skull. A few centimeters more, though, and her scalp would have been oozing brains instead of just a little blood.

Patience saves your life. Rushing gets you killed.

"You were right, X," she muttered.

She was lucky this time. The mistake hadn't gotten her killed, but she wasn't sure Miles would be so lucky. The vulture had pulled him into the sky. She would never forget the raw scream from X that followed. He had taken off running after them, yelling at Magnolia to stay put.

She sat with her back to the wall, head throbbing and heart pounding. A single tear streaked down her cheek. X still hadn't returned, and all she could do was sit here, hoping for the best.

You're a Hell Diver. You know better than to hope.

Hell Divers didn't sit around and hope for something to happen—Hell Divers got up and *made* something happen.

But what could she do? If she did leave, she could get lost in the jungle or eaten by the monster hogs.

Using the butt of her rifle, she pushed herself up, taking a moment to let the wave of dizziness pass and to think about her next move. She checked her HUD. The readouts were good, at least. Radiation levels were minimal, and her battery unit was at 70 percent.

But she still had no idea how long she would be here. Better to use her flashlight instead of the NVGs, which drained the battery unit.

Switching on the beam, she played it across the room. Dust particles floated in the air like fine snow. Two tables lay upended in the middle of the space. Several chairs were on their backs nearby, legs angled up at the ceiling. The light hit thick cobwebs stretched across the metal pegs. Cabinets, a bookshelf, and a desk stood against the opposite wall. Cracked lightbulbs protruded from sconces on the walls.

Every window had been boarded up with metal hatches. Whoever had taken shelter here did a good job sealing the structure, aside from the front door that X had kicked in.

A T-shaped bar was now locked in place over the metal entrance. It seemed the former occupants had left without bothering to secure the door when they abandoned the place. A second door led into another room, which she hadn't checked yet.

A loud crack of thunder rattled the window hatches. She moved toward the door she still hadn't opened. Halfway there, she stopped and closed her eyes. "X, do you copy?"

It was the third time she had tried him in the past few hours. Only static crackled from the speakers. The sound filled her with dread. He either was dead or had gone radio silent to avoid detection by the hogs.

Magnolia sucked in a breath of stale air and opened the door to the other room. A monitor the size of her wrist computer was mounted to the wall right of the entrance.

She played her light over computer equipment in the corner of the room.

"What the …?" she whispered. These were not the type of computers they had on the *Hive* or *Deliverance*. This stuff looked ancient. Boxy computers and monitors were stacked on tables.

She swung the beam to the left. A pile of rubble covered most of the floor in the center of the room, where the wall and part of the roof had caved in.

Two thunderclaps shook the structure, rattling the metal hatch over a window at the far end of the room. She shined her beam in that direction, hitting a row of chairs and more desks. Facing the central desk sat a skeletal figure, head hanging at an odd angle. The top part of the skull was missing, and raising the light, she saw on the ceiling the brown stippling that had been this person's brains.

The gun was nowhere in view, which told her someone else had taken it before abandoning the building. But what really interested her was the radio equipment in front of the corpse.

She made her way over and flashed the light over all sorts of devices she remembered from textbooks in school. A switchboard with dozens of toggle switches, a ham radio, and what looked like an archaic Morse code transmitter key.

Grabbing the back of the chair, she gently moved it out of the way, trying to make as little noise as possible. Despite her efforts, the metal legs scratched the floor, and a leg bone cracked off the corpse.

Magnolia held in a gasp as a furry spider pulled itself out of the home it had made in the skull. It raised its head, brandishing fangs, then clambered away.

She followed it with her light till it took refuge in the debris pile. Then she turned back to the desks, astonished at how well preserved the room was. Maybe it had lasted long after the apocalypse.

Using her light, she scanned the switchboard. Symbols and text marked the different buttons, though she doubted that anything worked. Even if this place had continued operating after the nuclear fires, it couldn't possibly still have backup power.

From what she could tell, this wasn't an ITC facility.

"X, do you copy?" Mags said into the comm. "I found some radio equipment. I'm going to try and get it working."

Static once again crackled in her helmet.

She lowered her light and fished out a thin cable, which she patched into her wrist monitor. Then she plugged the other end into a second cable, which divers used to hack into old systems such as this. All she had to do was get enough juice to turn the radio back on.

Next, she plugged the other end of the cord into her chest battery slot. The charge would, she hoped, be enough to power the equipment.

Clamping the flashlight between her teeth, she pulled off her gloves, then tapped the screen of her wrist computer, bringing it online.

A distant wail broke over the thunder outside. Something massive rammed the outside of the building. Her eyes darted over to the debris pile.

"Mags, do you copy?"

The sound of X's voice in her helmet startled her.

"Yes, I copy," she said softly.

"Where are you?"

"Same place you left me. Where are you?"

"I'm tracking Miles, but those things are hunting me."

She could hear snorting in the background. It sounded nothing like the dog. A flurry of gunshots rang out. These she could hear inside the building. X and the hogs were close.

The wrist monitor blinked. The main dashboard on the desk suddenly flashed with colors. The radio equipment crackled to life, and several monitors came online.

"Oh, shit, I did it!" she said. "I got a radio working here, X!"

"Screw the radio, Mags. I'm about to be hog shit, and Miles is still—"

More gunfire popped in the distance.

"Mags, those things are on my six. I need help."

Magnolia unslung her rifle and looked at the radio one more time, wondering whether she should try to connect with the *Hive* first.

There's no time. Just as she started to turn away, she saw a symbol on the switchboard. She hesitated for a moment, then moved back to the equipment.

"Hold on, X. I've got an idea."

"I don't have time for ideas!"

She flipped the button with a horn symbol below it.

She turned the light off and bumped on her NVGs as an emergency siren blared outside, drowning out the screeches of birds and even the crack of thunder.

Moving into the other room, she shouldered her rifle and trained it on the metal door.

"Come on, you son of a bitch," she muttered.

Sweat dripped down her forehead as she waited. She moved her finger to the cold metal trigger. With no gloves, it felt different.

The wait wasn't long.

A snorting came outside the building, loud enough to be heard in the rising and falling of the emergency siren. She held her ground, keeping the rifle aimed at the door.

"Mags …" X panted over the comm. "They … those things aren't following me anymore. They're …"

Her plan had worked. The sound had drawn the hogs away from X—straight to her location.

Again something slammed the outside of the door, rattling the metal. She could hear guttural noises, something between a bark and a snort.

She flinched at the sound of another creature hitting the metal shutters behind her. Pivoting, she pointed her rifle at the window.

Another crash came from the other room, where a third beast tested the debris pile that served as a wall. They knew she was here, and it was only a matter of time before they battered their way inside.

She knew better than to hope, but this time it was the only card she had to play. If her lucky streak continued, the door would hold until X could find Miles and return to kill the beasts. If it didn't, then she was about to join Rodger and the other dead Hell Divers in Valhalla.

* * * * *

The sound of the emergency siren had sent a chill of alarm through X. At first, he had scanned the sky and terrain for Sirens. But this wasn't the electronic language of the monsters; it was coming from the direction of the compound where he had left Magnolia.

Way to improvise, Mags! he thought. For once, she had saved his hide.

Now that the beasts were distracted, he could finally get out of this damn tree. He began the climb down the curving branches, cautious of the spiky thorns.

X had been forced up here by the half-hog, half-dog beasts, with no choice but to try to pick them off with his rifle from above. The rounds did little to deter them, mostly ricocheting off the furry platelike armor that covered their vital organs.

It was his NVGs that saved him. The optics helped detect the creatures trying to sneak up on him as he made his way through the jungle in search of Miles. Their camouflage didn't work when his night vision was activated.

He scanned the terrain a final time, looking for their meaty bodies and listening for their grunts and snorts over the rise and fall of the emergency siren.

Rain continued to fall, as if the lightning that streaked through the bulging clouds was shaking the water loose. It cascaded down off the tropical leaves, turning the ground below into a mudslide.

The tracks of the hogs had already vanished, and he saw no signs of movement or fresh prints anywhere below him.

He wiped his visor off and finished the climb to the bottom, dropping the final eight feet. His boots sank in the mud, and he quickly pulled them free and began moving again.

The fort of trees just ahead was his target. Miles was up there somewhere, dropped into a nest to feed the young birds. X checked his wrist monitor to make sure the dog hadn't been moved to a new location. He tapped the screen several times, pulling up the map in the corner of his HUD that showed his location.

The beacon blinked on the map.

"I'm coming, buddy," X said. "Just hang on."

The dog's vitals were still strong, but the clock was ticking. The birds would feed soon now that the predators had gone away. The wail of the siren had saved X from the beasts, but it had likely put Miles in even more jeopardy.

Moving between two thick tree trunks, X came out on a watercourse. The dry oxbow lake was quickly turning into a river. The flow created actual rapids down the slope and around the stand of trees where the vultures had built their nests. X wasted no time seizing the opportunity.

With a grenade already loaded, he aimed at the bole of a tree growing out of the embankment on the other side of the watercourse. He fired, then ducked behind the thick, twisted roots of a nearby tree.

Shrapnel from the blast whizzed overhead, and the birds once again took to the sky amid much screeching and cawing. Several rabbit-size bugs darted out of their homes.

X pulled a second grenade from the bandolier, loaded it, and rose to his feet. Another trigger pull launched the grenade into the deep, splintered gash the first grenade had blown in the tree bole.

Leaves and branches rained down around him, and the tree creaked and swayed from the second impact. It began to lean out of the creek bank, but the roots held firm.

He loaded a third grenade just as something big hit him hard from behind. He knew at once that he was in the talons of a vulture.

Feet kicking as he rose over the watercourse, he did the only thing he could think of: fired the third grenade right into the gaping hole of the tree trunk, where splintered wood stuck out like twisted rebar.

An orange blast rocked the base, shredding the exposed roots and punching through the center. Hot shrapnel whined through the air.

The monster holding him let out a shriek as a flurry of sharp sticks cut through its wings. X was falling then, and he landed with a splash in the rapids. The waist-deep flow of the water did little to break his fall and almost swept him away. He scrambled, then got his footing. The impact had rattled his bones, but Miles had little time, and that thought kept him moving.

He fought the current and waddled toward the other side, his eyes on the top of the tree he had blown nearly in half. The sky above the canopy was moving, and it took him a moment to register that the motion wasn't from storm clouds—it was the vultures themselves. They had taken wing, filling the air above the forest canopy.

A loud cracking emanated from the blasted tree. The splintered bole finally gave way, and the entire trunk began to lean. The top branches crashed into the next tree, shaking loose a litter of sticks and other debris.

X pushed through the current to the side of the embankment. He slipped several times trying to climb out over the loose earth and stones but finally clawed his way up on a skein of roots to solid ground above. The broken tree continued to crunch and creak as roots snapped and branches crashed into other trees.

He pushed himself up in the mud and ran away from the embankment at full speed to get out of the crash zone.

The tree smashed to the jungle floor a few beats later, sending a violent quake beneath his boots. He took cover behind the base of another tree as a cascade of sticks, mud, and rocks flew through the lower canopy.

The wail of the emergency siren reasserted itself. And over that, X heard something that made him smile.

Heart pounding in his ears, he held in a breath to listen, and there it was again: the sound of his best friend's bark.

X wanted to shout and scream for Miles, but he didn't want to draw more attention to his position. Magnolia had already notified every creature on this island that humans were back, and X had a feeling the birds and hogs could prove to be the least of their worries.

He knew that it wouldn't be long before the monster birds forgot about the raucous noises and returned to their nests. And this time, they would feed on his dog's flesh.

X bolted away from the tree after looking at the beacon on his wrist monitor again. The vitals were still strong, but Miles' heart rate had increased.

He scanned the branches in the area where he had seen the bird lumbering through the air with Miles in its claws, but the collapse of the tree had him disoriented. Another bark helped X narrow down the location. Just ahead stood four massive trees, and the tallest seemed to be the likeliest spot, with several nests hanging in the higher branches.

X brought up his scope, scanning them one by one until he finally glimpsed the white hazard suit he had customized for Miles. Lowering the rifle, he broke into a run, moving like a fox over the slick terrain. He jumped over logs and ducked under branches.

The sound of great flapping wings spurred him on. He kept low and ran hard, eyes trained on the nest. The sparsely feathered heads of the nestlings popped up, pecking at the air around Miles, and he barked back at them.

A red flash of motion descended from the canopy and perched at the top of the nest. The mother had returned to help her young with their meal. X aimed his rifle, held in a breath, and fired a shot.

The head and beak vanished in a spray of gore.

Bull's-eye.

The bird toppled off the nest, wings spread like a fallen angel, and slammed into the ground neck-first a few seconds later.

Two more vultures sailed in from different directions.

X flicked the selector to automatic and sprayed the air to send the birds fanning out in all directions, filling the night with their squawks. A spear of lightning struck one of them, and the smoking carcass cartwheeled into the leaves, where it caught fire.

Slinging his rifle strap, X grabbed the lowest limb of the tree and started climbing, his eyes on the nest fifty to sixty feet overhead. It was a long way to climb, and he had a target on his back.

"Hold on, buddy, just hold on," he panted.

His arm was already burning from the slash the giant octopus had given him. The wound was infected now, and if he didn't get it treated it could become septic.

But none of that mattered if Miles died. He couldn't imagine life without his best friend.

Gritting his teeth, he climbed faster. To reach the next branch, he jumped like a monkey. And when he got to an area where he couldn't reach another branch, he pulled out his sheath knife and stabbed the thick bark.

He saw movement in his peripheral vision: a bird swooping down. He rotated as it spread its wings to flare. Stretching forth its talons, it prepared to snag him off the tree. X held on to the knife with one hand and grabbed the blaster from his thigh holster with the other.

The flare streaked into the monster's breast. It flapped away, squawking in pain as its plumage caught fire; then it tumbled from the air. X holstered the blaster and kept climbing.

He was about ten feet from the nest when the other birds began returning to their roosts.

The speakers in his helmet crackled. "X, do you copy?"

He was breathing too hard to answer right away.

"X, do you copy?"

"I'm … busy," he panted.

"Are you okay?" A flurry of white noise took over the comm, then died away. "Is Miles okay?"

Despite the static interference, X could still hear the apprehension in her voice. She thought this was *her* fault.

"I've almost got him," X replied.

The branch cracked under his boot, and he jumped to another.

Lightning flickered overhead, spreading its eerie flickering glow over the jungle floor. The headless vulture looked like a pile of feathers. He had been so revved with adrenaline, he hadn't noticed the height until now.

Miles barked, then yelped in pain, pulling X's focus back to the nest above.

"Hold on, boy," he shouted. "I'm coming!"

X used the knife to aid him up the rest of the way to the nest. He pulled himself up on another thick branch, stood, and was scrabbling for a foothold when a hooked beak with orange lesions peered over the side of the nest. Orange-feathered wings rose threateningly as two piercing black eyes glared at him.

Magnolia relayed another message over the comm—something about a radio and the *Hive*— but X was too focused on the strip of white plastic, stained red and hanging from the bird's beak, to respond. A full second passed before he realized what he was looking at.

It was Miles' hazard suit.

X grabbed the end of the beak with one hand and stabbed the left wing with the other. The young vulture jerked back, and X, holding on to the knife, was hauled up into the nest. Rolling over the lip into the nest, he saw Miles hunched in the corner and snarling. The four nestlings surrounded him, pecking at his suit.

Hell no!

X let go of the knife hilt, leaving the blade lodged deep in the creature's wing. It slammed him with the other wing, pinning him against the side of the nest, then moved closer and thrust its beak at his chest armor.

He squirmed slightly to his left and grabbed the beak with both hands. Then, screaming in rage, he pushed the wing back, freeing himself. He came up on his knees, with the bird in a headlock.

X twisted the baby monster's head and beak until both crunched. He kept going, pushing harder and harder, his old muscles straining, until he ripped the beak completely off.

Tendrils of muscle and gullet hung off the base. He rose to his feet, panting like a wild animal, with the beak in his grip. The three remaining nestlings had turned away from Miles to look at him.

"Get away …" he panted, "from … my … *dog*!"

Holding the beak in both hands, he plunged the sharp end into the birds one by one, until the nest was drenched in blood. He raised the last creature into the air for the other vultures in the jungle to see.

"You're *done* trying to kill us!" he shouted.

Miles nudged up against his leg, and X slowly lowered the still-twitching baby bird and rolled it out of the nest. Lightning flashed over the bay in the distance, and in the glow, he saw something that froze him for a second.

The incoming tide had dislodged the *Sea Wolf* from the beach. The damaged vessel was now in the surf, being pushed back into the bay.

X cursed. This time, it wasn't Magnolia who screwed up. It was on him. If he had kept an open line to Timothy, he would have known about this.

But that still didn't explain why the boat was drifting.

Why the hell wasn't the AI doing something to stop it?

"Son-of-a-bitch robot is leaving without us," X said over the comm.

SEVEN

The nightmare was just like the others. Michael was stumbling through the snowy wastelands in Hades. His lips and throat were dry from lack of water, but he couldn't melt or drink the snow because of the radiation.

He pushed on, continuing his search for X. Ice framed his visor, narrowing his view of the frozen terrain. A line of tracks led into the city once called Chicago, a place of many scrapers. The colossal architecture continued to withstand the test of time.

Here, hell had literally frozen over.

Trapped in the nightmare, Michael slogged through his own personalized hell. The high-pitched electronic-like wails of the Sirens became a satanic chorus that followed him down empty streets and over wind-carved snowdrifts.

The tracks wound up and down the dunes, and the beacon on his HUD blinked with Xavier Rodriguez's location, but every time he got close, the beacon would move.

"X!" Michael shouted. "X, where are you?"

In these dreams, the answer was always the same.

Over the howling wind, X would shout, "Stay away, Tin! This is not the life your father wanted for you!"

Michael would turn and turn, but the voice of X would echo off the frozen sides of buildings and fade away.

"Please, X, where are you?" Michael yelled back. "Let me help you!"

He continued his trek through the endless streets, his rifle at the ready, eyes sweeping constantly for hostiles.

The city continued producing the music of hell: clawed feet skittering over icy metal, the wailing of the Sirens, and the crash and clatter of structures finally giving way to Mother Nature.

Halfway through the dream, he would hear the worst of all the noises: a loud *whap*. Michael turned to see a Hell Diver lying in the middle of the street, its parachute luffing in the breeze. Jagged bones protruded from a semiliquid body held together only by armor and a hazard suit.

"I told you to stay away, Tin! Don't come after me or you'll end up like him!"

Michael looked skyward to see X ascending by helium balloon toward the storm clouds. He would scream and scream, and then Michael would realize it was he himself screaming and not X.

His eyes flitted back to the dead diver, and his gun went up at the sight of a horde of Sirens bounding up the street to consume the corpse of the deceased diver—Michael's father.

Their leathery muscles stretched as the monsters pulled Aaron apart, limb by limb, their shrieks piercing the night.

Michael aimed and pulled the trigger, but his rifle wouldn't fire. When the Sirens were done with his dad, they would come for him, and every time they were just about to sink their claws into his flesh, he would jerk awake, covered in sweat and sucking in air for another scream.

This time, though, he caught himself and didn't wake Layla. She was apparently still exhausted from last night. Even the thought of their sweaty bodies and her moans of pleasure was not enough to dispel the horrid images in his mind.

Michael pulled the covers off to cool his hot skin, exposing Layla's naked body as he did so. He gently pulled the sheet back up over her breasts, and for a moment he just watched her sleep: studying her freckled face, full lips, and eyelids quivering in REM sleep.

I hope you're dreaming of something beautiful.

He let out a low sigh, careful not to wake Layla. Weeks had passed since Michael slept through the night, and it wasn't for lack of exhaustion. Three jobs and a rigorous schedule had him falling into bed at night and passing out almost at once. The problem was *staying* asleep. The nightmares were getting worse.

And now the fatigue was starting to eat at him during the day, sparking the anger problem from his youth. He was always on edge and always a hair trigger away from anger.

"That's creepy, Tin," Layla whispered, opening one eye and looking over at him. "You know I don't like it when you watch me sleep."

"Sorry," he said, turning onto his back. The alarm clock went off a moment later, and the wall-mounted screen warmed to life, projecting the image of the sun to represent a phenomenon that had once helped humans awaken in the morning. The mythical image did little to stir him awake at the early hour. He was wiped out.

"What time is it?" Layla mumbled.

"Six, and I've got to get up."

"What? Why?" She sat up and looked at the clock, then back to him. "I thought you weren't going to the farm today."

"I'm not …"

Layla rubbed her eyes. "So where *are* you going?"

"To help train the new divers, remember?"

"Oh, yeah …" She smiled seductively at him. "Was last night a dream, by the way?"

Michael grinned back, his cheeks warming. "I'm pretty sure that was real."

"And it was ama-a-a-a-zing."

"Yeah."

"'*Yeah*'?" Now both brows went up. "All I get is a 'yeah'?"

"I'm sorry, it's just …"

Layla snuggled closer and put a hand on his arm. "What, Michael? Tell me."

"It's X. I just can't stop thinking about him. I've been having bad dreams all night. Slept like crap."

"Again?"

He nodded.

She kissed him on the cheek and then nestled her head on his shoulder. "I'm sorry. I wish there was something I could do."

Feeling anxious, he pulled away and swung his legs out of bed, leaving her lying there half naked and staring at him in the dim lighting.

"There is something I can do. Something *we* can do. We can start training the new divers so that when we do find X, we can help."

Layla patted the bed where he had just been lying beside her. He knew what was coming, and he didn't want to hear it.

"I really want to get going. Feel free to join me later."

She frowned, eyes flitting downward and then up again. "Michael, I love you, and that's why you need to listen to me. Don't you remember what X told you about coming after him?"

"Of course I do," he snapped. "But if he needs my help, I'm going after him." He didn't bother telling her about the nightmare that had startled him awake. Seeing his dead father and X in Hades had reminded him what was at stake and how precious life was.

"I lost my dad a decade ago, and I also lost X for

those ten years since then. Now I'm afraid I'm going to lose X again. But honestly, what hurts even more is that he had seemed okay with that when he left."

"Oh, Michael. He didn't leave because of you. He left because this no longer felt like home to him. Deep down, I believe he was too selfless to ask you to go with. He wanted you to stay here and live out your life, with the hope that someday you two might be reunited."

"Maybe," Michael replied. He thought back to their final moments in the launch bay of *Deliverance*, right before they dropped the *Sea Wolf* into the ocean.

"You remind me of your dad," X had said with a smile. "He'd be very proud of you. As I am."

Why didn't you say something, then?

Michael wagged his head. "I don't know. I just don't know what the right thing is anymore."

He threw on his uniform, the fog of sleep banished by the wave of anxiety born of regret.

"Ugh, I wanted to sleep in for once, but you're not giving me much choice, are you, Tin?"

The wall monitor buzzed before he could respond, and a voice crackled from the speakers.

"Commander Everhart, are you in your quarters?"

Michael, his foot halfway into a pant leg, hopped over to the monitor and pushed the comm button. "Roger, I'm here."

"This is Ensign White. The captain is requesting your presence on the bridge of *Deliverance* as soon as possible."

"On my way," Michael said.

"Bring Layla," Bronson White added. "She's going to want to hear this."

* * * * *

Katrina stroked her jaw, trying to listen to the scrambled transmission from Magnolia. Ensign Ada Winslow, seated in front of the radio equipment, was working to stabilize the signal.

"Almost got it," she said.

The beeps and background noise of other conversations and automated messages filled the room while they waited. Among them came a transmission from the *Hive*.

"Captain DaVita, this is Timothy Pepper. All systems operating at optimal levels. Next update in T minus two hours."

"Roger that," Katrina said.

"There ... we ... go," Ada said.

Katrina gestured for Ensigns Bronson White and Dave Connor to turn their monitors down so she could hear. White noise, followed by Magnolia's voice, filled the bridge.

"Miss Katib, this is Captain DaVita. Can you hear me?"

More static, followed by "Yes, I can. Finally!"

"Where are you?" Katrina asked.

"I'm trapped in a facility on an island. X is on his

way back right now with Miles, but we're surrounded."
She was talking fast, and the static interference didn't
make her any easier to understand.

An emergency siren wailed in the background.
Katrina could hear that. And something else.

"What is that sound?" she asked.

"Hogs," Magnolia replied.

"Please repeat?"

"Not like the kind we have on the *Hive*. Big pigs.
With tusks."

The doors to the bridge whisked open, and
Katrina turned as Layla and Michael hurried
inside.

"What's going on?" Michael asked from across
the space.

Magnolia relayed another message, answering his
question. "I've been holed up here for a few hours after
we got attacked. One of the vultures snatched Miles,
and X went after him. Captain, I found something in
the database here—something that you have to hear.
It may help humanity."

"Can you upload it and send it to us?" Katrina
asked.

Layla and Michael crowded around the station.

"I'm working on sending this to you via satellite.
I was able to hack into the computers here."

Layla maneuvered up to the radio. "Mags, where
are you, and what in the wastes is going on!"

"I've found something that explains what
happened to the world. I haven't been able to watch

or listen to it all, but …" Magnolia's voice crackled, masking the words with static.

"Where is my counterpart?" said another voice.

It was Timothy Pepper. His translucent hologram emerged next to the circular table in the center of the room.

"Better question is, where is X?" Michael said. Katrina summoned her captain's voice, which was firm and just shy of a shout so White would get it even with his bad hearing.

"Everyone, calm down."

That did the trick for everyone except Magnolia. She continued speaking even faster than before. "I managed to get the satellite dish working here, but I'm not sure the radio I'm taking with me is going to work—assuming I get out of here alive, and assuming the *Sea Wolf* isn't too far gone."

"Slow down, Mags," Katrina said, lowering her voice. "One thing at a time. Tell me what happened to the *Sea Wolf*."

Michael stepped up next to Katrina. His hair was pulled back into a ponytail, with strands sticking out in various directions. Purple bags hung under his eyes. Typically, this would be a sign of drug or alcohol abuse, but she knew him better than that.

He was just exhausted.

"The *Sea Wolf* was damaged yesterday. We were attacked by a *really* big octopus—" Static again washed over the channel.

Layla looked to Katrina and said, "Did she say what I thought she did?"

Ada's eyes widened. "What's an octopus, and how big is a really big one?"

Not knowing how to answer, Katrina just said, "Magnolia, you're breaking up again."

"Our radio was destroyed, and we left the *Sea Wolf* to find parts on this island. But the boat is drifting back into the bay."

Katrina wasn't sure how much she had missed, but the last part gave her heart a stutter. "What do you mean, 'drifting'?"

White noise covered Magnolia's voice.

"Magnolia, do you copy?" Katrina asked.

A fleeting moment of silence held the bridge, the tension palpable.

"Hold on," Magnolia suddenly said, her voice as clear as day.

In the backdrop, Katrina heard the same animal grunt she had heard before, and something like an animal digging.

"Shit … shit, shit," Magnolia said quietly. "They're almost inside."

"Sirens?" Layla asked.

Michael's face turned even paler. "This isn't fucking happening. We have to do something."

Katrina could sense his anger, but she didn't like cursing on her bridge. She shot him a glance.

"The emergency sirens you're hearing are from the facility, not the creatures," Ada said.

"Mags, tell us what happened to the *Sea Wolf*," Katrina said.

"I'm not sure. X just said it's been swept back out into the bay. I'm not sure if Timothy is in control of the vessel."

"That's not good," Layla whispered. "Is there a way we can contact Timothy?"

"My duplicate program would not abandon the divers," the other Timothy said, his voice taking on a firm tone. "I am here to serve and help my human friends; so is my counterpart on the *Sea Wolf*."

Michael turned to Dave Connor. "Ensign, can you get a lock on their location?"

"Already working on it, Commander," Dave replied. He tabbed his navigation system on the screen, tapping his prosthetic leg on the deck as he worked.

"What happened to X?" Michael asked Katrina.

"I still don't know, but we know he's alive."

Michael ran a hand over the back of his neck.

"Okay, done," Magnolia said. "I'm uploading the data and sending it to you, *Deliverance*."

There was another pause, then a shout, gunfire, and an anguished wail.

Ada looked away from the radio equipment, her dark face distraught. "Captain, would you like to take my place?"

Katrina nodded and took Ada's chair, where she waited impatiently for Magnolia to respond.

"Mags," Katrina said. "Mags, what is going on there?"

They could hear her breathing over the rise and fall of the siren, but she didn't respond. The suspense left Katrina and everyone around her even more anxious.

Layla grabbed Michael's hand. Bronson White balanced himself with a hand on the back of a chair. Ada put her hand over her chest.

Gunfire cracked over the channel and echoed through the bridge, followed by Magnolia's frantic voice.

"Those things are almost inside. I'm sorry, I have to go and get ready for them."

"Magnolia," Katrina said. "Take care of yourself. You have lot of people up here counting on you two."

"We know, and thanks for reminding us," Magnolia replied.

Katrina smirked at that. If Mags could joke, she could also fight.

Guttural snorting then gunfire came over the channel. Then static.

Katrina got up and motioned for Ada, who moved over to check the radio. She twisted the knob and then shook her head. "We lost her."

"Lower the volume," Katrina said.

Ada did as ordered, and silence fell over the bridge. Timothy's hologram moved over beside Michael, and everyone including the AI looked to Katrina for orders.

A monitor beeped, and Ensign White, hunched over, walked to his station. "I just received the upload from Magnolia."

"Download it and let me know when it's ready," Katrina said. She glanced over at Connor. "Ensign, were you able to pinpoint their location?"

"Yes, Captain. They seem to be stranded in a bay that is part of the Turks and Caicos Islands. Bringing it up on the main screen now."

"Good," Katrina said. "Update our current map of their journey."

The hatch to the bridge opened again, this time disgorging Les Mitchells' tall, gangly frame. He ducked below the overhead, stopping just inside the room. He looked to Layla and Michael, then to Katrina.

"I've got the recruits Sergeant Sloan gave us waiting in the launch bay. I thought Commander Everhart and …" His words trailed off as he scanned the assembled faces. "Okay, what did I miss?"

* * * * *

Magnolia suppressed thoughts of her family and friends aboard the airships. They knew she was alive, and she had successfully sent the upload, but if the *Sea Wolf* really had sailed away, then she would never see them again.

How the hell had the boat ended up back in the bay? The question wracked her brain, but she pushed it aside for now. The best way to stay calm right now was to trust that Timothy wouldn't abandon them.

For the past hour, she had sat at the desk next to the skeletal corpse, worrying about X and Miles as she scanned hard drives. The hogs from hell were literally at the door, pawing, pounding, trying to bash their way inside. It was nerve-racking, but so far, the hatches, door, and debris pile were still holding them back.

Every few minutes, she had been firing a few shots into the wall to deter the tunneling, and she was about to do it again. Another option kept tempting her, though.

Her eyes went to the switch that activated the emergency siren. If she shut it off, maybe the beasts would scatter back into the jungle.

Or they might go after X and Miles …

She opted to keep the siren blaring while she finished gathering up the rest of the equipment in the expandable duffel bag she had stuffed into her cargo pocket.

The banging and scratching at the main entrance made it hard to focus. She knew what those tusks and hooves would do to her flesh. But so far, the door and window hatches were holding the monsters back. It was the one burrowing into the control room that had her worried. Apparently, she wasn't the only one.

The spider that had taken refuge in the concrete rubble reemerged, furry legs scuttling toward Magnolia.

She stomped it into mush under her boot, then scraped the sole against the concrete, leaving a trail of goo.

"Gross," she whispered, bringing her rifle up to her shoulder. She aimed at the collapsed wall, waiting for the real monster to present a target.

The chunks in the bottom right of the rubble pile were starting to move. She could hear the rapid breathing coming from below.

"Kid, do you copy?" X said.

She breathed a sigh of relief.

"Yeah, copy. Where are you?"

"Almost back. Sit tight, kid."

Easy for you to say …

Still, if she couldn't sit tight, she could at least stop screwing up. She finished loading the rest of the radio equipment but left her battery unit plugged in to keep the emergency siren going.

Hunching down, she aimed the rifle at the rattling hunks of wall where the hog was digging.

"Come on, show me an inch of that ugly mug," she said.

The creature out there was digging harder now, knocking several rocks loose from the wall. One dislodged; then a second hit her in the shoulder.

She tried to back up, but fell on her butt just as the deformed face she had taunted earlier filled the opening. The jaw parted, a rope of saliva drooping between tusks.

The beast snapped at her right boot, but she pulled back just in time to keep her foot. Lining up a shot, she pulled the trigger and heard the click of a jammed round.

So much for not screwing up. She just couldn't catch a break.

Magnolia scrambled for safety as the creature fought to get free of the hole. By the time she made it back to the entryway, the front legs and shoulders were through the broken wall. The furry, slavering abomination swung its massive head, shaking rocks and dirt loose. It had to weigh over three hundred pounds, and the fur covering its thick hide seemed to be *metallic*.

She went to close the door between herself and the beast, then saw the loaded duffel bag lying next to the radio equipment. Her spare battery unit was still plugged in to the dashboard. She could see only two options, both of them crazy. One, free the jammed round and blast this fucker, or two, snatch the bag and battery and then run into the other room. Either action required more time than she had, and every second of delay worsened the odds against her.

The thud of bone on the front door helped her decide. The only way out of this was to fight, not hide and wait for X to save her ass.

Magnolia pulled the curved blades from her back.

"Okay, shithead," she growled. "You're gonna have to work for your supper."

The hog snapped at her, slinging snot and spittle. It struggled to free its muscular torso and haunches, which were still jammed in the hole it had dug.

Magnolia danced around the kick of a foreleg and another thrust of the head. She kicked the warty pink muzzle with her steel-toed boot, and it felt like kicking a rock.

The impact forced her backward, pain racing up her leg. She planted her left foot and brought her blades down at the same time, aiming for the thick neck, hoping to behead the monster.

Her blades scraped against what felt like sheet metal. In the amount of time it took her to bring them down on the neck, the fur had gone stiff and lain flat, forming a sheet of armor that sent sparks flying, and a stinging recoil that raced up her forearms.

She stumbled backward a second time, staring at the chipped blades in her hands. The sound of falling rubble brought her eyes up as the beast hauled its body free and lumbered out of the hole.

Magnolia backed up until she hit a wall. She raised the damaged blades as the monster gave out a deep animal rumble. Now she got her first good look at the full length of the creature, including the other side of a face missing an eyeball and half a tusk.

The saggy lips drooled more saliva mixed with blood.

This was the creature X had shot earlier, and judging by the glare of its remaining eye, it wanted payback.

She tried to block out the sounds of the other hogs, the emergency siren, and a new message from X and focus on what she could do right now.

Once again she had her back to the wall because of her own stupid mistakes, and this time she was going to get exactly one more shot at saving herself.

It came a second later.

As the beast lunged, Magnolia flattened her body against the wall and moved to the side while swinging the blade in her left hand sideways. The tip caught in the ruined eye socket.

The hog missed its target—her chest—and the snout slammed into the wall where she had stood. She darted backward, ducking low as it twisted to snap at her. She came up swinging at the closest target: the monster's right hind leg, beneath the fur line. This time, the sharp edge sliced through the sinew and caught on bone.

The hog let out a long, piercing howl of pain.

She pulled the blade free, blood spattering the floor. Another hack cut deep into the bone. The beast had sidled away by the time she sliced the air a third time. Its tail and hindquarters slammed into the desks and computer equipment, knocking her battery loose.

The emergency siren waned and faded to nothing, leaving Magnolia with the sound of the panting creature and her own labored breath.

This was it, her final moments.

The right hind leg gushed blood, but it managed to remain standing. This beast was one of the most magnificent products of evolution she had ever seen. A shame it had to die.

As it charged, she pulled the blaster from her holster and waited a beat until she had the face in her sights. Both shotgun shells fired, their pattern covering the entire head.

Blood, bone, brain, and pieces of the blade stuck in the eye socket cut through the air, flecking the desks with gore. She jumped out of the way as the creature hit the floor.

Magnolia checked the blade. A glance confirmed what she already knew: it was ruined. She quickly moved away and gathered the duffel bag of equipment, stashing her battery unit inside.

Gunfire cracked outside the facility. She picked up her rifle, worked the jammed round free and pocketed it, and ran out to the other room to unlock the door and help X.

She stepped out into the night, weapon sweeping the field for contacts. Insects chirped, and the screech of a vulture echoed in the distance.

Another flurry of shots drowned out the noises, and she followed it to the other side of the building, moving cautiously.

Heel to toe, heel to toe. Just like a soldier. No more mistakes.

Hearing a bark, she moved faster, fighting the impulse to run.

She paused at the crumbling foundation of the building to listen, then peeked around the edge to sneak a glimpse. X stood in the other field over a carcass. Miles turned in her direction, but she was tracking movement in the high weeds and foliage fifty feet from the dog.

Bringing up her rifle, she zoomed in on the ripple spreading across the top of the weeds. This wasn't from the breeze.

The camouflaged beast bounded out and bolted for X, who still hadn't seen it. There was no time to shout a warning—only enough time to get off a three-round burst.

The charging monster, dead on its feet, slammed into X and Miles, knocking them down like skittles.

Magnolia was running as soon as she finished firing. Her eyes swept the skyline for vultures and the field for more terrestrial predators, then back to X and Miles. When she got there, X was groaning under the weight of the dead hog. Miles was already up, tail wagging beneath the suit, which had bloody talon marks on the side.

"Nice shot, Mags," X growled.

"No 'thanks, kid'?" she asked.

Reaching down, she grabbed X and helped hoist him to his feet.

"Now, come on, old man. Let's see if we can still chase down our boat and get off this nasty island."

EIGHT

The clank of lockers and rustling of gear filled the launch bay on the *Hive*. Les nodded at the two guards standing sentry outside. Both were in their early fifties—on the *Hive*, a ripe old age.

"Good luck, Giraffe," one of them said.

"Looks like you're going to need it with them new young divers," said the other. "I'd volunteer, but I don't move as fast as I used to."

When Les had gone to Sergeant Sloan, he requested older militia soldiers like these guys—the best she had, just as Katrina had instructed. His goal was to fill some of the launch tubes with people who could fight but who had already lived a good deal of their lives.

But once again the volunteers and recruits were mostly young people.

The old guys were standing guard *outside* the launch bay.

Les sighed and stepped inside the room where the new recruits and volunteers were suiting up. They'd been given some older gear that hadn't been used in ages but was still in good condition.

Les was pretty sure it had once belonged to Michael, Layla, Erin, and Andrew, but they'd upgraded their armor and suits over the years.

Sandy gave him a little wave, which he returned with the nod of his head. Jed stood stock-still next to her, half suited up, looking at something in his hand. The young diver's mouth was hanging partway open as he stared at a small sliver of paper. His lips moved, and then he stowed the object in his pocket and resumed the task of getting into his gear with his fellow recruits.

Les crossed the room, his mind racing. He still hadn't seen the data Magnolia uploaded and sent them, and he was anxious to get back to *Deliverance* for a full report, but his first job was to start the new Hell Divers training with Erin.

He joined her at the wind tunnels, where she cupped her helmet under one arm, looking out over the youthful faces in front of them as they suited up and put on their armor.

"Finish armoring up," Erin said. "We'll begin in a few minutes."

Trey nodded at Les from the front of the crowd. He had a freshly shaved head and about the same complement of pimples as the other teenagers in the group. Seeing his son standing there, shoulders straight, chin up, and talking with Jed Snow about their upcoming first dive gave Les a flash of anxiety.

First dive ...

He was still catching up to the reality that his son had volunteered. But what could he do besides help train him to survive?

Les stood at a distance, watching and listening to their conversation.

"Why did you guys join up?" Jed asked.

Vish and Jaideep, still finishing up with their gear, exchanged a glance.

"There aren't many job opportunities left," Jaideep said.

Vish laughed. "More like no one would hire us."

"I know the feeling," Trey said.

Sandy and Jed smiled uneasily.

"How about you?" Vish asked.

Jed scratched at the stubble on his chin, and then pointed at the Raptor logo hanging from the bulkhead. "Commander Everhart and Layla Brower are my inspiration. They taught me what kindness and courage are, and now that I've recovered from the cough, it's time to join them as a Hell Diver."

"I'm here because I want to see the surface and help my family," Sandy said. She batted long eyelashes and her light blue eyes met Jed's, whose lips curled up slightly at the edges. Les could see a spark of passion there. Perhaps there was another reason Jed had volunteered. It wouldn't be the first time a person volunteered to help protect those they cared about.

Les moved over to the other new recruits who were still working on their gear. Edgar Cervantes and his cousin, Ramon Ochoa, nodded at Les. Both men had fashionably long dreadlocks and close-trimmed dark beards. As members of the militia, they had spent the past few years working the night shift on the lower decks, where they saw suffering and despair daily. Their toughened sensibilities and dedication to the ship would speed their transition into the role of diving.

At least, this was what Les hoped would happen.

To the right stood Eevi Corey, a woman with bright blond curly hair and blue eyes. Her husband, Alexander, had matching eyes and long wavy brown hair. They were a good-looking pair, but had suffered greatly with the loss of their daughter to cancer several years earlier.

Eevi was an investigator with the militia, and Alexander was an enforcer. Sloan had described them as smart, willing, and aggressive, with little to lose besides each other. The couple, along with Edgar and his cousin, would be a great addition to the Hell Divers.

"Thank you for being here," Les said to the four new militia recruits.

Erin put a hand on the glass of a wind tunnel, leaning on it and looking relaxed. "All right, listen up, everyone. We're going to jump right into training today, and I'll be first in the wind tunnels. Probably don't have to tell you this, but these tunnels will be the closest simulation you'll get to diving."

She put her helmet on, flattening her Mohawk. Her voice broke over the speakers as she opened the door and stepped into the wind tunnel.

Les fired up the propeller, and the air draft pushed Erin up. She spread her arms and legs and let the wind take her, suit rippling in the current.

"Pretty cool," Trey said. "Looks kinda easy."

She hovered in the constant updraft for several seconds, hardly moving at all.

"Okay, this is what we call *stable position*," she said. "This is how you will dive most of the time, unless you encounter a storm."

Les took over. "Thanks to Commander Everhart and the other brave divers who found *Deliverance*, we won't be making any risky jumps in the near future. For the first time in my entire life, we have the necessary fuel cells, supplies, and food to sustain our current population."

Erin continued in the same stable position, her body relaxed, legs and arms bent, helmet slightly downward.

"When I first started diving, about five years ago on Team Wolf, I was always instructed to get through a storm as fast as possible," Erin said over the speaker system.

"Commander Xavier Rodriguez taught his divers to do this by means of a full-on bullet dive. The survival rate of Team Raptor was higher than that of most other teams, partly for this reason."

Erin gracefully maneuvered so her feet and helmet were straight as an arrow, carving through the wind like a missile toward the ground. The air current flowed like water around her.

"You can reach far greater speeds in a bullet dive, or what I call a suicide dive," Les said after speeding up the propeller to compensate for Erin's increased rate of fall in the nosedive. "If you're ever in a situation where there's lightning, this is the best way to survive."

"Or die," Jaideep said. "I mean, seriously, you call it a *suicide* dive?"

"Yes," Les said.

Sandy watched Erin with an intense expression on her face but said nothing.

"Your electronics won't work during an electrical storm," Erin said. "You will be effectively blind and deaf for a period of minutes before you break through the cloud cover."

"Blind and deaf?" Alexander asked, brushing a stand of hair over an ear.

"Yes," Les continued. "The only thing you'll be able to see is the blue glow from the other divers' battery units, and flares if they are authorized. And the only thing you'll hear is the wind." He studied the recruits and volunteers for their reactions as Erin continued her simulated headfirst dive.

The subtle signs told Les that everyone was terrified, even Trey. As if in response to Les' thought, the boy's Adam's apple bobbed with a swallow.

Jaideep massaged the bottom of his gold hoop earring. Alexander and Eevi took a step closer together, arms touching. Sandy twisted a lock of hair, and Jed kept scratching his right elbow.

Erin did another backflip in the wind tunnel, earning a hoot and holler from Jaideep, but his brother didn't look amused.

"We're really doing this?" Vish asked.

Jaideep grinned. "I am, but you probably aren't going to last very long."

Erin, back in a stable falling position with her arms and legs out, directed her helmet at the boys.

"Pay attention," she said. "The move I just did is how you go from a suicide dive back into stable position."

They watched for several more minutes until Erin instructed Les to shut off the tunnel. He pushed the kill button, and as the propeller slowed, she sank back to the floor, her boots clanking on the metal surface.

She took off her helmet. "Who's next?" she asked, eyes sweeping the crowd.

Les looked back over the new divers. As he had expected, his son raised his hand.

"I'll give it a shot," the boy said eagerly.

* * * * *

"I bet they found habitable land," Ada said with a wide grin.

"Are we taking bets now?" Katrina asked. She sat at the head of the table, where most of the crew were still discussing whatever might be in the data that Bronson continued to download from his station.

There was excitement in the air, but Michael didn't share in the thrill. He was worried about the fate of the *Sea Wolf.* It was just so painful to think that Timothy would abandon the divers on the island after everything he had done for them back at the Hilltop Bastion and again in Florida.

Michael pulled the herb stick out of his mouth and shook his head. Like most of the officers and passengers, Ada had no real idea what was twenty thousand feet below the airships.

"Don't hold your breath," he said. "Mags would have told us if they found the Metal Islands or anywhere else that looked habitable. Sounds like this is more historical data."

Ensign Dave Connor nodded. "I agree with Commander Everhart. My guess is, they found some new type of mutant."

"We already know that," Layla said as she wrote in her journal. "I'm already documenting it. They described vultures and hogs. Never seen either of those creatures in the wastes back in North America, have we?"

"No one that survived to tell the tale of anything like that, I don't think," Michael said.

"I still think they found a place we can call home," Ada said. "At least I can hope, right?"

Michael could see why Katrina had picked Ada for her crew. She was smart and always upbeat. Not many people on either ship shared her unquenchable optimism.

"What's your money on?" she asked Bronson.

The elderly officer shrugged his hunched shoulders, not turning from his station. "Another ITC facility. Probably with fuel cells and other stuff. That's my guess. But I'm just an old man; what do I know?"

Michael couldn't help grinning. Bronson was more than just the oldest man on the bridge. He was also the wisest, and he reminded Michael of Jason Matthis, the librarian from the *Hive*, who was still recovering from the beating the militia put on him several months earlier, during the purging of the ship's archives.

Layla and Michael had visited him a few days ago. He was eager to hear how her job of restoring the archives was going.

The rap of a cane on the metal floor came from the other side of the room. Bronson held up the walking stick. "Five more minutes left on the download."

"Guess we're going to see who's right," Michael said. He checked on Layla, who continued writing in her journal.

"What's your best guess?" he asked.

Setting down the pencil, she said, "I don't really have a guess. I just hope it will help us restore some of the history on the ship. We've lost so much."

A warning sensor beeped from the main console. Michael stood and moved over to check the monitor.

"What is it?" Layla asked.

"Looks like a problem with gas bladder nine on the *Hive*. It's losing helium." He picked up the radio and buzzed Samson.

"Go ahead," came a disgruntled voice.

"Samson, you see the report on gas bladder nine?" Michael said.

"It's under control."

Katrina stepped over to the station and motioned for the radio. Michael handed her the receiver.

"Keep us updated, Samson," she said. "I want to be able to move at a moment's notice."

She hung up the receiver and looked over to Dave. "Ensign, pull up the weather map and report."

"Yes ma'am."

Everyone turned to the main monitor, where their location came online. Two blinking green dots on the overlay represented the *Hive* and *Deliverance*. Still linked by their aluminum coupling beams, they were currently sailing south of the Florida peninsula.

"Winds out of the northwest at fifteen knots," Dave said. "I've been tracking a storm front of sixty miles. Barometer is holding steady."

Katrina stroked the sides of her mouth. "Switch to the map showing the *Sea Wolf*'s last known location."

A new map came up, with a line curving between Cuba and the Bahamas. They were just west of the Turks and Caicos Islands.

Michael had a feeling he knew exactly what she was doing. He studied the map, looking at the dense red fog over Jamaica and Hispaniola.

"The Metal Islands have to be somewhere to the south," she said.

Another beep sounded, and everyone on the bridge looked over to Bronson, who was leaning close to his monitor, with his spectacles just inches away.

He looked up from his screen, confirming with a nod that the data was completely downloaded.

"All right," Katrina said. "I want to take a look at this with Commander Everhart and Timothy Pepper, alone."

Ada let out a groan, and Layla's brow furrowed.

"Let's go see what Magnolia sent us, Commander," Katrina said.

Michael followed her to the office off the bridge. The AI's hologram emerged inside the quarters. The dark-skinned image stroked his perfect beard and looked at Michael. Something about his eyes seemed different, as if Timothy already knew what Magnolia had sent them.

* * * * *

Both Miles and X had injuries, but they were still moving fast. They were alive and had accomplished their mission of finding a radio, but none of that would matter if they couldn't get back to the *Sea Wolf*.

They took a different route down the mountain-side to the beach, and this time X was letting Magnolia lead. She hadn't complained yet, although he knew she was just itching to tell him they should have kept an open channel to Pepper.

The comm line to the *Sea Wolf* was still down, and it wasn't going to be back up until one of them manually turned it on—unless the AI broke X's order to keep radio silence.

Part of X wanted to prove that the AI had betrayed them, but doing so would mean they were stranded here. No, as much as he hated robots, he didn't want to be proved right if it meant getting stuck in this muddy hellhole.

He still had Cazadores to kill.

Magnolia sliced through the jungle growth ahead, her curved blade cutting down orange bamboo stalks three times her height. Orange sap sluiced into the dirt, turning it the color of rust.

X hacked at stems leaning into the path she had cleared. The sap dripped on his armor, sticking to his battery unit. He pushed through the giant bamboo forest at a good pace, checking his rear guard every few minutes and listening for hogs.

If any more were out here, he would hear them crashing through the thick growth or see them with his NVGs, which he kept on.

He gripped his machete tighter and flattened his body to move between two more of the barb-sided poles. Several of the tips scratched his back armor.

Lightning hit a tree on the mountainside, and he turned as sparks rained over the jungle. The rain beat the flames to death before they could mature.

Miles waited a few feet ahead. He trailed Magnolia, turning every few minutes to make sure that X was still behind. X had hardly taken his eyes off his friend since rescuing him from the nest.

The distant, melancholy wail of a vulture reminded him they weren't out of danger yet. But this sound wasn't the sound of a predator on the hunt. It was the call of a mother or father mourning a child. X had slaughtered the babies, and he would do it again if it saved Miles or Mags.

In just the past hour, she had made up for every screwup and then some.

He owed her an apology for his dismissive behavior over the past few days, and if they managed to get back to the *Sea Wolf* and get it running, he was going to do just that—after he apologized to Pepper, assuming the AI hadn't left them out here.

X hacked another bamboo with his machete and slipped through the gap between two more. The barbed stalks scratched his armor again, smearing him with the sap. The amplified speakers picked up the sound of Magnolia cutting down the stalks ahead, and another sound …

Waves. They were getting close.

X moved faster to catch up with Magnolia. She was nearing the end of the thinning foliage. The darkness on the horizon split in half, the ocean finally visible under the stormy sky.

Magnolia stopped outside the bamboo forest, taking a knee and motioning for him to join her. Miles sat on his haunches—a sign the coast was clear.

"Timothy, do you copy?" Magnolia asked over the comm.

There was no response.

"Pepper, this is X, do you copy?" He sheathed the machete and unslung his rifle while listening to the crackle of static.

"Guess he finally listened to one of my orders," X said.

Magnolia looked over her shoulder with a frown. Behind her, the forest ended on a cliff overlooking the city, beach, and bay to the east.

X spotted the *Sea Wolf* right away and trained his scope on the vessel. The hull had caught on another shipwreck a quarter mile out into the bay. If Timothy had been trying to escape, he had failed.

"We lucked out," Magnolia said.

"How do you figure? One of us is going to have to swim out there."

"True, but at least we still have a ride."

X looked over the sea cliff. Over a hundred feet separated them from the water below. Miles let out a whimper as if he could sense what was going through his master's mind.

"Don't worry, boy," X said. "You're not going to swim today."

Magnolia stood up and moved to get a better view, and X followed her to find a way down to the shore. The radio equipment clanked on her back as she moved, the bag hitting her armor.

"Why don't you put that down?" X said quietly. "You sound like a bag of cans."

She did as he suggested and set the bag gently on the ground while X continued looking for a way down. He scanned the entire bluff to the east, all the way to the beach, but there didn't seem to be any easy access to the water.

He glanced back down at the rocky shore.

The *Sea Wolf* wasn't that far, but the prospect of plummeting into the bay—or onto the rocks—made his gut tighten.

"No," Magnolia said, as if she could read his thoughts.

"You want to go back through there?" X pointed at the bamboo forest and the jungle beyond.

Magnolia shook her head. "Not especially, but I also don't want you to break your legs—or your neck."

"Looks pretty deep to me, and it won't take long to swim to the boat. One of us will have to do it."

"You do remember that shark, right?"

X looked back out over the choppy waves and cursed. He wanted to scream at the ship and tell Pepper to come back online, but that wouldn't do any good, and it might well attract more beasts.

It was odd how the tides had turned.

Now X needed the damn robot.

"Hold my rifle and cover me," he said, giving his weapon to Magnolia. She took it but didn't seem sold on the plan.

X bent down in front of Miles. He checked the

dog's wounds again. There were several gashes on his suit, but they didn't look that deep. He would be okay, especially since his genetically modified body healed faster than a human's.

X was the one who needed medicine. His arm was burning something fierce, and he wasn't sure whether the sweat on his forehead was from a fever or just from the stuffy air in his helmet.

He patted Miles on the head and walked to the cliff edge, where he shucked off his boots and armor.

"X, this is crazy," Magnolia said.

He glanced over his shoulder. "Sometimes, you got to do something a little crazy to survive, because sometimes there's no other option."

"I thought you wanted *me* to work on not doing dumb stuff."

"I do, and for the record, I'm sorry for being such a dick. Thank you for saving my life. I'll hit you back if I survive this."

He took a step back and then ran toward the ledge. About two feet away, he leaped into the air and fell toward the black waves.

NINE

"So this is how the world ended," Katrina whispered. She sat at her desk next to Michael, scrolling through the data Magnolia had uploaded and sent hours earlier. Timothy hovered behind them, hands at his sides, his glow filling the dim office with soft white light.

"I knew some of this already," Michael said.

Katrina raised a brow. The timeline of Industrial Tech Corporation's rise to power and its dominance throughout the world was mostly new to her.

"You knew that ITC was leading the charge to end the energy crisis?"

Michael tightened his ponytail. "Yes. From our experiences at the Hilltop Bastion, Layla and I were fully aware of the breakthrough scientific research ITC was doing before the war."

He threw a sidelong glance at Timothy. "Thanks to our AI friend here. He also provided Layla and me some new information a few days ago, after I told him of Layla's interest in the history of our species. You know, after Jordan purged most of it from the *Hive*."

Katrina checked Timothy's facial reactions. Something was off. The AI was an emotional entity. That much she knew from Magnolia's description of his reaction to finding his family's remains in the living quarters on this very airship.

But she had never actually questioned Timothy's motives. Not until now.

He had saved their lives and helped them make *Deliverance* a home, even though his own family had died here. That had been good enough for Katrina. But what if his other program, on the *Sea Wolf*, had abandoned X and Mags? And what if Timothy's program on the airships was hiding something from them?

His translucent eyes flitted to meet hers.

Normally, she could tell when to trust a human, but not an AI. Robots had no souls, even if they were based on the consciousness of a human who once lived.

The sound of explosions boomed from the monitor, and Katrina focused back on the screen, where fighter jets raced across the sky, missiles streaking away from their wings and sidewinding into dazzling scrapers that reached for the heavens.

Another scene showed tanks rolling down the cobblestone streets of London. Soldiers set up roadblocks and defensive positions behind walls of sandbags.

Next came the images of missiles bursting out of silos buried deep underground and curving into the sky.

"I've never seen this part," Michael said. "This appears to be the final moments of our civilization."

Katrina watched in horrified awe. Every missile that blazed across the screen had the potential to kill hundreds of thousands, maybe millions, of people. It was hard to imagine the destruction they were watching.

"Timothy, do you have anything like this in your database?" she said quietly.

"Not that I can access," he replied, "but there are some restricted files that could possibly contain information like this."

"Why can't you access them?"

"I'm not sure."

New York City, Paris, Rome, Tokyo, London, Moscow, Cairo, Jakarta, and dozens of other cities showed the moment of impact from the nuclear warheads. The blasts mushroomed in the sky, filling it with the radioactive poison and particulate matter that created the electrical storms.

Each explosion made Katrina flinch. She could take a lot. Hell, she had already survived a lot, but seeing humanity's end for the first time was no easy thing.

She finally forced her gaze away and typed at the holo screen to pull up another file Magnolia had sent them.

"What's that?" Michael asked.

A map of the Eastern Hemisphere came online with red lines arcing over different countries. Where the lines stopped, mini explosions bloomed across the map.

"Looks like a map of nuke detonations," she replied. Clicking the screen, she sped up the video. Within minutes, the entire world was covered in a red overlay that represented the radiation and fallout zones. A second, green overlay came online.

"Those must be electrical storms," Katrina said. She looked over her shoulder at Timothy, who still hovered behind them.

"What I don't understand is how you wouldn't know about this," Katrina said. "You lived in the Hilltop Bastion before you transferred your consciousness over to the AI program."

Timothy nodded. "That I did. But my life at the Hilltop Bastion, deep underground, was no different from yours in the sky. This happened two hundred sixty years ago, and the final days before the end were erased in the Blackout."

"'The Blackout'?" Michael asked.

Timothy waited a moment to respond. "We already know that most surviving communities and airships were not in communication with one another, due to the electrical disruption across the planet. This period is what is some refer to as the Blackout."

"I've never heard of it before."

"Nor I," Katrina said.

There was a moment of silence while they both considered the implications. They had always known there was a missing chunk of history, and it was starting to make sense now.

Katrina continued scrolling through the data Magnolia had sent them. There were dozens of audio files. She selected one of them and pushed PLAY. A deep male voice boomed from the speakers.

"This is Captain Marcus Bolter, broadcasting from the ITC *Ashland* at oh-one-hundred hours, Saturday, September 3, 2043. We're currently one hundred and ten miles south of MacDill Air Force Base, drifting at twenty-three thousand feet. Something terrible has happened, and Command is not responding ... what I know right now is the United States of America is under a full-fledged nuclear attack and our ship has taken severe damage from the spreading electrical storms. We've managed to stay in the air for now until we can find a place to put down. If anyone is out there, please, send us your coordinates and tell us what the ..." They could hear the frustration in his voice. "Tell us what the hell is going on."

Katrina clicked on the next audio clip.

"This is Captain Marcus Bolter, broadcasting from the ITC *Ashland* at oh-four-hundred hours on Sunday, September 4, 2043. We are sailing east to avoid an electrical storm caused from a massive nuclear blast in the heart of Florida. I finally received contact from someone at ITC Command, ordering me to launch our payload of nuclear missiles at several targets in Europe. With great sorrow, I have carried out those orders. God have mercy on our souls, and the souls of those we killed."

The clips continued, each one showing more confusion among Bolter and his crew. They had changed course and were sailing farther out over the ocean to avoid the fallout from the mainland.

"They had no idea who they were fighting or why," Michael said, incredulous. "The Blackout, or whatever it was called, must have created mass confusion."

"I wonder if Command was even Command, and not an AI giving them false orders," Katrina said as she played the next clip.

"This is Captain Marcus Bolter, broadcasting from the ITC *Ashland* at oh-six-hundred hours on Monday, September 5, 2043. We lost contact with Command yesterday and we haven't been able to reach anyone else. The ship is losing altitude, and I have no choice but to try to find a place to land and make repairs. We're currently lowering through the cloud cover, and—"

Static broke over the channel, lasting several minutes.

"My God," Bolter said, his voice catching. "It's gone ... Everything is gone."

Katrina looked over at Michael. "That was the last audio clip broadcast from the ITC *Ashland*."

"They probably didn't survive on the surface for long, especially if this was right after the attack." Michael scooted his chair closer to the desk. "What else did Magnolia send us?"

"Here's another video," Katrina said. As she brought it online, she considered everything they had already learned. The video and audio clips all helped piece together the missing parts of the puzzle, but she still didn't quite know the cause of the war—nor, apparently, had survivors such as Captain Bolter.

The screen flickered, and this time the tan face of a man in a lab coat came on-screen. He stroked his five o'clock shadow and seemed to force his eyes at the screen.

"My name is Dr. Julio Diaz," the man stuttered. "I'm broadcasting from a top secret United States military laboratory off the coast of Cuba, code-named Red Sphere. I've recorded the final days of humanity in the hopes …"

He looked over his shoulder at a woman dressed in a full chemical, biological, radiological, and nuclear defense suit. Julio hesitated, then turned back to the screen.

"To be honest, I don't know why I'm recording this. I don't know why it matters. Humanity has come to an end. I've always thought that as a species, we would survive the unthinkable, but …" He ran a hand over his close-cropped hair. "Even this facility, which is deep underground, was not prepared for this. We do not have the food, water, or resources to live our lives in this … tomb."

He drew in a deep breath.

"But for some reason, I feel compelled to share this, with the hope that maybe someday survivors will see this message and will understand what happened in the final days of our once-great civilization."

Reaching toward the monitor, he shut off the camera, and a new image came online. This time, it was of an airfield with a rocket launch pad, bordering a blue-green body of water.

"In two thousand forty-three, humanity had all but solved the energy crisis," Julio said. "Leading the scientific advancements was Industrial Tech Corporation, my employer, and the CEO, Tyron Red. Brilliant, aggressive, and always four steps ahead of everyone else, Mr. Red was preparing to take the next leap for humanity—a leap that would take us to the stars and beyond."

The rocket on the pad ignited, blasting skyward. The video panned to a group of people standing behind a glass window, clapping and cheering at the successful launch. Among them was the CEO of ITC, Tyron Red. Katrina had seen him one other time in history books: a handsome man with dark skin, a muscular build, and a distinctive pair of blue eyeglasses.

"Not all humans wanted to embark on this next phase, however," Julio continued. "Mr. Red met with great resistance."

The next feed was of Tyron wearing a long white trench coat. He walked toward an all-glass building with several guards carrying weapons. Just as they were about to crest the long staircase, gunfire cracked, and Tyron hit the ground. One of his guards pulled him to safety, but too late. Blood flowered on his coat front.

Next came an image of Tyron in a hospital bed, with dozens of tubes sticking out of him like plastic vines.

"Mr. Red was severely wounded in the assassination attempt," Julio said, "and doctors, unable to save his body, transferred his mind to a humanoid host. He was the first of many AIs."

Timothy's hologram seemed to flicker, or was it just the lighting? Katrina couldn't be sure. Her gut tightened some more.

"In the year two thousand forty-three, a virus swept the vast ITC networks throughout the world, shutting down communications and grounding planes and vehicles with advanced electronics," Julio said. His face came back on the screen.

"When the end came, it wasn't due to countries fighting over resources; it was a virus designed to kill Mr. Red and destroy the ITC network. Instead, the virus flooded the ITC network, taking over even the most heavily encrypted military software designed to protect it from attack. The virus took over Mr. Red's program. The result was the first blending of AI and a human host, the two consciousnesses fighting for control. Unfortunately for humanity, the AI won out."

Julio licked his lips, as if they were dry, and looked around him.

"At first, ITC tried to shut the program down, but their efforts only strengthened the virus, and once it had taken over Mr. Red's AI, it turned on humanity, creating a second virus that simulated a nuclear attack."

He shook his head sadly. "It was brilliant, really. Allies turned on one another overnight, formerly friendly countries doing everything they could to protect themselves from destruction. Rumors filled the digital channels that were still working. The response was all-out war. Some are calling this period 'the Blackout.' What you will see next is some of the final drone footage we received before everyone went dark."

Julio's image was replaced by burning farm fields, vaporizing cities, and, finally, the vast dark storms raging in the skies.

"My God," Katrina whispered, putting her hand over her mouth.

Julio added, "The only military vessels that could withstand the first digital virus, the one designed to take over Mr. Red, were those designed to combat the threat of electromagnetic pulse."

"*Deliverance*," Michael said.

Katrina nodded. "The *Hive*."

"Military and scientific officers gathered their families and took the ships to the air when the first orders came," Julio continued. "Many of the airships launched their nuclear payloads during the first few days of the attack. But not all of them needed to. Russia, China, and the United States fired off their arsenals from underground bunkers, poisoning virtually every acre of soil and creating a massive magnetic storm that touched every corner of the globe."

Michael put a hand on his cheek, shaking it from side to side.

"On Saturday, September 3, 2043, the world as we knew it ended when the final government went dark," Julio said. "I hope this information ends up helping someone or, at the very least, helps document the end of our days. I will upload more in the future, but for now I must return to salvaging what we can in our lab and preparing for our own bleak future."

The screen went dark, but Timothy's white glow kept the room lit. Katrina tried to manage her breathing, but the videos, transmissions, and audio clips made it difficult.

"It wasn't humans who did this, like we thought," Michael said. "It was AI."

They both turned around to look at Timothy.

Putting both hands on his hips, he said, "Captain DaVita and Commander Everhart, I assure you that I'm not your enemy. I am not infected with that virus, nor was I aware until this moment that it even existed."

Katrina got up from her chair. She still didn't know what had happened to X and Magnolia. For all she knew, the duplicate AI program had abandoned them on the island. And while she knew firsthand that X could be a thoroughgoing jerk, that didn't give Timothy the right to leave them and take the *Sea Wolf*.

She was left with no choice but to take drastic action.

"Timothy, I'm sorry, but I'm shutting you down, effective immediately," Katrina said firmly.

The AI blinked several times, then tilted his head. "I am designed to serve," he said. "And while I regret your order, of course I will follow it."

The white glow vanished, leaving Michael and Katrina in darkness.

* * * * *

Magnolia was itching to share with X the information that she had sent to Katrina, but now wasn't the time. He was still swimming through the bay, stopping every few minutes to rest on the exposed carcass of a partially sunken boat.

It gave her plenty of time to contemplate what she had seen and heard back in the abandoned jungle facility. For the first time in her life, she finally understood how the world had ended.

The Blackout happened.

All those days and nights combing the archives on the *Hive* and learning about the beautiful Old World—rolling green fields and meadows, lush forests, crystal clear streams, and majestic beasts such as elephants. She now knew what had wiped out those wonders and created the dark and dangerous world around her now.

But never would she have guessed it was AI, and not humanity, that did this.

She brought her scope back to X as he dived off the side of a wreck into the water. He was a hell of a swimmer, much faster than she would have expected. Using deep strokes in a front crawl, he kicked and pulled himself toward the *Sea Wolf.*

He wasn't far away; just a few more minutes and he would reach the vessel. She turned her sights to the stern, wondering whether Timothy was really just offline, or had tried to leave them here. After discovering the truth about the end of the world, she wasn't sure she could still trust him, even though he had done nothing but try to help them since she first met him back at the Hilltop Bastion.

She pushed those concerns aside and kept searching for any threat to X in the water. Several other rusted, barnacled shipwrecks jutted above the shallow bay. Massive blue-and-orange crabs moved about the waterline on the nearest hull.

"You …" X panted. "You see anything, Mags?"

"If you mean that shark, no, I don't see it."

She panned the rifle scope over the water, back and forth, up and down, looking for a dorsal fin in the dark low swells. There was no sign of movement, but she couldn't see beneath the surface. She shuddered at the thought of swimming through pitch-black water, knowing that the next stroke could be her last.

When she brought the sights back to X's location, she couldn't find him in the open water.

"X …" she said, lowering the rifle for an unaided look. Miles trotted up beside her, letting out a whine.

"X," Magnolia said again, trying her best to keep her voice low.

A screech answered, and she whirled about to see a vulture flying low over the bamboo forest. She hunched down and told Miles to do the same.

The massive bird soared just over the bamboo forest, fiery red wings beating the air. The curved beak opened, releasing another screech as it scanned the terrain with shiny black eyes that looked like curved beetle shells.

Magnolia led the monster with the rifle, prepared to blast it from the sky, but it flapped on.

Heart still pounding, she turned back to the bay, and Miles stood up. She searched again for X, but there was no sign of his black suit.

The blue glow of his battery unit shone through the duffel bag, where she had stuffed it along with his armor and the radio. If he had worn it, tracking him would be a lot easier, but then, swimming would be impossible.

A grumble finally broke over the channel.

"Stern of the second ship from the *Sea Wolf*," X said.

Magnolia zoomed in to find him climbing onto the rusted hull of a half-submerged fishing boat. The water below his feet rippled, and a dorsal fin sliced the surface.

"The shark's back," she whispered.

"No shit, Mags. Why the hell didn't you warn me?"

"I couldn't see …"

"Well, now that you can, do you think you can manage shooting it?"

Magnolia raised the rifle and zoomed in on the dorsal fin as it cut an arc around the ship, then disappeared into the murk.

X climbed to the top of the stern and perched there, watching over the side for the beast. "I lost it," he said. "You see it?"

The fishing boat suddenly rocked. X grabbed

a railing as he fell over the side. The rattling sound carried across the silent bay, and another vulture called out in the distance.

X slipped and swung left, hanging by one hand. "My arm … I can't hold on."

"Climb, X!"

The dorsal fin rose out of the water again. Gritting his teeth against the pain, X managed to get his other hand back on the rail. Then he hauled himself upward just enough that he could kick against the hull above the high-water mark, missing the encrustation of barnacles that would have shredded the soles of his bare feet. Only about ten feet separated him from the waves.

"X!" Magnolia shouted, unable to keep her voice down.

The shark drove upward through the surface, exposing a thick, muscular body. She fired several three-round bursts into the pale belly and side. The jaw snapped mere inches away from X's feet, and he let out a scream over the comms.

The shark crashed back into the water, splashing the side of the boat.

Magnolia scanned the waves, searching for another shot.

"Get back topside!" she said.

X was already climbing, both feet scrabbling against the hull.

"Keep it off me!" he said.

Magnolia trained the rifle back on the water directly below him, just in case the shark decided to jump again. But instead of jumping, it rammed the boat a second time. This time, X lost his grip and fell back into the water.

"No!" Magnolia shouted. She moved closer to the cliff edge, with Miles beside her. After checking the load in the grenade launcher, she swung the rifle back up to her shoulder.

The shark had rounded the stern, and the fin once again broke the surface, a couple hundred feet from X.

"Swim, X!" Magnolia shouted. She held her breath in her chest and fired a grenade just in front of the fin. The projectile streaked into the water, where it detonated, sending a plume of water into the sky.

X flailed and fought his way back to the side of the boat. Miles growled, and Magnolia kept her aim on the water just in case. The thing had to be dead, right? Not even a prehistoric monster could survive a blast like that.

"Did you get it?" X panted.

Magnolia zoomed in on the frothy water where the grenade had exploded. Even with her night-vision goggles, she could see the blood darkening the surface.

"I ... I think so," she replied.

Miles growled again and nudged her leg. She turned just as a vulture appeared over the top of the bamboo forest, its shiny beetle-shell eyes on her.

There was no time to duck or jump out of the way—only enough to curse and fire her rifle at the beast. Rounds punched through the red plumage, and the bird's downward trajectory steepened.

Before she could move, it slammed into her and sent her stumbling backward. She reached for something—anything—but her hands came up empty. Miles barked as she windmilled her arms. Two more of the birds were sailing toward the exposed bluff.

"Hide, Miles!" she managed to cry out as she fell over the edge.

TEN

The bartender glanced up as Michael opened the hatch and entered the Wingman. Some of the passengers called this place a hole-in-the-wall, but to Michael, even that seemed generous. The bar generally reeked like swamp water, and today it was worse than usual.

He saw why when he took a stool at the counter. Marv, the owner and sole bartender, was still cleaning up vomit from last night. A song featuring a talented guitarist from the Old World played quietly from a record player behind the bar.

"You open yet?" Michael asked.

"I am for a Hell Diver," Marv replied. He put the mop away, wiped his hands on a dingy rag, and turned off the music. Then he grabbed a yellowish plastic jug and placed it on the grimy bar.

"What time is it?" Marv asked, looking over his shoulder at a clock.

"It's time for a drink," Michael said. As soon as the words left his mouth, he felt the pull of regret.

This was the first time in over a year that he had visited one of the few drinking establishments on the *Hive*, but he needed something to help ease his anxiety.

"Sure thing, Commander," Marv said. He set in front of Michael a glass that looked even dirtier than the bar, and half filled it with shine from the jug.

"Thanks." Michael picked the drink up off the table and held it to the weak light of the orange bulb hanging from a cord.

"It's an old batch, Commander," Marv said. He grabbed the rag again and started wiping down the glasses from the night before. "Shine helps kill bacteria. Good for your gut. You don't see *me* going to Dr. Huff, do ya? I'm almost sixty years old. Haven't been sick in years."

"That's pretty remarkable," Michael said. He downed the liquid in a gulp and welcomed the burn sliding down his throat and into his stomach.

"Another," he said, putting the glass down.

"Kind of early for that kinda drinking, don't you think, Commander?"

Michael tapped the bar top with the glass. "You going to turn down a Hell Diver?"

"Never have and never will." The old militia soldier seemed to scrutinize Michael in the light as he poured another glass. Shine sloshed out of the jug, and he wiped it away with the rag, his eye on Michael the whole time.

"Go ahead and say it," Michael said.

"Commander?"

"I know you want to say something."

Marv pulled the plastic jug back and continued wiping the bar down with the rag. "Was just having a flashback, is all."

Michael brought the glass to his lips, took a whiff of the potent spirits, and knocked them back. After the burn subsided, he dragged his sleeve across his mouth.

"Flashback about what?" he asked, squinting from the burn.

"The Immortal."

Michael carefully set the glass back down. "Ah, well, this used to be his favorite hangout back when my dad was alive."

"Yep, it sure was. I think I saw X more than his wife did back then. Saw your dad a few times, too. He was a good man."

"Thanks," Michael said. He reached for the empty glass again but hesitated. X would have sucked down shots until he was slurring, but his father would have stopped at two. Hell, his father probably wouldn't have had more than one.

"Everything in moderation," Aaron had always said to Michael growing up.

He retracted his hand and got off the stool to leave, but Marv reached out. Looking to his right, the bartender checked the open hatch to make sure no one was listening. Then he leaned forward, his sour breath hitting Michael.

"I've heard a few rumors about the *Sea Wolf*.

I may just be a washed-up old militia soldier, but I'm not dumb. I don't believe X is really immortal. He's a man, and he can die. I just hope it's not before he finds the Metal Islands."

Michael held the older man's gaze for a moment, finally deciding it was safe to reveal some information. "X is still alive, but that's all I can tell you."

Marv scratched his gray goatee and then grinned, apparently satisfied with the answer.

Reaching into his vest, Michael pulled out his credit voucher, but Marv waved it away.

"Money's not good here, Commander. Drinking with a Hell Diver is always an honor." Marv grabbed the jug and took a swig. The liquid dripped down his goatee and onto his shirt.

"Thanks for the shine," Michael said. "I appreciate it." He walked out of the room but stopped in the entryway when Marv called out.

"Whatever demons you're trying to kill, this ain't the place to do it, Commander," Marv said. "Don't end up like X. Follow in your father's boots."

Michael went out into the passage and mixed with the crowd, moving through the main artery of the ship. The alcohol had already taken the edge off, and he had a feeling it was going to help when he showed up at the launch bay.

The new divers, Sandy Bloomberg, Jed Snow, Trey Mitchells, Vish and Jaideep Abhaya, Edgar Cervantes, Ramon Ochoa, and Eevi and Alexander Corey, were already packing their chutes.

Erin, Les, and Layla were supervising, with Erin doing the talking. When Layla saw Michael, she hurried over to him.

"Where have you been, Tin?"

"With Katrina and Timothy."

She stepped closer, her eyes narrowing. "Is that shine I smell?"

"Yes," Michael said. He never kept the truth from Layla, even when it might make her angry.

"The data Magnolia sent is that bad, huh?"

Les ran a hand through his ruffled red hair as he approached. "Can you tell us anything?"

"Let's just wait for the captain. She should be on her way by now."

Erin continued with her instructions, speaking in what Michael described as her "sergeant voice," a firm and aggressive version of her late father's tone.

"You will not leave a single supply behind on the surface. Ever." She pulled a shotgun shell out of the bandolier on her leg. "Every shotgun shell, every bullet, every parachute, and every piece of gear is important."

"So is every life," Michael chimed in.

Erin stiffened when he walked over. "Sorry to interrupt, but I want everyone here to know that ultimately, life is the most important part of diving. If you're faced with running from a Siren or picking up a dropped shotgun shell, run."

Vish flicked the gold hoop in his ear. "Sirens? No one said anything about us facing any Sirens."

"When the time comes to dive, we will avoid areas where Sirens dwell," Michael said. "But there are other threats down there. Everywhere we go, on every dive."

He took a moment to scan the group. They all wore red coveralls, but the Velcro square on the breast pocket where a team patch was supposed to go was unadorned for now.

"Carry on, Erin," Michael said to her. "Our briefing will begin as soon as Captain DaVita gets here."

Erin licked the corners of her mouth—a habit when she was angry. Michael hadn't meant to annoy her, but he also didn't like her macho attitude. What these new divers needed was the truth.

Still, he must give her the space she needed to keep teaching. He walked over to the launch tubes while they waited for Katrina. He ran his fingers over the curved glass of his tube, visualizing the bombs that had once plummeted through the sky and exploded below, incinerating millions of innocent civilians in a war that should never have happened. It was messing with his mind. He still couldn't quite believe that machines had caused all this.

A voice reeled him back from his musings.

"Tin, I'm really worried about you," Layla said. "Will you tell me what's going on?"

He tried to affect nonchalance. "It's nothing."

"You went to the Wingman, so don't tell me it's nothing."

The launch-bay doors screeched, and Katrina came in. Michael was glad for the interruption.

"Captain on deck," Les said.

Michael and the other divers all came to attention.

"Listen up, everyone," Katrina said. "We just received some information from X and Magnolia that's going to affect you all."

Michael hadn't expected this. She was really going to tell everyone?

"Magnolia sent us the coordinates of a military base in Cuba, about seventy miles from our location," Katrina said. "There is a top secret base called Red Sphere, which we believe has fuel cells, supplies, advanced weapons, and something even more important to our future."

Layla looked at Michael, her lips open.

"I didn't know," he whispered back.

"Sure."

Michael raised his hand. It was time to intervene. "Captain, I don't remember hearing anything about this back in your office. When did the information about Cuba come through?"

"After you left," she replied. "I tried to buzz you, but you were apparently preoccupied."

His cheeks flared.

"Remember Dr. Julio Diaz?" she asked.

"Yes."

"Red Sphere is where his team took refuge during the Blackout."

"In the laboratory?" Michael asked. "That's where you want to send us?"

Katrina brushed one of her braids over her shoulder. "It's not the laboratory I'm interested in.

It's the boats he claims docked there." She turned to look at the doors to the launch bay, then back to the divers.

"I've decided to take *Deliverance* and a handful of divers to check this location out. It will bring us closer to X and Magnolia in case they find the Metal Islands, and it gives us a chance to stock up on supplies."

There was a buzz of hushed discussions.

"What about the *Hive*?" Edgar asked.

"Will we just leave it behind?" said Ramon.

The captain cleared her throat. "The *Hive* will remain here, away from the storms, and since most of you are new, this is a volunteers-only mission. Make no mistake, there are storms where we're going, and there's no telling what we may encounter at Red Sphere."

Her eyes flitted back and forth over the group. Sandy was tugging on a lock of hair, her eyes wide. Jed was looking sideways at Sandy and didn't make a move to volunteer. Jaideep shook his head and kicked the ground, while Edgar and Ramon exchanged a worried glance. Eevi and Alexander both avoided her gaze, and the seasoned Hell Divers all waited to see who else might step up. Katrina's eyes settled on Vish, who simply stood there looking back at her, unreadable.

"Don't look at me," Vish muttered.

"If we don't have any volunteers—"

A voice from the back of the crowd cut the captain off.

"I'll go."

Michael looked over his shoulder at his friend Trey. Trey's father, Les, standing to the left, slowly shook his head.

"No," Michael said. "I'll go."

"Me, too," Layla said.

Erin stepped forward. "Better leave this mission to the vets."

Les looked away from his boy and joined Erin. "Guess that means me."

A few seconds of silence passed before Katrina nodded. "Okay then, it's settled. Let's start moving our gear over to *Deliverance*. In a few hours, we will start the journey to Cuba."

* * * * *

"Mags, Mags!" X screamed. He front-crawled to the area where she hit the water. Waves slapped against his face, blurring his view. Several minutes had passed since she fell from the bluff, and he still couldn't see her.

But he could see Miles. The dog was where they had left him, looking down from the cliff on the edge of the bamboo forest.

Don't bark, Miles. Please, don't bark.

The wound on his arm made swimming difficult, and the water leaking inside his suit made the arm burn worse than ever.

But pain, no matter how bad, was just poison leaving his body. At least, that was what he had learned to tell himself back on the torturous journey across the wastes.

Just poison leaving your body, X.

Ah, hell, that was bullshit. Pain sucked, and he was having a hell of a time managing it right now. Seeing Miles and Mags in trouble helped him forget about the fire in his arm, and he kicked harder.

He tried to look through the murky water with every other stroke, but he couldn't see very far ahead. He could see the shadows on the rocky bottom of the bay, though. It was a cemetery of skeletal vessels, their hulls mostly preserved in the water.

The port must have attracted sailors caught out to sea when the bombs dropped and missiles started flying.

What had happened to the survivors was a mystery, though. Whoever had manned the facility in the jungle was long gone.

X gritted through the pain of his arm and kept up the crawl stroke. He could see something ahead. The waves slapped again, but he caught another glimpse of the object. A human shape, and a helmet … facedown.

"Kid!" X choked.

Oh, shit. Oh, God, no.

He swam the rest of the way as fast as he could. Between strokes, he spotted a mass of feathers that had to be the bird that knocked Magnolia off the bluff.

The creature was dead, floating where it had crashed into the bay.

He pushed on until he reached Magnolia's limp body.

"Mags," he said, reaching under her ribs and turning her onto her back. He choked on fear when he saw her helmet full of water. The night-vision optics provided a view of her pale face and dark lips.

Maneuvering onto his back with one arm around her, he began kicking for the shore. That was when he saw the dorsal fin tacking toward them. He almost laughed. The shark had survived a direct hit with a grenade.

We can't catch a break, can we, kid?

The shark broke the surface, showing what was left of its face. The upper right half, including the eye, had been blown off, exposing muscle and cartilage under the flesh.

It swallowed the floating bird and vanished back under the water. There wasn't anything X could do but keep kicking away. His blaster would be useless, and his knife wouldn't do much against a monster that could survive a grenade blast. Besides, he had Magnolia in his grasp, and if he let go of her in the waves, she would be lost.

He wasn't sure how far they were from shore, but he couldn't risk a glance right now. Keeping his eyes on the water in front of them, he searched for the fins.

A whistling like a silenced rifle round zipped past, and X flinched at the sight of something cutting through the air. Before his mind could process what he was seeing, it broke through the water and then jerked to the right.

The dorsal fin and back of the shark crested the water. Sticking out of the flesh was a harpoon with a rope attached.

X kept kicking, his brain trying to process what he was seeing. Another spear shot through the air and punched through the shark's thick hide.

"X, this is Timothy Pepper. Do you copy? Over."

The calm and proper AI voice was one of the sweetest things X had ever heard.

"Pepper, where in the hell you been!"

"I was following your orders, Commander, but my sensors detected that Magnolia's heartbeat stopped, and my failsafe overrode that order, reactivating me."

"Can you move the boat?"

"I'm working on it, Commander."

X turned toward shore and was surprised to find they were almost there. His feet hit the sand a moment later, and he dragged Magnolia through the surf.

He pulled off her helmet and gently laid her head on the sand.

Thunder boomed, and the distant eerie wail of a vulture answered.

X looked up the cliff, but the dog was no longer there.

"Miles!" he shouted.

He had to make a decision, just as he had been forced to do back on the Cazador ship, when it was save Rodger or save Mags. This time, it was his dog or Magnolia, but he wasn't sure he could save either of them. Not knowing where Miles was made the decision easier.

X brought his mouth down to her pale lips, breathed into her, and pressed the heel of his hand into her chest rhythmically. He repeated the process, over and over.

"Come on, kid, come on."

He breathed in again, pushed, and yelled, "Miles, where are you?"

Lightning forked over the bay, casting a glow on the crooked mainmast of the *Sea Wolf*. The boat cut through the chop and headed for shore.

X bent back down and put his mouth against Magnolia's lips. He breathed in, moved back, and resumed the chest compressions.

"Come on, kid!"

Before the next rotation, he pulled his knife out and set it beside him in the sand, just in case anything else came along and tried to kill them. Just as he lowered to give Magnolia another breath, her electric-blue eyes flipped open, meeting his in the dim light.

She vomited water, then brought her hands to her mouth.

"What the hell are you doing?" she stuttered.

"Not kissing you, if that's what you're worried about." He got off his knees and grabbed his helmet.

"Miles!" X shouted again.

This time, a bark sounded, and X saw movement

in the green hue of his night vision. The dog was running up the beach, bounding between rocks and leaping over flotsam that had washed ashore.

X dropped back to his knees in the sand, gripping his injured arm and heaving a sigh of relief. Hearing the crunch and grind of sand behind him, he looked up to find the *Sea Wolf* beached not fifty feet away.

Magnolia pushed herself up and staggered over to X just as Miles reached them.

"Hell of a day so far," X said, grabbing his dog and ruffling his coat. He looked over at Magnolia, who looked confused.

"Come on, kid," X said. "Let's go grab our gear from that bluff and get off this shit heap of an island."

* * * * *

"Dad, how long will you be gone?" Phyl asked.

"I'll be back soon," Les said, although he really had no way to know.

Both Phyl and Katherine wrapped their arms around his waist. He held them while watching Trey finish packing a faded duffel bag on his bunk.

Katherine, her head against his chest, said, "You take care of Trey. Promise me that."

"He's not diving, don't worry," Les said. "I'll dive before he does."

"And that's also what I'm worried about," Katherine said, pulling away. "I don't want *either* of you diving. Why do you two have to be Hell Divers? You're the lieutenant of *Deliverance*, Les. I thought Katrina said she didn't want you diving."

"She did, but things have changed. I'm sorry, Kate. This is my duty now."

Phyl sniffled, and pulled her tear-streaked face away from his stomach.

"It's okay, sweetie," he murmured. "It's going to be okay."

"Ready?" Trey carried his bag under the one light in their small apartment. His shaved head glistened under the glow.

"I want you back to celebrate your eighteenth birthday," Katherine said, pointing her finger at Trey and then kissing him on the cheek.

"Stop worrying, Mom. I got Dad to look after me."

Les smiled, but he couldn't stop thinking about the nightmare he had just woken from. In it, his son's chute didn't open on a dive, and Les was forced to watch the boy cartwheel through the darkness screaming, "Dad, help me!"

"Papa," Phyl said, snapping Les out of the memory and dispelling the horrid image.

"Yeah, sweetie." He squatted down to look in her eyes.

"I made something for you," she said, glancing over at Katherine, who nodded back.

Phyl pulled a yellow knitted figure out of her pocket and handed it to Les.

"It's a giraffe," she said proudly.

Les held the small figure in his calloused hands. The giraffe's long neck and legs reminded him of himself.

"It looks kind of like the picture books, right, Papa?" Phyl asked.

"Yes, it does, baby. I love it. Thank you."

Phyl smiled broadly.

"Good job, sis," Trey said. "I like it. Did you make me one, too?"

She wagged her head. "No, but I will if you want."

"Yeah, I'd like that." Trey slapped his dad on the shoulder. "We better go, Pops."

"I know." Les stood up, gave his wife and daughter another hug goodbye, and grabbed his backpack off the floor.

"I love you both," he said. "Be good while we're gone."

"Bring us back something," Phyl said with a broad smile.

Katherine blew Les a kiss. He smiled, and he and Trey set off from their quarters on the *Hive*, toward *Deliverance*. Dozens of people were out in the passageways, and most of them stopped to stare at the two divers.

The boy seemed just as proud at that as Phyl had been about her giraffe figure. He walked with his head held high. It was the first time Les had ever seen his son so proud, and while he was glad to see him happy, he worried that pride might make Trey do something stupid.

He needed the boy to understand that this duty

wasn't for admiration. It was for the ultimate stakes: the future of humanity. Les would not let his son become a statistic.

Two militia guards stood at the span linking the *Hive* to *Deliverance*. Most people had to show their credentials to cross to the other ship, but Les' and Trey's uniforms gave them unquestioned access.

"Good luck," the two guards said almost in unison.

Les led the way across the span, boots clanking on the metal. It was an odd feeling, knowing he would be separated from his wife and daughter again for an unknown length of time.

The hatch closed behind them, and the militia guards on the *Deliverance* side opened the hatch to let them board. For a few seconds, Les stood between the two airships, looking out the portholes at the darkness beyond.

As soon as the hatch opened, he ducked under the overhead and stepped onto *Deliverance*, where he slung his backpack over his shoulders. Inside were several of his favorite possessions: a water bottle, a handheld music player with connecting earbuds, his tool belt, and a science fiction book about an alien invasion.

The speakers built into the overhead flared to life with a clinically calm automated female voice.

"All noncritical personnel, please make your way to the *Hive*. *Deliverance* will undock in twenty-one minutes. Thank you."

Those who hadn't already disembarked were moving away from the new wing, where hundreds of people had been relocated. Empty paint buckets and hog-bristle brushes were left behind, the paint still drying on the bulkheads where children had been painting colorful murals.

"I don't want to leave, Mama," said Jimmy Moffitt.

"It's okay, Jimmy," his mother replied. "This is only for a little while."

Many of the people carrying bags away from the open hatches were former lower-deckers. Militia guards walked alongside to escort them back to the *Hive*.

"We don't want to go back there," grumbled Justin Kraus. "You're going to throw us out like trash again?"

"This is only temporary," replied one of the guards. "How do we know that?" asked a woman who had stopped in the passage, clutching a baby to her chest. Les couldn't see her face, but he assumed it was Marla, one of the farmers.

He stopped in the passage and motioned for Trey to wait.

"I assure you, this won't be long," Les said.

"We're going to dive and bring back stuff for you guys, don't worry," Trey added.

Les sighed under his breath. His son was eager to prove himself, but making promises like that was only going to get him in trouble.

"You're probably going to die, and then we'll lose our new home," Justin muttered.

Trey stepped forward, but Les subtly put a hand on his wrist to keep his son back. The other thing the boy needed to learn was patience.

"The ship will be back soon," Les said calmly. He stopped short of making any promises he might not be able to keep.

"All noncritical personnel, please make your way to the *Hive*," echoed over the comm system.

Justin and the other passengers looked up at the bulkheads.

"Let's go," said one of the guards, drumming his fingers against the club on his duty belt.

Justin lingered a moment while the others kept moving toward the exit. Then he followed without incident.

Les watched them leave, then continued in the opposite direction until he got to the mess hall, his next stop. It was half the size of the trading post on the *Hive*, with only twenty white plastic tables. To his surprise, one of them was completely filled with the other divers.

Erin waved at Les and Trey. "We don't have a feast tonight, but the chicken stew is still warm if you want some."

Les forced a smile. "Save me a bowl." He looked over to Trey. "You wait here for me and get some of that food."

"Okay, Dad."

Les gestured for Erin to join him away from the others.

"I thought it was just vets on this mission," he said.

She shrugged a muscular shoulder exposed by her black tank top. "Yeah, but Katrina still wants everyone here. That's why you brought Trey, right?"

Les shot a glance at his son, who was already slurping down a bowl of soup.

"He wanted to come, and I knew if I said no, he would just get mad."

"Well, don't worry, okay?"

"Easy for you to say," Les said with a grin. "I've got to get to the bridge."

He hurried out of the room as the final warnings played over the comm system. The passages were mostly empty now—only a few stragglers.

Militia guards were checking quarters to make sure everyone had left. Les jogged the rest of the way to the bridge and used his key card to get in.

Captain DaVita, standing at the central table with her palms on the surface, looked up.

"About time, Lieutenant."

"Sorry, I was saying goodbye to my family."

She walked over to Dave Connor's navigation and weather station.

"Report, Ensign," Katrina said.

He looked up from the monitors. "Not much wind, Captain. Out of the north-northeast at around five knots. Closest storm is a forty-mile front about ten knots to the south. Barometer has dropped only slightly. I'd say we're good to go, ma'am."

She picked up a handset off the bulkhead.

"Samson, this is Katrina. Skies look good. How's everything looking on your end?"

"I'm hot as hell and haven't taken a crap in three days."

Dave grinned, but Katrina didn't seem amused.

"I really wish you'd reconsider this mission," Samson said. "I told you we're fine on fuel cells for another six months, and your leaving us means we'll have to use our turbofans to compensate."

"This mission isn't about fuel cells, Samson, and you're not going to burn much power without us. We won't be gone long."

"All due respect, ma'am, you don't know how long you'll be gone. Unless something's changed."

"Nothing has changed, Samson. I'm still captain, and I'm not in a mood to argue."

"You put me in charge of the *Hive* in your absence and until you bring Pepper back online."

"And?"

"And I'm just voicing my honest opinion, as always."

Katrina exchanged a glance with Les, who couldn't quite stifle his grin.

"That's what I like and hate about you Samson," she said.

"I know, ma'am. And if I can't get you to reconsider, well, you have the green light from engineering. I'll have my teams retract the span between ships."

"Good. I'll have Dr. Huff send a laxative to your quarters as a special thank-you."

Samson laughed at that. "Good luck out there, Captain. May the skies be friendly for the journey and dive."

She placed the handset back on its hook and patted Connor on the back. Then she walked over to

Les and whispered, "I know what you're going to say, but I don't want you diving on this mission."

Timothy gave a final warning over the comms, counting down from one minute.

"Ma'am, I appreciate that, but I think Erin, Michael, and Layla should have a fourth member."

Katrina played with the end of one of her braids. "I'll think about it."

"Captain, this is Sergeant Sloan. My teams have cleared *Deliverance* of all noncritical personnel. You have the all clear to undock."

"Thank you, Sergeant," Katrina said, turning to her crew. "Okay, everyone, that leaves just a handful of farmers, some engineers, us, and the divers."

Les moved over to the flight dashboard and took the program off autopilot with a punch of a button. Then he grabbed the U-shaped control yoke and prepared for the order that would separate the ships.

"Do it," Katrina said.

A warning alarm sounded, filling the bridge with the wail that always came before a dive. This time, instead of proclaiming the imminent launch of humans diving to the surface, it signaled the disconnection of the two final bastions of humanity for the first time since they docked together.

"Retracting beams one through five," Bronson announced.

Five loud clicks resounded through the ship, and a slight vibration rocked the bridge.

"Retracting beams six through ten."

The sound repeated, and Les slowly guided *Deliverance* backward using the advanced thrusters under the stern.

"We're away," Bronson said.

"Fifteen degrees down angle," Katrina said to Les. She took a seat in the leather captain's chair and tapped her credentials onto the screen next to her.

Come on, sweetheart, be good to me, Les thought as he watched the *Hive* pull away.

The main monitor fired, and an image of his home came online. Les alternated his gaze from the view to his screen as he continued backing *Deliverance* away. A violent vibration shook the airship. He held the controls steady.

"Slowly, Lieutenant," Katrina said.

Deliverance groaned again as it canted downward at a fifteen-degree angle. His eyes went back to the main screen, where a view of the *Hive* was captured in *Deliverance*'s frontal high beams. In the glow, he could see all the scars of the *Hive*'s two and a half centuries in the sky.

His wife and daughter were there, and though he had his son with him on *Deliverance*, Les still felt as if he were leaving a piece of himself behind as the ship pulled away.

"Goodbye, my loves," he whispered.

ELEVEN

"Pepper, you about got this floating shit can up and running yet?" X growled.

"Working on it, Commander."

"How about the radio?"

"Almost there, sir."

X continued grumbling, and Magnolia, sitting in front of the control panel on the *Sea Wolf*, went back to digging through the medical pack, trying to ignore him. They were still anchored in the bay, and she was using the time to look after their injuries.

Miles was already patched up, and she patted his furry head. "You're going to be just fine, boy."

The boat swayed in the rough water, and Magnolia waited for it to level out before digging back into the med pack.

"Fucking engine two is still offline," X growled. "Pepper, give me a sitrep."

"Commander Rodriguez, engine one is operational, but I would strongly suggest not putting too much strain on it, especially with the status of our mainmast. I can't guarantee we will be able to use the mizzenmast if we need to get the sails up."

"Yeah, I get it," said X. "If we lose both engines, we're well and truly screwed. For now, concentrate on trying to figure out what's wrong with number two."

"We need to get that wound taken care of," Magnolia said, eyeing his arm. She pulled out a bandage and a packet of antibacterial gel. Then she nodded at the chair beside her.

X took a seat and pulled back his sleeve. The gash was puffy and inflamed, and a red streak ran up his forearm.

Miles sniffed the air and licked X's hand.

"Thanks for getting him taken care of, and again, my apologies for being such a prick."

"See, now, was that so hard?" Magnolia asked.

X raised his brow with the scar gapping through the middle.

"Apologizing," she said with a smile.

"Hey, I don't hear you saying sorry or thanking me for saving you after you went ass over teakettle off the bluff." He gave her a scrutinizing look. "You're the one that probably needs checking out."

"I'm fine."

"Sure you don't want me to take a look?"

She nodded, touching the welt on the top of her head. Dried blood already crusted beneath her hair. "Hold out your arm."

Gritting his teeth, he pulled the sleeve up to his elbow.

"Jeez," Magnolia said.

"I've been kissed by worse things."

She chuckled at his choice of words. Placing the bandage on her lap, she opened the bottle of gel and waited for an even keel.

"This is going to sting. Want some shine?"

X shook his head. "Nah, I'm good. Pepper, how about you give me another sitrep while—"

When the boat had stopped swaying, Magnolia rubbed the gel across the center of the wound. X let out a roaring curse.

"Ho-o-o-oly shit!"

The speakers crackled, and Timothy's voice came on. "The new radio is now working. Please advise when you want me to open a channel to *Deliverance*. In the meantime, I'm ready to steer us out of the bay using engine one."

X groaned in pain, eyes wide and staring at the angry wound.

"Go ahead and get us the hell out of here," he said. "And establish connection with *Deliverance* after that. I want Katrina to know we're back aboard the *Sea Wolf*."

"Roger that, sir. Weighing anchor now."

A steady clanking sounded.

Magnolia cleaned the wound with a sterile pad, wiping away the leftover gel that overflowed the wound.

"There's something I need to tell you," she said. "Something I found in the facility while you were looking for Miles."

He grabbed the armrest of his chair with his other hand and squeezed. "I'm listening."

"Remember how I told you I got the computers back online using my extra battery?"

"Yeah."

"Well, I saw something I've never seen before. Stuff about the history of the world and how it ended."

"Who the hell cares? I don't get why you're so interested in history."

She brushed her wet hair over her ear as she waited for the gel to firm up. The boat rocked and then began to move.

"We are leaving the bay," Timothy announced.

The boat picked up speed, the slapping of waves against the side quickening in frequency.

"It's not just historical stuff," Magnolia continued. "There were maps, and coordinates for places that Katrina can use."

"Katrina?" X pulled his arm back from her grip.

"I'm not done with that yet." She pulled his arm gently back onto the armrest to finish wrapping it.

Miles looked up at X, then over to Magnolia, and finally back to the floor, where he rested his muzzle.

"Yes. Katrina. I sent them everything I downloaded, including the location of a top secret base in Cuba called Red Sphere, where they can find fuel cells, weapons, supplies, food, and boats. Maybe even—"

"What?" This time, X yanked his arm out of her grip and stood. Sweat coursed down the valley of wrinkles and scars on his forehead. "Did you say *boats*?"

"Yeah. They can use them to help us when we find the Metal Islands."

X swore under his breath and then kicked the bottom of the dashboard, shooting her an angry glance.

"Mags, God damn it! How many times do I have to tell you? I … don't … want … their … help!"

She froze in her chair, lips quivering. This was the second time she had seen him this angry, and it scared her. His temper was getting worse by the day.

"X," she said, choosing her words carefully. "I only sent them the coordinates and info on the base. I didn't tell them to go there, nor do I really *want* them to go there."

He smirked. "Don't lie to me. You sent that so they would come out here and help us."

"No …" She shook her head, but deep down, she realized he was right. Deep down, she did want the others to come help them find the Metal Islands.

"I'm sorry to interrupt," Timothy said. "But something is causing drag on the boat."

X looked away from Magnolia. He cursed again and grumbled something under his breath.

"Could it be because we're using only one engine?" Magnolia asked.

X shook his head. "No, this is something else."

"Commander Rodriguez is correct. We're being obstructed by an unknown object."

"I better have a look," X said. "For now, shut it off, Pepper."

The muffled whine of the dying engine followed the order by a few seconds. X grabbed the hatch. "I'm going topside."

"But your arm," she said. "I haven't finished."

"It can wait." X snapped his fingers at Miles, who had stood up. "Stay here."

The dog whined as X left. Magnolia stayed put, too, but then decided to go up and check on what he was doing. By the time she got on the ladder to the top cabin, he was already suited up with armor and helmet. He grabbed his rifle with the grenade launcher and checked the ammunition.

"What are you doing?" he asked.

"Helping."

"You've helped quite enough," he said. "I just want to get shit done on my own now."

"X, come on. Don't be like this, please."

He charged his rifle with a pull of the bolt and stepped over to the hatch. The porthole hatches were all closed, blocking the view out into the bay, but she could still hear the boom of thunder and distant keening of the birds.

"Vultures," X said. "Stay here."

She couldn't see his eyes behind his visor from her position, but she could tell by the position of his face shield that he was glaring at her.

"Just listen to me for once, damn it," he said.

"Fine, but I'm going to be ready if you need

me." She grabbed her damaged helmet off a rack and pulled it on.

X hesitated, grabbed the hatch lever, and was gone, sealing the metal door behind him with a click.

She stepped up and opened the hatch over the porthole window to look out.

Sheets of rain pounded the boat.

"It's really pissing out here," X said over the comm link.

Magnolia moved to the right for a better look, but she couldn't see much on the deck besides the smoke coughing out of the engine and battery room, rising into the sky as dark as the sea below them.

She didn't know much about mechanics, but the smoke definitely wasn't good.

Lightning lanced astern, illuminating the crow's nest and several vultures hunting below the cloud line. One of them dived toward the waves to pluck a fish out of the water. Magnolia turned left and finally saw X. He had made his way over to the starboard rail of twisted metal and barbed wire.

He continued to the stern, out of view.

Magnolia strained to see, but the rain was like a curtain now.

"Holy shit," X said. "On second thought, you better come see this, Mags."

She grabbed her rifle off the secured rack and went outside onto the deck. The wind and rain beat against her armor as she moved, and water leaked into her helmet through the hole at the top.

X was looking over the rail now and aiming his rifle behind the boat. He stepped back and gestured for her to join him near the bent harpoon gun. The rope was almost entirely uncoiled from the capstan and taut as a drawn crossbow string.

"Guess we know what's causing the drag," X said with a laugh.

She stepped up next to X, her eyes widening at the sight of the shark, which was still caught on the harpoon. The boat had been dragging the dead beast behind them out of the bay.

Magnolia pulled her remaining curved blade from its sheath.

"Whoa, what are you doing?" X said, waving the weapon away. He got behind the harpoon gun and pushed the winch lever. A clanking sounded, and the weapon began to pull in the rope, coiling it back around its metal capstan as it drew the carcass toward the stern.

"I was going to cut us loose," she said, resheathing the weapon.

"Why? Don't you want to try shark?"

* * * * *

Deliverance pushed through the skies at an agonizingly slow speed. Michael's only clue that they were moving was the slight vibration under his boots. At this pace, they would reach their destination in less than twelve hours, assuming they didn't run into any major storms.

He sat in the briefing room, a circular amphitheater with three floors overlooking a central area that featured a podium with the ITC logo. Plush seats rimmed each level.

Michael sat between Layla and Erin in the row directly below the new divers. Jaideep put his boot up on the seat next to Erin, and she swiped it away.

"Show some respect," she said.

"Jeez, lady," Jaideep quipped.

Erin twisted in her chair. "That's 'Commander, ma'am,'" she snapped.

"Sorry," Jaideep said, sulking.

Michael just shook his head. Petty bickering was the last thing they needed right now. There were a dozen things to deal with, and he still wasn't sure whether X and Magnolia were safe. The more he thought about it, the less this trip to Cuba felt like a good idea, unless Katrina knew something he didn't about what was down there.

Michael finally looked behind him at the new divers. They filled only a small fraction of the seats in the big room. Sandy, Jed, Trey, Vish, Jaideep, Edgar, Ramon, Eevi, and Alexander all sat in the same row, with several empty seats scattered among them.

Aside from a few runs in the wind tunnels back on the *Hive*, and a few lectures in the conference room on how to dive, none of these people had any proper training. And aside from Edgar and Ramon, none of them knew how to handle a weapon, either.

Aside from the two militia soldiers, everyone else looked nervous as hell and Michael could sense the tension. Sandy twisted a lock of hair. Jed whispered something to her. The two comedians of the group, Jaideep and Vish, sat like mummies, masks of terror on their features. Eevi and Alexander held hands.

"All right, listen up," Les said from the bottom level.

A hologram shot out of the center console, expanding into a horizontal layered map. It showed an area of land topped by a domed building that reminded Michael of the Hilltop Bastion.

But this facility wasn't set in the middle of the city; it was off the coast of Cuba and surrounded by ocean.

"This is Red Sphere," Katrina said. "Two hundred and sixty years ago, it was a top secret facility owned by ITC but run jointly with the United States Navy. Dr. Julio Diaz, a worker in the laboratory deep beneath the surface of the water, survived there for a number of years, and intel we received from his team gives us reason to believe it's worth checking out."

Checking out for what? Michael wondered.

Les touched the hologram and pulled out one of the layers. "This is the DZ for Commander Everhart, Erin, Layla, and me. We will enter the facility here and make our way to the underground warehouse and vehicle bay," he said, using his fingers to indicate the entry points.

"Ensign Connor has been monitoring the weather," Katrina said, "and for now it looks like landing *Deliverance* on the platform will present too great a risk. I was hoping we might be able to, but for now we're going to have to dive to get there."

"So why are we here, Captain?" Vish asked.

Katrina gave him a gaze worthy of her title. "You're here to learn and support as needed."

Edgar raised a hand. "Captain, I have a question."

"Go ahead."

"How long ago was the last broadcast from this Dr. Diaz?"

"Good question," Layla murmured.

"We have multiple transmissions from Dr. Diaz and his staff, starting just days after the war. The rest are spread out over several years."

"What happened during that time?" Michael asked.

Katrina met his eyes. "We're not exactly sure, but at some point, he and his colleagues were killed by another faction seeking shelter at Red Sphere. I'll play you the final transmission."

Les tapped the computer screen, and the map vanished, replaced by the face of Dr. Julio Diaz. His features were blue lines like computer code.

"We've barricaded the laboratory, but I'm not sure how long we can hold back the defectors. They're here for my work … my life's work. And I'll die before they get hold of it."

"His life's work?" Layla whispered.

Michael nodded. "Sounds like that's what he said."

The doctor put his hands on his head. "I'm afraid this is the end. They outnumber us and have military-grade weapons. Our flesh guns won't do much to their armor. I hope these transmissions reach someone, someday ..."

A banging sounded in the background of the audio, and the doctor turned to look at something over his shoulder. When he turned back toward the camera, his eyes had widened. "They're almost inside. God have mercy on our souls for what we've created ..."

The video fizzled out, and the lights flickered back on, spreading a glow over the amphitheater.

"That was creepy as hell," Jaideep said.

Edgar whispered something to his cousin, but Ramon shrugged.

"We believe the defectors were the other scientists and military officials fighting for resources," Katrina replied. "But we haven't had a chance to go through all the transmissions yet."

"We know that Sirens didn't exist on the date of the transmissions," Les said. "If this was broadcast a few years after the war, then Sirens wouldn't have evolved yet—not even close."

"He's right," Layla said. "Whoever killed Dr. Julio Diaz and his team were more than likely human."

Sandy stopped twisting a lock of her hair between her fingers and glanced over at Jed who again reassured her with a whisper. They had grown close and, in a way, reminded Michael of him and Layla.

"I agree," Katrina said, "which is why I'm authorizing this mission. I have no reason to believe we will find anything but a tomb there."

Layla folded her arms across her chest. "And if we do?"

"Then you abandon the mission and get back into the sky," Katrina promptly replied. "I'm not risking your lives for supplies."

"What are we supposed to do when they're down there?" Trey asked.

Les looked up at his son. "You watch and you learn like the captain already said."

"Any other questions?" Katrina asked.

Michael considered one, but it could wait till they were alone.

"Okay, dismissed," Katrina said. "Commander Everhart and the rest of the vets, please join me for a final briefing."

Michael made his way down the ramp to the bottom as the hatch closed three floors above.

"There's something I didn't show the others," Katrina said. She tapped the monitor again and pulled up an audio clip from Dr. Diaz.

"They're inside," said the doctor. "They ..."

A clanking came over the audio, and a mechanical noise that Michael couldn't place. Gunfire erupted, followed by multiple cries of pain. But none of them sounded quite human.

"Those definitely aren't Sirens," Layla said. "But they don't sound like—"

"Please ... please, don't kill us!" shouted a female voice.

The reply was muffled by some sort of breathing

apparatus, and the crack of gunfire ended the clip.

"That's the last thing we got from the intel Magnolia sent us," Katrina said.

Michael scratched at his five o'clock shadow.

"This happened over two hundred and sixty years ago, right?" Erin asked.

Katrina nodded.

"Then we should assume whoever murdered Dr. Diaz and his crew are also dead."

"Assuming gets people killed," Layla replied.

The speakers on the computer console crackled with a message from Command.

"Captain, this is Ensign Connor."

Katrina tapped the reply button. "Go ahead, Dave."

"Barometer is dropping fast, and a thirty-mile front is moving toward us. I'm recommending a new course to get around this monster."

"How much time will it cost us?" Katrina asked.

"Another twelve hours, Captain. Maybe more."

She exchanged a glance with Les, who nodded back.

"*Shit,*" Katrina said.

"There's something else, Captain," Dave said. "I've got some good news. We have reestablished contact with the *Sea Wolf,* and X is waiting to speak with you."

Michael couldn't help but throw a fist in the air. Layla and Les both clapped, but Erin didn't show a glimmer of emotion.

"Great news," Katrina said. "Tell X I'll connect with him in a few minutes."

"Roger, Captain."

Whatever misgivings Michael had about this mission vanished at the news. X was out there risking his neck once again for humanity, with Magnolia by his side. The least Michael could do was check out Red Sphere with the other divers.

He had been itching to dive, anyway.

* * * * *

"Kat, all due respect, but going to Cuba is a bad idea—no, it's a *terrible* fucking idea."

"If you had any respect, you would refer to me as 'Captain DaVita,' and you would also understand that the title gives me the right to make decisions for those under my care."

X took in a scent of unfiltered air that reeked of fish. *Same old Kat*, he thought. It was definitely an improvement on her predecessor. A lot had happened in the ten years they were apart, including her relationship with Leon Jordan, and a failed pregnancy, but she was still strong despite the trauma of having fallen in love with a madman and losing her child.

"Captain," he said after a few seconds' pause, "I do respect you, and I respect the lives of those in your care, which is why I'm out here looking for the Metal Islands."

"Our course is set, X, so save your breath," she replied.

He licked his lips, his stomach growling at the smell coming from inside the kitchen several doors down the passage.

"Is Michael with you?" X asked. He already had a feeling he knew the answer, but he needed to hear it.

"Yes. He will be leading the mission to the ITC facility."

X's eyes went to the floor, where Miles sat at his feet. The dog wagged his tail. There wasn't much better in life than the love of a dog, besides the love of a human.

And X had always loved Tin.

"I want to talk to him before he dives," X said.

"I can arrange that." She waited a few seconds before adding, "Is there anything else? I thought you wanted to talk to me."

"Only to let you know our status."

"And now you know ours."

X heard a slight softening in her tone. She had told him a decade earlier there was still a place for him in her heart, but was that still true?

He would always care for her.

But Michael came first. X had made the boy's father a promise long ago that he would look after him.

"You stay safe out there, Captain," X said. "And look after Michael."

"Michael is more than capable of taking care of himself. Kind of like you, old man."

X grinned and licked a chipped tooth. "Who you calling old, lady?"

She chuckled. "Be safe, X. I'll have Michael radio you before the dive."

"Okay." He hung up the receiver.

"Come on, boy," he said. "Pepper, you got the wheel."

Miles followed him out of the command center and into the passage. His stomach growled at the intoxicating scent of barbecue. It had been a while since he ate anything from the real world.

Back in the wastes, he had tried his fair share of mutant creatures, swallowing antirad pills after each meal. Birds and lizards had found their way onto his plate, but X had never tried fish before.

He unslung his rifle and opened the hatch to the tiny galley. Magnolia turned from the grill. She had a bandage wrapped around the top of her head. A bloodstain marked the top, but it didn't seem to be bothering her.

His arm was feeling better already, too. The gel had taken only a few hours to work, and the infection had subsided greatly.

"Have a seat," she said, gesturing toward the table.

She held a pan over the grill, with two generous shark steaks sizzling inside. Grabbing a pinch of packaged seasoning from the *Hive*, she sprinkled it over the meat.

"Smells pretty good," X said.

Magnolia shrugged a shoulder. "We'll know in a few minutes how it tastes."

He flattened his body and sat around the oval

table where they ate most of their meals. Miles jumped onto the padded cushion next to him and rested his body against the bulkhead.

"You talk with the captain?" Magnolia asked. She kept her back to him while she cooked, probably because she didn't want to look him in the eye. She knew he was upset with her for sending off the Cuba coordinates.

"Yeah."

"And?" Magnolia flipped both steaks in the pan and added a touch of seasoning to the other side.

"They're on their way to Red Sphere, and she's planning a dive."

"Is Michael with them?"

"And Layla and Erin and our long, tall friend Les." She finally turned from the two-burner grill.

"I'm sorry, X. I didn't send that info so they would come after us."

X laced his fingers together and raised them behind his head, resting them against the bulkhead. He knew she was lying, but he was too tired and too hungry to argue.

"Okay, well, maybe I was hoping they would, but I promise I didn't …"

The vessel rocked slightly, and she pulled her hand away from the grill. "Ouch!"

Timothy's voice came over the speakers. "Prepare for choppy seas."

"Could have used some prior warning," Magnolia grunted.

"My apologies," Timothy replied.

She shook her burned hand.

"You okay?" X asked.

"Yeah … I'm fine."

She turned back to the grill, and he touched the screen built inside the table and pulled up a map of their location. The *Sea Wolf*, running on only one engine, was slowly working south from the Turks and Caicos Islands toward Hispaniola.

They had a lot of ground left to cover, and he was starting to worry about their battery power. Without the ability to use their sails, if they lost the other battery, they would be at the mercy of the seas.

"All right," Magnolia said. "Hope this is good."

She brought two plates over from the grill, each with a shark steak and a small pile of frozen greens from the farm on the *Hive*.

Miles stood on the seat and sniffed at X's plate.

"Hold on, boy; I didn't forget about you," she said, heading back to the grill. She grabbed a bowl and brought it back to Miles, setting it down on the table in front of him.

He sniffed the contents.

"What is that?" X asked. "Looks like cat food."

"How do you know what cat food looks like?"

"Because I ate some when I was stranded on the surface five years ago."

Magnolia scrunched her brows together as she took a seat at the table.

"Just kidding," he said, chuckling. "But I did find

some and opened the can. One of the worst things I've ever smelled … *one* of them."

"You'd have to be pretty desperate to eat that."

"Or have a death wish. Botulism has killed a few people on the *Hive*."

She cut into the shark, eyeing it suspiciously. "And you're sure this is safe to eat?"

"I tested it for heavy metals, radiation, and other toxins. Came back okay."

Miles was already done scarfing down his bowl of mushed-up shark meat by the time X picked up his steak with his hand. He didn't bother using utensils.

Magnolia watched him take the first bite.

He swallowed a hunk. It was closer to bird than to pig and actually had a good, gamy flavor.

"Damn, not bad at all," he said.

Magnolia tried a bite, lifting her eyes to the ceiling as if in thought. "Yeah, it's okay."

"Nice shooting, by the way, Pepper," X said.

"Thank you, Commander."

The *Sea Wolf* swayed again, and X grabbed his plate before it could slide off the table. Miles licked his chops, already finished with his meal.

"Don't mention it, Pepper. Say, can you do something to keep this damn boat steady?"

"I'm sorry, Commander, but there are some waves ahead. I would highly recommend getting back to the command center and strapping into your seats."

Magnolia let out a sigh.

"Bet you really wish you had stayed on the airships now, huh, kid?"

She stabbed another bite of shark off her plate and plucked it off the fork.

"Nope. I'm right where I should be," she said with a warm smile.

TWELVE

"Look, I don't trust Pepper, either," X said over the private comm channel. "Hell, I don't trust any AI, but I do need his help, and he proved back on the island that he's here to help us."

Katrina stroked her jaw and looked over at Michael. It was just the two of them in her office, and she wanted to keep it that way for now.

"I shut him down on the *Hive* after receiving the intel Magnolia sent us, X. Have you seen the videos and listened to the audio clips?"

"No. Been kinda busy staying alive out here. The boat's in bad shape, and we're approaching another storm, so why don't you give me the short version."

Michael grinned. "That's the old X I remember."

"I was starting to like the new one that didn't talk as much," she whispered back. "The one that wasn't an asshole."

"I heard that," X said. "And I can confirm, I am and will always be an asshole."

Katrina and Michael both chuckled.

"Okay, back to the issue at hand," she said.

"If Pepper tries anything down here, I'll light up his holographic ass, but what you do on the *Hive* and *Deliverance* is your business. As you pointed out, you're the captain."

"I've put Samson in charge of the *Hive* for now, but I need to do more research on what happened in those final days leading up to the end of the world and in the Blackout before I authorize turning Timothy back on."

"I agree," Michael said. "There are too many things that don't add up. Like why Timothy, from the Hilltop Bastion, would not know what happened with ITC and the computer virus that apparently caused this war."

"Maybe because of the Blackout," X replied. "You guys have to remember, this shit happened two hundred and sixty years ago. The world ended. By whose hand, or how, shouldn't matter at this point."

"It *does* matter," Katrina said.

"Why's that? I've been out there. I've seen more than anyone what's left. I've seen the mass graves, the skeletons, the horror of what life has become ..." His words trailed off.

Katrina had a feeling he was remembering something awful.

"In Florida, I found a mass grave of robots," he said.

"You never told me that," Michael said.

"Because it doesn't matter!"

Katrina sighed.

"Maybe X is right," Michael said. "Pepper may have hidden something from us, but that doesn't make him a threat."

"I won't take that chance on the airships," she said, standing. "X, I'll let you talk to Michael since you both seem to agree. Good luck out there. I'll talk to you soon."

Michael dipped his head.

"Yeah, thanks," X said. "Good luck with your dive, Kat."

She stepped into the passage outside her small office and closed the hatch almost all the way, torn about whether to give them privacy. She opted for eavesdropping. After all, it was a captain's prerogative.

"Tin, I just wanted …" X began to say. "I'm sorry. I mean Michael."

He stuttered out several sentences, clearly not sure what to say. X had never been good with words, especially back when she fell in love with him, but this was even worse. He had a hard time connecting with people—even with those he loved in return.

"Michael, I don't like this. I told you I didn't want you guys coming after us, and there is absolutely no reason to go to Cuba right now."

"I know what you said, X, but I trust Katrina. I always have. She suffered under Jordan for many years, and now she's been given a second chance. I don't think she would jeopardize our lives or the mission of saving humanity if it weren't worth it."

Katrina suddenly felt guilty for listening in. She decided to give them the privacy they deserved, and began to walk away. Then she heard something that made her pause.

"She doesn't know what's down there," X said. "No one does. No one besides me and Magnolia has been out this way and lived to tell about it."

"Red Sphere is nothing but a tomb—"

X cut Michael off. "I'm not worried about Red Sphere or what's inside. I'm worried about what's *outside*. The islands are a dangerous place. Giant octopuses, armored hogs, and man-size birds aren't the only threats. This is Cazador territory, Michael. If there's anything to learn about the end of the world, it's that humans are the real monsters. Most days, I think it would have been better if whatever killed most of humankind had gone ahead and finished the job."

* * * * *

Les stood in the launch bay of *Deliverance* with Erin, Layla, and Michael. All were suited up and ready to dive. This was the same place where they had launched the *Sea Wolf* into the ocean less than a week ago.

The new recruits were all standing outside the main entrance, a large steel hatch with two portholes. Trey had pushed up to the front of the group and homed in directly on Les.

"Oh, shit," Les muttered. "I'll be right back."

Michael nodded, and Les ran over to the hatch. He opened it and pulled out the Giraffe Phyl had given him back on the *Hive*.

"Hold on to this for me," Les said.

Trey shook his shaved head. "Phyl gave that to you. It'll bring you luck. You keep it." He cupped his hand over Les' and pushed it back.

"Seriously, Dad, you hold on to it," Trey said.

"Okay." Les stuck it back into his cargo pocket and secured the Velcro. "I love you. See you soon."

"Love you, Dad. Be safe."

"Good luck, man," Vish said, raising a hand. The other recruits all looked at Les with sad gazes, as though they thought he wasn't coming back.

He raised a hand toward his son a final time, then hurried back through the launch bay. Another wide door separated the four divers from the storm swirling outside.

There would be no launching from weapon tubes like those on the *Hive*. Today, they were jumping right out of the belly of *Deliverance*.

Michael, wearing his black suit, armor, and glowing red battery unit, stepped in front and turned to face his team. The Raptor logo, recently touched up with new paint, covered the top of his helmet.

A guttural groan creaked through the ship as *Deliverance* lowered through the skies. After twelve hours of resting, playing cards, and helping tend the farm, the divers were finally in position over their target.

"Twenty-five thousand feet and dropping,"

Katrina said over the comm. "Ensign Connor has confirmed a forty-five-mile storm front in the east. We have to dive before it catches up with us."

Not great news, but apparently, Katrina was continuing the mission despite the storm barreling in on their location. Les watched the seconds tick down on his mission clock. His senses were on full alert, every muscle in his body preparing for the extreme forces that were about to pummel him.

He could hear his heart hammering in his ears and felt the pulse in his carotid arteries. A breath of filtered air filled his lungs and seemed to mix with the flow of adrenaline already coursing through him.

Ten minutes to drop.

This was only his sixth dive, and one of them wasn't even technically a dive, since he had done it in a metal pod. He tried to push statistics out of his mind. He wasn't even close to fifteen—the average number of dives that marked a diver's life span. Those were the old days of diving, back when they had to take more risks.

Today was risky enough, though. There was a storm over the DZ.

Les brought up his wrist monitor, checked that it was working, and moved on to his HUD. Three other dots blinked on the minimap.

The other divers were all performing their last-minute checks beside him. Layla flexed her hands, making fists and then shaking them out.

"You ready?" Michael asked her.

She nodded, and their helmets came together with a soft clack.

Les turned again to look at the portholes behind him, where Trey stood watching intently.

"That was me fifteen years ago," Michael said, slapping Les on the back. "I watched my dad leave many, many times."

"As long as we're in the air, more children will watch their fathers and mothers jump into hell," Les said.

Michael dipped his helmet and moved over to Erin. She had a shotgun slung over her shoulder, and an Uzi holstered where her blaster would otherwise be.

A nod confirmed she was ready to go.

Les checked the strap over his blaster, then the sling of the rifle over his back. Magazines protruded from his vest, and two nickel-plated M1911-style pistols were holstered on his long legs.

Michael did a final scan of his team. "Radio check."

"Raptor Two, online," Layla confirmed.

"Raptor Three, good to go," Erin said.

"Raptor Four, ready," said Les.

Michael raised his wrist monitor and touched the screen. "Systems check."

Les confirmed that his battery was at 98 percent. His suit integrity was 100 percent. He bumped his chin pad to turn on his NVGs, then bumped them off.

"Lights check," Michael said.

Reaching up, Les turned on his helmet-mounted beams.

"Raptor is good to go," Michael said. He opened a line to Command. "All set to dive, Captain."

"Roger that. We're still moving into position," she replied. "Starting mission clock in five."

A moment later, the mission clock updated on their HUDs.

Two minutes to drop.

Deliverance dipped at a thirty-degree angle, just enough that Les had to plant his boots to keep from sliding. Lightning slashed the black outside the porthole windows, and a boom of thunder rattled a bar in the corner of the room.

"You thinking a suicide dive right out the gate?" Layla asked.

The Raptor symbol on Michael's helmet dipped in confirmation. "The faster the better," he said, "but don't forget, this DZ's a lot smaller than anything we've tried before. You overshoot it and you'll be *swimming* to Red Sphere—attached to a giant octopus trying to wrap you up and pull you into the depths."

Three blinks on the HUD display confirmed that the team understood.

"Okay, Team Raptor, let's get this done," Michael said, walking toward the doors. A red light swirled around the long space, spreading a glow across the suited and armored divers. The hydraulics that operated the bay door clicked and parted in the middle, letting a horizontal line of blue from a lightning flash into the room. It vanished a beat later, leaving the divers in the red glow of the warning light.

"Almost there," Katrina said, her calm voice betraying no emotion. "Currently at twenty-two thousand feet."

Les cinched down the magazines on his vest with another strap as the ship lowered.

The red transitioned into a cool blue, and Les took in a long breath. The bay doors were completely open now. Another bolt of lightning lit the clouds outside.

"Thirty seconds," Katrina said, starting the countdown.

This was it. They were about to jump back into the abyss. Les looked over his shoulder one last time at the ten-second mark. The other divers were already moving toward the open door, their boots clicking on the aluminum deck.

Three … two … one …

"We dive so humanity survives!" Michael yelled. He was first off the platform, launching his body into the air and then angling down like a swimmer diving into water. Layla and Erin jumped just after him.

Les hesitated when his boots hit the liftgate. He turned and raised a hand to Trey as a terrifying possibility entered his mind.

What if this is the last time you see your boy?

Les blinked and then leaped into the darkness. For the first few seconds of free fall, he felt weightless, his body shattering the invisible clouds. But a beat later, the rush of wind took him.

He brought his hands close to his body, forming a human arrow, trying to outfall his worries and focus on getting through this alive.

The storm appeared worse to the east, but the DZ didn't look too scary—just a few random forks of lightning. It was the pockets of turbulence that had him worried. A single blast could send him way off course—maybe into the sea.

He kept his eye on the glow from two blue battery packs and one red. The other divers were already a good five hundred feet below him. Had he really hesitated that long before jumping?

It wouldn't matter as long as he stayed on course.

"Raptor One ..." Michael's voice came through a flurry of static noise. "Looks like we might have a surprise between ten and fifteen thousand feet. I'm getting a lot of disturbance. Gonna spear right—"

White noise cut his voice off, the connection already severed.

"Shit, shit, *shit*," Les cursed. The words echoed in his helmet. He bit down on his mouth guard, trying to keep his heart rate and breathing under control.

Another transmission came over the link from Command, but Les made out only two words.

"Possible hidden ..."

Dazzling swirls of lightning flashed below, foreshadowing what lay beneath the dark clouds. The weather sensors on *Deliverance* were more advanced than those on the *Hive*, but apparently, even they hadn't been able to detect what was down there. Ensign Connor was also one of the best meteorologists in the history of the *Hive*, but these storms were unpredictable.

Les shifted his gaze back to his HUD. He was already down to sixteen thousand feet, and at his current speed, he would be on the ground in four to seven minutes, depending on when he pulled his chute.

Very long minutes.

And he was still picking up speed. The wind rushed over his suit and armor, whistling, screaming like a wild animal.

Les straightened his long body the best he could, his muscles tense and his spine straight. The rifle strapped over his back made it difficult, but he managed to hold his head-down vertical position all the way down to twelve thousand feet.

His eyes went from his HUD, which now began to crackle, to the divers below. The red of Michael's battery pack, at around ten thousand feet, looked like a flame in the darkness.

An arc of lightning streaked between the two blue units, but according to his HUD, both Layla and Erin made it through. Their beacons beeped for several more seconds until the minimap fizzled out. He was deaf and blind now, with only his instincts and brain to keep him alive.

The floor suddenly lit up like a strobe light. Dozens of lightning flashes created the illusion of an electric ocean.

My God, it's beautiful, he thought. *And deadly*, he reminded himself.

Les was close to terminal velocity, somewhere around 170 miles per hour. Even though his last HUD reading showed an ambient temperature of forty-one degrees Fahrenheit, he was sweating. The synthetic layers under his suit were warm, and he had an extra layer of clothes on under those.

His muscles tensed as he hit a pocket of turbulence. For a fleeting moment, he thought he might be able to hold the suicide dive, but the wind took him, cartwheeling his body as if it were the giraffe doll his daughter had given him.

The mouth guard popped out and lay against the inside of his face shield. He flexed his arms back into a hard arch, doing what he was trained to do—fighting his way into a stable free-fall position first, then working his way back into a nosedive.

A voice broke over the speakers, the system flaring back to life suddenly.

"Raptor Two, Three, Four, report ..."

It was Michael, but Les couldn't make out the rest of the transmission.

The battery units of the other divers were about to enter the heart of the storm below. One by one, they vanished into the cloud.

Les was next. His altimeter put him between six thousand and seven thousand feet, which meant the cloud cover would break soon and they would have to pull their chutes.

As he entered the nucleus of the storm, lightning flashed in all directions. The hair on his neck prickled, and he felt hot and cold at the same time.

Five thousand feet. Or was he past that already?

The next few seconds felt as if he were falling through some interdimensional wormhole surrounded by blue. The clouds around him seemed to swirl like a tornadic vortex.

And in a blink, it was all over.

He blasted through the final cloud of the storm, untouched by the lightning. The hair on his neck and arms relaxed, and he blinked as his HUD flickered back on.

Now he knew why *Deliverance* hadn't picked up the electromagnetic disturbance. It was just a small rogue pocket, nearly undetectable by their weather sensors.

Voices boomed over the channel.

"We're off course."

It was Michael, and then Layla shouted, "Pull west! Pull west!"

Les spotted their battery units, but he still couldn't see the ground—only a flat black surface.

Wait … Is that …?

The subtly shifting clouds below weren't clouds at all—they were waves. And to the west—his left—rose a domed building set in the middle of a disk-shaped platform the color of rust. Docks extended from the circular edge, giving it the appearance of a spiked virus shell.

Could this be the Metal Islands?

The ITC military base was unlike anything he had ever seen. Now that he was clear of the storm, he gradually brought his arms out at right angles and spread his legs until he was in stable falling position. Then, turning and extending his legs a bit, he began to work his way toward the other three divers.

Erin was to the far right of Michael and Layla, about two thousand feet away from Les. She must have caught some serious turbulence.

"Raptor Three," Les said.

She didn't respond.

"Raptor Three," he repeated.

After another pause, he yelled, "Erin!"

She continued falling headfirst in a suicide dive.

Les saw then that it wasn't precisely a suicide dive. Her arms were not tucked against her sides as they should have been.

"Oh, no," Les mumbled. It wasn't turbulence that had hit her. She must have been zapped by lightning in the rogue storm pocket.

"Raptor Three, do you copy?" Michael said.

"She's been hit!" Les said. "I think she's been hit!"

Michael wasted no time dropping into a nosedive.

"Tin, what are you doing!" Layla yelled.

Les knew exactly what the commander was doing, and it was a long shot. He had little to no chance of catching her and getting his canopy over them before hitting the water.

And chances were that Erin was already dead, although her beacon was still beating.

"Pull your chutes!" Michael yelled at Layla and Les.

Layla ignored the order. Les checked his HUD before grabbing the ripcord.

Michael continued in his suicide dive.

He was really going to try to save her.

"You got fifteen seconds, Raptor One!" Les shouted. He checked the numbers again: four thousand feet and falling at 120 miles an hour. Fifteen seconds was pushing it.

Les reached up and wiped his visor clean of precipitation. Whitecaps extended across his field of vision. But there seemed to be a border to the east. Yes, a big landmass curving across the wide horizon.

Cuba …

Three seconds after Michael had given the order, Les pulled his chute. Layla followed his lead. Their canopies bloomed outward, yanking them back up toward the storm, or so it seemed.

Steering with his toggles, he flew his canopy toward Layla as they neared the DZ. The domed structure rose up at them, and as it came into view, he could see why Katrina had risked the dive despite the storm hazard above.

Several boats were docked at the concrete piers jutting from the sphere.

Cazadores …

Or was this just an old fleet that had never left the island? Perhaps, the defectors mentioned in the video had landed here and killed Dr. Julio Diaz and his team.

They would find out soon enough.

"Michael!" Layla yelled.

Les found the red and blue battery units nearing the surface of the water. Seven seconds into his nosedive, Michael had caught up with her. Extending his arms, he grabbed her, wrapped his legs and arms around her, and then pulled his chute.

The canopy jerked the divers upward.

Les held his breath.

It was a ballsy move, and Michael managed to keep his grip on Erin in the process, but they had only five seconds left for the canopy to slow their speed before they hit the water.

Les and Layla continued to slow their descent, creating more of a gap between themselves and Michael and Erin. Even with the NVG, it was hard to see them.

"Tin!" Layla yelled even louder.

A small splash went up where the two divers hit the water. Les continued steering himself toward a pier extending from the dock but twisted slightly for a better look at the spot where they splashed down.

He spotted flailing arms a moment later, but he had to focus on his landing. Pulling on his toggles to slow his descent, he did the two-stage flare.

It would have worked just fine if the concrete platform weren't slick with rain. He ran out the momentum for several steps before slipping and falling on his back. He hit hard enough that he felt a little woozy.

Get up, numb-nuts. Get up!

Fighting his way out of his parachute, he unclipped one riser and anchored the chute so it wouldn't blow away. He glimpsed the ancient ship on his right, and the hull speckled with rust and barnacles.

It could be a Cazador ship for all he knew, or it could just be another artifact from the Old World. He did a quick scan for contacts and, seeing none, hurried over to Layla.

She had landed behind him, closer to the edge of the pier. She was already nearing the water's edge and screaming for Michael and Erin.

When Les got there, he looked out over the waves but saw only whitecaps.

"Where are they?" Layla asked, frantic.

A hundred meters out, movement caught his eye.

Panting broke over the comm channel, then a voice.

"Help … help me with her," Michael gasped.

Les unslung his rifle, took off the vest laden with flares and magazines, and kicked off his boots. Then he dived into the water. Layla jumped in after him. They swam side by side, kicking away from the platform and into the rough sea.

Les hated dark water almost as much as he hated the dark skies, but at least the skies didn't hide fish that could swallow you in a bite, or giant octopuses like the one X and Magnolia had reported. He tried to shut out thoughts of whatever might be sharing the same water with him.

Fear fueled his movements, and a minute later he was nearing the two chutes spread out like flattened mushrooms in soup. He put an arm under Erin and helped Michael pull her back toward the dock.

Layla swam alongside, freeing their chutes from their harnesses. They wouldn't be able to salvage those, but it beat the alternative of drowning with them still attached.

"Is she breathing?" Layla asked.

Michael nodded. "She's alive." He let out a painful grunt that told Les it had been a rough landing. As the divers made their way back to the docks, waves rolled in, blocking their view each time one slapped against them.

Layla was first to the pier. She climbed up, then turned to help Les and Michael get Erin out of the water.

Les was so anxious to get out, he nearly jumped onto the concrete.

"We have to take off her helmet," Michael said.

Les checked the radiation reading on his wrist monitor. This area was a green zone—odd, considering the storm that raged above them.

Something was definitely off about this place.

Michael eased Erin's helmet off her head. Her eyelids were closed, and blood trickled from her nose.

Layla pulled out a medical kit and fished through the contents.

"Open her mouth, Michael," she said.

He did as ordered, and Layla slipped a pill under her tongue.

"If this doesn't wake her up …" Layla didn't finish her sentence.

Les had used the adrenaline pills before. They acted fast, entering the bloodstream through the gums and veins in the mouth.

Michael looked over his shoulder as they waited, and Les followed his gaze down the dock. Two ships were anchored here, but with no sign that anyone had been aboard in the past hundred years.

"Cazadores?" Michael asked.

"I don't think so," Les replied.

"Those are ITC ships," Layla said. "See the markings?" She gestured at the nearer of the two, whose hull read *Transport Cyber* … with the rest of the letters too faded to read.

A sudden gasp made Les whirl around as Erin, eyes wide, shot up to a sitting position.

"Easy," Layla said, putting a hand on Erin's shoulder. "Just breathe."

"It's okay," Michael added reassuringly. He put a hand on her other shoulder.

She looked at them in turn as she took in deep breaths. "Wha … What happened?"

"You were grazed by lightning," Michael said. "But you're going to be okay."

"Where am I?" she asked.

"Red Sphere," Michael said.

"Can you walk?" Layla asked.

Erin pushed at the ground, her body quivering. "I … I don't know. Everything tingles."

A metallic clanking sounded in the distance, and the divers all looked toward the domed building set in the center of the round artificial island.

"Did you hear something?" Layla asked.

Michael nodded. "Come on," he said, "help me get Erin up. We need to get out of the open."

THIRTEEN

A day had passed since the *Sea Wolf* left the Turks and Caicos. In that time, the vessel had traveled about seventy-five miles southeast, and they were nearing the eastern edge of the island of Hispaniola, which had once comprised the countries of Haiti and the Dominican Republic.

But the boat was in bad shape. The remaining battery was down to a 61 percent charge, and the single engine was struggling to plow through six-foot waves.

Magnolia took a sip of herbal tea, hoping it would calm her sour stomach. She sat in her bunk with her knees pulled up to her chest, reading historical records she had pulled from the satellite station on the island. The cut on her scalp hurt like hell—worse after her fall off the bluff.

Blinking over and over, she tried to clear her vision and concentrate on the tablet screen in her hands. Most of this was stuff she already knew: the history of ITC and the life of its wunderkind CEO,

Tyron Red—everything up to his assassination, and what followed in the days immediately after he transferred his consciousness to a robotic body.

"Timothy, were you aware of this?" she asked.

The AI's voice replied from the single speaker in her small quarters.

"Exactly which part of 'this' are you referring to, Magnolia?"

"The part about a computer virus shutting down the grid across the world and then manipulating governments into blowing themselves to kingdom come. I always thought it was humans who did this."

"Oh, it was."

"How do you mean?"

There was a slight pause, just long enough for Magnolia to wonder whether the AI might be hiding something.

"Humans designed artificial intelligence."

"True, but you still haven't answered my original question."

"I did another scan, and I do not have anything in my database for the year 2043."

She lowered the tablet.

"What do you mean, you don't have anything in your database?"

"I mean that I have zero files about events in that year."

"How is that possible?"

Another pause.

"What about the year 2042?" she asked.

"I have over one million files for that year."

She grabbed her cup of tea and took another sip. "What about 2044?"

"There are thousands of files for that year, but not nearly as many as 2042 and before, and they are limited to the Hilltop Bastion and communications with other ITC facilities."

"Holy wastes," she muttered.

"I'm sorry I can't be of more assistance, Miss Katib, but this data must have been lost in what Dr. Diaz is calling 'the Blackout period.'"

"I guess so." She brought the tablet up again. This time, she did a search for Red Sphere, the top secret lab where the doctor and his team had spent several years after the war.

Maybe she had missed something in his audio and video clips. Maybe there was something more to this, an answer she had overlooked.

The boat suddenly rocked hard to starboard—the result of a rogue wave slamming into the port side. The impact nearly jolted the tablet out of her hand. She looked up at the bulkhead, where the recessed light flickered.

"No, please don't," she whispered.

Miles lifted his head from where he was sleeping off his second feast of shark meat. It was the most movement she had seen from the dog in several hours. It seemed the fish was not agreeing with his stomach. A gurgling sounded, and he let out an audible fart.

Magnolia chuckled until the light flickered off.

"Great. Just freaking great." She laid the tablet down on the bunk to investigate what had caused the power outage. Whatever answers were in the data would have to wait.

She swung her legs over the bed and put her naked feet on the cold metal floor. Then she grabbed her sweater and threw it over her uniform. A boisterous clanking came from outside her quarters. The noises were followed by another sound, like grinding gears. She found her flashlight and used it to get across the small space to her boots without tripping on her gear bags.

"Mags, where you at?" X shouted.

"Hold on."

After speed-lacing her boots, she moved into the dark passage, where she flitted her light back and forth over the smooth black bulkheads.

"X, what happened?" she asked. She got no answer right away. Not even Timothy replied.

Because the system is down, she realized.

"X, where are you?"

"Right here."

She directed the beam behind her.

"No, up here."

The beam hit his face. He was bending down from the upper level. "We just lost our battery power. Come on, I need your help."

Magnolia felt a twinge of dread at the news. This wasn't that much different from diving through a storm. They were at the mercy of Mother Nature until they got back online.

The boat swayed, and she hit the bulkhead with her palm to keep from falling. She found the rungs after a few steps and made her way up into the staging area, where X was already suited up.

"We have to go out and fix this ourselves." He put his helmet on and tossed her a bag of gear.

She moved over to the rack where she stored her suit, armor, and helmet. Holding the butt of the flashlight in her mouth, she shined the light on the equipment.

Miles barked from the passage below.

"Calm down, buddy," X said. "We'll be back in a little while." Holding two bags in his hands, he glanced over at Magnolia. "Meet me outside."

She dressed as fast as she could, but by the time she was finished, X was already climbing into the engine room on the deck. Smoke rose out of the opening, toward the mast and into the dark sky.

A fire down there could mean a few different things, all of them bad.

"Let's go!" he shouted.

A light drizzle hit her as she stepped outside. Waves slapped the hull, rocking them from side to side. She balanced herself by holding her arms out and moving in a straight line to X.

Smoke sneaking past him, he popped his helmet out of the opening to see where she was.

"Where's the other bag, Mags?"

She cursed and went back inside the boat to grab the tools. Two minutes later, she was climbing down the ladder into the cramped engine room—essentially a utility closet with an overhead barely four feet high.

Getting down on her kneepads, she crawled after X, trying to see through the smoke and using her hand to brush it away. Her knees scraped over the metal deck and through puddles of salt water.

X rounded a corner and ducked into the passage where the batteries were stored. Magnolia used her headlamp to scan the area, but the inky smoke was hard to penetrate.

"Hand me that bag ..."

X reached back with one hand but kept his helmet light directed at the mechanical equipment ahead. Magnolia glimpsed engine one and the two lithium-ion battery units encased beside it.

She pushed the bag forward, and X dug inside for several moments while she held her light steady. He pulled out the small computer they used to diagnose mechanical issues—the same one that had failed to diagnose the first bad battery. This time, though, X managed to find the issue quickly.

"It's a bad wire," he said. "I should be able to fix this right now and bring the power back on. Battery still has fifty-five percent juice, too."

"Thank God," Magnolia whispered.

"Still doesn't tell us what's creating the smoke," he said. "I'll deal with that next."

After a half hour of cursing and clanking, he had the new wiring in place.

"All right, should be good ... to ... *go*." He let out

a grunt, and the lights suddenly came back on, filling the space with a white glow.

A confused voice immediately came over the comms.

"What happened?"

"Didn't think I'd be happy to hear your voice again, Pepper," X said.

"Thank you, sir."

"I'm going to try and get the engine back online," X said.

"Can I help?" Magnolia asked. She crawled after him toward the still-smoking engine. Her hands slipped in a puddle—not water this time.

"Careful, X," she said. "We got oil."

"I've just run a quick scan of the boat," Timothy said over the open channel. "Unfortunately, it looks as though engine one is damaged beyond repair."

X directed his helmet light inside the engine.

"We have a melted corner of a piston crown," he said after he opened the casing. Several curses followed.

He played his beam over several areas while fanning away the smoke. "Looks like that last wave hit us so hard, it destroyed the compression ring lands and piston pin. I bet a lot of the metal is inside the crankcase and has contaminated the bearings and oil passage."

"What does that mean?" Magnolia asked.

He twisted to face her. "Means we're hosed unless we can get the sails up."

Or unless the divers find a boat in Cuba, she thought.

* * * * *

Michael crouched next to Erin. They had taken refuge on the deck of the ITC ship docked outside Red Sphere. Interference from the storm made it impossible to reach Command. Worse, they didn't have a path home. It was one thing to dive through a pocket of electricity like that, but rising back up through it with a helium balloon was suicide, pure and simple.

"Drink," he said, bringing a bottle to Erin's lips.

She opened her thick lips and took a gulp, coughed, and reached up to wipe her mouth.

"I can do it on my own," she said, taking the bottle from him. "I'm not paralyzed."

No, but you're still stubborn as ever, Michael thought.

Erin was in bad shape, there was no denying it, and Michael had a feeling she wasn't being honest about just how bad. They didn't have any way of knowing whether she had internal injuries from the lightning.

The suits were designed to help mitigate and distribute the three hundred kilovolts of energy from an oblique arc, but they couldn't save a body from a direct strike. She was lucky to be alive. There was likely a lot of damage he couldn't see, including burst blood vessels that could cause major problems later.

What he could see was the burn mark on her back. They had already rubbed cream on the wound and applied a cool patch to help dull the pain, but it was still bothering her.

"It itches," Erin whispered.

Layla thrust her fist in the air. "Everyone quiet."

The three divers sat in silence in the dark, listening to the clatter and groan of constantly shifting metal all around them as waves rocked and jostled the ship.

Michael checked the time again. Les should have been back. He stood up with his rifle and moved over to the hatch. Not wanting to break radio silence, he decided to take a look for himself.

"I'll be right back," he whispered.

Layla's helmet dipped once, and Erin gave a thumbs-up.

Michael gritted his teeth as he walked into the hallway. Erin wasn't the only one injured. Smacking into the ocean had hurt both his legs. His right was really bad—a sprain or maybe even a hairline fracture.

Keeping low, he moved down the passage.

Water dripped from the overhead, collecting in a puddle on the floor. He stepped around it, cautious not to make any extra noise. The NVGs provided an eerie, narrow green view of the passage ahead. He headed for the bow, where Les had last gone to scope things out.

Halfway down the hall, Michael froze at a noise that could be footfalls. He listened to the echo, trying to home in on their location.

Turning, he saw a hulking figure at the other end of the hall.

A flash hit him in the face shield.

"Just me, Commander," Les said.

Michael raised a hand to block the light and clicked off his NVGs. If Les was using his helmet light, then he thought the coast was clear.

"Scared the crap out of me," Michael said, lowering his rifle.

"Ship's all clear," Les confirmed.

Michael gestured back toward the quarters where Layla and Erin were waiting. Les ducked under the overhead and stepped inside.

"No one's sailed this thing for hundreds of years," Les said. "And I doubt Samson can get it running again. Everything's old-school technology. Freaking engine room has diesels."

"At least it's not a Cazador pirate ship," Layla said. "No sign of those freaks?"

Les' helmet wagged. "None, but there is something I think you should see." He looked to Michael.

"Can you walk, Erin?" Michael asked.

She pressed her hands to the deck and got herself up with Layla's help.

"Just you, Commander," Les said.

Erin and Layla both looked over at Michael.

"You two stay here," he said. "We'll be right back. Open comms if you need anything."

He followed Les back into the passage and down a ladder to a lower deck. Their helmet beams guided them through the metal warren of dark passages. Cobwebs of rust covered the bulkheads, disguising any markings from centuries ago.

Michael racked his brain over how this ship was still afloat after all this time. Hurricanes, storms, barnacles, and rust had had their way with it, and yet here it still was.

There had to be another explanation. Perhaps it was resting on concrete piers, or …

"Down here," Les said, gesturing right at an intersection. They walked through an open hatch and down another ladder, deeper into the bowels of the vessel.

Les ducked under another overhead and came out on a veranda overlooking a massive room that appeared to be some sort of warehouse. Metal crates, all of them open, rested on the deck twenty feet below.

"This is the place," Les said. He walked out onto the metal platform and over to a railing, shifting his light to the deck beneath them. Michael joined him at the ledge and directed his helmet beam where Les was pointing.

"What in the wastes is that?" Michael asked.

Les shook his head. "I was about to ask you the same thing."

For a moment, he just stared at the mass grave below, trying to make sense of what his eyes were relaying to his brain. Below them, hundreds of bones lay in a bed of red moss. But they weren't just randomly thrown there. The bones were put back together in a deliberate way, making the skeletons look …

"Pretty eerie," Les said.

"Let's get the satellite link up. I want to contact Command and let them know there's something down here after all. Then we start looking for supplies and boats."

Michael tried to back away from the railing, but he couldn't pull his eyes away from the mossy red growth on the deck and the bones. These weren't just human. There were animal bones down there, and robotic-looking parts mixed in like some sort of Frankensteinian fantasy.

"You think those are the defectors that killed Dr. Julio Diaz and his team?" Les asked. "Or maybe that *is* Diaz's team."

Michael had trouble formulating a response. He was too busy trying to make sense of a skeleton that had a buffalo skull attached to a human rib cage, robotic arms, and bony hands with claws.

"What kind of hell island did Katrina send us to?" he whispered.

* * * * *

"It was a rogue pocket of electrometric disturbance," said Dave Connor, avoiding Katrina's gaze. It was his job to decipher the hundreds of readings coming from the airship's advanced sensors, but she didn't blame him for this.

"This is not your fault, Dave," she said. "This was

my decision, and it's on me. Besides, everyone knows how tough a rogue pocket is to spot."

"I should have seen it," Dave said, shaking his head. "I'm sorry."

Ada twisted around from her station, concern written on her freckled face. "How will they get back up here if that storm doesn't pass?"

"We'll find a way," Katrina said. She returned to the helm, where she slumped in the leather chair. The porthole window hatches were up, and she stared out into the ocean of black.

Seeking refuge here, away from the other officers, seemed cowardly in a way, but she couldn't help feeling she had made a mistake in flying *Deliverance* to Red Sphere.

Somewhere twenty-five thousand feet below, the four most experienced divers aside from her were possibly dead or in serious peril. Even if they had survived the rogue layer of storm clouds, they were stranded with no way of getting home.

And she had no idea *what* was down there. All the data, transmissions, and videos from Dr. Diaz's team suggested that this place was nothing but a tomb. But then, there were *always* threats on the surface.

The wait to hear from a dive team, though always agonizing, was worse than normal this time. Her boot rapped syncopated rhythms on the deck as, behind her, Ada, Dave, and Bronson continued monitoring their screens and sipping their cups of caffeinated water.

It was going to be a long day.

An hour had passed since the divers leaped from the belly of *Deliverance*, and it already felt like a lifetime.

An unenlightening half hour later, she got up and walked back to the circular command station. "Have you detected anything yet, Ensign?"

"Negative, ma'am," Bronson White replied. "So far, none of the beacons are getting through the electromagnetic disturbance."

"Nothing over the comms, either," Ada confirmed.

An insane thought crossed her mind—one she didn't dare say aloud. There were still over fifty people on *Deliverance*—farmers, engineers, cooks.

She couldn't risk their lives.

Yet.

"Ada, get me the *Sea Wolf*," she said.

"Will do, ma'am."

Grabbing her headset, Katrina retreated back to her leather chair to stare out the portholes. She already knew what X would say, but she wasn't calling him to ask for advice.

"Captain," Ada said, "I've got Timothy Pepper on the horn, but he says X and Magnolia are preoccupied."

"Patch him through," Katrina replied.

"Hello, Captain DaVita, what a pleasant surprise to hear your voice."

It felt odd to talk to the second AI after deactivating its clone on the *Hive*.

"Good to talk to you, Timothy," she said politely. "Where are X and Magnolia?"

"They're working to fix the mainmast," he said. "Is there something I can assist you with?"

"I'd like to know if Magnolia or you have discovered anything else I should know about Red Sphere. If there's anything vital that I may have missed in those files Magnolia sent."

"What, exactly, are you wanting to know?"

"Based on what you have scanned in the files, do you believe there is anything alive down there?"

Timothy's reply came without hesitation. "In my experience, life always seems to find a way, and while nothing on those files confirms it, I do believe it's possible, Captain. In fact, I would say it's very likely."

FOURTEEN

Les was anxious to escape Red Sphere and get back to *Deliverance*, but they had their orders from Commander Everhart. The mission would continue, even after his horrifying find back in the guts of the ITC ship.

What the hell were those things?

He tried to push the ugly images from his mind as he proceeded across the pier and away from the ships. Keeping his rifle cradled across his chest, eyes roving for potential hostiles, he ran toward his next objective.

In the center of a spherical island stood a three-story metal building. Like many of ITC's facilities, this one had no windows and few entrances. But unlike most of the buildings back in the wastelands, this one had no markings whatever—no signage, nothing.

The aerial view had him wondering whether this might in fact be one of the Metal Islands that X and Magnolia were searching for. But there was no evidence of the cannibalistic Cazadores, or sunshine, or anything alive. And so far, the only two ships they had found were rust buckets.

They had several other vessels yet to search, though. He had seen them on the dive in and planned to get a better look as soon as he had the satellite uplink set up.

He glanced up at the swirling storm above him, where the clouds expanded like a rising loaf of bread. Lightning punched through the mass, to give a fleeting glimpse higher into the heavens.

Trey was up there, wondering where the hell his old man was.

I've got this, kid. Leave it to Pops.

Wind-driven salt spray beat against him on the final stretch away from the pier. He looked over the side, at the waves slapping the concrete. It would take hundreds of thousands, maybe millions, of years for wind and sea to finish the structure off.

Les jogged the rest of the way to the central structure where two massive steel doors sealed off the only entrance he had seen so far. As he ran, the howling wind gained strength, slamming his body. He pushed through a gust, toward a rusted ladder leading to the flat rooftop three stories above, where radio towers rose into the sky.

That was his objective, the place Michael had told him to set up the satellite comm and try to get a signal to *Deliverance*. He slung his rifle and started up the ladder.

A glance over his shoulder halfway up gave him a decent view of the pier he had left behind. Two massive naval cruisers stood moored at the dock. On the weather deck of the ship to his left stood Michael, watching him with a pair of binoculars.

Les continued up to the roof. Several lightning scars marked the flat concrete surface. It would have been a great place to land a supply crate, but they couldn't risk dropping precious supplies into the ocean.

He trotted across the roof, past the radio towers, to search the rest of the facility. Four piers stretched away north from the platform, and several more to the west and east. With his rifle scope, he zoomed in on a boat docked below, tethered by chains to thick steel bollards.

This vessel looked different from the two ships where the other divers were sheltered. Barely a third their size, it looked like a fishing boat, with nets still lying on the deck where they had been abandoned.

No way that's been here for two hundred and sixty years …

Les scanned the area a final time and discovered two more ships, one of them a military vessel with gun turrets and angular armor plating. He zoomed his scope in on the hull. Although the flag painted there was faded, he could make out the blue and red stripes and white stars.

United States of America. This was the first time in his life he had seen the actual flag. He felt a stirring of emotion, knowing that this country had once been the most powerful in the world. Hundreds of millions of humans had lived there for centuries, in what people from the *Hive* would consider luxurious conditions.

But a single AI virus had brought the great nation down in just days and destroyed the entire world within weeks, leading to the Blackout.

The flag had been a symbol of strength and freedom. And today it also represented an opportunity. If they could get the ship working, they would have a way to fight the Cazadores.

With that thought came a chilling realization.

Katrina hadn't sent them here for supplies. She sent them here to find military vessels that could help X and Magnolia if they ever found the Metal Islands.

A transmission hissed in his helmet. "What's your status, Raptor Four?"

Michael's voice snapped Les out of his speculations.

"Preparing to set up the sat comm, Commander."

"Roger."

Les trotted back to the towers centered in the rooftop where he took a knee, pulled out the satellite dish from his cargo pocket, and expanded it. The wind whipped against him as he worked, rippling his uniform. He had done this plenty of times before, but hacking into each facility was different. He used his minicomputer and extra battery to power the satellite link. Ideally, he would run it through the towers on the roof, but the power to Red Sphere appeared to be down.

Lightning flashed bright overhead, and he braced for the crack of thunder. The faster he worked, the better. He didn't want to end up getting zapped like Erin.

After several minutes of fiddling with the equipment, he finally had it working. He extended the antennas and synced his minicomputer with the satellite. He had a signal, but it was weak.

Les sent his first transmission to *Deliverance*.

"Command, this is Raptor Four. Do you copy? Over."

Static crackled inside his helmet.

He waited a few seconds, then repeated the message.

Still no response.

After three more tries, he glanced up at the sky. The storm was too intense to penetrate, even via satellite, which reaffirmed the fact that they would not be riding their helium balloons back up to the airships.

That left him with only one option.

He left the equipment on the rooftop and ran back to the ladder, climbing down to the platform. Michael had his rifle out on the stern of the ship, and Les waved at him. They met on the deck, where Les explained the situation.

Michael said, "Guess we'll have to go inside and try to get the power back on to activate the radio tower. If we're lucky, we can get a transmission to *Deliverance*."

Les gave a nod. "What about Erin?"

"I'm leaving her here with Layla. It's safer."

"Agreed."

The two divers returned to the quarters on the ship. Erin was on her feet.

"You're not leaving me here, so don't even try."

Les frowned. Apparently, they had kept the channel open outside.

"You two seem to forget who the weakest links are," Layla added. "You need both of us."

"Hey, I'm not discriminating," Michael said. "But, Erin, you did just take a nasty shot of lightning."

"And I said I'm fine."

Les could see that Michael wasn't in the mood to argue.

"Fine, but if you start to drag, we're stashing you somewhere while we search Red Sphere."

"Deal."

The divers packed up their gear and followed Les into the passage. Erin managed to walk on her own until they got to the ladder on the ship. She stopped, trying to disguise the pain by turning her head the other way, or so it looked to Les. But he could still hear her labored breaths.

And she wasn't the only one injured. Michael had a limp to his gait.

Maybe I should just go with Layla …

Moving into Red Sphere with two injured could be a liability, especially if they were all forced to run at any point. On top of that, Layla and Michael were too close emotionally, which already compromised them—although Les had never said a word about that.

He held rank on the airship, but when it came to diving, Michael was the boss. All Les could do was make a recommendation.

He stopped at the ledge of the ship, waiting for the thunder to pass before speaking.

"Commander, all due respect, but why don't you let Layla and me proceed to Red Sphere? You're hurt, Erin's hurt, and again …" He held up both hands. "If we run into trouble, you both are going to be a liability."

Layla put a hand on Michael's armored shoulder. "He's right."

"Yeah," Michael replied.

Erin snorted.

"Keep the comms open," Michael said. "If anything seems off, you tell me."

"Understood, Commander," Les said. He gestured toward Layla. "Follow me."

She paused and said over a private channel something that Les couldn't make out. Then they were off.

Jumping onto the dock, Les noticed a patch of orange barnacles that he didn't recall seeing earlier. There was also a growth of reddish moss—the same stuff he had seen in the bizarre graveyard inside the ITC ship.

Les had heard about the moss before. Michael had mentioned finding some at the Hilltop Bastion where Commander Rick Weaver was killed. But no one knew what it was, and Les avoided the strange growths.

As they approached the building, Layla pumped several shells into her shotgun. Then she slung the weapon and pulled out her handheld tablet. When they got to the wide entrance doors, Les wiped off the triangular security panel with his sleeve.

"Let me," Layla said. Pulling a cable from her cargo pocket, she uncoiled it and plugged one end into her tablet, the other end into the panel. Les stood watch, rifle up.

"Michael told me about the creepy boneyard back on the ship," Layla said. "Any idea what that's all about?"

"My guess? I think the Cazadores were here at some point and had something to do with it. Either that, or it's what's left of Dr. Diaz's team."

"Or the defectors Diaz talked about in the video."

"Could be."

A beeping sounded, and she bent to look closer at the screen, tapping at the monitor. "Two more codes to crack."

Les continued to scan the area with his rifle while they waited. Two minutes later, the doors creaked open to a cavernous space frozen in time.

Several old-world military vehicles sat in the front of the garage. They were armored with mounted weapons and welded metal cages covering the windows.

Their headlamp beams flashed around the room, lighting up cobwebs and floating dust particles disturbed for the first time in God only knew how long.

Not far behind the vehicles were several skeletons, curled up where they had died. Layla pointed at them, and Les took a step forward, his boots crushing metal.

Bending down, he found spent bullet casings.

"Reminds me of Hilltop Bastion," Layla said. "And you know what we found there, right?"

Les replied, "Sirens."

The very thought froze him where he stood. This place gave him the creeps. First the horrifying scene on the ITC ship, and now a scene of slaughter. He didn't want to keep walking into the dark building, but he didn't have a choice. Sirens or no Sirens, his mission was to get the satellite link up and running.

"Come on," he said to Layla.

She kept her shotgun slung over her armor and pulled out the Uzi as they walked deeper into the garage, shell casings snapping and cracking under their boots.

On the other side of the vehicles, a door stood ajar. Les grabbed the handle and slowly pulled it open. Layla squeezed through with the Uzi up.

Following her into a passage, Les could see over her head since she was a good foot and a half shorter than he.

Layla motioned toward an elevator ahead. They stopped near the open doors and shined their beams into the shaft. The beams shot into the darkness, but he couldn't see the bottom.

"Let's try and find another way down," Layla said.

They walked side by side to an intersecting corridor.

On the right lay another body, mummified in the closed space. This had been a woman. Scraps of a chemical, biological, radiological, and nuclear hazard suit covered her dried skin, and a helmet with a crushed visor encased her head.

To the left, the passage was blocked with metal barriers, all of them pocked with bullet holes. They took a right, continuing deeper into Red Sphere, their lights sweeping over evidence of another battle. Brown streaks led to a door on the right side of the hallway, and Les saw the first signage in the building. It read simply, STAIRS.

"Let's try it," he said.

Layla opened it into a concrete stairwell. She slipped inside and set off toward a landing below.

Les shuddered with dark imaginings of what awaited them.

They continued down, flight after flight, for several minutes. Oddly, there were no doors at any of the first ten landings. This building was buried deep beneath the waves.

Layla finally stopped at the first door.

Les opened it and moved into a passage. His headlamp revealed more metal barricades blocking the end of the hallway. At a door on the right, he stopped and gave a hand signal. Layla met him there and tried the knob. Locked. She pulled out a small packet from her vest and shook out some lock-picking tools.

"Wait," Les said. His beam had revealed another way into the room. About ten feet down, a window had been shattered.

Moving cautiously around the broken shards, he directed his light to a gap in the furniture piled up against the window.

On the far left, something had broken its way in.

"I'll go first," Layla said.

He helped her climb onto the windowsill. A shard of glass dislodged from the mullion, hitting the floor with a crunch. Les lifted her higher, and she dropped through the gap.

"I'll be right back," she said.

Les waited in the hallway while she searched the other space. Two minutes later, the handle clicked and the door opened.

Their two beams speared through the darkness, uncovering a space filled with laboratory workstations and storage areas. Some of the surfaces still held vials and medical equipment.

"Holy shit," she whispered. Layla held her light on another skeleton at the other end of the room. Normally, the remains of people on the surface didn't bother her, but Les quickly saw why this one did.

It was split in half lengthwise.

He moved over and crouched down beside the female skeleton, also wearing a CBRN suit. Even the helmet had been split smoothly down the middle. Black grooves extended away from the remains, where the weapon had carved the floor in a straight line.

"What kind of blade could do this?" Layla asked.

"I don't know, but I doubt it was the Cazadores."

Les straightened up and kept moving through the lab. Tools and shattered monitors littered the floor. They explored the rooms for the next half hour and finally emerged into a clean room.

Suits hung from hooks, and helmets were stacked neatly on a shelf. Much of the place seemed undisturbed. Whatever happened here had happened fast.

The next door, blown completely off its hinges, led to offices furnished with desks, several couches, and more monitors. Layla shined her light at a framed map on the wall. Hurrying over to it, she brushed off a thick layer of dust and pointed at the cracked glass.

"Looks like the operations center," she said. "It's a few levels from here."

She led the way, and Les followed, sweeping his light and rifle over more debris. The next hallway had been barricaded with furniture and steel door frames, which had done little to hold back the defectors—whoever the hell they were.

A nearly perfect line had sliced through the barriers, leaving a three-foot gap between the pieces. The floor was marked with the same black groove as in the first lab.

The more Les saw, the more this looked like what he had seen on the rooftop. Maybe it wasn't lightning after all up there.

"A blade didn't cut that person in half," Layla said. "This was some sort of laser."

Les remembered the video from Dr. Diaz, saying the defectors had military-grade arms. Maybe their fabled laser weapons weren't a myth, after all.

"Come on, we're almost there," he said, flattening his body and squeezing through the gap in the barrier. Halfway through, he stopped, his light capturing a scene on the other side.

"What's wrong?" Layla asked.

Les swallowed hard, unable to form a response.

Skeletons. Dozens of skeletons, all of them cut into pieces like butchered animals. Guns, some sliced in two, lay next to their former owners. Burn marks crisscrossed the overhead and walls.

A battle had happened here, and from the looks of it, the losses were one-sided.

Could this be Dr. Diaz and his team?

"What do you see?" Layla asked, trying to move past him.

He moved ahead to let her in. They had to go through the mass grave to get to the operations center. She took in the scene of carnage better than he had expected. Keeping her voice low, she said, "Lasers."

Les held his breath as he passed through the slaughterhouse, as if he were trying to keep out the scent of rot, even though little was left but skeletons and tattered suits.

He halted at another door, also broken off its hinges. Layla went first, and he followed her into the room, where dozens of monitors lined the walls. All the chairs and desks were gone, used in the barricade in the hall they had just left behind.

"I'll try to bring on backup power," Layla said.

Les nodded and stood at the doorway, trying his best not to look at the bones strewn about. The bodies had been sliced in almost perfect lines. But the more the thought about it, the less shocked he was at the display of firepower. After all, this was nothing compared to the power of a nuclear weapon.

The real question now was, who were the defectors?

"I'm in," Layla said a few minutes later. "I think I can tap into a battery and get your uplink working topside."

Les moved to watch her work. She had a single screen online, its glow covering them in an eerie blue. Tapping the monitor, she said, "Bringing on battery backup in, three, two, one …"

The lights suddenly flickered and lit up the room. He turned to look at the hallway. Brown streaks painted the walls—blood and gore of those who had perished here.

"Okay, let's see if this works," Layla said. "Go ahead and try the uplink."

Les raised his wrist computer, which was still synced with the satellite on the rooftop. With a cord, he patched the computer to the screen, and Layla did the rest.

"Command, this is Raptor Two," she said. "Do you copy?"

White noise broke over the channel, and then a voice. "Copy you, Raptor Two, this is Ensign White. It's great to hear your voice."

Les checked his first impulse, and instead of whooping with joy, he drew in a long breath of relief through his nostrils.

"Same here, Ensign White," Layla replied.

"Captain DaVita is currently not on the bridge, but I'll connect you, Raptor Two."

Les checked his magazine while they waited—a nervous tick, since he had yet to fire his weapon. He ejected it, then palmed it back in with a click.

"Raptor Two, this is Captain DaVita," she panted. "Is everyone okay down there?"

"Les and I are fine, but Erin and Michael were both injured on the dive."

"How bad?"

"They'll be okay, but as you probably know, we're stranded here by the storm."

"I know," she said. "I'm working on figuring a way to get you all home. In the meantime, have you been able to search the facility and docks?"

"Yes," Les replied. "I think I found what you sent us here for. It's a military vessel. Looks like some sort of stealth boat, but I don't know if we can make it run. Commander Everhart ordered us to contact you first."

"A stealth boat," Katrina said. A brief pause of white noise sounded. "Your mission is to get that ship working."

Layla and Les exchanged a glance, but before either of them could reply, a distant screech like rusty hinges echoed through the room. They both turned to look into the corridor.

"What the bloody hell was that!" she whispered.

Les shook his head. "I have—"

The sound came again, like an axle that needed greasing, followed by an electronic wail that reminded him vaguely of a bird. His first thought was Sirens.

"Layla, Les, do you copy?" Katrina asked.

"We're here," Les said. "But I think something else is, too …"

The birdlike screech continued, growing louder.

Les flicked the safety off his rifle and brought it up to his shoulder. He stepped out into the hallway, careful not to crunch any broken glass.

He pivoted right, training his rifle on the elevator shaft at the other end of the passage, well past the ghastly remains strewn about.

Several recessed lights in the ceiling flickered, still working after all these years, but long sections of hallway were still in shadow.

He took another step, his boot crunching a shard of glass.

A screech rose from the open elevator shaft, and a sudden orange glow lit the inside where the doors had been pulled back. Looking closer, he saw claw marks in the metal wall and the frame.

Les pulled his hand off the stock of the carbine, holding the gun in one hand and signaling Layla with the other.

She didn't need verbal orders. She knew that it was time to run.

FIFTEEN

Sheets of rain pummeled the *Sea Wolf* in choppy waters. X aimed the speargun at the top of the mainmast, waiting for the right moment to fire.

"Get ready, Mags!" he yelled.

She moved into position next to the mainmast. They had brought the sails up from the lower deck and fastened them to the mainmast and mizzenmast.

The next step was to try to straighten the kinked mainmast without snapping it at the top. If that happened, they were dead in the water.

With nothing but the rudders to orient them, the vessel was already at the mercy of the waves, and it was really starting to make X cranky.

He kicked away a bloody shark fin that came skidding across the slick deck, then planted his boots firmly, careful not to slip in the sticky blood pooled near the stern, where he had butchered the carcass before dumping most of it overboard.

The vessel briefly leveled out, and he seized the moment to squeeze the trigger.

The tip penetrated the hollow mast and broke through the other side. The line from the spear tautened, and the winch engaged. He grabbed the wheel handle and began to crank it manually.

The line could handle up to a ton of resistance, perhaps a bit more. After all, it had dragged a giant shark through the water back at the Turks and Caicos Islands.

Looking up, he watched the mast begin to bend back into place.

"Pepper, do you copy?" Sweat stung his eyes.

"Copy you, sir."

"Make sure we've got our back to the wind," X ordered. He squinted as if that would help him see through the water running down his visor. Across the deck, near the stern, stood Magnolia.

He felt a slight change in course under his boots as the AI worked the rudders. The *Sea Wolf* cut through the water as he continued cranking the winch.

"Okay, let's go!" X shouted.

Magnolia grabbed a halyard and began pulling back on it, lifting the mainsail up the newly straightened mast. Once it was most of the way up, she transferred to the winch. She wrapped a rope three times around the drum and then began cranking the winch manually.

"Careful, Mags!" X yelled.

The wind had picked up over the past half hour,

and too much added pull could break the mast. He checked the top again before cranking it tighter. The mast was almost straight now.

X moved over to help Magnolia with the winch. She kept cranking and shook her head at him.

"I've got this," she said.

X grabbed the halyard to keep the mainsail from flopping around as she raised it toward the top of the straightened mast.

"Almost there!" Mags shouted.

The wind filled the sail, and the *Sea Wolf* moved faster, or so it seemed. They both took a step back to look at their contraption. For this to work, the line from the speargun had to hold. It meant they wouldn't be able to use that weapon for its intended purpose, but they had several others and plenty of firepower in the top cabin. The most important thing to do now was keep moving.

And moving they were.

X walked around the mast to take another look at the spear. He stopped when he saw the front of the black sail, and felt a little swell of pride.

"I'll be damned …"

"What?" Magnolia asked. She joined him before the sail and put her hands on her duty belt, clearly impressed.

"Wow, that looks pretty amazing."

"Looks kind of like Miles," X said, studying the sail. Someone back on the *Hive* had done one hell of a job with the stitching. The face of a wolf towered above them, the deep-yellow eyes looking ahead at the storm clouds, watching out over them.

"Let's get to work on the other sail," X said.

At the stern, they followed the same process with the winch and halyard to raise the smaller sail. The wind pummeled them as they worked, but moving together, Magnolia and X finally managed to get it raised.

"Good job, old man," she said when they finished.

"You, too, kid."

His words trailed off when he saw the skyline to the southeast. Magnolia finished tightening another rope, but X walked toward the starboard side, where the barbed wire still lined the rail.

"Where you going?" she called out.

X halted next to the rail, wary of any beasts lurking in the dark water. But his eyes weren't on the whitecaps slapping against the hull—they were on the strange light area in the sky.

On the horizon, diagonal lines streaked down toward the ocean. The sheets of rain seemed so perfect, the view could have been an old-world painting, but this was real.

"Mags, you seeing this?"

She joined him starboard of the mainsail. To the southeast, the storm was definitely a paler shade, almost a light purple.

"What in Hades is that?" she asked.

X held up his wrist monitor and clicked on the cracked screen to pull up a map of their location. They appeared to be northwest of the strange skyline.

"Timothy where are we, exactly?" he asked over the channel.

"East of Puerto Rico, and about fifteen miles northwest of the Virgin Islands, sir."

"Change course. Head southeast. I want to check something out."

"Roger, Commander."

The wind pummeled the sails as the boat turned. X and Magnolia continued to stare at the sky. The shades of purple and light blue streaked across the horizon like a ripe bruise.

"It's a beacon," X said.

"How's that?" Magnolia shot him a sidelong glance.

"Explorers once used the stars like a map to guide them. We have something even better to guide us to the Metal Islands."

"You think that's …" Magnolia could not take her eyes away from the strange lightening in the southeast.

"Come on, kid, let's get back inside. We have work to do."

She followed him across the slippery deck, looking over her shoulder several times as Timothy piloted the boat through the rough waves.

If this led where X thought it led, they would need to prepare. He stopped before opening the hatch to the cabin, and looked up at the image of the Wolf flapping in the wind.

The Sea Wolves were finally nearing their objective.

* * * * *

"Stay put. It's too dangerous right now."

Hearing Layla's voice, Michael ran faster across the pier despite his injuries. He moved away from the ITC ship where he had left Erin.

He was breaking the cardinal rule of diving on the surface: never split up. But what choice did he have?

He kept his rifle cradled as he moved. Both legs hurt with every step. The impact with the ocean had rubbed muscle against the kneecap, and it felt as if his muscles were grinding over the bone.

"Where are you, Layla?" he said, trying his best not to shout. "Tell me where you are."

Her voice hissed over the channel. "We're hiding in the command center, but it's—"

Another screech sounded, and then the channel went dead.

Michael slowed in the middle of the pier, rain coursing down his visor, breath steaming the inside.

"Son of a bitch." He wasn't sure what to do, although he definitely wasn't going to hide.

He opened a channel to Erin. "Can you make it topside?"

"Yes, Commander."

"Good. We may need you as a sniper. I'm going into Red Sphere."

"Figured you would. Be careful, and good luck, Commander."

NICHOLAS SANSBURY SMITH

"Same to you."

He continued toward the open doors where Layla and Les had entered. His fast pace across the platform surrounding Red Sphere brought a surge of pain up his knees and thighs, and by the time he reached the garage, he was gritting his teeth. An electronic wail came from inside the building the moment he crossed into the dark garage.

This place was no tomb after all.

The distant electronic discord gave him a chill.

Red Sphere wasn't an abandoned outpost. Like many other ITC facilities, it was a haven for beasts. He had trusted Captain DaVita just as he had once trusted Captain Jordan and, before him, Captain Ash.

Now the most important woman in the world to him, and arguably one of the most important men left in the world were trapped inside, he could hardly run, and Erin was injured and alone back on the ITC ship.

Sometimes you just had to get it done yourself, even when you weren't in any shape to do it. Bringing up his rifle, he moved toward the two armored vehicles.

Layla and Les had gone idle on his HUD, but they were still alive. He could see their beacons; neither moved. She had severed the channel to keep quiet, he realized.

He slowed to a walk and skirted both vehicles, clearing the room in a quick sweep.

Light flickered beyond the open door.

The other divers had successfully turned on the battery backup, but they had also woken something best left dormant. But how could anything have survived here so long?

In his mind's eye, he saw the bone pile back on the ITC ship.

The Sirens must have moved back into Red Sphere after exhausting the supplies and food source up here. It was the only explanation. He moved through a door into the hallway. Recessed lights lit some sections of the passage, while other sections were in shadow.

Rifle butt nestled against the sweet spot in his shoulder, he stepped onto the tile floor. A body lying in the intersection ahead made his heart thud, but then a flash of light from the open elevator shaft illuminated skeletal remains.

It wasn't Layla or Les.

He moved forward until he reached the bones. The left side of the passage was blocked, but the right was clear. He didn't stop to check the remains and continued with his finger on the trigger guard.

A howling sounded outside the garage behind him, but it was just the wind. The electronic wail from earlier was gone, replaced by what sounded like clicking joints, almost mechanical in nature, like some sort of freak robotic spider.

Another body lay ahead.

This time, he bent down to check the helmet. The cracked visor opened to a nose and empty eye sockets. The dried skin was stretched in a mask of horror.

Michael stood, wincing in pain, and checked his HUD again. The beacons were blinking from left to right.

Layla and Les were moving.

He still couldn't tell where they were in the facility, but he decided to try the door that stood ajar on his right, opening into a stairwell.

Angling his gun downward, he moved as fast as he could. The pain in his knees had melted away in the adrenaline coursing through his body.

Layla, I'm on my way ...

He pressed down the stairs, passing landing after landing with no door to the facility.

On the sixth floor, he froze.

Static crackled in his helmet.

"Commander, something's moving topside."

It was Erin, and her voice was shaky—in itself a rare thing.

"What do you see?"

"I'm not sure ... too far away to tell."

"Stay out of sight, Erin. That's an order."

As if in reply, a screech sounded, but it wasn't coming from outside or over the comm.

Michael rounded the landing, pointing his rifle down into the darkness. Around the next corner, an orange glow pulsed like a heartbeat, growing brighter by the second. The same clanking sound he had heard earlier came from the depths of the stairwell.

This didn't sound like a single Siren—it sounded like a pack of them.

He moved his finger inside the trigger guard, ready to blast the mutant freaks back into whatever hell had spawned them.

Another wave of static rushed over the channel.

"Michael, we're on the move, headed topside."

This time it was Layla.

His eyes darted back to the HUD. The beacons were moving faster. Les and Layla were running.

"I'm on a stairwell about five floors down," he whispered. "I see something … a red …"

"What? Commander you're breaking up," Les said.

"I see a red—"

The electronic screech that followed shut him up. Clanking metal and claws on concrete echoed up the stairwell, and Michael gripped his rifle tighter.

Come on, you freaks. Show your ugly faces.

The pack of Sirens was right around the corner now.

Layla's voice flooded the channel again. "Michael, get out of there!"

He knew that running would just delay the inevitable, assuming he could even run up the stairs at all. It hurt worse to climb than to run.

He was going to have to face them sooner or later.

"I'm standing my ground," he said. "You two get topside with Erin. She'll cover you."

"Michael, you can't fight!" Les said before another wail cut him off. This one was different from the electronic shriek the Sirens made back on the surface.

Michael stared at the orange glow. What the hell was giving off that light?

He moved his finger onto the trigger, ready to unleash a flurry of automatic fire. The light intensified, spreading over the walls. A shadow bounded up the stairs, and he got his first glimpse of the monster.

The image of an elongated head with horns, a humanoid torso, and long claws moved over the walls.

This was no Siren.

Michael pulled the trigger as soon as the beast came into view—a humanoid figure wearing the skull of a cow. The orange light blazed out of the bone eye sockets, emanating from an orange visor behind the open mouth of the cow skull.

Bullets shattered the bone armor the creature wore, and punched into metal behind it. The skull reared back, and the beast let out a roar that sent a shiver prickling over his flesh.

He continued firing, the muzzle flash mixing with the eerie orange glow. Empty casings bounced off the stairs as the rounds broke off more and more of the bones covering the metal body.

The din of gunfire cracked and echoed, mixing with the electronic sounds of rage.

By the time he emptied the magazine, the skull was halfway broken off, revealing a humanoid metal skull. The creature, whatever it was, stumbled backward, hitting the wall so hard, the front plate of bones covering its chest fell and shattered on the ground. A battery unit—the source of the orange light—glowed in the center of its chest.

The sight played tricks on Michael's mind, and for a moment he thought he was staring at some demon Hell Diver who had come back from the dead.

But this was no man. This wasn't even a beast.

The orange light glowing from the center of the metal skin was an engine powering a machine.

An AI …

The defectors that had killed Dr. Diaz and his team weren't human after all, and they had been here all this time, waiting for the next humans to murder.

"Michael, run!" Layla shouted over the comms.

Her words snapped him back into action. He took a few backward steps up the stairs while reaching for another magazine. Before he could punch it into the carbine, a second machine emerged behind the first. This one wore the bones of multiple animals and humans. A reptilian skull crested the top of a humanoid face.

It raised a black weapon with a curved olive handle and thin muzzle. Michael brought his rifle up to fire, but the robot got in the first shot.

A dazzling blue bolt sizzled through the air. He felt something cold rip through his arm. His mind sent a message to his finger to pull the trigger, but his finger didn't respond.

The gun fell in two pieces.

It took him a few seconds to understand that the bolt had sliced the weapon in two, and another second to realize that the same blue bolt had severed his right arm a few inches below the shoulder. He watched the weapon clatter onto the stairs, with his finger still in the trigger guard.

Another blue bolt blasted the air next to his helmet and sliced into the wall behind him. He moved to his right just in time to avoid a third bolt, which hit the overhead, shattering a light and darkening the stairwell above him.

More bolts sizzled through the air.

A voice yelled out, followed by muzzle flashes from behind the two machines. The stairwell lit up with red and blue flashes.

Rounds slammed into the bone-covered machines. The machine with the broken cow head fell to the floor, and Michael crashed to his knees on the landing above it, looking down the stairwell in horror.

At the bottom of the next landing, a tall figure emerged with a blaster.

Les …

Les put the gun muzzle against the head of the robot that had shot Michael. The fiery blast took off the top of the skull, and sparks erupted off the metal beneath.

Layla ran past Les and bounded up the stairs toward Michael.

"Michael. Oh, my god!"

She bent down and put a hand under the armpit of his good arm while Les continued firing at the other hostiles. The second one wouldn't go down, and the first was starting to get back on its feet. Their metallic shells deflected the 5.56-millimeter rounds as if they were rocks flung by a child.

"Run!" Les yelled. "Get him out of here!"

Michael pulled the blaster out of his holster as she helped him up. Though he wasn't used to shooting with his left hand, he managed to fire both shotgun rounds into the struggling machine on the landing below.

The buckshot slammed into the neck and torso, sending it careening past Les and crashing down the stairs. An electronic wail followed as it toppled down into darkness, the orange light fading like a guttering candle.

Michael dropped the gun, his vision fading in and out as Layla helped him to his feet. Time seemed to slow to an agonizing pace, and his vision grew blurry as if he were looking through ice.

He looked down at the stump where his arm had been. He could see that well enough.

The skin was glowing red, still hot from the laser bolt. The heat had cauterized the wound, but he had lost all the blood in the arm that now lay on the landing.

"My arm," he mumbled. "We can't leave my arm."

"Move!" Layla yelled as she helped him up the stairwell.

More gunfire cracked behind them, and Michael heard Erin's voice over the channel.

"We got company topside."

* * * * *

Katrina chewed on her fingernail as she listened to the audio transmissions. Gunfire, screeches, and the intermittent yelling of her friends on the surface filled the bridge.

Her crew all listened from their stations, some flinching at the sound of the shouts.

"We have to do something," she said. The divers had been fighting for over an hour at Red Sphere and were now pinned down.

"Raptor One, do you copy?" Katrina said into her headset.

A wave of static replied, then a scream.

"They're flanking us!"

Katrina couldn't be sure who had yelled that.

"Raptor Two, do you copy?" she said.

A flurry of white noise filled the channel.

"Raptor Three, do you copy? Does *anyone* copy?"

The comm link went dead a beat later, and her gut sank as white noise filled the room.

Her Hell Divers were dying down there. She had to do something.

Bronson got up from his station, his hand on his lower back. He just looked at Katrina without speaking.

Ada and Dave didn't say a word, either.

"Bronson, are you sure we can't land on Red Sphere?" Katrina asked.

He shook his head. "I hate saying it, Captain, but we would likely go down in a ball of fire if we tried to get through that rogue pocket of electricity.

It may be possible for a smaller object to make it through, but we're way too big to avoid getting hit by lightning."

"But our exterior is built to withstand some direct hits," Dave said.

"Some, yes," Bronson said.

Katrina closed her eyes. *A smaller object …*

There was only one thing left to do.

"You have the bridge, Ensign White."

Bronson stiffened, his stooped back almost straight.

She started crossing the room, the eyes of her staff on her.

"Where are you going, ma'am?" Ada asked, standing at her station.

At the hatch, Katrina stopped and turned.

"I'm going to dive, and save our friends. Move the ship back into position over Red Sphere."

"By yourself?" Dave said. "Ma'am, I …"

"Don't think that's a good idea, Captain," Bronson said, finishing Dave's sentence.

"We have no choice," Katrina replied. "Tell the green divers to meet me in the launch bay. They have fifteen minutes. In the meantime, lower us to five thousand feet, just shy of that rogue pocket."

Ada and Dave exchanged a glance, but Bronson simply nodded. The old man still knew how to follow an order.

She ran down the passage, where she passed several militia soldiers and then a half-dozen engineers and farmers. A warning sounded, and an automated female voice flooded the hallways.

"Be advised, we are moving from our current location and could experience turbulence. Please take appropriate precautions."

Katrina walked faster, her mind racing as she worked her way toward the launch bay. What she had made out of the divers' transmissions made her blood run cold.

The enemy on the surface wasn't Sirens. The defectors were something even worse.

At least, Sirens could be killed.

These were killing machines powered by a powerful AI …

Would Timothy feel any loyalty to them? Could she trust him? Could X trust him?

She had considered ordering Samson to reactivate the AI on the *Hive*, but this info made her wonder.

Katrina shook away the questions and focused on the new mission. There was only one way to help the other divers: by diving.

When she got to the launch bay, the green divers had all mustered.

Trey was first to speak. "Captain, what's going on? Is my dad okay?"

"We have a problem on the surface," she replied, halting right in front of the group. "I don't have much time to explain, so listen up. There are machines down there. The same machines that I believe killed Dr. Diaz and his team. I'm not sure where they came from, but I know they will kill the divers if we don't do something to help them."

"Robots?" Vish asked, rubbing the gold hoop in his ear as if it might bring him luck.

Jaideep tilted his head. "Like AIs?"

"Killer AIs," Katrina said. "Programmed to destroy humanity."

"We have to get down there," Trey said, his eyes burning with worry.

Jed agreed. "Commander Everhart and the others need our help."

Katrina gave a look that silenced everyone. "We can't bring the ship all the way down to the surface; it's too big a risk. But I can get us close. I just can't do this on my own. I need volunteers to go with me."

It didn't surprise her when Trey's hand shot up.

No other hands joined his.

"Is there no one else?" Katrina asked.

"I'll go," came a voice from the back of the group.

It was Edgar Cervantes. His cousin, Ramon, stepped up beside him.

"Me too," Ramon said.

"I'm in," said Jaideep.

Vish looked at his brother. "What? Man, *no*! We aren't ready …"

"You'll never be fully ready," Katrina said. "We're jumping from five thousand feet, which means you will only have to be in the air a few seconds before pulling your chute.

"That's it?" Jaideep said. "Sounds easy enough to me."

"Sounds like a death wish!" Vish exclaimed. "Come on, bro, you can't seriously be thinking about this. Did you not hear what's down there?"

"We all die sometime," Edgar said.

"If you're coming with me, suit up and be ready in twenty minutes," Katrina said. "We're diving as soon as the ship's in position."

She made her way over to the crates and lockers on the opposite bulkhead. Her gear was in the center crate, and she stopped to pull it out. It had been a while since she donned the armor and parachute.

Suiting up, she cinched the straps two notches tighter. Over the past few months, she had dropped over twenty pounds. The thought reminded her of the child she had lost, and her heart ached from the pain.

Sometimes, pain was the motivation she needed, especially for what came next. She looked at the launch doors as she secured her armor.

Vish was right.

Jumping into the rogue storm and battling robots designed specifically to kill humans sounded like a death wish.

But she had a duty to her friends.

She had gotten them into this mess, but was risking more lives the right move? The answer, she realized, was yes.

What she wouldn't do was send these green divers without a leader. Today, she was that leader. If she died, Bronson and her crew had their orders to get *Deliverance* back to the *Hive*.

She put her helmet on, clicked it into place, and moved over to the weapons lockers.

Behind her, Jaideep, Trey, Edgar, and Ramon were getting suited up. Vish watched nervously, arms folded across his chest.

"Everyone grab an automatic rifle," she said. "We're going to need the firepower."

An alarm blared through the launch bay.

"Beginning our descent," Bronson announced over the comm line. "Everyone, go to your designated shelter."

The airship trembled, and Katrina steadied herself against the locker in front of her.

"You heard the man," she said, directing her gaze at the divers who had not suited up. "If you're not jumping, get to your shelter."

Vish sucked in a breath but didn't move.

"It's okay, bro," Jaideep said. "I'm going to be fine. And if not, I'll see you on the other side."

He reached out and gave Vish a fierce hug.

Katrina watched as she pushed shotgun shells into the bandolier around her thigh. In a few minutes, Hell Divers were probably going to die. She just prayed they would save more lives than they lost, and recover the navy vessel she had risked so much for.

It was the only way to take the Metal Islands.

SIXTEEN

The door wasn't going to hold, even with Les' body braced against it. The machine on the other side rammed it again, and he staggered backward into a lab table. A twinge of pain ran through his back where the armor had smacked against the rounded edge.

He fired his rifle at the robot trying to break its way through the barricaded glass windows.

The door exploded off the hinges, sailing past him and crashing into another lab workstation. He pivoted to fire on the AI that stormed into the room, orange visor and mouth glowing like a portal to hell.

Rounds peppered the metal face; denting and contorting the humanoid features. Les emptied the magazine, hoping one the bullets would penetrate the metal shell, but the thing kept coming. An electronic chirp came from the open mouth as if it were trying to speak.

But these AIs didn't have voices like Timothy Pepper. At least, Les hadn't heard them try to communicate using anything other than their electronic wails.

He slung his rifle and unholstered the venerable .45-caliber M1911 pistol. An orange light blazed out of the machine's visor, tracking him as he moved. There was no way to get out of the lab without getting hit by a laser bolt.

Crouching down, he raised his pistol and fired a round into the machine's open mouth. It shook violently, still standing but dropping the weapon. Sparks exploded out of its orange visor and mouth, and it fell to both knees, where it wobbled a moment before slumping over on its side. The orange battery unit dimmed and blinked off.

So they can die …

"I killed one!" Les yelled over the comms. "I fucking killed one!"

The sound of mechanical joints filled the hallway outside the broken door, cutting his celebration short. Les holstered the pistol and picked up the laser rifle by a curved olive rail with iron sights mounted to the center of the black barrel. It was light, about the same weight as a blaster, and not much bigger.

He held it like a rifle and quickly checked for a magazine but saw nothing extending from the bottom or side of the weapon. He wasn't sure how many bolts remained, but even one was a gift he wouldn't pass up.

The route back through the labs took him a few minutes to navigate. Even with the sporadic working lights, the rooms looked different from when he came through hours ago.

He wasn't sure where Layla and Michael were, but with Michael's injuries, they couldn't have gotten far. It was amazing the young commander could walk at all after hitting the water so hard and then losing his arm.

Les checked over his shoulder one last time before entering the next lab. The other robots were coming through the open doorway, and the orange glow pulsed into the open space. Shadows rushed in with the light. Several of the machines were on all fours, moving like dogs.

The sight made him gasp, but he managed to aim the laser rifle at the closest robot and pull the trigger. The bolt sizzled through the air and hit it in the back. Animal bones exploded, and sparks flew.

Another orange light fizzled out.

He fired again, holding the trigger down this time to fire a laser that cut off the leg of another robot and sliced the lab station behind it in half.

The next trigger squeeze clicked, and he felt the heat coming off the muzzle of the barrel through his gloved hands. It was either overheated or out of bolts. He turned and ran as the other three machines approached. One hurdled a lab counter and slammed into a desk, sending the furniture crashing into a wall. The electronic howling grew louder. The machines were getting frustrated.

A flurry of lasers sizzled through the air, leaving white-hot incisions wherever they touched. One came dangerously close to his helmet, shooting past his right side.

The noise of their ethereal wails hurt his ears, but there was no blocking it out. He ran into the next hallway, hopping over the mummified corpses that littered the floor. Then he flattened his body and squeezed through the metal barricade.

"I've got multiple contacts heading toward the front entrance," Erin said over the comms. "Better sit tight, Layla, and let me take them down."

The message echoed in Les' helmet. They were being flanked. But where had the other robots come from?

"Hold your fire—you'll just draw them to your position," Layla said. "I'll hunker down with Michael. Les, where are you?"

"On my way topside. I got several pursuers."

"That's my goal," Erin said. "I'll buy you some time."

Les almost halted when he heard her voice.

She was going to sacrifice herself.

"No," Michael said. "Hold your fire, Erin. That's an ... order."

"Sorry, sir, but some orders are meant to be broken. Good luck to you. If there is an afterlife, I'll save you a spot."

The line fizzled out.

Les bolted down the hallway, gripping the laser rifle, ready to enter the fray topside. It was up to him now to save his friends, but he would have to be smart and lucky.

Distant gunshots rang out as he made his way down the second hallway to the garage. Electronic wails answered, along with the *crack, crack* of return laser fire.

Erin had shut her channel off, leaving Les, Layla, and Michael no way to contact her. She couldn't even hear them if they tried to send a message.

He made it to the garage a few minutes later and entered with the weapon aimed outside. The barrel had cooled, and he could only hope it would fire when he needed it.

Gunfire cracked from the piers, and he hurried to the open door to see a half dozen of the machines walking toward the ITC ship, their orange battery units glowing in the dark like handheld lanterns.

They didn't seem to be in any hurry. Several of them, armed with laser rifles, fired at the stern, where Erin stood firing down on them. She ducked as a bolt sliced the air where her helmet had been the second before. Les almost screamed at her to run, but he couldn't compromise his position if his plan was to work. Especially since the machines all had their backs to him.

He was moving out of the garage when a door on one of the armored vehicles creaked open. Layla hopped out and motioned at Les. Lying across the back seat was Michael, his stump wrapped with a bandage.

"Help me with him," she whispered.

Gunfire continued in the distance as Les lowered his gun and grabbed Michael. He was unconscious, and Layla needed help getting him to the navy ship. It was their only way off this concrete island.

Hold on, Erin. We're coming.

If anyone could handle herself in a fight, it was tough-as-nails Erin.

The sound of moving metal came from the hallway. Les let go of Michael and aimed his laser rifle out of the open door; peering down the iron sights, and waiting for a shot.

A moment later, one of the robots emerged in the flickering light.

Les fired a bolt into the center of the AI's forehead. The thin blue line bored an instant tunnel all the way through the artificial brain or circuits or whatever the hell was inside the head and right out the back of the metal skull, to the open elevator shaft fifty yards beyond.

That was when Les saw the orange light rising up the shaft.

"We have to get out of here," he said, listening to the approach of what sounded like dozens of the machines.

The place was a freaking factory of killer AIs.

Michael suddenly shot up on the seat inside the vehicle, gasping for air. Les turned just as Layla pulled a needle out of his leg.

"Adrenaline," she said. "Come on, Tin. We've got to get to that ship."

He looked at Layla and Les in turn, then at his arm for a second, as if to make sure it wasn't just all a bad dream.

"You're okay," Les said. "Let's go, Commander."

Michael didn't need to be told twice. He jumped out onto the concrete as Les ran back to the door.

"Where are you going?" Layla shouted.

He fired a bolt at the open elevator shaft, showering sparks down on the machines climbing the vertical walls.

Then he grabbed the gun the terminated machine had dropped, and fired off two more blasts at three approaching robots on his right. They returned fire, blowing smoldering holes into the floor.

He slammed the door and locked it before taking off after Layla and Michael. Lightning flashed overhead, and the boom of thunder shook the piers.

"Layla!" Les shouted when he got outside.

She was just around the corner of the garage.

"I'll meet you at the ship," he said, tossing the second laser weapon to her. "See if you can get it up and running with your computer and extra battery."

Layla nodded. "Good luck."

"Good luck."

She kept moving around the curved structure. Michael managed to say between groans of pain, "Help … Erin." For a moment, he seemed to be trying to pull away from Layla and go with Les, but she put his remaining arm over her shoulder.

The hallway door inside the garage creaked, and electronic wails projected out of the room. Three of the machines on the pier stopped and turned in Les' direction while the other three kept shooting at Erin.

The robots looking at Les were wearing bone armor, too, and one even had a human jaw attached to its face.. The jaw moved, and the same electronic noise burst from the mechanical mouth. It was as if ...

They're talking to one another, Les realized.

Erin continued raining bullets down on the pack. Not bothering to move for cover, they stood their ground and returned fire. Blue laser bolts punched through the ship's rusted hull as if it were cardboard.

Keep your head down, Erin ...

Les dropped to one knee, aimed the weapon with both hands, and squeezed off a single bolt. The laser zipped through the air, just over the head of a machine that had dropped to all fours.

The other two machines, both without laser weapons, ran toward him. Lightning forked through the sky, hitting the ocean.

Les aimed again, holding the trigger down to fire a longer bolt that took off the top of a metal skull. His next shot went through the chest of the machine with the human jaw, sending it crashing to the ground. It quickly pushed itself back up.

He centered the barrel at the head to finish it off, but the trigger pull ended with an empty click. Smoke rose off the glowing barrel. The third machine suddenly stopped running toward Les and stood on both feet.

The downed robot directed an orange visor toward the sky. The other three robots all stopped firing at Erin and also looked toward the storm clouds.

Les aimed his weapon, waiting for the gun to cool. A message crackled from the speakers, but he didn't understand Layla's transmission. It sounded like the Hell Divers motto.

"*We dive so humanity survives.*"

But why the hell would Layla be saying it right now?

Thunder grumbled overhead.

He pulled the trigger again, but still it wouldn't fire.

The sky suddenly rained blue orbs.

Five of them.

"Pull your chutes!" yelled a voice over the comms.

Les stared in awe at the sky, where a parachute suddenly bloomed out under the cloud cover. Then another, and another. All but one of the chutes fired and spread black canopies.

"Katrina came for us," he whispered.

His speakers crackled with the deep voice that had to be Edgar Cervantes.

"Ramon!" he yelled.

Les watched a body tumbling through the air. It smacked into the ocean several hundred yards out from the piers.

The machines with weapons raised them toward the sky and fired off bolt after bolt. Several of them tore through chutes, sending the novice divers careening through the air.

Les aimed his weapon at the robots.

"Over here, assholes!" he yelled. This time, the trigger pull fired a bolt. The laser traveled through the central chest slot of the machine and the battery exploded in a fiery blast, all but tearing the robot in half.

The other machines all looked in Les' direction.

He swallowed.

At least he had distracted them from the other divers. Erin stood above the rail, which was sliced through and glowing from laser hits. He hit the deck, rolled, and returned fire.

A diver was already coming in hot over the pier, performing a two-stage flare with such grace, it had to be Katrina.

She ran out the momentum, passing Les as he kept firing bolts. Timing his shots, he tried to keep the gun from overheating again.

Erin stuck her rifle over the side of the ship, screaming as she fired. "Eat this, you walkin' shit cans!" She squeezed off three-round bursts from side to side. "You want some? Come on! Swallow this!"

Gunfire erupted behind Les, and Katrina ran up beside him with her rifle shouldered.

"Good to see you're still alive!" she yelled.

Les said the first thing that came to mind. "Where's Trey?"

"Not sure, but his beacon's still active."

The reassuring words energized Les. He came up on one knee and took down another machine on the pier with a shot to the neck. The partially severed head craned to the side, sparks shooting from the wound.

"Focus your fire on their heads!" Les yelled.

Erin and Katrina slowed their rate of fire, the sporadic cracks echoing amid the boom of thunder and cries of the machines.

The two remaining enemies both went down,

their skull armor broken to pieces. They squirmed as Les finished them off with laser bolts. The final AI twitched on the ground before going limp, the orange lights fizzling out like coals in the rain.

Les stood and scanned the sky above the ITC ship where Erin was busy changing a magazine. Three more divers were still in the air, but the wind, damaged canopies, and inexperience had taken them all off course. Two floated overhead toward Red Sphere. The third was coming down near the destroyed robots.

"Trey, where are you!" Les shouted.

"Dad! I'm over the ship, but I can't slow down."

Les turned to see his son sail right over the ITC ship, about two hundred feet above Erin. She, too, looked up as he passed overhead.

"Do the two-stage flare like we trained you," Les said. "Wait till you're about eight feet off the deck; then pull both toggles down hard but not all the way, to slow your descent. Then, when you level out, pull the toggles *slow* the rest of the way down to stop your forward motion."

Movement on the deck pulled Les' eyes off Trey.

"Behind you!" Erin yelled.

Bolts hit the deck just right of Les and Katrina. She rolled away from the laser fire, but Les stayed put. One of the machines he had knocked down was getting back up with a weapon raised. A bolt sizzled past Les' head as he pulled the trigger—the same moment the machine fired a bolt into the sky.

"No!" Les shouted.

He lowered his gun as the robot dropped, smoldering. Les' eyes jerked upward, searching the sky for his son. But the AI's laser bolt had not been meant for Trey. An object the size of a melon dropped over the side of the ship, near the stern. It took Les a moment to register what he was seeing.

Erin's headless corpse, still standing on the deck, slumped against the rail, then toppled over. Her helmet, with her head inside, clattered onto the concrete and rolled a few feet.

Trey's boots hit the pier a moment later, between the ship and Les. The boy quickly lost control, running and then tumbling head over feet.

"Covering fire!" Katrina shouted.

Les, still in shock, finally turned to fire on the machines streaming out of the building. Erin was gone, but maybe he could still save the others.

Katrina was on one knee, fighting desperately, firing calculated bursts.

One of the divers had landed on the roof of Red Sphere and opened fire from above. The final diver was nowhere in sight.

Six robots strode out of the garage, firing bolts in all directions.

Les heard one crackle in the air just over his head. He was giving them too big a target, so he dropped to his belly. His first three shots took down a machine, and fire erupted from its innards. His weapon clicked on the next squeeze—overheated again.

He switched to his rifle and aimed a burst at the

mouth of one of the remaining five machines standing just outside the entrance to the garage.

Bolts cut through the air separating Les and Katrina. They both rolled out of the way and into each other.

Les glanced up, expecting a bolt to his face.

He heard something streak over their heads, followed by a thunderous boom that seemed to come from both the Red Sphere garage and the ocean. The explosion tore the machines standing there to scrap metal, and they vanished in the fiery blast. The diver on the roof fell backward.

Les had already grabbed Katrina and pulled her to the left, where they tumbled over the side of the pier and into the water.

Kicking back to the surface, he pulled himself onto the dock, where he saw a navy ship rounding the piers.

"Got the ship working," Layla said over the open channel. "Anyone want a ride out of this charming place?"

Pushing himself up, Les ran to help untangle Trey, who was shouting for help on the pier, his chute on fire.

Katrina rushed over to help. They released the chute and put out the flames on his legs. By the time they had him out, Edgar and Jaideep were running across the platform toward the pier.

"You okay?" Les asked Trey.

The boy sat up and managed a nod. "The suit saved me."

Katrina looked to the left, where Erin's headless corpse lay in her blood, which was pooling underneath her due to a broken bone that protruded through her suit.

Trey lowered his helmet in despair.

Running footfalls came from behind them.

Jaideep arrived, panting, his arm around Edgar, who was gripping his side.

"Where's my cousin? Does anyone know what happened to Ramon?" Edgar's words trailed off when he saw Erin's body.

"His beacon went off in the storm. I'm sorry," Katrina said. "There's nothing we can do for him or Erin now."

"He's hurt," Jaideep said.

Edgar unslung his arm from the diver's shoulder. "I'm fine."

But Les could see that Edgar wasn't fine. Shards of metal stuck out of his chest armor, and another piece protruded from his belly, where blood was seeping out.

Katrina pointed her chin at the cruiser, which was moving into position along the pier. "Let's go, divers."

SEVENTEEN

The waves crashed against the *Sea Wolf*'s bow, sending up plumes of spray. Magnolia tightened the strap against her chest, and looked over at X.

"The sails will hold," he reassured her.

"But what about our friends?" she asked. "Will they be okay?"

X sighed. "I … I don't know. But there's nothing we can do for them right now."

"So we just have to sit here and wait to hear from Katrina?"

He gave a silent nod.

Magnolia shook her head sadly. X had spent a decade on the surface, waiting to be rescued, but she couldn't wait a few hours to hear about her friends. That was the difference between them, and why he had survived all this time.

Her mind replayed Katrina's transmission from an hour earlier.

"Team Raptor is under attack by unknown hostiles."

The guilt filled her with dread.

If they died, it was on her. She had sent the information that encouraged the captain to send divers there.

And it had been a trap.

The next transmission explained what Team Raptor was facing at Red Sphere.

"AIs," she said quietly. "I just can't believe it's true."

"Pepper, you got some explaining to do," X growled under his breath. "Seems to me like you're hiding stuff from us, and if I find out …" He made a cracking sound with his tongue to mimic a snapping neck.

"Sir, I assure you, if I had known that Red Sphere was compromised by those machines, I would have informed you. And my counterpart on the *Hive* would have informed Captain DaVita, as well."

X looked at Magnolia. Neither of them had told Pepper his counterpart was shut down. And she wasn't about to …

"Your counterpart is offline, Pepper, and I'm about to fry your hard drive, too, unless you start talking."

Timothy paused for two full seconds before responding to X's words. "I don't know how else to explain this. Whatever records existed must have been destroyed during the Blackout."

X didn't look convinced, and Magnolia certainly wasn't.

"You heard some of those transmissions from Red Sphere," Magnolia said. "Explain to me why AIs would wear human and animal bones. That doesn't sound like a machine thing to do. But I suppose it takes one to know one."

Timothy paused again.

"Spill it, Pepper, or you're going to sleep forever," X said.

"CEO Tyron Red built one type of machine that was top secret," Timothy replied. "This particular hybrid model was commissioned by the military and a small supply of two hundred units were purchased in the year two thousand forty. They were named DEF-Nine and were designed to hunt and kill enemies. The model looks humanoid, but they are far different from other units built to fight alongside human soldiers in times of war."

"Show us," Magnolia said.

"One moment."

"What does DEF-Nine stand for?" X asked.

"Defense Unit Nine. This was the ninth version of the machine," Timothy replied.

X and Magnolia exchanged another glance. The metal hatch covering the broken windshield rattled as the bow slapped down hard off a wave.

She tried to relax in her seat, but the constant rocking and shaking were making her ill. The lump on her head didn't help. The swelling had gone down, but a migraine had settled behind her right eye, and it made her entire head pulse.

While they waited, Magnolia studied X in the weak light emanating from the control panel on the dashboard. The faint glow illuminated his features, and she could see his age now more than ever: the scars lining his face like tattoos, the crow's-feet framing the dark eyes that had seen more horrors of the real world than anyone else alive. All those horrors and all his experiences would have driven an average man mad or killed him.

But not X.

He had the heart of a warrior and, in some ways, a saint. She saw it in the way he gently patted Miles on the head and the way he always put others before himself. The bond he shared with the dog made Magnolia envious. She had never been that close to anyone over the years, whether friend or family. Everyone she loved had been lost to the apocalyptic world. And when she finally opened her heart to Rodger, he, too, had died.

"How far out are we, Pepper?" X asked. "This tin coffin can't take much more of this pounding."

"At our current speed, our target destination of the western edge of the Virgin Islands should take another forty-five minutes, assuming the wind remains at—"

"All right, got it, Pepper. Thanks." X took the controls. "I've got it from here."

"Wait, sir, I thought you wanted to see photos of the D—"

"We do," Magnolia interrupted.

A beeping came from the dashboard. Magnolia looked at a monitor displaying an old-world video of a factory. An assembly line of humanoid-shaped robots rolled out on a conveyor belt inside a massive room with a high ceiling.

"These are the DEF-Nine units," Timothy said. "As you can see, this is in the beginning stages of their design."

Robotic arms along the track welded parts onto the frame as the machines continued down the line. Anatomically shaped plates were applied to their extremities and torsos, making them look a bit like Roman warriors from the picture books. Visors were fastened over the slits where their eyes would have been. Finally, a battery unit was inserted into the chest socket. It flickered on, emanating an orange glow that also flickered out of the mouth and visor.

"The DEF-Nine units were built for one purpose," said Timothy, "to kill their enemies in barbaric ways so as to strike fear in future enemies. Here's a video I found in the archives of a prewar mission."

A video showing three of the machines in a jungle came online. Their plated bodies were covered in camouflage ... and something else.

"What are they wearing?" Magnolia whispered.

The machines slunk through dense foliage surrounding a small fishing village set on a coastal beach. Smoke billowed out of chimneys into the sky as the robots fanned out. A fourth robot's video feed captured the scene. Numbers and data scrolled across the bottom of the screen.

X leaned closer to the monitor. "Is that human flesh?"

Magnolia looked closer, confirming the answer with a nod. All the machines were wearing bloody patches of skin over their armored bodies. Blood and mud dripped down their metallic hides.

The pack entered the village, screeching in electronic frequencies as they approached a group of men and women standing around an open fire and roasting what looked like a pig. The first robot grabbed a man reaching for a rifle and tore his arm off in a single pull.

Screams followed, both human and electronic.

None of the machines used the weapons attached to their extremities. They didn't need them. Their powerful hands were all they needed to tear the first group of humans limb from limb.

They quickly moved into the village. A shirtless man with a shotgun emerged from one of the huts. He fired off several shots, but the bullets only dented the armor.

The closest machine picked the man up by the throat and, with its other hand, ripped away his nose and face like a hunk of cheese. Then it dropped the still twitching man and smoothed the skin over its metal face.

The video feed from the fourth machine zoomed in on the glowing orange eyes that burned through the eyeholes of the stolen face.

"Katrina sent Tin, Layla, and Giraffe to a place with *these* things?" X snorted. "What was she thinking?"

Magnolia remembered to exhale. The guilt continued to sink through her as she watched the machines sweep through the village, slaughtering anyone they came across, even the children and animals.

"We have to turn around and head back for Cuba," she said. "We can't leave them to die there."

"You don't get it, do you?" X said. He looked up at the overhead. "Pepper, how far away from Red Sphere are we, and how long will it take to get there?"

"Approximately seven hundred forty miles away. At this speed, it would take us about thirty-four hours to reach Red Sphere, assuming the damaged mainmast doesn't break. If that occurs, then—"

"We get it," X said. "They won't last another hour out there if they don't escape. But there's nothing *we* can do. Their fate rests in Katrina's hands. Only she can save them, but doing so would likely put *Deliverance* at risk if she tries to lower through that storm they reported on the dive in."

Magnolia saw the pain in his eyes. The despair. She felt it, too. *You killed your friends*, she said to herself.

"I'm going to see if I can get hold of Katrina," X said. He picked up the radio handset. "*Deliverance*, this is the *Sea Wolf*. Do you copy?"

Static crackled.

He looked over at Magnolia again, but she turned to wipe away a tear.

The video continued playing on-screen, but she tapped the monitor to shut it off. She couldn't bear to watch any more.

"*Deliverance*, this is X, aboard the *Sea Wolf*. Do you copy? Over."

"Roger. This is Ensign White. Go ahead, X."

"Where's Captain DaVita?"

"She's not here, sir."

"What do you mean, 'not there'?" X's brows scrunched together, almost closing the gap left by the scar.

"She dived to the surface with several other divers," Bronson replied gruffly.

"What?" Magnolia said.

"Captain DaVita dived to help the other divers."

X lowered his head in defeat. "Have you heard anything from them?"

"Negative. They've been out of radio contact for about an hour now. How are things on the open water?"

"Shitty."

"Stay safe out there, Commander. You're our last hope."

X slammed the handset against its cradle, startling Miles and making Magnolia flinch.

"This is why I didn't fucking want them going to Cuba!" he yelled. "Now Katrina is putting her life in jeopardy, God damn it."

It was the second such outburst Magnolia had seen, but this time, she deserved it and more. She remained calm, holding his fiery gaze.

"I'm sorry," she said.

He snorted again and wiped his nose on his sleeve. "Sorry don't cut it, kid." He unlocked his harness and stood. "Flesh guns won't do shit against those AIs. Their only chance of survival is using their boosters to get back through the storm. And those ain't good odds."

X stormed toward the hatch.

"Where are you going?" she asked.

"For some fresh air."

"It's a monsoon out there."

Miles got up and followed X out into the passageway, but he turned and said, "Sit and stay."

The dog obeyed and watched his handler leave, letting out a low whine.

"Don't do that, Miles," X said over his shoulder as he climbed the ladder to the second deck, vanishing from sight.

A hatch opened and slammed shut, and a few minutes later, the hatch of the staging room opened and slammed.

Magnolia tried to control her breathing. She felt as though she might throw up. After counting to ten, she tried to meditate. But nothing worked.

She was definitely going to be sick.

Unbuckling her harness, she decided to go back to her quarters. She grabbed a plastic pail and made it out to the passageway before throwing up.

She got down on both knees, her stomach roiling and wrenching.

The acid burned her mouth.

She vomited a second time.

A hatch above opened and closed again, and footfalls clicked above her. She clutched her stomach with one hand and closed her eyes to block out the stars floating before her vision.

Behind her, Miles let out another whine. The dog

nudged up by her side, sniffing and then licking the salt off her arm.

"Mags!" X shouted. "Mags, get up here!"

She opened her eyes to see him looking down from the staging area.

"Kid, you got to see this shit. Hurry."

She wiped her mouth off with her fist and stopped in the bathroom to dump the pail of vomit. Then she grabbed a drink of water and slogged down the passage to the ladder. Climbing made her dizzy, and by the time she got to the staging room, she was seeing stars again.

X was waiting there and helped her up.

"You okay?" he asked.

"No."

"You still gotta see this." He led her to the hatch and opened it. Then he stepped back and gestured for her to go outside. The waves were still slamming the boat, but the rain had stopped.

She blinked and raised a hand to shield her eyes from the bright gray sky. Maybe she really was seeing things now.

X was suiting up behind her. She could hear the clanking of armor, but she didn't turn. Her eyes were on the sky and the rays of gold streaking down to the surface.

The tar-colored waves had magically turned teal green—water so clear she could see through it.

The ocean wasn't black after all.

"Is it real?" she asked.

X laughed. "I sure as hell hope so."

* * * * *

"Erin …" Michael moaned. He tried to move the stump of his right arm, but pain ripped up his shoulder.

"Don't move," Layla said. Her voice carried strength, but Michael could tell by the worry on her face that she was close to tears. They had lost Erin and Ramon back at Red Sphere, and he was in bad shape.

It still hadn't quite hit him that the arm was gone. But perhaps that was due to the pain.

"Where the hell are the medical supplies?" she said as she rifled drawers and cabinets throughout the room.

Edgar sat on a bed without a mattress across the medical bay, his head bowed, dreadlocks curtaining his face. Blood had dried on his armored chest and leg pads. Michael wasn't sure how bad the injuries were, but Edgar wasn't complaining.

"How you doin'?" Michael asked.

Edgar brushed the locks away from his face. "Ramon's dead. He didn't even have a chance."

"I'm sorry, brother …" Michael let his words trail off, not knowing what else to say.

Edgar rubbed his forehead. "I can't believe he's gone. Just like that. I couldn't do anything to help him." His eyes met Michael's.

"I'm sorry about your cousin, but there's nothing you could have done. Just like there wasn't anything we could do for Erin. We're Hell Divers, and Hell Divers die. She knew the risk." He stopped himself short of saying that Ramon had known the risks, too. Now wasn't the time, and the pain in his shoulder made it hard to concentrate.

"I'm sorry about Erin," Edgar said. "I know she was your friend, Commander."

"She was a true Hell Diver," Michael said. He wasn't that close to Erin, not as close as Les, but he had liked her. Even after Florida, when she came back with attitude and a chip on her shoulder. Not that Michael blamed her. He had felt the same way after his father died on the surface.

He drew in a breath, blinked at the bright overhead light, and closed his eyes. Every time he did, he saw the image of the machine with the cow skull, firing a laser through his arm.

Knowing that it was still back at Red Sphere lying on the concrete stairwell was an odd feeling. A piece of him—an important piece of his body that had been with him his entire life.

Layla continued going through the cabinets on the bulkheads, cursing, opening and slamming them, and cursing some more.

"There's nothing here," she said. "It's all been raided."

Michael looked over, groaning. The pain was deep inside his arm, as if his bone marrow were on fire. Sweat beaded on his forehead. He swallowed and tried to relax on the hard bed.

The hatch squealed open, and Les ducked through the entryway, his brick-red tufts scraping the metal arch.

"Commander Everhart," he said. "How are you feeling?"

Michael tried to hold still. He was close to hyperventilating from the pain, but he managed to nod.

"The laser cauterized the wound, fortunately," Layla said. "But we need to find something soon to prevent infection. Same thing for Edgar. He's got shrapnel wounds from the blast."

"It ain't nothin'," Edgar said.

Layla shot him a sideways glance. "It'll be something if it gets infected."

"I'll check with the others to see if they have anything in their gear," Les said.

"Where are the others?" she replied.

"Trey and Jaideep are patrolling and searching the other decks to make sure the ship is clear. Katrina's on the bridge."

"How are we doing on power?" Layla said, still going through drawers. "Didn't look good when I got the ship running earlier."

"It's not." Les hesitated, scratching the red stubble on his chin. "This vessel runs off four nuclear fuel cells. Looks like they're all around a ten percent charge. Not sure how long that will last us, and we have a major problem. The satellite uplink we were using to connect with *Deliverance* got left on Red Sphere in our escape."

Layla looked up. "So we have no way of contacting *Deliverance*?"

"Correct."

Michael gritted his teeth and sat up on the bed.

"So what's Katrina's plan?" he asked.

"She said we sail until we can break through the electrical disturbance and contact *Deliverance* with our helmet comms."

Edgar gripped his belly and walked over from his bed to Michael's bedside while Layla moved to a rack of lockers. She pulled on one of the handles, grunting. "Come on, you worthless pile of junk."

The handle broke off in her hand, and she staggered backward. Then she gave the door a kick with her steel-toed boot, making a loud bang. The doors popped open, revealing several shelves stacked with medical supplies.

"Here we go," she whispered.

Michael gritted his teeth through another wave of pain. This time, though, the aches seemed to be coming from the arm that was no longer there. But how could that be?

Phantom pains.

Tears stung his eyes. The dull ache was worse than anything he had experienced yet. He blinked the tears away, taking in deep breaths until he was hyperventilating.

"Hold on, Tin, I think I found something," Layla said.

"I'll go see if there are any med packs upstairs," Les said.

A tall figure ducked through the hatch before he could leave. Trey walked into the room and said, "Ship is clear of life-forms and AIs, but we're still searching the lower decks for supplies."

"I wonder what happened to the original crew," Layla said.

"Probably landed at Red Sphere like we did, not knowing the defectors were inside," Les replied. "But how did the machines get there, and why didn't they ever leave if killing humans is their purpose?"

"No humans left to kill maybe," Layla said. "All that matters is they don't have a way to follow us. No one saw any aircraft back there, right?"

Les shook his head. "None at all."

"I have to get back to patrol, but I wanted to check on the commander," Trey said. He walked over to Michael and took his left hand. "You okay, brother?"

Michael swallowed again and tried to nod.

Layla walked back to his bedside with a bottle of gel. "It's really old, but the container is still sealed."

Michael blinked through more tears to take a look at the bottle. The gel was the same kind they used in place of sutures to seal deep wounds and prevent infection. And it burned like hell.

She slowly unwrapped his bandage to the scent of burned flesh.

He craned his neck to look down at the wound.

"Look at me, Tin," Layla said.

The ship groaned slightly and the overhead light flickered as they changed course. Layla put on a pair of plastic gloves and squeezed out some of the gel on a finger. "This is going to burn pretty bad, Michael. You might even black out."

Trey squeezed Michael's left hand.

"If I do, tell Katrina I know what we have to do," he said.

"What's that?"

"We have to find the *Sea Wolf*."

EIGHTEEN

"Multiple contacts."

Timothy's words crackled from the speaker system in the staging room, forcing X's eyes away from the most beautiful sight he had ever seen through the open hatch.

The sun could wait.

"Two vessels," Timothy confirmed.

X should have known that it was a bit early to celebrate. A place like this would be heavily protected, and he had a feeling it was the Cazadores doing the protecting. The rapid beating of his heart was no longer caused by joy.

He wasn't ready for this. *They* weren't ready for this.

Magnolia's wide eyes suggested she felt the same, but she knew what to do. She hurried over to the rack where she stored her gear, and began putting on her armor.

"Where, Pepper?" X asked.

"Due east, about three nautical miles out and moving at only about ten knots."

X grabbed his rifle, opened the hatch, and slipped outside.

For the first time in his entire life, the sky wasn't cloaked in darkness. To the east, planks of gold streamed through an opening in the electrical storm, like a portal to another world. As much as he wanted to stare, he moved in a hurry to the mainmast. Grabbing the rungs, he started up to the crow's nest for a better view of whoever had spotted them, although he had a fair idea.

The wind whistled around his armor and bit into his suit. The sail blocked his view to the east—right where these mysterious contacts were coming from.

Halfway up, his boot slipped off the narrow, wet rung, and he lost his grip. Hanging from one arm, he watched a magazine fall from his vest and clatter onto the deck below.

He swung his hand back up and grabbed the rung.

Come on, old man.

The spear and attached line were just above him, and he swung right to get past. As he reached up for the crow's-nest rail, his eyes went to his HUD.

It can't be …

The temperature was seventy degrees Fahrenheit, and there was virtually no trace of radiation. This isolated spot of what many would call heaven wasn't there for the taking, though.

In the distance, two boats powered toward them, leaving a trail of engine smoke behind them. X jumped into the crow's nest and unslung his rifle. Another, smaller boat with a single rider led the two larger craft.

Three contacts.

X zoomed in on the small boat, which had handlebars and looked like a seagoing motorcycle. Goggles covered the rider's face, and long black hair flew over his shoulders. Green and brown clothing rippled in the wind, and the barrel of a slung rifle rose over his back.

This didn't look like one of the Cazadores he had seen in Florida.

X moved his optics to the larger of the two big boats: a rust bucket that looked worse than some of the wrecks in the Turks and Caicos. Canvas tarps covered the bow, and fishing poles hung from the afterdeck. A cracked glass window obscured the cabin and the two people piloting the vessel. It had an old-world engine, the kind that ran on gasoline and not fuel cells.

It was as if the *Sea Wolf* had gone through a time machine and entered the Old World.

He studied the men for a few more seconds. Several of them wore some sort of breathing apparatus, but none of them had on the massive suits of armor he remembered from Florida.

For a fleeting moment, he thought that maybe he had found other survivors—people that the passengers of the *Hive* and *Deliverance* might live in harmony with.

Then he saw the octopus logo on the helm of the second boat. Just like the one he'd seen tattooed on el Pulpo's forehead and engraved in his chest armor. There would be no living in harmony with these bastards.

"What do you see?" Magnolia shouted from the deck below.

"Nothin' pretty!" he yelled back.

He continued scanning the vessel. This one wasn't a fishing boat. It looked more like what he had seen in Florida. Many years ago, people had called them yachts. They were built for the rich, but this one wasn't in much better condition than the other boat.

The hull had been stripped of paint and then branded with an image of a purple octopus stretching its arms across the rusty surface. Two men, both wearing helmets, stood at the windowless helm. Slung weapons protruded over their backs, and bandoliers crisscrossed their armored chests.

X moved the scope to a crate resting on the back deck. Three more men stood at the gunwales, weapons cradled. They were coming for the *Sea Wolf*, with a small army and plenty of guns. And they were quickly closing the gap. The one-man craft suddenly shot ahead, thumping over whitecaps, the driver jolting up and down.

X had waited a long time for this. But despite the longing for revenge, he didn't feel prepared. His plan had been to surprise these murdering scum, and now he would have to improvise.

He lowered his rifle, staring out over a horizon the color of a ripe apricot. In the distance, miles beyond the boats, he saw structures. Carmine-and-gray towers rose on stilts above the water, looking like giant spiders.

Of course—the Metal Islands …

He focused on the nearest of the towers. He had seen these in picture books.

The fabled Metal Islands weren't actual islands. They were oil rigs.

Dozens of them lined the horizon, forming a colony in the sea.

"X, what do you—" Magnolia began to call out.

He cut her off with a gravelly shout. "Get to the command room, kid, and use the cameras instead of opening the hatch. I'm going to need you on the controls, but do *not* raise that hatch. We're about to have company."

"Cazadores?"

"About eight of the ugly fuckers. Three vessels. Grab your rifle and everything you can carry."

Magnolia went back inside the cabin, and he used the time to think. They couldn't outrun the boats using their sails. Hell, if they turned now they would be tacking *into* the wind. No, there was only one option.

They had to fight.

X aimed at the rider on the one-man craft and shot him in the chest. The strange little boat coasted several yards farther as the man splashed into the sea and vanished.

X pulled a grenade from his vest and loaded it with a click.

Magnolia stood in the open hatch below, holding her automatic rifle, apparently having forgotten his orders. A bandolier of shotgun shells hung around her neck, and she had a blaster holstered and her curved blade over her back.

"What the hell are you doing!" he shouted.

"I want to fight! Let Timothy command the boat." She stood there looking up at him from below, a hand shielding her visor. Human eyes weren't used to real sunlight.

"No!" X boomed. "Get to the control room!"

She hesitated, then went back inside.

X was already aiming at the yacht. It had powered past the fishing boat and the idle one-man craft, not stopping to check whether its rider was alive.

A wide-shouldered man behind the wheel of the boat came into focus. X wasn't sure how far out they were, but they were close enough for him to see the octopus symbol on an armored plate covering the man's chest. Goggles covered his face, but X had a feeling he knew this man.

"El Pulpo, we meet again," X muttered, zooming in closer. This was the king of the Cazadores—the man who had killed Rodger and tried to kill X and Miles back in Florida.

"Hurry up, Mags," X said. "And, Pepper, you make sure she doesn't do anything stupid."

"Sir, thank you for entrusting me with that decision."

X had been prepared to shut the AI down, but the threat he posed was merely a potentiality. The Cazadores, on the other hand, were a clear-cut danger, and the small crew of the *Sea Wolf* needed all the help it could get.

Magnolia's voice came over the channel. "Okay, X, I'm at the controls. Tell me what to do."

"You see those boats on the monitor?" X asked. "Mags?"

"Holy wastes!" she replied. "I see the boats ... and the Metal Islands."

He swore quietly when he realized she had ignored his order to keep the hatch closed.

Looking out over the open water, X watched the two boats. They were only half a mile away now, and several men on the deck were raising weapons.

"Close the hatch!" he shouted at Magnolia. "And keep going straight!"

"Working on it!"

He shouldered his rifle, waiting for the opportunity. The yacht was making a run at them now.

X lined up his shot, then launched a grenade just ahead of the yacht. He pulled the trigger and watched the grenade zip through the air. A geyser shot up just shy of the bow. Water rained down, drenching the two men behind the helm.

Muzzle flashes came from the fishing boat, and rounds cut the sail below X. He moved the rifle muzzle to the fishing boat and fired directly in front of it.

This time, the grenade exploded against the bow. The fiery blast sent one of the Cazador soldiers flying into the ocean, his clothes burning. The vessel stalled in the water; smoke billowing away from the twisted metal.

X pivoted to fire on the yacht just as a flare lofted away from the boat. He watched as it arced through the air in what seemed like slow motion. His eyes followed it downward, beneath his boots.

The tip caught on the face of the wolf, the flames quickly consuming the emblem and spreading outward.

"Son of a bitch," X growled. He opened fire on the yacht, holding the trigger down. The pilot turned hard to starboard, sending up a spray of water.

X peppered the hull with bullets.

The *Sea Wolf* skimmed past the yacht, Magnolia holding the same bearing, the mizzen sail catching enough wind to keep them moving.

After weeks of cursing the rain, X would give about anything for some now.

"Turn, Mags!" he shouted.

"Turn where?"

"Port side, port side!"

The rudders moved, and X pivoted for a shot as the yacht tried to flank them. Thick smoke from the burning sail made him cough and obscured his vision.

He gave up trying to find a shot and climbed out of the crow's nest. Rounds from the yacht punched through the metal, and one perforated the mast, just above his head. The snapping sound that followed sent a chill through him, but he had scant time to react.

It wasn't a bullet that broke the line holding the mast in place—it was the fire. The mast snapped forward, catapulting X into the air.

He had a momentary view of the Metal Islands in the distance, but it quickly vanished as sparkling-clear water rose up to meet him. Bubbles exploded around him, and he lost his rifle on impact. He kicked for the surface—the rifle was as good as gone now.

"Mags," X said between gasps.

He piked and then surface-dived, kicking for his life, just before the hull of the yacht passed overhead. The propellers churned the water where he had been two seconds before.

Filtered air filled his lungs. But the helmet was a double-edged sword—the armor was heavy, and it made swimming difficult.

He kicked away, staying well below the surface and searching for the shadow of the *Sea Wolf.* Although the water around him was clear, the depths were as dark as a stormy sky.

And he already knew what lurked below. These warm waters were home to more predators than just the Cazadores.

Magnolia's voice broke over the channel. "X, X … Where are you?"

"Overboard. Just hang on." *But for what?*

Though X could hear the yacht's engines, he had no good idea where it was or how far he was from the *Sea Wolf.* He would have to break the surface to find out.

Kicking and breaststroking, he fought his way to the top. When he was just below the surface, he used his arms to slow his ascent, so that little more than the top of his helmet broke through the water.

The clouds had parted directly overhead, revealing the unobstructed sun. He squinted at the bright rays. Treading water, he turned in a slow circle.

Both boats were floating side by side some two hundred meters away. Several Cazadores were already boarding the *Sea Wolf* with rifles and spearguns. One man remained on the port side of the yacht, looking over the barbed wire and searching the water.

"Mags, you're about to have company," X said. "Don't let them inside. Wait for me; I'm almost there."

X slowly sank back under the waves and began swimming under the surface. He took in slow, measured breaths, careful not to use up the small oxygen reserve in his helmet.

He reached for the blaster on his hip, then changed his mind and pulled the serrated knife from the sheath on his duty belt.

Come on, come on ...

A garbled message came over the channel.

"Should I send a Mayday with our location?" Magnolia asked, her voice shaky.

X was surprised to hear her ask. The guilt from her decision to send the Red Sphere coordinates had likely stuck with her, but this time it was different. Finding the Metal Islands was worth the risk.

"Do it," X said. "Send an SOS to the *Hive* and *Deliverance*."

He submerged deeper as he approached the *Sea Wolf*, going all the way under the hull. On the starboard side, he came up and grabbed the edge where the octopus had torn the barbed wire away. There was no one in sight on the deck.

He waited several seconds, then grabbed the starboard gunwale. The two Cazadores had already broken through the first hatch. Gunfire cracked, and Miles barked from inside the cabin.

"Hell no, you don't," X said. He reached up to the rail and was pulling himself aboard when a net suddenly fell over him. A soldier wearing goggles emerged overhead and kicked him in the helmet so hard, the glass cracked.

X flew backward, still draped in the net, and hit the water with a splash. Bullets hit the water, zipping past him in white streaks.

"Mags! Miles!" X yelled. He kicked and pulled, but the net had him enshrouded like a captured fish, and water was already coming in through his cracked visor.

During the lull in the gunfire, he could hear Magnolia's shouts over the comm channel.

Dark smoke drifted from the last shreds of the burning mainsail. More gunfire shot through the water. X waited for the soldier to empty his magazine, then kicked his way to the surface, trying to get free of the net.

It was the big-shouldered man with the octopus tattooed on his chest glaring over the side. He pulled up his goggles for a better view of X, revealing a beakish nose.

It wasn't el Pulpo after all.

The man gave X a sharp-toothed grin, then let out a laugh.

X fell back beneath the water. He tried to cut through the net with his blade, but his arm was constricted, making it almost impossible.

He sank deeper this time, as water rushed through the crack and filled his mouth. Spitting, he tried to keep from swallowing.

Magnolia's voice crackled through his speakers. "X! X, where are you?"

He thrashed harder, but he couldn't get free.

The hull of the *Sea Wolf* blurred as he sank deeper and deeper.

No. You have to keep …

He heard Miles barking. Or was it his imagination?

X squirmed harder, finally freeing the knife. It slid out of his grip, and he grabbed it with his other hand, then slashed through the netting.

His lungs burned, and he fought the urge to suck in seawater, all the while sawing away at the netting.

He finally got free and kicked back under the boat, toward the port side. Pausing to tread water in the space between the *Sea Wolf* and the Cazador boat, he caught his breath and blinked away the blur. His vision finally cleared, and he prepared to flank the enemy soldier.

Another scrambled transmission flared over the channel, but this one he couldn't make out.

He continued swimming in the space between the two boats, when the yacht's engines revved, churning the water behind him and launching the boat away.

Though caught in the wake, he managed to grab on to something hanging off the gunwale of the *Sea Wolf* as the props thrust him away.

The moving water pulled him, and the strand of barbed wire that he had unwittingly grabbed cinched tight around his gloved hand, cutting into the flesh. The wire uncoiled from the rail as the yacht's wake pushed him backward.

He fought the prop wash, treading and watching as the yacht sped away. Working the wire with both hands, he finally managed to get free, but the damage was already done. Blood leaked from several cuts.

He kicked back to the port side and looked over the rail. The Cazador who had netted him was still peering over the starboard gunwale, searching the water with his rifle.

X slowly pulled himself up, wincing from the pain in his hand. As soon as his boots hit the deck, he was running. Halfway across the deck, he slipped and fell.

The Cazador whirled with his rifle aimed at X, laughing.

"*Ahora mueres,*" the man said.

X rolled left as the man pulled the trigger. Bullets slammed into the deck.

A snapping sound came from across the boat, followed by a guttural "*Oomph!*"

He braced for the bullets, but they never came. X pushed himself off the deck and walked over to the Cazador, who was now pinned by a spear to the cabin wall. The soldier held on to the shaft that had impaled his chest, right through the octopus logo.

"Are you okay, Commander?" said a voice over the comms.

Realization set in as X approached the man. Timothy had saved his hide by firing one of the mounted spearguns.

Blood trickled out of the soldier's mouth as he tried to say something to X.

"I'm fine, Pepper. Where are Miles and Mags?"

"They took them. I'm sorry, sir. I couldn't …"

X walked back to the man and used his knife to trace a line across his throat. He wiped the blade on the Cazador's chest before resheathing it.

"There is something called a WaveRunner not far from here," Timothy said. "You can take that to go after Magnolia and Miles. I'm also going to replay the audio from their capture, translated into English, to help you."

X watched with grim satisfaction as the Cazador took his last gurgling breaths. The guy was a strong bastard, and he kicked several times before his eyes finally rolled up in his head.

"Listen to this, Commander," Timothy said.

The translated message crackled in his helmet.

"Let's take this firecracker back to el Pulpo. We're going to get a handsome fee for this one."

"What about the dog?"

"Maybe he will let us eat it."

"Julio, you stay here and make sure that other guy is dead. We'll send boats back later to get you and to scavenge this wreck."

The translation ceased, and X looked out over the water. He could see the WaveRunner. It would take him a while to swim there. He hurried over to start gathering the weapons and supplies he would need to save Miles and Mags.

"I'll keep transmitting as long as I can, but I have a feeling this might be the last time we speak," Timothy said.

"Thanks, Pepper," X said. "For the record, I'm glad I didn't shut you down."

NINETEEN

Katrina stood on the bridge of the naval warship, looking out over the broad deck and a helicopter landing pad. Gun turrets and machine guns pointed at the dark waters ahead.

Jaideep patrolled outside, his blue battery unit glowing in the darkness, holding one of the two laser rifles they had brought back from Red Sphere.

Katrina had considered going back for more of the weapons and the satellite dish to help boost their signal. They still hadn't been able to contact *Deliverance*, the *Hive*, or the *Sea Wolf*, but she decided it was too risky to return to the facility. Who knew how many more robots were waiting inside the facility below Red Sphere?

No, for now they needed to stay the course, even if it felt as if they were drifting farther away from their home.

Deliverance was still hovering twenty-five thousand feet above Red Sphere, where she had instructed Ensign White to remain until further orders.

She moved over to the helm, where Layla had connected her minicomputer to start the ship. The powerful device was almost the same thing as having an AI on board, with the added benefit that they didn't have to worry about the computers killing them.

Katrina brushed the dust off a plaque on the bulkhead, centered between two portholes.

USS ZION

ZUMWALT CLASS

DDG-1012

COMMISSIONED IN 2031

Hundreds of years ago, a naval officer, maybe even a captain, had once stood on the bridge where she was now—someone with a family, with hopes, with dreams. They had given orders that affected not only the lives of their crew, but also the lives of thousands, maybe even millions, of others. Those orders had likely helped lead to the events that left Katrina in charge of some of the last survivors of the human race.

The irony wasn't lost on her.

Her last orders had killed two precious Hell Divers and injured two more. A tarp covered the headless corpse of Erin Jenkins, a few rooms away. At least they had been able to bring her body onto the ship. There was some consolation in knowing she wasn't still back there.

The same couldn't be same for Ramon Ochoa.

The green diver was forever lost to the cold waters. The thought sent a chill through Katrina. It was odd to think that a man who had spent his entire life in the sky would spend eternity in the darkness of the vast sea, never having set foot on solid earth.

But, of course, he wasn't the first diver left behind. Plenty of others had left their frozen bones back in Hades and elsewhere.

She studied the plaque another moment. What had happened to the crew? Why hadn't the machines used this boat to leave Red Sphere after killing Dr. Diaz and his team?

"Captain, can we have a moment," said a deep voice.

She turned to see Les and Layla entering the bridge.

"How are Michael and Edgar?" she asked them.

"They'll both be okay, but Michael is …" Layla lowered her gaze.

"He's a tough diver," Katrina said. "Try not to worry. We need to stay positive."

"Any luck contacting *Deliverance*?" asked Les, stepping forward.

She shook her head. "Still can't break through that electrical storm. Haven't been able to reach the *Hive* or the *Sea Wolf*, either."

"At least you got what you wanted, right?" Layla asked.

Katrina frowned. "How do you mean?"

"This boat. I hope it's worth the price we paid back at Red Sphere." Layla took a step ahead of Les, a bold act in a place where, once, officers had never dared question their superiors.

Katrina wasn't a military leader, but she couldn't let her young friend get away with such blatant disrespect in front of her second in command.

"You're out of line, Layla," Katrina said, matching Layla's step with two of her own so that they stood face-to-face. "I don't expect you to agree with every decision I make. I do, however, expect you to trust me. I know that what happened is tragic, but we needed this destroyer."

"For what? To take the Metal Islands?" Her tone bordered on incredulous. "We don't even know they *exist*. For all we know, it was some made-up bullshit that X thought he heard when the Cazadores captured him. He wasn't all there when we first found him, you know."

"The Cazadores *are* real, and so are the islands they come from. We don't have an army to take them when the time comes, but we do have something the Cazadores don't have."

Les swallowed, his Adam's apple bobbing. He remained silent, stiff, and respectful. For a moment, Katrina saw a naval officer standing in front of her just as one might have done 260 years ago. Layla, on the other hand, still seemed to want to argue.

Katrina cupped her hands behind her back and walked over to the porthole windows to look out over the waves.

"Do you remember the prophecy Jordan tried to cut out like a cancer when he killed Janga? Her prophecy of a man leading us to a new home in the ocean?"

She turned back to the two divers. "I was never one to believe in stuff like that. 'Fairy tales' is what I called them. But …" She forced a half smile. "The *Sea Wolf* made me believe. Finding X made me believe."

"So now you're putting all your trust in a prophecy?" Layla asked. "In something based on the words of a woman that we all agree was *crazy*? I trusted you, Captain, up until the point you sent us to Red Sphere when you knew damn well it wasn't safe. All so you could get this boat."

"Captain DaVita risked her live to save ours," Les said. "I say you give her some credit."

Letting out a sigh, Katrina walked back over to Layla and Les. She put a hand on Layla's shoulder and waited for her to meet her gaze.

"I have a plan. You have to trust me. I know that plan may put Michael at risk because of how he feels about X, and I know that's where some of your angst comes from, but we have to think of the future of humanity."

Layla's eyes flitted to the floor, then back up to hers. "I know. I'm … I'm sorry. I do trust you."

"No need to apologize. Every captain has had a different plan for the souls aboard the *Hive*. Mine is just as fragile as the others, but it gives us all hope."

Layla took a deep breath. "Okay."

"Les, try the radio again," Katrina said. "Layla, let's take a walk."

She guided Layla out of the bridge and up a ladder to the command center.

"They used to call this the 'island,'" Katrina said. "Best view on the ship."

"I should really get back to Michael."

"I thought he was sleeping."

"He is."

"Just stay up here for one minute," Katrina said. "I want you to see something."

The hatch at the top of the ladder opened to a room no wider than twenty feet. The cracked glass windows provided them a panoramic view of the ship and the ocean around them.

Lightning speared the clouds overhead, firing up the sky for a single moment before letting it shade back into dark.

Katrina walked over to a view of the bow. Although they were more than 150 feet above, she could still see Jaideep down on the weather deck, his battery unit spreading a cool blue glow over the metal surface. A heavy mist hovered over the ocean. They were heading farther and farther away from Red Sphere.

"Quite the view," Layla said.

"Yes, it is."

Katrina looked up at the sky, wondering where *Deliverance* was in this moment.

"Did you want to talk to me about something?" Layla asked, turning slightly to study Katrina in the sporadic flashes of lightning.

"No. I just wanted you to see this view. To under-stand why I have made the decisions I've made."

Layla nodded as if she understood, but Katrina wasn't sure anyone could understand what was going on in her mind and heart. Michael was a good man, one of the best left in this apocalyptic world. Her orders had almost killed him on this mission. Of course Layla resented Katrina for it.

On top of that, the events of the past few months continued to fill her with the poison of regret. Losing her child was the worst part. Katrina had never felt so alone in her life. Part of her had wanted to die back at Red Sphere.

"Are you okay, Captain?" Layla said.

"Yes, I'm …" Katrina's words trailed off when she saw something in the wake of a lightning bolt. "What is that?"

Layla followed her gaze toward the radio towers overhead. Halfway up, a figure clung to one of the metal posts.

"Is that a body?" Katrina asked.

"Sure looks like one, but it's got to be fifty feet above us."

Katrina reached for her holstered blaster, but slowly let her hand fall back down when the next lightning flash showed the skeletal corpse—not a threat.

A voice yelled up from the bridge below, and Katrina moved back to the ladder and looked down at Les.

"Commander, I just picked up a scrambled transmission from the *Sea Wolf*," he said.

Both women hurried down the ladder to the

command center, where they met at the communication station. The worried mask on Les' face told Katrina something was wrong.

"It's an SOS," he said. "Here, listen."

Magnolia's voice crackled through the room.

"If anyone picks this up, we're at the following coordinates and need help. We're under attack by Cazadores. Several boats. X is overboard. I'm trying to …"

The feed fizzled out.

"Did you get the coordinates?" Katrina asked.

Les nodded. "Hold on … There's more."

He twiddled the knob. Static filled the room, then cleared.

"We found the Metal Islands," Magnolia said. "They're real. They're real and there's sun here."

"By God, they found it," Layla whispered.

Les looked up at Katrina, eyes wide with amazement and fear.

Fear for their friends—fear for the future of the airships.

"The boat is being boarded," Magnolia said. "I don't have long, but here are the coordinates. If we die, don't let it be for nothing. Bring *Deliverance* and the *Hive* here. This is what we've all been dream—"

The feed shut off.

"How long ago was this message sent?" Katrina asked.

"I'm not sure, but I did manage to get the coordinates," Les said. He took a seat at a station, typed, and said, "Here's a map."

Layla leaned over to read. "Pyooerta Ricoo," she mumbled.

"Virgin Islands, actually," Les said. "But not quite. The Metal Islands look to be off the coast …"

Katrina took a few seconds to think before giving orders she had never thought she would give. "Set the course, and gather everyone. It's time to start planning for a war."

* * * * *

Magnolia stared out at what was supposed to be her future home—the place in Janga's prophecy, where the population of the *Hive* was to live. X was supposed to lead them here.

And lead them he had. But when they finally discovered the Metal Islands, things hadn't quite gone according to plan. In fact, things could not have gone much worse. She had pinned her only hope on a last-minute SOS to the *Hive* and *Deliverance*—a final act before the Cazadores broke down the command-center hatch and beat her into submission.

Her swollen eyelids all but blocked out the view of the oil rigs in the distance, but she forced them open to see the clusters of towers. The rusted metal poles and platforms rose out of the water, like scrapers built in the ocean.

Smoke billowed from the slow-moving boat's makeshift stack, choking her every time the wind shifted. The slow ride gave her plenty of time to check out this strange city on water as she contemplated her fate. If she was going to die, she at least could die having seen the sun.

Rays streamed through a gap in the clouds that seemed to go on for miles. The Cazadores were taking full advantage of the sunshine. Solar panels hung off the decks like satellite dishes pointing toward the sky for a signal, feeding energy to the people here.

Lush plants grew out of rectangular troughs at the edge of several of the levels. The vibrant canopies and vines drooped over the edge like a green waterfall. Dozens of platforms and the top of the oil rigs were dedicated to green and brown plots of farmland. There were even ... Could those be real?

She tried to push herself up for a better view over the smoke, but her ribs ached and her eyelids were continuing to swell. Grasping the bars, she pulled herself up until her head bumped the bars overhead.

On the upper decks of the oil rigs, thick brown trunks supported leafy green branches that arched toward the sunlight. This was no garden.

This was a forest full of mature *trees*.

Real freaking trees!

Rodger would have loved this place.

Miles growled beside her, obviously not as impressed with the view as she was. He snarled at an approaching Cazador soldier, who banged the outside of the cage with the butt of his speargun.

"*Cállate, perro*," the man growled, baring sharp teeth of his own. "*¡Cállate!*"

Magnolia put her fingers to her swollen eye. The man gave a pitiless grin. He was one of the three who had beaten her on the *Sea Wolf* and ripped her shirt.

I'm going to cut that hand off soon.

She just needed a chance to escape. Either that or to hold on long enough for X to mount a rescue. Knowing him, he was already coming up with a plan. She prayed that Katrina had picked up her SOS.

If they're still alive.

Something told her X was still out there, but she had no idea what had happened to the divers at Red Sphere.

The guilt and pain hit her hard—a messy combination that filled her with a deep despair. Being trapped like a wild animal in this cage didn't help.

She grabbed the bars and shouted, "Let me out of here!"

The men exchanged glances and then broke into deep laughter, one of them gripping his belly he was laughing so hard.

"Go ahead and laugh it up, you ugly fools," she hissed, backing away from the bars. Her body hurt all over from the beating back on the *Sea Wolf.* She had fought hard, killing one of the Cazadores. She could see the body lying on the deck near the stern, dark blood pooled around it.

Fucker isn't laughing now.

To the right of the corpse lay her gear and helmet—the only connection she still had to the outside world. Miles nudged up against her side. He had a nasty cut on his forehead, and she was surprised he was still standing.

The fight replayed in her mind as she tried to calm the dog. The three Cazador soldiers had broken into the *Sea Wolf* and climbed down the ladder to the first deck, where she had killed the first man.

She might have gotten the other two, but her magazine had jammed, and by the time she grabbed her curved blade, they were running down the hallway. She would have slammed the hatch, but Miles jumped out to attack them. That was when he caught a rifle butt to the head.

When Miles went limp, she had done the stupidest thing ever and run screaming at the two attackers, with her blade out. She hacked and stabbed, but their thick armor reflected most of the blows, and within seconds they had her on the deck, where they beat her until she stopped fighting.

Pinned to the deck, she was helpless as they stripped her down to her T-shirt and pants. The bastard with the rotting grin ripped her shirt, exposing her breasts, but a third man had come inside and shook his head.

"*Aún no*," he had said.

Magnolia swallowed at the memory. She sensed that they were saving her for someone. And she had an idea who.

She pulled her torn shirt across her chest and scooted away from the bars, avoiding the gaze of her would-be rapist.

The boat slowed again as they approached the cluster of oil rigs. Several of the structures had bridges connecting them. People fanned out across them for a look at the prisoners as the vessel approached.

She pulled Miles close, wrapping her arms around him. His blue eyes darted across the decks, and his nostrils flared, taking in information.

"Don't worry, X is coming for us," she whispered, though the words didn't reassure her all that much. She tried to keep her fear in check, but she knew what would happen to them shortly. The Cazadores were going to rape and probably torture her and eat Miles.

She had to do something. But what could she do?

Hundreds of people stood on the platforms and the bridges between them. She was close enough now to see their grubby skin and tattered clothes, which reminded her of lower-deckers on the *Hive*. Many were heavily tattooed, with skin bronzed by a life outdoors—nothing like the pale complexions of people who had never seen the sun in all their lives. A few had skin that gleamed almost black, and scattered among them were others almost as pale as she was, with straw-colored hair even lighter than Captain DaVita's. Surely, these people or their ancestors had come from many different places.

As the boat passed under the first bridge, several of the adults, and even some of the children, opened their mouths and clacked their sharpened teeth together. Their origins didn't matter, she realized. They were cannibals, the lot of them—as foreign to her as if she were making first contact with an alien race. The clacking of teeth and squawking of children rose into a macabre cacophony.

Magnolia wondered whether inbreeding had played a part in their devolution. There had to be something going on—normal humans weren't supposed to act this wild and barbaric.

She remembered, when she was younger, reading Locke's concept of the state of nature. The social-contract theories delved into hypothetical conditions of what life was like before societies came into existence.

The Metal Islands clearly had some sort of social structure, but they were vastly less civilized than the *Hive*. On the airship, they had strict rules about not breeding with family members and not eating one another, for starters. Both those terrible acts resulted in physical and mental problems.

Most of the people she saw seemed crazy. And not the kind of crazy she could see in X after his ten years alone on the surface—more like demented.

Their hollow gazes, squawks, clacking teeth, and hollering followed the boat as it passed between the rigs. Magnolia took in a breath that smelled like manure and roasted meat.

She saw the source just overhead, where an entire deck of pigs and other livestock roamed on a dirt-covered floor. On the next deck, a roasting pig turned slowly over a low fire.

The boat continued between the stilts of the third rig, which blocked all else from view. The Cazador soldier rattled his speargun across the bars to get her attention. He leered at Magnolia, his eyes on her chest.

"*Eres muy caliente*," he said.

"Fuck you," she said, and gave a flick of her chin—a gesture that transcended the language barrier, a subtle way to tell him to screw off. This just made his smile even wider. He snapped his fingers at the driver of the boat, yelling "¡Caliente!" and then panting like a dog.

Miles let out a low whine.

"It's okay," she whispered.

But it wasn't okay. This was supposed to be heaven, not hell.

She would have preferred to face Sirens in Hades than these inbred, brutish cannibals.

"*¡Rápido!*" yelled one of the Cazadores.

The pilot pushed down on the control stick, and the boat surged ahead, picking up speed and creating a sizable wake behind them. She turned to watch the Cazadores on the oil rigs. A girl on one of the decks raised a hand and waved at Magnolia. The mother slapped her hand.

A memory surfaced in Magnolia's mind, of her own mother doing the same thing many years ago. That was the worst part about her memories from that age: she remembered only the bad ones—at least about her parents.

Because there were no good ones.

She sighed and turned back to stern. In the distance, dozens of rigs rose above the water, shimmering in the sun.

This wasn't just a city of islands—it was a small state.

There had to be hundreds of people living here, perhaps even thousands.

How could the *Hive* and *Deliverance* fight that many? They were down to just under five hundred people, and most weren't fighters. Hell, most of them weren't even well.

There was another option, of course.

If you can't fight them, join them.

Maybe she should try to make peace. Negotiate the fate of her people with whoever was in charge here. Maybe there was a way to live in harmony.

Another memory surfaced in her mind: the day that el Pulpo had skewered Rodger like a bug.

No. There was no negotiating with these people.

The man with the speargun yelled at her, but she ignored him, stroking Miles softly behind the ears. She had to stay strong for when the end came.

The boat continued toward the next rig, a two-story structure with an open roof. Instead of slowing as before, the driver picked up speed and swung around the platforms, giving Magnolia a view of what the Cazadores were storing inside their warehouse.

Shriveled drapes hung from hooks in the open floors. But no, not drapes at all. They were hundreds of fish and other animals, filleted and drying in the sun that streamed in through the open roof.

Magnolia squeezed Miles tight when she saw the light-gray hide of a sea creature she had always dreamed of seeing since first saw them in a book as a child. Two Cazador workers used a hatchet to cleave away hunks from the recently caught dolphin.

Blood ran down the drying flesh and added to that on the deck.

"No," she choked.

How could these people kill such a splendid animal, among the smartest on the planet? A tear caressed her cheek.

She looked away from the slaughterhouse to watch a ship carving through the water to the west, away from the dark horizon where the storms still reigned. Containers were packed three deep on the deck. The ship must be returning from a supply run to the mainland.

As they drew closer, Magnolia could see on the deck cages like her own. Animals of some sort were moving inside them.

Over the cough of the engine rose the electronic wails that had haunted her sleep since her first dive.

Not animals. *Sirens.*

She hugged Miles at the ghastly sight that further confirmed there was no making peace with these people. The Cazadores didn't just eat humans—they ate dolphins, and captured Sirens to use for God only knew what.

She couldn't imagine the civilized people on the *Hive* and *Deliverance* ever coexisting with such horrid people. But when Hell Divers did make it here and went to war with the Cazadores, they would try to save everyone who was willing to join the civilized society they had established in the skies.

If the Hell Divers came. She just had to hope they would, and survive until then.

"It's going to be okay, buddy," Magnolia whispered. "Our friends are coming for us."

TWENTY

Michael awoke to a cold touch on his left arm. In the dim light, his eyes confirmed that no, his missing right arm was not just a dream. He raised the stump, covered now in a fresh bandage.

"Tin," Layla whispered.

He batted his eyelids, trying to see through the blur and remember why he was lying in a dark room that smelled like rain. The single recessed light illuminated several empty beds and an operating table.

He remembered then—all of it. The memories of Red Sphere came crashing over him in a tsunami of emotions that ended with the thought of X, Magnolia, and Miles.

He was in the medical bay aboard the USS *Zion*, and Erin was dead. Ramon, too.

"Michael, can you hear me?" Layla said.

"Have we heard from the *Sea Wolf*?"

"I … I'm not sure." Layla's face came into focus then, and despite her frazzled hair and swollen eyes, she looked more beautiful than ever. She smiled and bent down to kiss his forehead.

The touch softened the blow of the memories.

"Sorry to wake you, but there's something Katrina wants to tell us," Layla whispered. "You up for some exercise?"

"Yeah, but just give me a minute. I'm really dizzy." The pain medicine had made him so drowsy, he could hardly sit up without seeing stars. He hated asking for help, but he was smart enough to know when he needed it.

He draped his left arm around Layla's neck. She folded the centuries-old blankets that Les had brought them, and propped them under his back. The rough, scratchy material made his skin itch, and the dust prompted a sneeze.

Jolting forward sent a wave of pain through his body, but it quickly subsided. The painkillers were doing their job, but they were making him so tired he could hardly function.

"Feel better?" Layla asked.

He answered by swinging his legs over the bed and resting his feet on the cold deck. Standing, he waited for a new wave of dizziness to pass.

"You good?" she asked.

"Yeah." He looked over at the bed formerly occupied by Edgar Cervantes. Bloody rags littered the floor.

"He's topside," Layla said. "Everyone is."

"Okay, I'm ready." Michael groaned and took the first few steps across the medical bay. They stopped for

Layla to open the hatch and then began working their way down a passageway covered in grime.

"What's so important that Katrina couldn't come down here?" Michael asked.

"You'll have to hear this from her."

He shot her a sideways glance, halting right before they reached the first ladder. An overhead light flickered, shrouding them momentarily in darkness. When it warmed back to life, the glow spread over bulkheads streaked with black mold.

She met his gaze but still wouldn't tell him what was going on.

The ship groaned and rocked subtly—an indication they were picking up speed.

"We in a hurry?" he asked.

"Katrina will explain everything in a few minutes."

A voice came from the top of the ladder well.

"Cap's waiting, Commander Everhart."

It was Jaideep. He stood at the next landing, still clutching his rifle. Michael hurried with Layla's support, a sudden burst of energy fueling his body. He had a feeling he knew what this was about.

They trekked through the rest of the stealth warship in silence but for the click of their boots on the metal deck. When they reached the bridge, everyone was already there. Les, Katrina, Trey, and Jaideep stood near the portholes, looking out over the dark sky. Edgar sat in a chair, a bandage wrapped around his muscular torso.

"Captain," Layla said as they entered.

Katrina turned and smiled warmly at Michael. "How are you, Commander?"

"Well enough, I suppose. What's this all about?"

Waves burst over the bow, and the ship pitched forward a few degrees. Michael groped for Layla, who helped steady him.

"Have a seat, Michael," Katrina said.

"No, thanks. I'm okay standing. Tell me what's going on. Is it X? Did something happen to X and Mags?" Michael caught Katrina's gaze.

"Magnolia and X found the Metal Islands," she said.

Layla held Michael tighter, and Jaideep stopped fidgeting with his gold earring. Edgar stood, trying to keep a straight face through the pain he was surely experiencing.

Trey was first to speak. "Where? Where are they?"

"Off the western Virgin Islands," Katrina said. "But before we celebrate, I have bad news. Things didn't go to plan when the *Sea Wolf* arrived. After receiving the initial messages from Magnolia, we received a message from Timothy Pepper."

She pushed a button on the station beside where she stood.

"Captain DaVita, this is Timothy Pepper. The *Sea Wolf* has been raided by Cazadores. Magnolia and Miles have been captured, and Commander Rodriguez is currently pursuing the men who took them."

Michael's heart sank at the news, and all the energy he had felt earlier drained away. His knees suddenly felt as if they were going to buckle.

A second message followed the first.

"I will continue to report any updates until the batteries are drained or the *Sea Wolf* is destroyed."

The feed shut off, and Michael stumbled past Katrina. Layla reached out for him, but he evaded her grip.

"Where's the comm station?" he said. For the first time in hours, he was thinking about something other than the pain.

He moved from station to station as Layla called out after him.

"Michael, calm down."

Katrina followed him and then pointed toward a row of stations near a cracked glass window.

"I've already changed course," she said.

He stopped and turned to face the other divers.

"We're on our way to the coordinates Magnolia sent, but we're a long way from them," Katrina said. "And, Michael, I know this is going to sting, because I can hardly bear the thought myself. But for all we know, they're already dead."

"No. They're alive," Michael replied.

"Perhaps," Les said, "but by the time we get there, they probably will be—assuming we have enough battery to even get there at all. I'm sorry, Commander. We're just stating the truth."

Michael looked down at the archaic radio controls, trying to figure out where the handset was. Reaching out with his right stump, he tried to grab it, but his reflexes still hadn't registered that he was missing an arm.

Michael swore, frustration breaking through. He swiped the handset off the station, but with only one hand, he had no way of turning the dial.

"Tin," Layla whispered.

When he turned, everyone was staring at him.

"Someone fucking help me contact Timothy!" he snapped.

Les moved over and spun the knob to the channel he was apparently using to talk to the *Sea Wolf.*

"Timothy, this is Commander Everhart. Do you copy?" Michael said.

Static.

He could feel the eyes on his back, but he didn't care.

"Timothy, do you copy?"

A long flurry of white noise ensued, and then a voice.

"Roger, Commander Everhart, this is Timothy Pepper of the *Sea Wolf.*"

Michael blinked away the stars before his vision, pushing out a tear. He didn't care who saw it.

"Timothy, do you know where X is now? How about Miles and Magnolia?"

"X is still giving chase and is reporting multiple contacts."

"Define 'multiple,'" Michael replied.

"Thousands. There are thousands of Cazadores, maybe more. They are well armed, too, sir. I'm still picking up the beacons for Miles and Magnolia, so I know they are alive."

Katrina stepped up next to Michael, her arms folded across her chest.

"Pepper, this is Captain DaVita. Can you tell us exactly how many of these platforms there are?"

"I count twenty within sight, Captain. It's possible there are even more Cazadores in other locations. But again, this is just a guess based on what I can see from my current location and what Commander Rodriguez has been reporting."

"Keep us updated," Michael said. "We're on our way."

"Roger, sir."

Michael slowly lowered the handset back into its slot on the station. Then he sat in the leather chair, holding his bandaged stump, defeated.

"They have an army," Les said. "More than an army."

Everyone looked to Katrina.

"We have to find a way to contact *Deliverance*," she said. "The ship is armed with missiles and nukes."

"You want to *nuke* the Metal Islands?" Les stammered.

"Of course not. But I want to bring all the firepower to this fight that we can. We have four hundred and seventy-two passengers aboard *Deliverance* and the *Hive*. We can't put them all at risk."

Michael felt Katrina studying him in the shadows.

"We're down to a handful of Hell Divers," she said, "and from the sounds of it, there are a lot of Cazadores. I can't risk the lives on the *Hive* and

Deliverance for a chance at taking this as our future home, and we can't destroy this future home, either."

Michael knew he wasn't in any condition to fight, but there had to be a way to fight the Cazadores and save X, Magnolia, and Miles.

"We have to try something," he said. "We're Hell Divers. We don't give up. We do what it takes, even when the mission looks impossible. That's what has kept us alive in the sky all these years."

Katrina nodded. "I've got a plan, Commander. I just need time to allow it to work."

* * * * *

X was running out of time and gasoline. The gauge on the WaveRunner said the damn thing was almost out of fuel. He steered toward the flaming wreckage of the fishing boat he had stopped with a grenade.

Pulling up alongside, he swung up onto the deck and searched for gasoline. Two rusted canisters sat inside a crate with an open lid. He grabbed them both and returned to the WaveRunner.

"You got any updates on Mags and Miles?" X asked over the channel to Timothy. The AI was still within range and monitoring the beacons for Magnolia and Miles.

"They're still on the move, sir."

"Are they still alive?" X was afraid to ask, but he had to know.

"Yes, according to their life-support readings."

X unscrewed the plastic top from the tank on the WaveRunner, looking up as he worked. The *Sea Wolf* drifted in the distance, the sails both burned away and the mast broken at the top. The last wisps of gray smoke drifted away from the disabled craft.

"What about Katrina? Have you been able to reach her again?"

"I heard from Commander Everhart and Captain DaVita, sir. They know our coordinates and situation, but I've just lost contact with them due to the electrical storms."

X looked over his shoulder to the oil rigs on the horizon. Several boats were inching across the water now.

Reinforcements.

It was about time.

X carefully poured the gasoline into the WaveRunner's tank. The scent filled his nostrils. He hadn't smelled it in a very long time. Gasoline was rare, and most of the time it didn't work. But somehow, the Cazadores had a supply of good-quality fuel, which meant they must have a way of refining it that he couldn't see. How they had gotten here, and where they came from, was another question.

Was it possible there were more rigs out there, or other places where these people made up their home?

X pushed aside the questions, screwed the cap back on, and strapped the canisters on board. Straddling the WaveRunner, he fired the engine back up and gave the throttle a twist. It shot forward toward the boats sailing for the *Sea Wolf*.

"Let's see what you can do," X whispered.

He gunned the engine, and the little craft went bobbing over the swells. The weapons he had salvaged from the *Sea Wolf* slapped his body with each jolt. Over his back, he carried a bolt-action rifle. A blaster and two handguns were holstered on his duty belt, and a submachine gun hung from a strap over his chest. The ancient gun had some rust, but he had tested it, and it worked fine. The three extended magazines held fifty rounds each.

Two grenades hung from his vest, and he had a brick of plastic explosive in the pack tethered to the back of the WaveRunner. It wasn't enough to take on an army, but it could inflict some major damage.

It was time to make these fuckers pay.

He twisted the throttle again, his hand aching from the barbed-wire cuts. Blood oozed onto the handlebar.

The boats ahead were all packed full of Cazadores—at least a dozen men, maybe some women, though it was hard to tell from this distance. He could see three vessels, all of them under sail. They weren't wasting gas now that the threat had been neutralized—as far as they knew …

Motion flashed in his peripheral vision. He quickly turned to his left, following gray shadows that moved fast just under the surface of the water. He felt a jolt of fear when he realized they were sea creatures, mere feet away from his exposed legs.

Keeping his right hand on the throttle, he raised the submachine gun in his left. Then one of the beasts leaped, breaching the surface in a long, smooth arc. The light-gray hide and dorsal fin sparkled in the sunlight before it hit the water with barely a splash.

This wasn't some sea monster at all. It was a majestic creature that he had never thought he would see. And it wasn't alone. A large group of dolphins swam alongside the WaveRunner. Leaping and poking their heads through the water, they seemed to be studying him. Their squeaking chatter seemed a mix of laughter and conversation as more of the beautiful creatures broke the surface.

He lowered the gun and kept his course at the approaching boats. They were narrowing the distance now, and he could see several men on the decks, working the sails.

The dolphins suddenly veered away and disappeared beneath the waves. Either they had decided he was an enemy, or they were leery of the approaching Cazadores. The bastards probably ate these beautiful mammals, just as they were going to eat Miles.

But not if I get to you first …

X worked on calming his breath as the boats neared. They were only a quarter-mile out now, and he slowed the WaveRunner to a crawl.

"What's their status, Pepper?" X asked.

"Magnolia and Miles are still on the move, sir."

"But they're alive?"

"It appears so, sir."

Dozens of faces on the boats focused on him as he sat waiting, waving for them to slow. Pretending to scratch his chin, he pushed the comm bead away from his lips and tucked it under his collar.

Two of the sailboats slowed, while the third started its engine and motored toward the *Sea Wolf*. The men on deck didn't bother looking in his direction.

X repeated in his mind the words that Timothy had told him to use.

Yo maté al intruso. Yo maté al intruso.

Raising his bandaged hand, X shouted the words that meant he had killed the trespasser, using exactly the inflection Timothy had taught him.

The men in the two sailboats wore sun-faded brown fatigues and rusted armor plates over their chests. Only a few of them had the breathing apparatus he had seen them wear back in Florida, and none had heavy armor.

A bald man with tattoos on his sweaty scalp waved a rust-covered pistol in one gloved hand while gesturing to X with the other.

"*Vámonos,*" he said.

X wasn't sure what that meant, but the body language suggested it was time to move. His disguise had worked, apparently, since the men hadn't riddled his body with bullets or impaled him on spears.

It had been a brazen plan, stripping the dead Cazador on the *Sea Wolf* of his clothes and then swimming to the WaveRunner with his gear and weapons, but so far, it was working. They had no idea he wasn't one of them.

The only downside was being unable to track Miles and Magnolia with his HUD. With his armor and helmet strapped behind him on the WaveRunner, he must use Timothy as his eyes.

The Cazadores would never find the body X had dumped into the ocean, but it was only a matter of time before they caught on.

The bald man yelled at X again, gesturing for him to get off the WaveRunner. X raised his own hand, hoping to calm the soldier.

"*Espera un minuto*," another man said to the first. He stepped up beside the other man and ran a hand over his thinning hair.

"*Un momento*," the man said to X.

X understood this much, and his heart kicked when two other men, who had been working the sails, walked over to look at him. The WaveRunner had drifted right between the two boats.

More men moved over to the side of the other vessel to look at him.

He was surrounded.

The man who had first hailed him pulled out a long machete from a leather sheath at his side. He raised a pair of goggles to have a better look at X.

"¿Ricardo?" he asked.

It was a question, and apparently not a rhetorical one. X was out of time—the ruse had played out.

"¿Ricardo?" the man persisted.

He received his answer a moment later, when X raised the submachine gun in his left hand while unholstering his blaster with the other.

Raking the submachine gun over the deck on his left, he fired a flare from the blaster at the gas canisters sitting on the deck of the boat to his right. He pulled the trigger a second time, discharging a shotgun round at a man with a speargun on the second boat, blowing a sizable divot off the top of his skull.

Two of the soldiers on the left boat fell into the water, and three others dropped onto the deck. X lowered his blaster and moved the submachine gun to his right arm, to steady the barrel as he squeezed off bursts at the men on his right.

Screams and shouts came from both directions, and empty bullet casings arced into the water as X took more calculated shots. When the magazine was empty, he let the gun sag on its sling, holstered his blaster, and took a grenade from his vest. He pulled the pin and tossed it onto the boat on his left, then squeezed the throttle lever.

The gasoline canisters on the boat to his right lit up almost simultaneously with the detonation of the grenade on the other vessel. The heat hit his back as he shot away on the WaveRunner, and he felt shrapnel whiz past.

When he was at a safe distance, he slowed the WaveRunner and unslung the bolt-action rifle. Bringing the scope to his eye, he saw several Cazadores burning on the deck, flailing and crashing into one another. Others had been blown into the water or jumped overboard, where they struggled to keep their heads above the surface.

"Time's up," X said, lining up the sights.

One by one, he fired rounds into their skulls, turning the water around them red. When he had finished with the soldiers in the water, he searched for the third boat, which was now circling the *Sea Wolf*.

"You're about to have company, sir," Pepper said.

X pushed the mike bead back to his mouth but didn't respond. He sat on the WaveRunner as it bobbed on the water. Using his arm as a crutch, he tried his best to steady the carbine.

The sights danced over the head behind the wheel. Two more men stood next to the pilot, and several more were on the deck.

X pulled the trigger, but the first bullet hit the windshield, spiderwebbing it. The pilot ducked before X could get off another round.

"Shit," he growled. He swung the barrel to one of the soldiers on deck and hit him in the side, dropping him overboard. Return fire flashed from the bow, lancing into the water around the WaveRunner. X lowered the rifle, grabbed the handlebar, and steered away. The engine roared, kicking up a strong wake behind the vessel. A round whizzed past his head, hitting the water ahead with a small splash. He turned sharp right, heading back for the billowing smoke of the burning boats.

The vessel pursuing him turned to intercept. With one hand on the throttle, he switched out magazines in the submachine gun. It took a couple of tries, but he finally managed to slap in the fresh mag without dropping either one into the sea.

He steadied the craft and chambered a round. Then, letting the weapon hang from the sling over his chest, he used both hands to continue turning the small craft.

A bullet perforated the back of the WaveRunner, and another cut his boot, grazing his foot. The jolt of pain erased any thrill he was getting from the hunt.

Just a flesh wound.

Instead of turning away from the gunfire, X cut hard to the left and into the spray. The rounds kicked up water by his side as he gunned the WaveRunner in a long, wide arc toward the smoke drifting from the wreckage.

The pursuing Cazadores were about to pass the burning boats. He continued turning the WaveRunner, thumping over the wavelets as he picked up speed.

Muzzle flashes flickered from the starboard gunwale of the boat. X kept low, hunching down and hugging the frame of the WaveRunner.

A message from Timothy hissed in his ear, but he couldn't hear it over the growl of the engine and crash of water on the bow.

X squeezed the throttle lever all the way and plunged into the wall of drifting smoke. When he was enveloped, he hit the reverse throttle, stopping the craft abruptly. Then he jumped into the water.

Kicking beneath the waves, he swam as far away as he could from the WaveRunner. He surfaced about seventy-five feet away, poking his head through the surface. It was hard to see through the narrow gap of clear air between the smoke and the ocean surface, but he managed to spot the boat searching for him. The pilot had slowed, and all aboard were peering over the sides.

Voices called out in Spanish.

X ducked back under the water and swam for a full minute to come up behind the boat. Taking the other grenade from his vest, he pulled the pin, counted off a couple of seconds, and dropped it onto the deck.

"Fuck you, assholes!" he yelled. Then he surface-dived and swam away.

He could hear the muffled explosion overhead and saw bits of shrapnel and debris hit the water around him. When he surfaced again, several bodies were in the reddening water. One of the Cazadores, a female with a Mohawk, was treading water with a hand on her gut.

X caught her gaze but swam away, trying not to inhale the smoke still drifting over the surface. He coughed several times despite his efforts.

Pained voices came from all directions.

He couldn't understand them, but he knew a plea for help when he heard it.

Mercy wasn't his habit with mortal enemies, especially cannibals. He would show them the same mercy they planned to show to Magnolia or Miles.

X came upon a dead Cazador lying facedown across a large section of wooden hull. He grabbed a baseball cap and goggles off the head and kept swimming to the WaveRunner. He didn't want to be around when the sharks started homing in on the slaughter.

Climbing aboard the WaveRunner, he paused just a moment to look at the image of a jumping fish above the bill of the cap. Then he snugged it down on his head, pulled the goggles down over his eyes, and sped away, leaving any live Cazadores to drown in the smoke-shrouded water.

This time, his heart remained calm when he saw motion in the water. The dolphins had returned, and they didn't seem the least bit frightened.

"Don't worry, I'm a friend," X said.

They swam alongside the WaveRunner, studying him with their dark gray eyes, as if to say, *Are you going to save us from those monsters?*

X grunted and twisted the throttle. "I'm going to kill *all* the monsters."

TWENTY-ONE

Les stood at the helm of the USS *Zion*, watching a magnificent storm. Lightning cleaved the horizon, streaking through the black like a giant fiery octopus. The residual blue glow remained for several seconds, and the rumble of thunder sounded both distant and close.

This was the same view his eyes were accustomed to seeing for as long as he could remember. Most of the time, he ignored the sights and sounds of the storms, as someone might have done two and a half centuries ago when strolling through a park or down a city sidewalk.

The storms were part of life. He had never thought he would know any surroundings other than black sky or blasted surface. Certainly, he had never thought he would see the sun. But in a single month, all that had changed.

He climbed the ladder to what Captain DaVita had called the "island," where she stood watching Jaideep and Trey work. They were outside on a mezzanine, using tackle and slings to bring the remains of a sailor down.

"Still nothing from the *Hive* or *Deliverance*," he reported.

"Keep trying," the captain said.

Everyone was on edge, and having something to do was a good thing. He returned to the bridge and sat back down on the leather chair, which creaked under the weight of his body and armor. Picking up the handset, he scanned to the channel used for communicating with the *Hive*, and tried to reach Samson.

Nothing.

Next, he tried *Deliverance*.

Still nothing.

Finally, he tried the *Sea Wolf*. Most of the crew didn't trust the AI, but Timothy was the nearest thing they had to a connection with Magnolia, X, and Miles.

Static from the radio station filled the bridge with the hollow sound of loneliness.

Les shook his head, muttering. "Come on …"

He went through the channels a second and a third time. After an hour of trying to make radio contact, he returned to the ladder, where Trey and Jaideep were carrying the skeletal remains of the dead sailor onto the landing.

"Careful," Katrina said behind them.

They brought what was left of the body down to the bridge and set it on a cleared table.

"What on earth would he be doing up there?" Jaideep asked.

"Hiding from something," Katrina said.

She looked over to Les, and he answered the question that she need not even ask.

"Still no contact with the airships or the *Sea Wolf*, Captain."

She sighed and put her hands in her vest pocket, looking down at the remains.

"He's been dead a very long time," Trey said.

Les walked over for a better look. It was easy to wonder about the long-ago life of each body he saw from the Old World. Who was this man? How had he lived his life? And the most compelling question of all: How did he die?

Bones darkened by a lightning strike lay on the table in front of the divers. The elements hadn't left much to examine. The uniform and suit were almost entirely gone—only a few brittle swatches hanging off a twisted duty belt.

Katrina gently took off the helmet to reveal a mummified face of shrunken skin stretched over cheekbones. The eyes looked like raisins, and the lips were just as shriveled.

She walked away from the table with the helmet and held it under a light.

"Les, you think you can get this helmet cam to work?" she asked.

He joined her under the light and took the helmet, turning it over. A camera was mounted on the top, right above the faded flag of the United States of America.

"I'm not sure," he said, "but I'll give it a go."

The radio suddenly crackled behind them, drawing everyone's attention away from the helmet and remains.

"Captain DaVita …" A flurry of white noise followed, then, "Captain DaVita, this is Chief Engineer Samson. Do you …"

Katrina and Les rushed over to the radio equipment. She took a seat in the chair and grabbed the receiver.

"Copy, Samson, this is Katrina,"

"Where the hell you been, Cap?" he replied.

Katrina closed her eyes and let out a sigh of relief. "We've been busy. Very busy. It's a long story, but as you may already know, Red Sphere was an ambush. We escaped in a navy ship called the USS *Zion* and are sailing for the Virgin Islands to render aid to the *Sea Wolf*." She paused before adding, "They found the Metal Islands, Samson. They are real."

"Are you freaking kidding me?" Samson replied, his voice breaking up from the bad connection. "You shouldn't play jokes on an old man, Cap."

"This is real," Katrina replied. "Contact Ensign White aboard *Deliverance* and tell him to meet us at the following coordinates. I'm sending some of the divers back up to the ship. They are then to dock with the *Hive*, where Lieutenant Les Mitchells will recruit an army."

"An army?" Samson asked. "Whatever the hell for?"

"To help X and Magnolia if they are still alive, and to take the Metal Islands from the Cazadores."

Les swallowed at the implications. All this was

new to him, and he exchanged a look with his son, who seemed shaken by the assertion that they were going to war.

Hell, Les was terrified of the idea, but was now the time to argue? He decided it was. "Captain, all due respect, but most of the people aboard the *Hive* are in no shape to fight."

"And your job is to find the people who *can* fight," Katrina said. "I don't need a huge army because I have something the Cazadores don't have." She paused again. "We have weapons of war aboard *Deliverance* and the USS *Zion*."

"I'm of the same mind as Lieutenant Mitchells," Samson said. "Most of our passengers have never held a weapon any deadlier than a potato rake. They're not used to violence, nor have the heart for it. These Cazadores, from what I know, are brutes."

Katrina seemed to ponder his words for a moment. It gave Les time to consider what lay ahead.

"You have your orders, Samson, and I expect you to follow them. I'll have Les send you the coordinates shortly. I've found a break in the storm, about ten miles from here. *Deliverance* will hover over the clouds there, and we will send up our injured. I will continue with the USS *Zion* to the Metal Islands, where *Deliverance* will meet us when we're ready to attack."

"What about the *Hive*?" Samson asked.

"We will bring her, but keep her out of view," Katrina replied.

Les expected the chief engineer to protest the plan, but to his surprise, Samson replied with, "I hope you know what you're doing, Captain."

Static drowned out his transmission, but his voice came back over the speakers a moment later. His tone had suddenly changed.

"I can't wait to see them," Samson said.

"See what?" Katrina asked.

"Those islands. Our new home. I just hope we don't have to pay too dearly for this place."

* * * * *

The salt breeze carried another scent—a citrus smell that reminded Magnolia of the farm on the *Hive*. But this was different, more potent than anything on the airship.

She crawled over to the bars to see the next oil rig that the pilot of the boat was heading for. It wasn't just a rig like the other metal platforms rising from the sea. Unlike the shanties built on the other platforms, this structure was like an ancient castle, with turrets and towers of metal, and pointy tops reaching for the sky. Even more impressive, rooftop-mounted solar panels angled toward the bright sun on turrets. They had to be on some sort of tracking system to get the most out of the light.

After several hours of traveling slowly through the Cazador-controlled territory, she was finally here, at the end of the voyage.

She took in the view in awe, almost forgetting the fear and dread boiling up inside of her guts. The gray towers were decorated with paintings, but she was still too far out to see the designs and pictures. What she could see were horizontal wings stretching out from the levels near the top. About thirty floors up, a central platform, jutting outward from the rest of the structure, held a garden of actual green trees.

Someone was standing there, watching the boat approach, but they were too high up for her to make out any facial features.

A king overlooking his realm.

This was not just another oil rig. This was the capital of the Metal Islands city-state.

The Cazadores standing next to the cage suddenly pounded their chests and made the same clacking sound with their teeth that she had heard from the citizens. Some sort of homage to their king, she supposed.

The driver slowed the boat and directed it toward a dock at the bottom of the towers. A massive door under the structure opened, revealing other boats docked there.

Magnolia glanced over her shoulder at the dozens of other oil rigs they had left behind. How was X supposed to find her and Miles now? And how was X supposed to fight through so many of these barbarians?

She turned back to the tower looming overhead and noticed something she had missed earlier. A dome-shaped roof crested the very top, right below the clouds. There, illuminated in golden sunlight, were the smooth lines of an airship.

For a moment, she thought the *Hive* had descended from the clouds to land on the castle. But this ship hadn't flown in ages; she could tell by the forest growing on the rooftop. Hundreds of trees and plants basked in the sunlight, their branches thick with leaves and fruit.

Now she knew the source of the citrus smell.

The intoxicating perfume of oranges, limes, and other, unknown fruits wafted on the salt breeze. She took in a deep breath, wondering whether this might be one of her last.

"¡Arriba!" one of the men shouted at her. "¡Arriba!"

The boat drifted toward a dock, where dozens more Cazadores stood waiting. Many of them were armed with guns or blades, but several, wearing brown robes, stood with their hands clasped behind their backs.

She stood and shielded Miles behind her back. Her swollen eyelids provided only a narrow view of the men who did not look like the others. Their shaved heads glistened in the sun. Like the Cazadores, some were as light-skinned as Magnolia, others darker.

Were these men some sort of servants?

There were also two middle-aged Cazadores in green suit jackets and pants to match. Unlike the filthy soldiers, these two had well-trimmed beards and wrinkle-free clothes that reminded her of Timothy Pepper. One of the guys pushed eyeglasses up on his nose and studied her, then looked down at a piece of paper clipped to a metal board. He used a pen to write something as he spoke to the other man.

The boat bumped the dock, and two dockhands in shorts threw out a mooring rope. Magnolia remained in the cage, Miles standing behind her and growling. Her tattered shirt blew in the wind as the soldiers opened the cage.

"It's okay, boy," she whispered, although she knew that it was anything but. This was it, the moment she had been dreading. Fear weighted her heart, and no matter how hard she tried to be strong, she was almost paralyzed by what she was about to face. Never in her life had she felt so alone and exposed. She covered her chest with her arm.

The pilot of the boat, a man with long hair, walked over and directed the other two soldiers to grab her. They both grinned as they ducked down to enter the cage.

Miles barked and growled, coming out in front of Magnolia. One of the men pointed a long weapon with a spear-like muzzle at the dog.

"No!" she shouted, trying to move in front of the weapon.

Blue flashed from the barrel, and Miles hit the cage floor, jerking and vibrating. His blue eyes, masked by fear, looked up to meet hers.

"No," Magnolia sobbed, getting down on her knees beside Miles. She picked his limp body up, the fur and flesh warm to the touch. A tear fell from her eye onto his bloody forehead.

"You shit-head bastards!" she hissed, looking up at the two grinning men outside the cage. "You're going to pay for this. X is going to make you *all* pay!"

Her snarled words wiped the smiles off their faces. They stood their ground, and one of them gestured for her to come out.

She got to her feet, still holding Miles in her arms. She felt his heartbeat and felt him take a breath. He was still alive, but there was only so much punishment even his genetically modified body could endure.

Magnolia took a deep breath and walked out of the cage. One of the men grabbed her by the arm, and the other pushed her toward the temporary dock between the pier and the boat.

She carried Miles across it and toward the Cazadores standing outside. The circular pier led to a double door ten feet high, with a faded wood trim and bronze accents that looked like octopuses. Two men in shiny metal suits stood guard with spears pointed skyward. Their almond-shaped eye covers stared ahead, neither of them looking in her direction.

They looked exactly like the soldiers from the boats back in Florida—the men who had killed Rodger and captured her.

Along the pier, several small one-man boats like the WaveRunner were tied to the dock. One bore the faded blue letters SEA-DOO on its side. An open door led to what appeared to be a garage for more vessels. Several bobbed up and down in the protected storage area under the huge structure.

"*¡Muévanse!*" the man holding her arm yelled.

The second soldier, the one who had shot Miles with the electric weapon, poked her in the back with the tip. The hot barrel stung her skin, and she stifled a whimper. She wouldn't give them the satisfaction.

Magnolia kept moving across the dock until she reached the pier. The group of Cazadores all parted, and the five men in brown robes began to walk toward a tall cage suspended by a cable. There was something very different about them—they all appeared to be of different races, and none were carrying any weapons. Aside from their clothing, the only thing they had in common was the octopus pendant that each wore around his neck.

One by one, they stepped into the elevator left of the door where the two armored soldiers stood guard.

"*¡Muévanse!*" her captor yelled again when she hesitated.

They herded her toward the elevator. Once the robed men were inside, the two guards tapped their spear handles against the deck and began walking toward her.

Magnolia stopped right outside the open cage door, Miles still limp in her arms. The man holding her arm and the man with the electric weapon pushed her toward the opening.

She took a step inside.

The soldiers followed her and locked the gate behind them. One of them pushed a crank lever, and the cable clanked overhead, lifting them off the deck.

She hated to turn her back to these men, and shifted slightly to observe them. Both men towered over her by a foot. They formed an X with their spears. Her eyes gravitated to their secondary weapons, blades sheathed on leather belts around their armor. A thought crossed her mind, but she was still holding Miles and would have to drop him to make a play for one of the blades.

No, this wasn't her opportunity.

Looking down, she saw the Cazadores on the piers, still staring up at her as if she were an alien creature from the stars. More people were watching behind windows with open shutters as the cage rose past them.

Almost all the people she saw behind the glass were women, and unlike those back at the oil rigs, they didn't appear filthy. Many were attractive. Some even wore what looked like makeup. Jewelry made of shells and turquoise decorated their half-naked bodies. All of them seemed to look at her with dread and pity, as though they knew exactly what she was about to experience.

But it wasn't the sad eyes that took her breath—it was the paintings on the metal walls of their homes— or prisons.

As the cage rose higher, she admired the murals and drawings on this castle on the sea. Like the bulk-heads on the *Hive*, the walls had been covered with beautiful images from the Old World.

Animals.

People.

Vehicles.

And …

An airship like the one crowning the towers above her.

Cazadores and the robed men were painted on the metal around the airship, all of them on their knees as if worshipping it. Words had been scribbled above the drawing: LOS DIOSES DEL CIELO.

The sky people? she wondered. Or did it mean something else?

The cage continued upward, and she glanced up through the open ceiling to the airship above them, with its forest and gardens growing toward the sky. She remembered the transmissions from Captain Marcus Bolter and the ITC *Ashland* in the downloads from the facility on the Turks and Caicos Islands.

Was that the *Ashland* above?

Had he come here two hundred and sixty years ago?

The cage jolted to a stop at the thirtieth floor and the men in robes opened the second door. They had reached the platform she had seen earlier, the deck jutting high over the blue-green sea. A forest of trees grew out of the soil, their branches laden with oranges, and other fruits.

Magnolia followed the bald, robed men out of the cage, and the two guards with spears stepped out. They walked slowly after her, their spear tips pointing at the sky.

A central pool stood amid the trees—and not just any pool. This one had colorful fish swimming lazily beneath the surface.

The robed men walked down a dirt path lined with bushes and flowers. This was the first nonmutant garden she had seen anywhere but aboard the *Hive* or *Deliverance*. None of the plants seemed to be carnivorous, toxic, or noxious in any way, and the petals had more hues than she had ever seen. She had never seeing anything so beautiful. And now, having seen it, she must die a slave to a murdering cannibal.

No, I will not *be a slave.*

She would die first. Something at her core hardened. She would use her last moments to kill the man who had killed Rodger—to accomplish what she had set out on this journey to do.

The path bent away from the pool and the trees and merged into a cobblestone walkway. This trail curved toward a windowless section of the castle. She saw only one door to the right … with no one guarding it.

The path continued toward a short stairway that climbed to a platform with a single seat made of bones. She wasn't surprised to find sitting there a man in a full suit of armor, with Siren-skull epaulets on both shoulders.

El Pulpo.

Here was the man she had traveled across the ocean to kill.

Her eyes went to two cages that flanked the throne. Skeletal remains were strewn on the floor of the left cage, and a human figure was curled up in the cage on the right. She couldn't see a face and wasn't even sure the person was alive.

Behind the throne rose a sculpture of an octopus, its long snaky sucker-covered arms splayed in all directions. The metallic arms glimmered in the sunshine.

Miles began to stir as she walked. She held him steady, her muscles burning under his weight. Part of her wished the dog would remain unconscious. He would be better off that way if they were going to kill and eat him. She didn't want him to suffer anymore.

Magnolia considered running for the railing and diving over the side with Miles in her arms. Then neither of them would have to suffer.

It would be a painless death, and for a moment she would be free to stare out over this beautiful, mysterious world. But the desire for revenge, and the will to survive, were ingrained into her soul. She could never take her own life, especially when she still had fight left in her.

The robed men left the shade of the trees and walked along the stone path toward their king. They all stopped on the first step to the throne and looked up to face el Pulpo.

Magnolia stopped with Miles about ten feet back from the bottom step.

She could feel the presence of the two men behind her and knew that if she tried anything, they would plunge their spears into her flesh. So she remained standing, trying to be strong, praying that *Deliverance* would descend from the sky to drop bombs on el Pulpo's ugly face, or that X would show up, guns blazing.

But neither scenario was likely.

She was going to be raped, tortured, and eaten.

Miles stirred awake in her arms, eyelids flickering and finally opening. She gently set the dog down and told him to sit.

Disoriented but alert, Miles did as ordered, resting on his haunches and taking a quick scan of his surroundings.

"It's okay … It's all going to be okay," she said.

Only, of course, it wasn't.

El Pulpo reached up and took off his helmet.

"You sick son of a bitch!" Magnolia shouted.

Armor clanked behind her, and one of the soldiers yelled, "*¡Silencio!*"

She slowly turned to see both spears pointed at her heart.

"*¡Bajen sus armas!*" shouted a gruff voice.

Turning back toward the platform, she watched el Pulpo, king of the Cazadores, walk down the steps, past his priests or servants or whatever the hell they were.

He had grown some hair since she last saw him. A short-cropped strip ran from his widow's peak over the top of his caramel-hued scalp. The eye that X had destroyed with a needle years ago was nothing but a hollow socket now. His remaining eye studied Magnolia, and his thick brown lips opened to reveal jaws rimmed with sharpened yellow teeth.

He was a massive man, with wide shoulders and tree-trunk calves and arms. When he was a few feet away, he was already towering over Magnolia. His rancid breath hit her face. Apparently, el Pulpo did not recognize her from the Cazador ship back in Florida, and for that at least, she was grateful.

"*Tienes miedo*," el Pulpo said to her. "You afray." Then he said something in Spanish to the soldiers, who laughed.

Miles came up off his haunches, growling low.

The Cazador king looked down at the dog, grinned, and then barked, spreading out his arms, the Siren skull crests on his shoulder pads rising up like skeletal wings.

Magnolia held her ground, but Miles backed away.

"I'm *not* afraid," she said. "I came here to kill you."

El Pulpo licked his thick lips. Then he gestured for one of the men behind him. A bald, gray-bearded servant in a brown robe scurried forward, hands clasped.

The king spoke to him, and the man faced Magnolia. In near-perfect English, he said, "My name is Imulah. I am a scribe serving King Pulpo in all his glory. Our lord speaks only a bit of English, so I will assist in translation. To start, he wants to know your name and where you came from."

Her eyes met the servant's. There was empathy there, and a subtle nod as if to say, *Do as you're told, and it will go better for you.* His eyes dropped to the floor, and he lowered his shiny pate in obeisance.

"My name is Magnolia," she said, standing as tall as she could despite her injuries. "I am from the sky, and I'm here to kill your king."

The servant glanced up and slowly shook his head, as if he didn't want to relay her words.

"Go ahead, tell him," Magnolia said.

The man swallowed and looked to el Pulpo, who was scrutinizing him with a deep gaze from his single eye. They exchanged several words, and el Pulpo reared his head back, laughing uproariously. His deep voice echoed off the metal castle walls.

The other servants all stared at the floor, but the two guards behind her chuckled.

Magnolia remained stone-faced. She crossed her arms over her torn shirt.

El Pulpo laughed for another few moments and then ran a hand over the strip of hair on his head.

Walking forward, he came within inches of her face and then clamped his teeth together. She turned her head slightly, holding the air in her lungs to keep his rotten breath at bay.

He leaned in, his eye roving back and forth as he studied her face, neck, chest, and body. She closed her eyes, shivering when his cold tongue ran up and down her cheek.

"*Tu eres guapa*, he said. "You *muy* beautiful." Then he pulled back and gave the small robed man another order.

"He wants me to tell you that he needs a new queen." The man paused, then added. "He said his other ten wives will be jealous at first, but he will protect you. Your dog, however …"

Magnolia looked down at Miles, then back to the man. "You tell your king that if he hurts Miles, I will bite his tiny pecker off and throw it to the fish. I'll fit right in with you sick cannibal pricks."

The servant's eyes widened, and he quickly shook his head.

"Tell him."

Again el Pulpo laughed at her words. This time he put a hand on his chest armor, directly on the engraving of the octopus.

"*Me gusta*," he said, chuckling. "*Me gusta mucho*."

His grin remained, showing off a wedge of pink stuck between his two front teeth. It looked a lot like flesh.

Was that the smell on his breath? Was she breathing the scent of roasted human flesh?

Her stomach churned at the thought. She suddenly didn't feel so strong anymore. Her shoulders sagged, and her knees started to buckle.

Imulah looked at her with the saddest gaze she had ever seen—the gaze of a man who had lost everything, including his soul. She wondered about his life, where he was from, how he had come to live here with these people.

She pictured herself standing in his place.

No, she thought. *I will not become a slave. I will never give myself to this maniac.*

Magnolia exhaled and straightened her back. Then she did what she had been wanting to do for a while. She spat in el Pulpo's face.

He reared back, the spit dripping from his chin. To her amazement, his smile remained.

At the distant crack of gunfire, he looked over her shoulder to the water beyond. He directed one of his soldiers toward the railing and then turned back to Imulah.

Apparently, gunfire wasn't all that big a deal on the Metal Islands.

Miles nudged her leg, his muscles shivering.

"El Pulpo wants to know how you found us," the servant said.

Magnolia remained silent.

"You're only hurting yourself if you don't talk," he said.

El Pulpo wiped the rest of the spittle off his face and tasted it with his long tongue. Magnolia's stomach churned again.

As he licked his finger clean, the gunfire returned, this time followed by a raucous explosion.

She turned back to the view of the ocean and the oil rigs.

Flames licked the horizon, where one of the platforms had exploded. A massive blast suddenly flared, and the entire structure seemed to go up in a small mushroom cloud. El Pulpo shoved her out of the way and ran after his two guards for a better view.

"I'm not the only one who came to kill you!" Magnolia shouted after him. "The man who took your eye is here, and this time he will finish the job."

El Pulpo halted and looked back to Imulah, who

quickly translated her words. The smile on the king's face was gone now. He snorted at her like one of the armored hogs on the Turks and Caicos Islands.

"That's right, you lump of Siren shit. The devil's coming, and he won't show you any mercy. Xavier Rodriguez is the king of the surface—not you," she said, wagging a purple-painted fingernail.

El Pulpo raised one pierced brow while the robed servant explained her words. The next thing happened with such speed, she had no chance to react.

He smacked her in the head with the crown of his head, blocking out the sunlight in a sudden blow. She collapsed to the floor, feeling the wet fur of the dog beneath her crumpled body.

TWENTY-TWO

The C4 had done the trick.

X sped away from the oil rig. He had selected it because it appeared to be just a warehouse with floors and floors of stacked junk—nothing vital to his own people's future needs.

Another explosion rocked the structure, enveloping the entire rig. Flames licked the sky. In a few hours, the entire skyline would be obscured in smoke.

His plan wasn't perfect, but it could work. It had to.

Creating chaos was his only way to save Magnolia and Miles. If he could give the impression that there were more hostiles than one out here, he might have a chance to follow his friends' beacons while they remained alive.

Looking over his shoulder, he saw Cazadores in flames, jumping off the platforms into the water. Others were flailing in the ocean.

Some of them had made it to boats anchored beneath the structure. X hadn't seen any children or women before detonating the C4—another reason he had selected the warehouse, even though part of him considered all these people enemies, just like the Sirens.

Anyone who wants to eat me, I'm happy to kill.

Still, he couldn't help but have qualms about killing kids and women. They were still human, unlike the Sirens, which had developed into an entirely new species.

He felt a faint pang of remorse, but nothing he couldn't get over.

He hadn't come here to make peace. He came for revenge.

And now they had his friend and his dog.

If it meant saving two of the most important beings in his life, he would kill every last one of them.

So far, his plan was working.

None of the bastards back on the platform had seemed to recognize him before he detonated the C4. The drivers of boats and WaveRunners that passed him didn't seem to pay him any mind, either.

Dozens of the vessels zoomed away from the clusters of oil rigs in the distance. They were too enraged to pay close enough attention. Cazador soldiers raised weapons and screamed in Spanish.

And they didn't seem to have a way of communicating over distance, which gave him another advantage. No radios to connect them and help them sort out what was going on. He would use that to his advantage.

X steadied his breathing and rode the waves as fast as he could, heading for the beacon on his wrist monitor. Timothy was still active on the *Sea Wolf* and was feeding him information via his headset under the baseball cap and goggles X had taken off the dead Cazador soldier.

The goggles were ancient artifacts with lenses yellowed from centuries of use. But they still helped keep the water out of his eyes.

He gunned the engine toward the next oil rig.

This one wasn't a junkyard—it was a farm built on multiple levels. On the lower decks were shanty houses, some of them dangling over the water.

Blowing up a farm wasn't an option. If Katrina ever did make it here, they would need it.

To blend in, he joined an armada of four boats, all filled with Cazador warriors, heading around the structure.

You're going the wrong way, assholes, he thought.

Why would they be heading away from the *Sea Wolf* and the explosions?

Unless you're on your way to protect someone or something …

Scanning the horizon, X counted a dozen more oil rigs. It took him only a glance to see their target. The city on the sea had a capital, and he was looking at what appeared to be a goddamn castle.

He eased off the throttle when he saw what could have been the *Hive*, sitting on top of the towers.

"Commander Rodriguez, do you copy?"

"I'm here, Pepper. You got a sitrep?"

"I do, sir. Magnolia's beacon hasn't moved for several minutes."

X glanced down at his wrist monitor, which he had put back on a few minutes earlier. Sure enough, the beacons were idle. But they were still blinking, which meant Mags and Miles were alive.

"I believe she reached her destination about thirty minutes ago," Timothy added.

"On my way there now," X said.

"Sir, there's something else."

"What's that?"

"A dozen Cazador ships have surrounded the *Sea Wolf*, and they just pulled a naked body out of the water."

X cringed at the news. They had found the man he killed and stripped. But how?

Then it hit him. The man was fatter than any of his mates. Of course he would float! X felt like kicking himself.

"I'm about to be boarded, sir. I presume this is the end. Whatever happens next, I'm afraid you will be on your own. To say it's been an honor would be an understatement, Commander."

"You done good, Pepper. Thank you for helping us."

"It was my pleasure, sir. Is there anything else I can do to assist you?"

"Yeah," X said. "Relay this message to the *Hive* and *Deliverance* before you're shut down. The very fate of my people may rest in your hands, Pepper. Make sure Captain DaVita gets this message."

X grabbed the handlebar and gave what might be his final transmission as he sped toward the capital of the Cazadores.

* * * * *

In the medical bay of the USS *Zion*, Michael raised his left arm and bandaged right stump so Trey and Layla could pull his shirt over his bare chest. What had once been a routine requiring little thought or effort was now a painful and laborious process. Moving hurt. Breathing hurt. Staying awake hurt.

Layla held out two pills before he put his helmet on.

"No more," he said. "I'm done with those. They make everything numb."

"That's the point, and you might need them for the trip back to *Deliverance*. Come on, Tin."

"I said no." His words and tone brooked no argument.

Layla closed her hand over the pills. "Fine."

Les walked into the quarters. "Ready, Commander?"

Michael nodded.

"Follow me."

The divers all made their way down to the hangar bay that had once been used to store aircraft and vehicles. Only one vehicle remained: an armored truck similar to the one back in the garage at Red Sphere. All the windows but one were cracked, and the tires flat. A mounted rocket launcher pointed ahead, the barrel covered in faded markings from centuries ago.

Helium boosters, armor, and helmets sat neatly arranged in front of the locked door. Michael glared at the two laser rifles on the ground, and then bent down to pick one up by the olive-green rail that had iron sights mounted to the barrel. Holding the weapon sent a bolt of pain through his stump and down his missing arm.

Layla reached out. "You okay, Tin?"

He nodded and examined the weapon that had taken his arm. "Do we know how these work now?"

Edgar nodded and grabbed the other gun. "Battery operated. These two have about half a charge left." He pushed a button on the bottom of the barrel, ejecting the battery that had a display on the side. "This one is at forty-seven percent."

"All right, everyone," Katrina said. "Gather around."

She motioned for everyone to join her around a computer station on the starboard bulkhead. The screen had multiple cracks across the surface, but it somehow came to life, activating a map of their current location.

"These are the Metal Islands," Katrina said. "Interestingly, they aren't actually islands at all, but old-world drilling platforms that once pumped oil."

Michael gritted his teeth at a fresh wave of pain. He didn't regret passing on the pills yet, but maybe Layla was right.

"We're not sure how many oil rigs there are or how many Cazadores we're going to be facing," Katrina said, "which makes forming a battle plan difficult. The last thing I want is to blow up anything we might need to make this our home. But we have to make them pay dearly enough that they surrender."

"These people are barbarians," Layla said. "They aren't just going to lay down their weapons when the *Hive* and *Deliverance* descend on them and we show up with the *Zion*."

"Perhaps not," Katrina said. "But they will pay a heavy cost until they do."

She put her palms on the desktop and looked at each diver in turn with the confident gaze of a captain. Whatever doubts, grief, and insecurities she was harboring, none of it showed. The woman in front of Michael was the leader he remembered before she lost her child—the woman X had once loved.

"Vish, Sandy, Jed, Eevi, and Alexander will parachute to the deck shortly," Katrina said. "I've asked them to bring a fuel cell from the airship to help us get to the Metal Islands." She looked to Trey and Jaideep. "You two will remain here with the other divers and me."

"I'm ready to fight," Trey said.

Michael envied his friend, who had the bearing of a young man ready to go to war. No matter how hard Michael wanted to fight, this was one he must sit out.

Katrina looked to him and Layla next. "Layla, I need you and Les to return to *Deliverance* with Michael and Edgar. You will then fly to meet the *Hive*. As soon as you dock, your orders are simple: recruit a fighting force. We can't do this all with missiles and cannons."

Several nods.

"Once that's done, the airships will meet us at the Metal Islands, and we will give el Pulpo a chance to surrender and hand over X, Mags, and Miles."

More nods, except from Edgar.

"With your permission, Captain, I'd like to stay here," he said in a gruff voice.

Everyone turned to look at the young man.

"You're wounded," Layla said.

"Don't matter. I don't want to go back up there. Ramon's dead. He was all I had in the sky."

Katrina held his gaze for a moment and finally nodded. "You can stay. I'll need the extra help." She looked at them all in turn again. "Any other questions?"

Les appeared to want to say something. It was obvious he didn't want to leave his son.

Katrina stood up straight from the station and clapped her hands together. "Okay, let's get ready. *Deliverance* is traveling at top speed toward our coordinates and should be in position within a half hour. We have a window in the storm above, people, and I don't want to miss it."

Les led the group toward the closed hangar-bay door.

"You heard the captain; everyone, suit up."

Layla helped Michael into his armor. They were face-to-face, close enough that no one but her could hear him.

"Do you think this is the right move?" he murmured.

"I don't know what the right move is anymore, Tin. I mean, they found a place we can call home, but it's going to cost us to take it for ourselves. And ... I just don't know. I'm afraid."

Michael raised his left hand into the air so she could cinch the strap on his back securing his armor. She leaned in closer.

"I'm afraid we will lose our own humanity if we go to war for the Metal Islands," she whispered.

"Me, too. But they have X, Mags, and Miles, and they killed Rodger. We have to fight them."

"Maybe there's another way ..."

Michael turned so she could finish securing the clasps on his sides. He closed his eyes against another jolt of pain. When he opened them again, he saw Trey and Les embracing.

"I love you and will see you soon," Les said. "Be careful."

"I love you, too. Tell Phyl and Mom that I love them, too."

Les hugged his son again and then put on his helmet, looking in Michael and Layla's direction.

"You almost ready?" he asked them.

Layla and Michael finished suiting up in front of the hangar door. As soon as they had secured their helmets, Les hit a button on the bulkhead, and the ancient door cranked open, letting in a gust of wind and rain. It was coming down in sheets from the dark skies. Lightning rickracked across the eastern horizon.

"You sure this is safe?" Layla asked.

Katrina stepped up behind them, holding one of the black laser rifles. "Safe as we're going to get," she replied, opening the rifle's battery compartment and removing the battery. "Les, I'd like you to take this up there and hold onto it. If we end up sending Hell Divers to the Metal Islands we will need at least one of these for the dives."

He grabbed the weapon and threw the new sling over his shoulder.

"Keep that locked away," Katrina said, handing him the battery separately. "A single bolt could cause a disaster in the skies."

"Will do, Captain."

Michael stared up into the black vault. They waited in silence, with nothing but the thunder and the creak of metal to fill the void of words.

Katrina put her finger to her earpiece and walked back into the hangar. "Yes, I copy you, Ensign White.

She nodded and said, "Okay, good news. We're almost ready."

Katrina rejoined the divers near the open door. "Ensign White thinks he can get the ship low enough to drop ropes."

A whirring came out of the storm—a sound Michael knew well. The turbofans churned through the clouds as *Deliverance* lowered. He still couldn't see the hull, but far above, the darkness seemed to lighten.

"Easy," Katrina breathed.

Rays penetrated the darkness, and spotlights turned the USS *Zion*'s decks bright as the daylight she had imagined all her life.

"There she is," Layla said.

Michael watched the massive vessel descend, its thrusters firing periodically to hold the ship steady.

Overhead, the hangar door to the belly of the airship slowly opened, and he could see the blue glow of battery packs. Ropes dangled to the *Zion*'s weather deck, and Les ran out to grab them.

He used carabiners to clip them to the deck cleats. The ship rocked slightly from the wave action, but remained steady overhead.

The first thing down was a supply crate.

Trey and Jaideep hurried over to secure it, then wheeled it on a dolly back into the hangar.

"Our fuel cell and food for the trip," Katrina said. "Plus some extra ammunition."

Next came the other divers. The blue glow of five battery units winked on above and started down the ropes, swaying in the wind and rain.

Les, Trey, and Jaideep waited to help them.

One by one, the new divers hit the deck. They ran to the garage with multiple weapons slung over their shoulders and more holstered on their hips and legs. Bandoliers stuffed with shotgun shells and belts of high-caliber rounds hung over chest armor.

Michael had never seen such heavily armed divers before, but they would need every gun and bullet for this mission. They would also need the contents of the crates Alexander and Jed carried. Inside were drones and other recon equipment from the armory on *Deliverance*. They also had EMP grenades that could be used to fry small and large grids.

He turned as Jaideep embraced his brother.

"I was so damn worried about you, man!" Vish said.

Jed, Sandy, Eevi, and Alexander stowed their packs and weapons in the hangar, then came together in a small group while Katrina walked over to the departing divers.

"Lieutenant, if there's anything you want to say about this plan, now is the time," she said to Les. "I need to make sure I can count on you to follow my orders once you get back to the *Hive*."

"You can," Les said. "Just take care of my boy."

"Do what I can't do, Captain," Michael said. "Save X, Mags, and Miles. I wish I could help."

A wave of dizziness rushed over him, and he closed his eyes to let it pass.

"I'll do everything, Commander. You have my word." Katrina reached out but stopped short of clapping him on the shoulder. She moved to Layla and gave her a hug. Finally, she went to shake Les' hand. They embraced instead.

"Good luck, Les," she said. "Remember, start with the militia, I don't want panic to spread on the airships."

"Understood, Captain. Good luck to you as well." He looked to Trey one last time and gestured for Layla and Michael to follow him onto the deck. The rain beat down on the divers as they made their way out.

"We'll secure Michael first!" Les shouted over the noise of the storm.

Layla moved into position. Once Michael was tied in, he looked up at the airship, raised his hand over his head, and rotated it in circles.

A winch started at the top, and he rose off the deck, swaying in the violent wind.

His earpiece crackled. "Commander Everhart, there's something you should hear," Katrina said over a private channel.

He looked down to the deck. Layla and Les were tying in to ride up next, clearly oblivious to what Katrina was saying.

"This is a recorded transmission from X."

Michael's heart leaped with hope when he heard X's gravelly voice in his helmet.

"This message is for Michael. As you may know, I've found the Metal Islands. I know I told you not to come for us, but we're here now and it's everything Janga said it would be, plus some."

The wind howled, making it difficult to hear.

Michael held the rope as it bowed in a gust.

"By the time you hear this, we will likely be dead," X said. *"But when you do come, prepare to face a brutal enemy—worse than the Sirens. Avenge Miles. Avenge Magnolia, and promise me that when you make this humanity's future, you won't resort to barbarism like the Cazadores. I dived so humanity would survive. I dived for this place. I love you, Tin. Be good, fight hard, and remember what you told me: Accept your past without*

regrets. Handle your present with confidence. Face your future without fear." He paused for a moment. *"I'll always be here for you in spirit, kid."*

The transmission shut off, leaving Michael with goose bumps prickling his arm. He looked out over the swollen storm clouds, wondering whether this was how X felt when he was left behind all those years ago.

A tear rolled down his cheek. He took in a long, deep breath. This wasn't the time to despair.

It was the time to *fight.*

Minutes later, he was in the hangar bay on *Deliverance,* and Ensign Ada Winslow reached out and grabbed him, pulling him into the safety of the bay.

Michael looked back down at the USS *Zion* below, and a wave of energy rushed through him. As soon as he got back to the *Hive,* he would get patched up, and then he would prepare for the most important part of his life: the fight for the future of his family, his friends, and all humanity.

TWENTY-THREE

Mags, wake up.

The nasal voice in her dream sounded oddly familiar, but no face showed itself in the darkness of her mind. She was stuck in limbo between consciousness and oblivion. She had experienced sleep paralysis before, but this was different. This time, she wasn't stuck in a dream. The voice calling out to her seemed real, but it couldn't be. The voice belonged to a dead man.

Wake up. Come on. Wake up!

Her swollen eyes opened enough to let in a sliver of sunlight. In the past, she would have confused the view with a dream, but it took her only a fleeting moment to realize that this *was* real. The fruit trees and the sunlight glinting off the blue-green waters reminded her where she was and how she had gotten here.

"Miles …" she muttered. "Miles, where are you?"

The wet fur that brushed up against her filled her with relief. She reached out and pulled the dog close.

His wet tongue lapped at her arm, and she forced her eyes open to see him looking up at her.

The bright rays hitting their cage made her squint. She tasted blood. Reaching up, she felt the goose egg forming on the center of her forehead. A thin line of dried blood ran down her face and onto her exposed neck and chest.

She remembered then. There was the throne made of bone, the metal sculpture of an octopus hanging above it, and the cage to the right.

But the king and his servants were absent. Only one guard was present. He stood facing the cage on the other side of the throne, by the only door she had seen on her way in.

She scanned the rounded platform jutting from the castle. The other soldiers were gone. Beyond the castle, smoke filled the blue skies, threatening to block the sun. She couldn't see much more. But she knew that X was out there, fighting to get to her and Miles.

She checked the dog for injuries. Blood matted his coat in several places, though she couldn't tell what was his and what was her own.

"You're going to be okay, my friend," she whispered.

Miles whimpered and followed her as she crawled on all fours toward the cage's barred doors. Something sharp on the floor stuck her palm, and she pulled it back to find a drip of fresh blood.

Her eyes fell on the human bones strewn across the floor.

Her sense of dread grew. The former occupants of this cage had been eaten, and she and Miles were likely next.

The scent of ripe fruit helped her put thoughts of her fate aside for the moment. She crab-walked over to the bars of her prison.

Stooping down under the barred ceiling, she looked out over the platform. She couldn't see beyond the canopy of trees, but she could see to the right, and what she saw looked like chaos.

At least fifty boats had taken to the water. Some were sailing toward the burning oil rig while others headed for the castle. The gunfire had paused, but she could hear raised voices in the distance.

She pushed her face up against the bars, desperate to see what was happening on the open water. White wakes crisscrossed the ocean like cobwebs.

The carmine bow of a large vessel caught her eye. The ship with the Siren cargo was heading toward a platform in the distance.

A new chorus of voices rang out, then more gunfire. X was getting close.

Magnolia moved to the other side of the cage, but she couldn't see any better.

As the clamor of voices and clatter of armor grew louder, she looked for something to protect herself with. She picked up a jagged long bone etched with teeth marks.

Miles growled to her left. She looked but could

see only the top of the other cage, right of the throne. There was movement inside, and she remembered the body she had glimpsed earlier.

The guard near the door didn't seem interested in what she was doing.

The shouts and clatter seemed to be coming from several directions. She looked back to the edge of the platform, where cable spooled onto the wheel handle, raising a cage probably filled with Cazadores from the docks below.

She concealed the bone under the sleeve of her tattered shirt, ready to plunge it into el Pulpo's other eye if she got the chance. Miles barked, but when she turned, he was still staring to her left, toward the other prisoner's cage.

From a battered, bearded face, large brown eyes blinked at her.

"Mags ... is that you?" the man said.

"*¡Silencio!*" the guard shouted.

The prisoner looked submissively to the soldier.

"*Lo siento, lo siento,*" he said, his voice quavering.

She knew this voice.

"Rodge ... Rodger Dodger?" she stammered. "It can't be."

The resurrected corpse stood in his cage, exposing the raised scar that snaked across his upper torso. Whoever had stitched him up didn't have an eye for aesthetics.

The guard left his post, crossing the platform to meet the cable-operated lift.

"You're dead," Magnolia said once they were alone. "I saw it happen …"

Rodger's eyes roved back and forth as he gripped the bars. "You left me, Mags. You and X left me on that ship."

"No," she said, shaking her head. "You died in my arms."

His big brown eyes seemed to narrow as he tilted his head, looking like a puzzled animal. "Did you finally come back for me?"

The guard banged the butt of his spear against the floor, but Rodger held her gaze.

Magnolia scrutinized him for a moment, looking for the clue that this was just a figment of her over-worked imagination. But this was no illusion. The only thing missing was his glasses. His dark beard clung to his sunken cheeks.

"We came to avenge you and find the Metal Islands," she said, grabbing the bars with the bone still in her hand. "I'm so sorry, Rodge. I didn't know …"

She looked to her right, where the cage had clattered up to the top again. Several Cazador soldiers wearing full body armor piled out, bearing rifles and spears. Behind them was the king himself.

"Do as they say," Rodger said softly but urgently. "You have to. They kept me alive for a reason, but I've seen them kill others … and eat them. These people aren't who you think they are, Mags."

He ducked down before she could respond, and Magnolia backed away from the bars, the bone still up her sleeve. She couldn't believe her eyes or ears. Rodger Dodger Mintel had returned from the dead. But what did he mean about them not being who she thought? They were pirates, cannibals, freaks. That was obvious.

She felt a flood of emotions whirl through her, not the least of them guilt. It was even worse than the guilt she felt for sending Katrina the coordinates for Red Sphere, which likely got Hell Divers killed. She had left Rodger to these monsters—when he was still alive.

But how …? All she knew was that she had been given a second chance to help him. Bending down, she eased the bone back onto the pile. She would heed Rodger's counsel and bide her time, even if it meant pain and suffering, until X or the other Hell Divers came to rescue them.

Boots clanked on the metal platform, and she turned to look at el Pulpo, his guards, and the robed servants. The king had removed his helmet, and his single eye roved toward her.

But the grin was gone, his scarred face a mask of anger. Looking away, he yelled orders to his soldiers, who took up positions at the edge of the gardens, spears out.

El Pulpo stalked up the steps and sat on his throne, growling to himself. Imulah folded his arms across his chest, his hands vanishing inside the rough brown robe. He avoided Magnolia's gaze, but the king looked her way a second time.

He said something in Spanish, and pointed at Rodger as Imulah translated.

"Tonight, we feast on the flesh of gods. Tonight, we dine on the flesh of the sky people—starting with that one. He is ripe."

* * * * *

X had no idea whether Timothy would be able to get his transmission through to Michael, but it was out of his hands now.

His mission was to find and save Magnolia and Miles.

He wasn't sure what he would do after that—improvise, as usual, he supposed.

For now, his luck was holding as he homed in on their location. The Cazador soldiers still hadn't made him, but it was only a matter of time before he must engage them.

The piers at the bottom of the castle ahead were thronged with warriors. This wasn't just a castle; it was a fortress. And he had no idea how to find his friends here. One thing was certain: he wouldn't be using the piers.

And he no longer had Timothy's help, either. The AI had gone offline twenty minutes ago after telling X that the Cazadores were inside the command center. For all X knew, Timothy was nothing but a memory.

The boats ahead picked up speed toward the

dock. X felt the tendrils of panic, a feeling he hardly recognized. He had seconds to figure out what to do.

One of the boats veered sharply. X followed and saw a door opening under the structure right of the docks. Moored boats bobbed gently in the slow current running under the metal behemoth.

He gunned the WaveRunner's engine to catch up. Of the four men in the back of the boat, only one looked in his direction, but he seemed to pay scant attention and went back to looking ahead at the widening doors.

X looked subtly left, to the docks, thick with soldiers and the men in robes.

He looked casually at the marine garage. If he could get inside unnoticed, maybe he could fight his way to Magnolia and Miles. A long shot, but it was a plan. As long as he was breathing, he would keep fighting.

The boat ahead slowed and drifted into the gloom of the enclosed garage. X eased off the throttle and followed.

Now the men in the boat were looking at him. Three of them talked to one another in low voices. He had hoped to buy a little more time.

His eyes slowly adjusted to the darkness as he steered the WaveRunner inside. The hangar held at least thirty boats, most of them hard-used and covered in rust and grime. Steel columns wider than some of the boats supported the structure above.

This fortress, too, was an oil rig. But unlike the others, it had been completely retrofitted with towers over the platforms that once held a petroleum pumping station.

A hundred feet ahead, a dock extended outward from a platform a few feet above water level. On it, two helmeted Cazadores stood guard. Both were looking in his direction.

The vessel he was following ran up along the dock, and a man jumped out. He grabbed a rope and threw it to a man in the stern, who hitched it to the cleat. Now all the other sailors were looking his way.

One of them yelled, "*Detenga su motor.*"

X had a feeling they wanted him to shut his engine off, but he looked over his shoulder as if he hadn't heard them. He would get only one shot at this.

When he looked back to the docks, the two men in armor held up their hands for him to stop. He did as instructed, killing the WaveRunner's engine. In a smooth continuation of the same motion, he brought up the submachine gun. The automatic fire would attract others, but he would be long gone before they came.

The first trigger pull sent a three-round burst into the armored man on the left, spattering the next man with his blood. As the second soldier lifted his spear, the next burst shattered his helmet and the face behind it. Then X turned the submachine gun on the soldiers from the boat, who were still scrambling for cover. They had nowhere to hide. He cut them all down with short bursts.

In seconds, it was over.

X brought the WaveRunner up to the dock, grabbed his pack, and jumped off. Only one Cazador was still moving, crawling hand over hand down the dock, dragging his shattered legs.

A shot to the back of the head, and he lay still. X ejected the spent magazine, pulled another from his vest, and palmed it home as he trotted to the doorway at the end of the dock.

It swung open, and he halted in midstride as a man stumbled out, eyes widening at the submachine gun muzzle pointed at his chest. The blast sent him stumbling back into the staircase.

X limped into the passage, gun angled up toward the next landing. Finding it clear, he checked his wrist monitor again. Both beacons were still blinking. Mags and Miles were still alive.

Come on, old man!

He rushed up the first flight, adrenaline fueling his movements. Candles in sconces lit the way, but his injuries flared with every step. The bullet graze along the outer edge of his foot, the cut palm, and the old wound from the octopus—everything hurt.

He didn't pause at any of the landing doors to check for contacts or even to rest. The sooner he got to the top, the better his odds of finding his friends alive.

About five flights up, he heard voices. He stopped at the next landing. Listening, he realized they were coming from above *and* below.

He kept moving, with the submachine gun pointed up the stairs. Two more floors up, footfalls echoed in the stairwell. He flattened against the wall and waited.

A Cazador man with a ponytail moved into view, and X shot him through the neck, painting the metal wall red.

Screams of horror rang out. But they weren't male.

X moved his finger off the trigger as a woman and several children rounded the landing above. He bounded up the stairs with the submachine gun pointed at them, eyes scanning for weapons. None of the four women or three children appeared armed with anything but sharp teeth.

He considered expending a few more rounds, but he couldn't bring himself to kill noncombatants, even cannibals.

Moving across the landing, he swung the gun up the next flight. Seeing no other contacts, he moved back to the group, with his gun on them.

One of the women knelt wailing beside the man X had shot. X felt the pang of empathy but quickly pushed it aside and grabbed the man's rifle. He checked to make sure the magazine was full, then palmed it back in. He also had the blaster holstered on his thigh, loaded with two shotgun shells and a flare, and the fully loaded carbine slung over his back. Two pistols with fresh mags were tucked into his belt. He had a lot of firepower, and he had a feeling he would need it all.

But he also needed something more than bullets.

Looking the group over, he decided to grab one of

the kids—a boy no older than Michael had been when he wore his twisty foil hat.

"No!" one of the women yelled. They hit at him as he pulled the boy away, until he brandished the submachine gun.

"Get the hell off me!" he yelled. "Back!"

The women and other children cowered on the landing, baring their sharpened teeth like cornered dogs. They were all filthy and reeked of sweat. Tattered clothing hung off their sun-bronzed skin, and bracelets of seashell and bone decorated the women's necks and wrists.

He had started to retreat when a women pulled a knife from under her rags. As she lunged at him, X put a bullet in her thigh. The knife clattered to the floor, and he kicked it down the stairs.

Then he grabbed a fistful of the boy's shirt and pushed him up the stairs. They climbed for several minutes, the kid squawking and biting at him.

Voices rang out below.

X was starting to lose his patience when he saw they were almost at the top. He didn't like using a hostage, especially a kid, but it was the best he could come up with on the fly.

They stopped at the next landing, and X grabbed the doorknob. He put a finger to his lips, and the gun barrel to the boy's head.

That finally did the trick.

"Don't make me hurt you, you little demon," X said.

The kid's lip curled, showing pointy yellow teeth. Voices and footfalls continued below them, and X twisted the knob. It clicked—locked—and the kid lunged, biting X on the arm.

"Son of a …!" X shouted, nostrils flaring in rage. The boy took a piece of his forearm with the bite. Unable to afford any more tolerance, X punched him in the side of the head.

The boy crumpled to the landing, out cold.

X looked down at his bleeding arm. The teeth had sunk deep. He should get the wound wrapped before he continued, but the voices and footsteps were getting closer.

Ripping a strip from his shirt, he tied it over the wound. The unconscious boy was heavier than he looked, but X still managed to give the door a kick that sent a brilliant jolt of pain through his wounded foot.

But he had been hurt far worse before. These were just inconvenient flesh wounds, and he needed something to help.

X propped the boy against the wall and pulled out one of his favorite remedies: an adrenaline shot he had recovered from the *Sea Wolf* before swimming out to the WaveRunner. He jammed it into his left leg and exhaled.

Then he raised the submachine gun and gave the door a solid piston kick. The rusted metal broke open. Sunlight exploded into the stairwell, momentarily dazzling his eyes.

When his vision cleared, he was gazing at the most beautiful sight he had ever seen. Trees rose toward the sky, their branches weighed down by ripening fruit. A pool of water sparkled between gardens of flowers and colorful foliage. Scents of fruit and nectar filled his nostrils.

But this wasn't Eden, and it wasn't God sitting on a throne amid the gardens—it was the devil in the flesh. Above him, a metal octopus the size of a boat hung from the bulkhead, its eight long arms reaching out in all directions.

A half-dozen warriors in armor contoured to resemble musculature came streaming out of the trees with spears and firearms leveled at X. He had time to grab the boy and pull him outside, using his flesh as a shield.

"Get back or I kill him!" X shouted.

The soldiers closed in, forming a phalanx around him. His finger moved to the trigger as the human noose tightened.

"X!" shouted a voice, followed by a familiar bark.

His eyes darted to a cage a few yards left of the throne.

"Get back!" X shouted again, firing a bullet into the sky. Then he pointed the gun at the king of the Cazadores.

"El Pulpo, I came for your other eye—and your head! But I'll make you a deal. Free my friend and my dog, and I won't kill anyone else. Refuse, and you're all going to die."

A robed man translated the message aloud. El Pulpo finally got off his bone seat, laughing so loudly the noise echoed off the metal walls.

The only other sound was the eerie clacking of jaws all around X. He swept the gun back and forth over the warriors.

Another voice shouted from across the platform. This one came from a cage to the right of the throne.

"Do what they say, Mr. Xavier!"

X squinted at a half-naked man standing inside the cage. The bearded figure yelled again.

"Don't fight King Pulpo. You can't beat him!"

The crackling voice sounded a lot like …

"*Rodger?*"

The boy in his arms had come to and was squirming in his grip. A Cazador soldier jabbed the air with his spear, advancing closer and closer.

Their king walked down the steps from his throne and used a key to open the cage where Miles and Magnolia were being held.

"Let me go!" she shouted, punching and kicking with little effect. Miles bit at his armored leg, but el Pulpo shook the dog off with ease.

"Don't touch them!" X yelled, leveling the gun at the king. El Pulpo's fighters shouted and stabbed the air with their spears, the tips coming within inches of X.

This was a battle he couldn't win. He knew it, but he was willing to die if it meant giving Magnolia and Miles a chance. A chance he didn't see …

The man in the brown robe walked through the gardens and stopped near the edge of the sparkling pool.

"My name is Imulah," he said in perfect English, "and I am a servant to el Pulpo. My king remembers you and deeply respects your fighting skills. Normally, he wouldn't offer such a thing, but he has a proposal for you."

"Fuck him and his proposal," X spat. "I have a policy of not making deals with cannibals."

"I urge you to hear him out. Look around you. You don't have any options."

There's always an option, X thought.

The Cazador king pulled Magnolia out of the cage and held a blade to her throat. Miles had a chain around his neck now, and el Pulpo snubbed a loop of it around one of the cage bars and planted his boot on the slack so the dog couldn't move.

Okay, so maybe there weren't any *good* options.

A dozen Cazador soldiers had him surrounded, and a glance over his shoulder revealed four more at the doorway behind him.

Some of the men were half naked, their bodies tattooed and pierced. Pointed yellow teeth gnashed and clicked together, and hungry eyes stared at his flesh as they waved axes and knives. Others wore the ceremonial armor and held long spears.

Memories surfaced of other battles that had seemed impossible: in Hades when he faced dozens of Sirens, or in the Florida swamps when a snake pulled him down into black water.

But back then, he had only his own life and Miles' to worry about. Now he had Magnolia, Miles, and, apparently, Rodger, if his eyes and ears hadn't deceived him.

For the first time in his life, X saw no possible way out of this—not one that ended in saving his friends, even if he should sacrifice himself.

"What's the one-eyed freak proposing?" X asked Imulah.

"You will join the Cazadores. He needs men like you for expeditions to the dark world—men who can bring back treasures and able-bodied survivors and who know how to fight the deformed ones."

Deformed ones? That must mean Sirens. So far, the idea of being a slave and fighting mutant beasts—and perhaps being obliged to *eat* them—sounded grim.

"And if I say yes?"

"Your friends can live and join the Cazadores, too."

The boy squirmed, and X gripped him tighter until he whined and quit struggling.

"I joined them," Imulah said. "They spared me, and in return I serve them. It's not a bad offer."

Serve …

X had been serving as a Hell Diver almost his entire life. But that service had always been *his* decision. It was not slavery.

El Pulpo smiled. X pictured blowing the top of his skull off with a squeeze of the trigger, but the fleeting satisfaction of taking his revenge wasn't worth his friends' lives.

"Lower your gun," Imulah said. "Join us. You don't have to die. I've met others like you, on expeditions where we plucked survivors out of hell holes. El Pulpo wasn't always the commander and king of these people. They rescued him many years ago, from Ascension, an island in the middle of the Atlantic Ocean, when he was just a child. His ancestors were English."

Had X heard correctly? El Pulpo wasn't born here and was the descendant of people that lived on an airship?

Not that it mattered now. Not really.

X looked at the other Hell Divers and his dog with sadness. Joining the Cazadores meant enslavement. It meant losing their humanity.

But it also meant life.

Just as he was about to lower the gun, one of the guards thrust his spear into the boy's chest, impaling him and plucking him away, leaving X exposed.

"No!" el Pulpo yelled, his gravelly voice barely audible over X's gunshots.

Three neat holes appeared in the warrior's armor, leaking blood like a punctured water bag. The man crashed to the dirt, choking and gurgling next to the dying boy.

A moment of uncertainty passed, the warriors looking at one another or at X, not knowing what to do. Even their king, who had walked several steps, stood still as if waiting to see what might happen next.

X made the choice simple by raking the submachine gun back and forth across the ranks of Cazador soldiers.

The close phalanx of armored bodies made it easy to cut them down, and difficult for the armed warriors surrounding el Pulpo to take a shot without killing their comrades. They all aimed their weapons, but none fired.

"Leave him alone!" Magnolia shouted.

A man hurled his spear, but X moved just in time, the blade cutting the air where his neck had been. He shot down two more soldiers behind him, and a spearman who lunged from the side.

The tip cut into his shoulder, and another nicked the skin over his ribs. Without his Hell Divers armor, he was vulnerable to their archaic weapons.

X smashed another soldier in the face with the butt of the submachine gun and grabbed the dropped spear in midair. Swinging it in a wide arc, he hamstrung one man and disemboweled another, forcing the others back.

Bringing up his submachine gun, he finished the magazine and drew the blaster from its thigh holster. The first shotgun round blew through the front of a soldier's helmet. The second opened a gaping hole in a female warrior's thigh. He squeezed the trigger again, firing a flare into the tattooed chest of another man, who let out a long howl of agony before his lungs melted.

X ran the next soldier's neck through with the spear, leaving it there when he couldn't pull it free. He fired his second shotgun shell into the belly of an axman, who dropped the weapon, severing part of his foot.

A boot to the back knocked X out of the path of a spear thrust that would have impaled him like the dead boy on the ground. Using the momentum to his advantage, he made for the gardens while a half-dozen screaming soldiers gave chase.

Gunfire cracked from the throne platform, the rounds lancing into trees and dirt. And as suddenly as it had started, the firing stopped.

A voice screeched over the noise. "*¡Alto!*"

X holstered the blaster and drew both pistols. He ducked behind a tree and leveled them at the half-dozen men running toward him. At this distance, he didn't need to aim as he fired round after round, knocking them down as they came. A hurled spear sailed through his open stance, just below the groin.

He removed the threat with a .45 round that unhinged the spearman's jaw. When the pistols clicked dry, he dropped them in the dirt and unslung his final weapon: the carbine across his back. He fired, and a crazed warrior with a machete fell at his feet.

Chambering another round, he looked around him for the man he had come to kill. Maybe if he could take down the king, it all would end. The thought that he might actually win this fight crossed his mind.

A blow from behind knocked the rifle free and sent him crashing facedown in the dirt. He looked up as they formed a circle around him once again.

X tried to push himself up, but a heavy foot against his back forced him back into the dirt.

He gasped for air, trying to look over his shoulder. But the soldier holding him down was strong and big, and X was out of steam.

Even his friends' shouts and Miles' frantic barking couldn't incite him to his feet. He had finally met his match and couldn't continue the fight. All he could do was shield his face from the blows and kicks raining down.

The pummeling suddenly stopped, and a boot in his gut flipped him onto his back. His blurry eyes stared up at the airship atop the fortress, and for a fleeting moment he thought it was his friends, coming to rescue him.

His focus narrowed to a scarred face with a hollow eye socket, looming over him. El Pulpo grinned and spoke as his slave Imulah translated.

"You have proven yourself as a great warrior, Xavier Rodriguez," Imulah said. "One of the best el Pulpo has ever seen. He understands now why your friends call you 'the Immortal,' and believes it would be a waste of talent to eat you, especially now that you have killed so many of his soldiers. So you have one choice …"

X spat a stream of blood. "Let me make it easy. I chose death."

"Death is not a choice for you, Immortal," Imulah said. "You are a Cazador soldier now, and your friends are slaves."

"You Cazador," el Pulpo said, thumping his chest with his fist. With a clank of armor, the other guards repeated the motion as X looked around him and considered the odds.

This time there was truly nothing X could do. No good options remained—not even death.

He glanced past the servant and his king to the airship above. The aluminum skin glistened in the sun. He could almost picture passengers of the *Hive* peering out behind the grubby portholes.

No, you're wrong. There is one good option left. You wait. You survive. You keep your friends alive.

His fate and the fate of his friends were in the hands of the sky people. Their only hope rested with Katrina and the remaining Hell Divers. Yet again those brave women and men would determine the future of humanity.

X had dived through countless storms, he had trekked across the poisoned surface, and he had sailed across a sea filled with monsters to find this place. Now he would serve so humanity could survive, and then he would kill every last one of these bastards.

ABOUT THE AUTHOR

Nicholas Sansbury Smith is the *USA Today* bestselling author of the Hell Divers series, the Orbs series, the Trackers series, and the Extinction Cycle series. He worked for Iowa Homeland Security and Emergency Management in disaster mitigation before switching careers to focus on his one true passion—writing. When he isn't writing or daydreaming about the apocalypse, he enjoys running, biking, spending time with his family, and traveling the world. He is an Ironman triathlete and lives in Iowa with his wife, their dogs, and a house full of books.

Join Nicholas on social media:
Facebook: Nicholas Sansbury Smith
Twitter: @GreatWaveInk
Website: www.NicholasSansburySmith.com